TRAIN MAN

TRAIN MAN

Andrew Mulligan

Chatto & Windus
LONDON

1 3 5 7 9 10 8 6 4 2

Chatto & Windus, an imprint of Vintage,
20 Vauxhall Bridge Road,
London SW1V 2SA

Chatto & Windus is part of the Penguin Random House group of companies
whose addresses can be found at global.penguinrandomhouse.com

 Penguin
Random House
UK

Copyright © Andrew Mulligan Ltd 2019

Andrew Mulligan has asserted his right to be identified as the
author of this Work in accordance with the Copyright,
Designs and Patents Act 1988

First published by Chatto & Windus in 2019

penguin.co.uk/vintage

A CIP catalogue record for this book is available from the British Library

HB ISBN 9781784742713
TPB ISBN 9781784742720

Typeset in 11/13 pt Goudy
by Integra Software Services Pvt. Ltd, Pondicherry

Printed and bound in Great Britain by Clays Ltd, Elcograf S.p.A.

Penguin Random House is committed to a sustainable future for
our business, our readers and our planet. This book is made
from Forest Stewardship Council® certified paper.

To Max

GOING NORTH

1

The first choice to be made concerned the 09.46.

The 09.46 meant no changes, whilst the 10.13 involved two – and deciding which one to take was a dilemma Michael had faced before because the two trains could be so very different. What made him anxious was the lack of control: you never knew what the 09.46 would be until it rolled up to the platform, and the type of stock made all the difference. The rail company had a tendency to switch the carriages, and the ones that Michael liked – which were roomy, with tables – were all too often replaced by those used for the commuter services. That meant no tables at all, and a lot less legroom. If things got busy you could end up squeezed against the window hardly able to move your elbows, and he so didn't want to be trapped like that on this particular morning.

He wanted space, and he wanted to think.

If a commuter-style train turned up at 09.46 he would wait on the platform, and take the later service. There was flexibility after all: he needed to be in Crewe for the 14.41. If he missed it, the through-trains were hourly, so he wouldn't be stuck.

He smiled. Was he always so particular about trains? The answer to that was an emphatic 'no', but he had been trying to learn from experience. He'd been making so many journeys over the last few months, taking advantage of off-peak tickets that sold in advance for next to nothing. As a result, he'd become very familiar with the different levels of comfort on different services.

There was a tannoy above his head, and it came to life even as he looked up at it.

'We are sorry,' it said, 'but the 09.46 service from Southampton will have no catering facilities today.'

You could hear the hesitations as a computer patched in the particular time and place. The apologies were pre-recorded, of course, the phrases selected for the constant stream of cancellations and adjustments.

'We are sorry for the inconvenience this will cause to your journey.'

Michael found he was smiling more broadly.

He had mouthed the words, giving the word 'sorry' the same heavy emphasis as the earnest announcer. Why would there be no catering services? It was because the trains had indeed been switched, which meant the person who wheeled the refreshment trolley would not be able to get along the narrower aisle of the replacement carriages. What would that person do now? Was he or she assigned to some other train, or did it mean that he or she had been advised to stay at home? The ticket price would be the same for Michael despite the absence of refreshments. There would be no refund, and no contingency plan – the train operator wouldn't scramble emergency rations in a cool-box. You'd be left hungry and thirsty, all the way to Gloucester. He glanced at a woman sitting at the end of the bench.

'Are you on the next one?' he said.

She was wearing tiny headphones, and had to remove them. 'I'm sorry?' she said.

'I was wondering if you were on the Great Malvern service. The 09.46 as it was meant to be.'

'Yes.'

'I got this train last month, and it wasn't on time.'

'Oh, they never are.'

Michael laughed.

'You wonder they don't change the timetables,' he said. 'If they simply changed the 46 to 56 they'd be so much closer. I suggested that on one of their customer feedback forms. Have you ever filled one of those in?'

The woman was smiling back. 'I really wouldn't bother,' she said.

'I'm still waiting for the reply,' said Michael. 'I'm an *important customer*, apparently. My opinions are very important to them, but they haven't quite got round to getting back to me yet. You know there's no catering service today?'

The woman shook her head. 'I never use it,' she said.

'I do, when I can. For fear they'll do away with it. You could say I'm trying to encourage them, but you can't encourage someone who keeps letting you down.'

She held the earbuds in her fingers, getting ready to reinsert them.

'Where are you heading?' said Michael – and there was a pause.

'Cheltenham.'

'Oh,' said Michael. 'A lovely town.'

'My daughter lives there.'

'Lucky her. Lucky you, in fact, because—'

'She was a student there, and never quite left.'

'Really?'

Michael nodded, remembering a postcard he'd seen of some fine-looking square, with bright, flowering gardens. He had a feeling that had been Cheltenham, or Bath – or somewhere similar.

'Why would she want to?' he said, quickly. 'There are worse places to live than Cheltenham. I had a bite to eat there years ago, and there's the most lovely tea room. Not that I spend all my time thinking about refreshments.'

He smiled, and the woman simply looked at him.

'Or trains, for that matter. It's not a hobby, but I suppose I've come to resent paying a lot of money for a cup of undrinkable coffee. The kind that... you know, if you were blindfolded, you'd genuinely wonder what it was in the cup. It's incredible how easy people find it to make bad coffee, and I don't know if it's because they don't use enough, or if the blend is a... a cheap one. I think you can store it for too long, of course – that's when it just goes stale. I used to work for the council, and you had to make sure it was fresh, because if you didn't use it up, you really noticed the difference. In the quality, I mean.'

'I don't drink it,' said the woman.

'You're more of a tea person, are you?'

'A what, sorry?'

'You're more into teas, are you? If you want a hot drink, you prefer tea.'

'I don't drink tea, either. I cut out all caffeinated drinks a few years ago, and I feel much better for it.'

'Good for you. I keep meaning to, or trying to.'

'It's blood pressure.'

'Yes, that's the worry. That is the worry. I went for one of those Health MOTs a little while ago – they were organising them through my local library. They said that my chief weakness, or... vulnerability, I should say, was blood pressure. If I could work to get the blood pressure down a bit, then... I'd have got the MOT, so to speak. They don't give you a certificate as such, it's just a printout and you can take it along to your GP if you want to follow anything up. A free service – I thought it was a really good idea.'

The woman nodded, but said nothing.

Michael remembered the young man who had interviewed him, though it hadn't actually been 'a little while ago' – it had been seven months previously, in February – just before Valentine's Day. A section of the library had been cordoned off, and there were two chairs and a small table. The man conducting the interview had been almost half his age – no more than twenty-five – and he was a fitness instructor on loan from the leisure centre, with the loveliest manners. The whole thing had taken less than an hour. In that time Michael had learned that the man had only recently changed jobs, having worked before in a department store, selling beds – a role that hadn't suited him at all. He'd become increasingly frustrated.

Michael went to speak again, but the woman was pressing the little headphones back into her ears.

He closed his mouth, and thought about Javed.

Javed was the young man's name, and he'd told Michael that his frustration had led to him having a bad diet. He'd put on weight, reaching nineteen stone – then he'd managed to shed five in ten weeks by going to what they called a body-modelling centre, which was much more intensive than an everyday gym. Michael remembered the details because he'd been so impressed by Javed's courtesy, and confidence. He'd been confident enough to take blood from Michael's finger. Then he'd been confident enough to give him advice, despite the fact that Michael was a total stranger, and so much older.

'And I lied,' he said quietly.

The woman didn't hear him. If she was aware that Michael had spoken she was pretending not to be. He was relieved, of course, for he was finding that now and then words, or short sentences, just slipped out like a soft belch. It was a kind of dribbling, and he tried to be careful, but one thought led to another and he could end up sliding sideways, or backwards. Wasn't it during the so-called Health MOT that he had made his decision? Yes, it was – he knew it was, though he'd been trundling towards it for months.

In that chair, talking to Javed, he had realised something terribly important, and had emerged knowing that he had to act quickly, and dismantle the thing he'd been accidentally constructing for the last three and a half years. He was going to make a huge change in his own life, and Amy's – both their present and future were to be transformed. He went straight to a café, to reflect on the consequences, but he knew the decision was made and it was simply a question of making the call, or writing the letter. He could absolutely not get married, for the whole thing was wrong – he'd been faking everything. He'd been trying and failing, so how could he imprison a woman in marriage, even if they were just seven weeks from the wedding, with Valentine's Day just round the corner? Even if it seemed unstoppable, it could and had to be stopped.

He could not marry her, and more than anything else in the world, he wanted *not* to marry her. The woman frightened him, and he had spent the last however long it was pretending that wasn't the case. Married life was too frightening, and he simply didn't love her.

She had given every impression of accepting the pretence. He had lied to her, and to the twenty-five-year-old health professional, too, whose name was not Javed, in fact, but Jared with an 'r'. Not that his life was tangled with Jared's, of course, because they hadn't invested in anything except an hour of irretrievable time. But he had lied, nonetheless, about how much he drank. He had lied about his intention to get an expensive bicycle, too.

He had no money – how would he buy a new bicycle?

The young man had seemed impressed, though, and they'd spent two minutes at least talking about road-bikes versus hybrids – the weight, the gears, the tread – and he talked on, trying not to think about Amy and what she would do. Perhaps she would sigh with relief, and shake her head.

'Do you know, I'd reached just the same conclusion?' she might say – and they would hold each other.

'Thank you for being honest, Michael.'

'No,' he'd reply. 'Thank *you*. We can still be friends, can't we?'

'Always, Michael – of course. I will always think of you as my best, *best* friend.'

'I am that, Amy. I will try to be.'

Alternatively, she might stand there blank-faced, unable to speak. She might simply fail to comprehend the silent collapse of all those plans, so lovingly and painstakingly made. She had dry lips, and he could see the words that would inevitably form on them.

'What do you mean? Why?'

Those were the words she would have to use. There were no others, really. They would precede more violent ones, of course, but she would spend the first few moments floundering. She would lean on the little breakfast-bar, and he could see her thin wrists holding up her almost skeletal frame – the frame he'd embraced and held against his own, and tried so hard to need.

'You lied to yourself,' said Michael very quietly. He went to stand up, but at that moment there was another announcement.

'The 09.46 to Great Malvern,' said the voice, 'is delayed by twelve minutes. We are sorry for the inconvenience this will cause.'

They were sorry again.

Michael looked at the woman he had been talking to, and smiled. She was attending to her phone, and didn't look up – the headphones were still in her ears. A small suitcase sat at her feet, and she was dressed in several layers, because it was a cold September day with rain forecast.

He had only a small, grey shoulder bag.

You lie to yourself, he thought. You don't believe your own lies, but you *hope* they might come true – or perhaps they simply distract you. You had a good enough bike, because it was Amy's brother who'd lent it to you. Why did you tell Jared you wanted a hybrid?

Jared had believed him.

Jared had nodded in an encouraging way, and Michael had looked at him, trying to imagine how he'd carried nineteen stone when he now looked so healthy and muscular – as he had to for the job he did. You wouldn't be employed in a leisure-centre gym if you were overweight, and yet that could never be a stated reason for rejection. The employer couldn't say, 'Sorry, Jared – you're way too fat to work here.' That wouldn't be allowed, though it would be the truth. 'You can't walk round in shorts and vest, man! – you'll set a bad example. We need thin people, so you're not on the team: we're not picking you.'

Michael found he was smiling again, because the sun was trying to break through and suddenly summer showed every sign of returning. The woman next to him would soon have to remove a layer.

Jared had lost weight, and shown real interest in Michael's lifestyle. For most of the hour Michael's habits had been his only focus. He had felt almost tearfully grateful as he left the library, for the wedding had been out there on the horizon for so long, swaying like a tornado. It had been a smudge in the air coming slowly closer, until he could feel the temperature changing and the wind on his face. He had to deal with it, somehow: three and a half years of fiction had to be confronted. The wedding could not happen, and all the investment... it was blasted away as the dreaming came to an abrupt and sudden end. He'd got off the train, as it were: he'd turned back. Having said yes, he was about to say no – and everything would stop.

He had written to her the same afternoon: *Dear Amy*.

He wrote on an old laptop, and then printed the document in the library's study section, horrified by the devastation a single sheet of paper was likely to cause. Would the pain turn into relief? It would do, in the end, because he was only confirming feelings she must have shared. They didn't know each other: they'd spent the years *not* getting to know one another. She couldn't know him, if only because she had no idea what he was about to do, and if she hadn't anticipated the letter then that proved the point: they were strangers.

They were strangers, and he had come to dread being with her. She was a good person, and he was a liar. They had worked on the whole nonsense together, planning and smiling – and what did it take to smash it all down? Twenty minutes of typing.

> *Amy*, he wrote. *There is no gentle way of saying this so let me at least be clear, so that there is no doubt. I cannot go through with our wedding, and I want to end the relationship because I am not good enough, or certain enough, or happy enough for you.*

She had called him that evening, but whether she had found the letter in the morning or later he didn't know. He didn't take the call. He turned his phone off, until he'd had two large glasses of wine – and then he called her back.

Her brother answered, and said simply, 'What are you doing?'

Michael was in his flat, sitting on the bed.

'Matt,' he said. 'Can I speak to Amy?'

'To say what?'

'She's been calling me.'

'I've been calling you. We want to know if what you've written is true. If you're serious.'

'I'm serious,' said Michael. 'It's all true and I'm afraid I am serious. Can I speak to her?'

'No.'

There was a silence.

'You are such a shit,' said Matthew – and he spoke so quietly that Michael had to press the phone to his ear, and hold his breath. He thought he might have misheard, for he could hear another voice in the background.

'Pardon?' he said.

'You're a total shit,' said Matthew.

That's when Amy took the phone, and Michael knew then that she hadn't anticipated the letter in any way at all. At once, he panicked. If she hadn't seen it coming, then perhaps her love for him was real? Perhaps they *should* be getting married. Perhaps he was wrong, and they did have something worth preserving. Maybe they had more than most people, and everything he couldn't feel or fake was about to burst into flourishing, nourishing life? He held his ground, though.

'Yes,' he said. 'I know.'

He had nodded, and he nodded on the platform bench – because Matt was right. Matt would have been sitting in his sister's kitchen, most likely – the two-bedroomed house that Michael had moved into for a little while, and then out of. He shuttled between her place and his own, so he left clothes and personal items there – items he would never see again, because she would get rid of them.

Had that been malicious, or appropriate? Because he had always contributed to the gas and electricity bills. He didn't help with the water or council tax for some reason, but he had bought things and invested in the relationship that way – even though he had to be so careful with his dwindling, disappearing stack of money. He had less money than she realised, which was another lie: he'd always avoided admitting just how dangerously poor he was.

He had lied about how he came to lose his job.

He had misled her about the loss of his first house, though he couldn't blame the council for that – that had been his own stupidity. He'd lent money to his brother, who'd failed to pay him back: when the council let him go, the mortgage was suddenly unaffordable. He'd sold up. He'd bought the flat, but now that was unaffordable too – which was one reason why he couldn't keep changing his mind and getting off the train.

No, to tell Amy the truth would have left him weak – and he couldn't do it because he'd made so many bad decisions. It was easier to pretend, so he pretended to be not affluent, but comfortable, paying for a new toaster and a fancy microwave, and – using one of the credit cards he should have cut into pieces years ago – he even bought her a bigger television.

Why had he done that when he hardly watched television?

It was really for Amy's youngest daughter, as a way of persuading her to join them downstairs in the evenings, when all she wanted was to stay in her room. He had paid for the carpets to be cleaned, and he'd picked up a succession of plumber's bills when the boiler stopped working. 'Helping out' was what he called it.

'You've got to let me help out,' he'd say.

'You're not rich,' said Amy. 'You've got your own place, too.'

He still had it, just about. He had a key to the front door, and a second to his own tiny upstairs hall which led to the one bedroom, which was all he needed as he had no children, and no old friends who rang to say they were passing, could he put them up? A guest room would have been just another fiction, and Amy was the last of his too-many fictions, or so he hoped: he would learn his lesson. Matt had called him a shit, twice – but that was a word from the playground, and it didn't even scratch the skin. Amy's words cut deeper, and he had to stand there with his ear to the phone as they sliced and burned.

'How have you kept it going?' she said. 'For so long?'

Her voice had a deeper register than normal, as if she'd spent the afternoon shouting or crying. He was about to reply, when her voice suddenly got louder and it was as if the woman's mouth was right up against his ear, forcing the words inside like little stones. 'How, Michael? How have you let it get this far? Is this your...?'

She paused.

'Is this what you like to do? Because...'

'No,' said Michael.

'How serious are you? About... cancelling? Is this – what? Is this you postponing, or saying you want some time? What are you doing?'

'No, Amy. Listen—'

'Michael, listen to me. You are throwing something away here. Have you any idea how much upset you're causing, to both of us?'

He nearly said it.

He nearly said, 'But I just can't talk to you. What I have to say isn't worth saying, but I still can't say it – and I do want to be with you, sometimes. Sometimes, when I close my eyes, when I ache – but that isn't a good enough reason, Amy. I can't talk to you!'

He had one hand over his face.

He held the phone away, and the voice became a furious buzzing that he knew he had to endure until she grew tired, or realised there was no reaction to be had. The assault would be over, probably soon: Amy needed to savage him, and Michael would sit there in silence, offering a handful of safe and meaningless words. The apparatus of lies was collapsing, and they were free of one another. They were both happier, ultimately, and definitely less doomed.

'I just can't do it,' he said. 'I'm sorry.'

'Sorry?'

'Yes. So terribly, terribly sorry.'

That had triggered more scorn and more rage. Eventually, Amy used up her fuel and the anger faded to tired, bitter contempt. Michael had listened, thinking how simple it was to move to the next phase of the relationship: total separation and wounded silence. That was what he'd been longing for, perhaps: silence was what he most wanted – and solitude of course.

But he had made love to her.

On every occasion he had done so with his eyes closed, and he knew what he'd been doing: he'd been trying to imagine she was someone else, which was the most appalling admission and it made him go cold to think of it. He wondered whom she had been imagining, for the idea of her finding him attractive or desirable in any erotic sense seemed ludicrous. They had met at an amateur choir, and held each other out of fear – two ugly, lonely people. Surely they'd both had their eyes closed, terrified that not making love would be an admission that something was fundamentally wrong. That was what normal people did, after all: they went to bed and fucked, and that was the playground word. It still swung like an axe: 'Fuck me. Fuck you, you worthless fucker.'

'Hey, Michael?'

'What?'

'Fuck off.'

He was clenching his teeth, and there was yet another announcement, breaking in and scattering his thoughts. It was a woman's voice this time, and she was talking to him, slowly, word by careful word as if he was a child of five.

'Report anything suspicious...'

He would, of course – why wouldn't he?

He would enjoy doing so, in fact, for everything could be made safe if you were vigilant and reported things. There was no need to be afraid – not when you could phone, or text or speak to a member of staff – the transport police were there to save your life. He waited for silence, and when it came at last Amy was beside him, and she sat there as if they were married. She could almost take his hand, and offer him a mint – and yet how had he ever thought marriage would be better than solitude? How had he believed that, when he recalled the relief as he finally rolled back onto his side of the bed, having learned nothing and given nothing because he didn't know what to give? After sex, they would adjust the duvet and sleep privately, dreaming separately – the touching was over. He felt wretched, but he'd done the right thing for her as well as himself – just as he would do the right thing at Crewe.

'*Crewe is the next station-stop.*'

Someone on a train would say that, soon enough.

'*We are approaching Crewe. We will shortly be arriving in Crewe: be sure to take all your personal belongings with you.*'

The voice might be male or female, and it would be as reassuring as the one he'd just heard.

'*Mind the gap between the train and the platform.*'

That was the announcement he loved most, for the man who said it always sounded slightly frightened, as if he thought passengers had tiny legs. He seemed to think Michael was about to trip or slip, and find himself wedged helplessly as the train rolled on and slowly crushed his pelvis. All these people wanted was to keep him safe: they wanted him to drink water, and buy his tickets online so as to make savings. They wanted him to plan his journey so as to avoid delays, and claim compensation should anything ever go wrong. When he got up to leave the train, they wanted him to stop and take that extra moment to check he had his bag. In this unpredictable, unknowable world, they could protect him.

Amy had gone.

The woman next to him was still busy with her phone, and her headphones sat neatly in her ears. The summer was definitely back, and Michael breathed out, relaxed and relieved. He had his own refreshments – they were in a bag at his feet. There was no need to worry, really, about the absence of a trolley service. In any case, he only had three to four hours left, depending on the progress of the 09.46 – if that was the train he caught. He had flexibility, and he knew what he was doing. There was no better place than Crewe: that, at least, was a decision. The platforms were long, and they let you onto the lines gently. Nobody would notice you walking along the tracks.

He took his spectacles off, and cleaned them with his handkerchief, breathing gently onto the lenses as he had done since boyhood. He exhaled again, and slowed his breathing down.

Then he widened his smile and closed his eyes.

What she wanted was not what he wanted, but he'd tried to want it and believed for a time that he did.

So what?

Yes, we will live together and share a bed. Yes, our lives will be full, and we will be like everyone else opening a bottle of very reasonably priced Bordeaux that's surprisingly good, sitting on the sofa we'll soon be paying for month by month because Amy got an interest-free deal that was too good to miss – she went for the more expensive fabric because the children are older, and the dog is well trained. We'll sit on that sofa, he'd thought – you'll even be in my arms, Amy, sometimes – and we'll look at the picture on the wall bought shortly after your sister's boyfriend had a stroke and needed a new hobby. It was a startlingly awkward picture, because he painted by numbers, copying photographs like a child as people encouraged him to keep using his left arm. It is a good picture, because the little cottage looks like a little cottage, and the sky is an interesting blue – and we know who painted it. Are there better reasons for buying pictures, and putting them on the wall? Probably not.

In fact, Amy would sit on the sofa more than Michael. He would sit in the armchair, where the reading light allowed him to see the words on the page.

'Michael,' she would have said – had they married, some day in the future. 'You know that job you had before I met you – working for the council? You didn't resign, did you?'

'Yes, I did.'

'Technically you did,' she would say. 'But something you said—'

'What are you asking me?'

He'd put down his book. He'd remove the glasses from his face and hold them still – if people really spoke to one another like that. 'What are you asking me, Amy?' The question would sound absurd, because it would have to be accompanied by a turning of the head, and a pause before her inevitable reply.

'I want the truth.'

'The truth?' he'd say.

'Tell me.'

'I resigned, love. That's the truth.'

Yes, it was and always would be – but only because they were about to take disciplinary action, Mr MacMillan. You resigned because you were about to be sacked, sir – it was the easiest way out. And that's why you don't have much of a pension, and that's why – after buying the toaster and the microwave and the big-screen television – you have nothing left, except debts. Here you are, with next to nothing, and you're probably about to lose even that. You can't say you haven't been warned: the letters in the drawer implore you to stick to whatever payment plan you last agreed, or call the helpline. Why weren't the station announcements urging you to do that?

'*Attention, please!*'

What voice would they use for that?

'*Always try to pay your mortgage, because if you don't – your home will be taken from you. Don't make yourself homeless.*'

Michael laughed quietly.

'You'll lose it,' he said. 'And who's to blame?'

'Mr Trace,' said a voice, and Michael laughed again.

He touched his wallet, and there were his bank cards, safe and sound. Two had accumulated so much debt they were almost warm to the touch, but card number three still worked. He should have done the right thing, and cut it in half – but it was a lifesafer now, and here it was in his pocket, and it would get him through the next few hours. He'd tested it, withdrawing sixty pounds in cash. Three brand-new twenties had emerged, unused and fresh, and he'd felt like a child again, with money to spend. A letter of explanation lay on the pillow, sealed. And here is a curious thing: you have taped a fourth card to the inside of your shoe, with parcel-tape. Haven't you?

A debit card that expired last month, and you did that last night.

Michael was nodding again, and his mouth was forming the words.

'Of course.'

'Why have you done that, old friend? Lay down your burden.'

Michael found his spectacles-case in his pocket, and set it on his knees. He would check his own itinerary again, and for that he needed his reading glasses – meanwhile, he could just feel the card in his shoe where the edges were rigid through his sock. It's there for identification, just like the capitalised name you wrote in the collar of your shirt. It's as if you were starting at school again, and some other boy might pick it up by accident and you'd need to prove it was yours as you stood bare-chested in the changing room, not thinking about Mr Trace. He could be erased so easily when there was so much else to think about. What is it, then? The fear of being left, alone in a fridge for however long it is they have to keep your remains. How long is it before some poor, overworked coroner can order the swift incineration of an unclaimed, unknown man? He didn't want to be some poor run-over dog, or fox.

They have to know your name, just to make the last phase as smooth as a last phase can be. Amazingly, he had a funeral plan and the paperwork for that was clearly marked in his filing cabinet. He hadn't kept the payments up, but there was at least a thousand pounds. They would have to find his name, and he had been told by someone years ago that shoes always survived the impact, because they were knocked clean off the feet: the card would be found.

He put on his reading glasses, and checked again. It was the through-train he wanted, and platform seven was used by diesels. There was no fear of electrocution. His train set off from Preston at 14.02 and it would roar through Crewe at – what? – about fifty miles per hour. That was enough to knock your shoes from your feet, and the brains from your head.

Amy was a truly good person.

She had enabled him to escape from Monica, who was also truly good – though he'd never been physically intimate with her: they'd just known each other, and turned slowly into friends. When Amy arrived, she had allowed him to pity Monica for being so alone: Monica had thus become truly pitiful. Amy was so very different: different in size, shape and sound, and totally different again from the only other woman he'd nearly married, and that was Elizabeth.

Elizabeth, Monica and Amy: his three main relationships, intersecting here and there in the strange scribble of life.

'So you met Monica where, exactly?'

'The council.'

'Same department?'

'No. We met at the coffee machine – she was in Parks and Recreation.'

Amy, he'd met at the choral society – where he sang badly, and had found himself standing behind her one evening making very little sound. He couldn't sight-read, so he had to familiarise himself with the tunes. There were always a few sections he could sing, and he waited for those and usually enjoyed himself. It wasn't the kind of choir that demanded perfection, which was why it had welcomed him. It was a sing-along choir, really.

People were cheerful, so he fitted in.

Amy had stood next to him in the refreshment room once, and they had found themselves talking. Monica he saw just twice a week, but Amy came along and within a short time he'd stopped pretending to himself that she was a romantic partner: that was Amy's new role, and she did become a kind of lover. She was stick-thin and wiry. She ate so little, and with a fuzz of curly hair there was something of a Peter Pan about her, except when she wore dark glasses, which she often did because of a mild and gradual macular degeneration. Monica, on the other hand, was altogether heavier, steadier and slower, with a face that seemed forever tired.

She had worked in the annexe.

'You know, I still believe in public service,' she said. 'Is that old-fashioned?'

'Not at all,' said Michael.

'People need us, I hope.'

He was thinking, They don't need me, because I'm not doing my job. I can't do it, Monica.

She was more generous than he would ever be, but he had ended up using her. She was thorough, dependable and Christian, and helped out in a food-bank. She responded to appeals, and was positive that everyone could do something to make the world a better place. That was Elizabeth, too – but he liked to keep Elizabeth locked up tight in his memory, where she couldn't be hurt or humiliated. His time with her had finished, long ago, and had been so rich and golden: the sun had blazed over them both, for a while. Elizabeth had 'loved life' – to use the phrase everyone reached for after a sudden death. She probably still loved life, since she hadn't died.

He had lived with Elizabeth, briefly – or stayed with her. He had travelled with her, but as for getting to know her, really? Never – and did it matter now?

He shook his head, knowing that he could sit on the station all morning, thinking it through.

He could sit on other stations too, missing trains. He'd been doing it for months, and he could sit on certain buses and miss his stop, because it didn't matter. If you had a day-pass, it didn't matter at all – and you could zigzag from A to B to C and come back by some other, circular route. You could head down the High Street, for example, and there was the library again. In you went, to join the old men who'd arrived earlier and were now staring at newspapers. Some researched local history, or studied maps. There was a stamp enthusiast, and the one with the wild, Karl Marx beard: they assembled like a club of silent bachelors, and Michael wasn't a member just yet. He was only fifty-six and he still laundered his clothes carefully. The library men were older, and smelled of neglect and sweat – deodorant was a luxury they could ill-afford, or a nicety they'd long forgotten, and they sat there waiting for him. One day his washing machine would break down, and he'd lose his flat. Then he'd be one of them.

Michael smiled, then frowned.

His reading glasses were surprisingly dirty, so he cleaned them harder with the little duster that had come with the case. When he put them on again, everything was so much clearer – including Monica, sitting opposite him on the other platform. There she was, or someone who looked just like her, and he was tempted to wave. She was hunting for something in her bag, even as the 09.46 came slowly and quietly into view.

It was the commuter train, and Michael knew he couldn't take it. The 10.13 was on its way, running just two minutes late: whether it would make those minutes up or experience further delays was impossible to say. He watched the train he'd intended to catch get closer, as the woman he'd spoken to stood up and moved further down the platform in readiness to board.

She hadn't looked at him.

'Excuse me,' she might have said. 'Excuse me, aren't you getting this one after all? Sorry, what's your name? I thought we were travelling together?'

'I'm Michael. Michael MacMillan.'

'I'm Henrietta, or Hilary – and as you know, I'm on my way to Cheltenham. Shall we sit together, Michael? We could talk properly.'

She didn't say that or anything else, because she had a daughter on her mind, who was probably starting an important job. She might even be getting a foot on the property ladder, though Cheltenham was expensive, of course – and they could have talked all the way north about just how difficult it was. They could have agreed that young people stood little chance these days, without their parents' help, and they could have laughed indulgently. Michael could have invented a daughter of his own. She'd be in Germany working as a translator, like the god-daughter poor old Monica supported.

The announcement came then, as he knew it must – and it was that wonderfully clear voice again: 'The train now standing at platform two is the 09.46 for Great Malvern...'

It was not standing at the platform.

The driver was just beginning to brake; the automated infor-mation-sequence had started fifteen seconds too early. He'd missed the previous one, but they must have played it – for that was the one that told everyone that the train was approaching. They would have made that claim when there was no train in sight, and Michael had once emailed the company to point it out. His real concern was with the last of the three, which came just as the doors opened: 'Stand clear of the train at platform two. This train is ready to leave.'

That was the announcement as people disembarked, and it induced not exactly panic but a certain anxiety. For how could the train be ready to leave when there were people on the plat-form waiting to board? Fifteen seconds later, it would have all made perfect sense: all they had to do was play the first one fifteen seconds later, and everything would be correct.

'As I get onto the train,' Michael had said. 'Or as I wait on the platform, you tell me to stand back. "The train is ready to leave," you say. The train is *not* ready to leave, because we're still getting on and off. I'd like to know if you play the message by mistake, because there's an error in the timing – or if it's delib-erate. Is it your intention to hurry people? If that's the case, I understand, but I think it's impolite. If it's not the case, please do your best to change the timing.'

The station clock was also wrong, but he hadn't mentioned that. The lift was often out of order, but he hadn't mentioned that. The ticket office seemed to be open for fewer hours, but he hadn't even mentioned that, even though he liked the calm, efficient men who sold tickets and knew their jobs were under threat. One thing at a time, and he had written politely and positively.

The reply had come in less than a week. The company was grateful for his message, but: *We have no control over the routine communications system on individual stations. We have therefore forwarded your communication to the operations department.*

Michael had gone to the library and researched that department. He found details for a first point of contact.

I expect by now you will have received my email...

I wonder if you have received an email that was forwarded to you...?

I am hoping to communicate with you about something that on one level is very trivial, but – on another – fundamental to how our railways run and how people use them. It is a small thing...

He had a vision of young men and women in the equivalent of a call centre, sitting at computers with headsets over their ears. The company would have outsourced the passenger-comment franchise, or whatever it was called, and those working would undoubtedly be on minimum wage. He had spoken to three workers in the customer-service department, about other things – and they always gave their names.

'My name is Stefan, how can I help you today?'

Michael explained – and this had been another incident, that had happened to him late one night the previous year. It came back to him now so clearly, and he closed his eyes. On that occasion he'd been in Southampton, having booked his return in advance for just five pounds. The train had arrived early. The carriage he'd stepped into had the most terrible smell, for it was nearly eleven o'clock at night and there were fast-food wrappers strewn around the tables. There was another smell over the top of that, though – much more distinctive.

'Don't tell me,' laughed Stefan. 'Was it dog shit?'

In fact, he hadn't said anything of the sort: Michael would amuse himself, sometimes, by imagining what call-centre people wished they could say, because it was clear that Stefan worked to a script. Michael knew that he had been trained never to be facetious – the poor man wasn't allowed even to interrupt.

'Don't tell me,' he might have said. 'Someone had pissed themselves, or puked? Vomit, perhaps? Tell me everything, Michael.'

The man sounded Polish, Romanian or Czech. What journey from the east had he made, in order to find himself hunched over a console listening to a fifty-six-year-old man recalling his experience on a stationary train in Southampton?

'It was a smell of permanent marker,' said Michael.

It had reminded him of school.

'Right,' said Stefan – listening carefully.

'It's unmistakable, isn't it?' continued Michael. 'So I looked up and down and I saw that two of the tables had been vandalised. With graffiti, you see – from the marker pen.'

Stefan said nothing now. Presumably he wasn't sure what Michael's point was going to be – or if, perhaps, he had made it. That was the probable reason for the silence, though Michael knew there could be others.

'The graffiti was actually quite obscene,' said Michael.

'Were you able to move to another carriage, sir?' said Stefan.

'Yes, of course. I could have done.'

He might have used the connecting door and forgotten about the images he'd seen. There were four carriages, and the train was still at the station, changing crew, so Michael could have disembarked. Instead, he had paused to study the graffiti, and that was how he'd come to see the large penis rearing up from a pair of pineapple-sized testicles. The penis had lips, which were pulled back to release a fountain of what had to be sperm – the globules looked like teardrops, bursting. *Suk my cock* had been written under the image, and the artist had signed his or her name below that. *Ejay!* was the name, shouting out loud in thick, black ineradicable ink. Michael had stared and reread the words, wondering how long it had taken Ejay to create the work, and what other passengers might have been thinking.

The other table had no picture at all: it had simply been scribbled on.

'I could have done that,' said Michael. 'I could have moved, but that's not what I'm actually calling about. I'm calling to tell you that when I spoke to the guard a bit later, he didn't seem to care. He told me that the train would be cleaned in the depot.'

Again, there was a silence. Michael could hear the very faint sounds of another operator taking a call.

'You've got CCTV,' said Michael, to Stefan. 'I asked the guard if he was going to find out who'd vandalised his train, and he said it wasn't worth it. "Ah," he said. "They'll clean it at the depot." "But it's vandalism," I said.'

The guard had laughed.

He had been a small, slight Sikh gentleman. He had the gentlest, most sympathetic face under his turban, and he'd walked up the carriage slowly in a little grey suit, treading lightly, as if he didn't want to disturb the passengers. Michael was used to Sikhs being very big, so this man seemed like a miniature – or even a little boy carefully made up to look old. He had told Michael that there was no point studying the CCTV film because the Transport Police wouldn't do anything.

'They would if it was an assault,' said Michael.

He sat on the bench, as the delayed 09.46 prepared to leave, and wondered why he had said something so stupid.

Of course they would act, if it was an assault. An assault was different. An assault was more serious than someone drawing obscene graffiti: everyone knew that, so what was the point of the comparison? Why had Michael thought, even for a moment, that a room full of Transport Police might want to sit studying the footage, hunting for images of Ejay as he or she fled the station with the marker pen in his or her hand? What would they do if they identified him – because it must have been a boy, surely? Would he be arrested and made to pay?

'You'll have to pay, I'm afraid,' said a smooth voice in Michael's head – sing-song, smiling, with glittering, fun-filled eyes. The smell of the pen had taken him straight back to the classroom, and there was the teacher's voice.

'I didn't know homework was due, sir.'

'Ah, but ignorance is no plea,' said Mr Trace as the other boys laughed. 'Come out here and pay the price!'

'Wouldn't they?' said Michael.

He was speaking to Stefan, who was still at his computer console, listening professionally and not interrupting. 'You have the CCTV footage,' he said. 'So I think something ought to be done. You ought to prosecute these people, because it's a crime. It's disgusting.'

Stefan did speak, then. He urged Michael to put his thoughts in writing, and send them to the company so as to open a proper complaint file that would receive further attention. He would need to document the case and detail the exact time and date of the incident.

'I haven't got the time,' said Michael – which was a lie.

Stefan said nothing to that.

I just want the world to be a nicer place, he thought, but did not say. I want it to be better and more decent, and I want… it's more than that, Stefan. I want big corporations like your train company to spend some of their profits on making our world less foul. I want Ejay to be confronted and helped. I don't want him fined or thrashed. He's only a boy and I want him supported, because you can't go through life drawing ejaculating penises on tables: it's not right.

Michael said, 'I don't have the time,' and he'd said it in a voice that suggested that even this call now had to be hurried. Perhaps Stefan was imagining Michael just as Michael had been imagining Stefan? – in which case perhaps Stefan had an image of a forceful person, neatly dressed and professional, sitting amongst files and invoices, his laptop chirping softly as the emails landed. The Michael that Stefan saw was a conscientious traveller who'd made the time to follow up on an experience that had disturbed his sense of propriety, but now – duty done – he had to return to the pressures of his demanding job and loving, needy family.

'I'm sorry your journey was made uncomfortable,' said Stefan – and there was no trace of irony. The man was humble and sincere.

'It wasn't really,' said Michael.

Silence.

'I just wanted to talk to someone about the incident. I mean… if young children had seen that picture, they would have been horrified.'

'I'm sure it will have been cleaned off, as a priority,' said Stefan.

'That's what the guard said. He said it would be cleaned in the depot.'

'They're pretty good.'

Stefan's English was perfect.

'I'm sure they are,' said Michael – and he wondered which young children might have been horrified. Why would young children have been up so late, and wouldn't the drawing have simply made them laugh – or put their hands to their mouths? Yes, it would have told them, subliminally, that the penis is a weapon – but they would have got over that soon enough and realised it needn't be. They would come to understand that if some penises go unused for long periods of time, shrinking and withering as the pubic hair moults and sensation proves ever more unsatisfactory, then *some* penises do not. Some swell and splatter the world, for some penises are like spears, because what's the best way of picking up a bird? That was a joke from school that clawed him back to boyhood. What's the best way of picking up a bird, Michael? On the end of your dick.

He hated that joke, but it was lodged in his head.

You lift her up on the end of your dick, and carry her into the bedroom! That's the best way, apparently. That's how it's done, Mr Trace – if a girl is what you want, sir.

'Thanks for taking my call,' said Michael politely.

'Not at all, sir. Is there anything else I can help you with?'

'Yes, please,' he wanted to say. 'Yes.'
Instead he'd said, 'No. You've helped me a lot.'

Courtesy meant dignity. Perhaps Stefan ended the call feeling better, because progress had been made. He would have felt worse, probably, if Michael had sworn at him – though once again, how could you know? Call-centre people buckled on suits of armour, surely: they made themselves impregnable. It was Michael who'd ended the call feeling better, and he knew it was because someone had taken him seriously for almost two whole minutes. Now he sat on the station bench, trying not to look down, for the 09.46 had departed.

To look down meant seeing his own feet, which were planted either side of his shoulder bag, there on the earth's crust. If he stood up too fast he'd go through, and slither down into the caverns of despair.

'The Caverns of Despair' was an image from a poem he'd written for his English teacher, who'd read it to the class:

Come with me, to the caverns of despair. . .

It had earned eleven-year-old Michael his first ever straight A grade, but he couldn't remember the next line. Now he was old, and he leaned forward carefully to open the bag. There were some easy-peel tangerines inside, packed into the front pocket in their net. He took one out, and it took less than thirty seconds to reveal the fruit, then sixty seconds to eat it. As a child, he remembered the peeling of an orange taking for ever, because skins were tight and there was always a layer of white stuff that needed removing. Now they were simple and they were seedless, too. They were ridiculously cheap, discounted at the supermarket he passed on his way to this particular station.

He is a lucky man, people might think, if they noticed him on the bench. He eats his orange, without a care in the world – no work for him today, and why not? Perhaps he's part-time, or even retired? Is that possible? He is going on some nice excursion, perhaps, this man of leisure... he is meeting a friend for coffee further up the line. Could he even be a grandfather? Yes, he's old enough – but he's probably an uncle joining a nephew and niece, with tickets to the zoo. The zoo? No, the space museum, or the science park, or the place people play Laser Quest, next door to the vast, warehouse-like space they'd opened full of trampolines.

So many people, it seemed, wanted to bounce up and down.

Michael sat, wondering if he looked like a grandfather, and he wondered who would have his watch, which he'd left by his phone. Both sat on the envelope: phone and watch, and his charger too. He'd made his bed. He'd even emptied the glass of water, and left it in the kitchen. What would happen to the things he kept in the fridge?

Ryan might have them, as he lived below. More likely, they'd be thrown away along with his paperbacks, his underwear, and his extra-thick jersey. Even his supermarket loyalty card would be wasted, and yet he'd accumulated so many points. Surely they could be transferred to someone?

Ryan downstairs – or nobody at all. But someone would have to take the duvet cover off the duvet, launder it and then fold it on a hanger so it could sit in the linen section of the charity shop, so that another someone, coming in, might pause and – if they only knew – recognise the clothing on the rack just behind. The jersey, the cap, the half-dozen shirts. The blue bedroom slippers! And they might, just for a moment, remember the man they'd seen walking to and from the railway station, and glimpse his ghost. Here were his remains on the two-for-the-price-of-one rail, raising money for Save the Children. God save the children: Michael was helping children, even after Crewe.

He looked up at the electronic-display sign, so much more efficient than the painted ones they'd used when he was younger. These were updated every second it seemed, for the 10.13 was on time again – it had made up some distance. He had eight minutes left to wait, and he was alone on the bench. Nobody had sat beside him, and there was orange peel on his knee.

A boy in school uniform stopped in front of him, wheeling a bicycle. Without thinking, Michael said, 'You're running late,' and the boy smiled nervously.

His instinct was to smile, even at a stranger.

Michael wondered why he'd spoken. All he'd meant was that at close to ten o'clock the boy was going to be late: a simple statement of fact. He was fourteen at the most, and dressed in the burgundy-coloured blazer of the academy one stop down, so it was safe to assume he wouldn't get there until half past or so. On the other hand, it wasn't safe to assume he was late, because there were many possible reasons for him missing the first two hours, and Michael realised he couldn't possibly know the facts and therefore shouldn't have jumped to conclusions. The boy's parents might have arranged their son's unavoidable absence. They might have come from the doctor's, or the hospital – the boy might have been visiting a loved one who had just had an operation, though surely visiting wouldn't take place in the morning unless it was urgent?

The boy had moved on. He was now checking his phone, so maybe it *had* been urgent.

'Who is it?' Michael wanted to say. 'Is it someone close?'

'My gran.'

Just a moment of connection.

The boy's eyes were filling with tears. The bike was gone, and he was beside Michael on the bench.

'Don't talk if you don't want to.'

'I do want to, mister. I feel like I've got to.'

The boy was himself, of course. Michael found he was nodding again, and he slipped an arm around his younger self's shoulders. Where was his friend, though? Where was dear old James? Because they'd caught the train together most mornings. Michael, James and Luke, who got on at the next station – they'd been close, with fine biblical names like three young disciples. Yatin was the fourth, whose mother and father were dentists. Four friends, inseparable in their smart blazers, black rather than burgundy: they looked out for each other, fighting off the bullies and getting into scrapes – what larks they'd had, learning about the world.

'Did you do the maths?'

'God, it was hard.'

'It's not in until Friday, is it?' It was probably James who'd said that, for he was just that little bit disorganised.

'Maths is today, James! The deadline's today! Copy mine...'

Now Michael sat alone, saying nothing to the child beside him. He passed him a segment of tangerine, and the silence went on. James wasn't coming to school today, perhaps: he was ill, and would miss period three, with Mr Trace. James was his own age now, if he was alive – which he should be. You shouldn't die at fifty-six, after all, unless you were unlucky. No James, and the whole platform was suddenly empty. A few people waited on the one opposite, though. A woman looked up and thought, That kind man is supporting a child who appears to be in distress. It's a moment of connection.

'Why did he do it?' said the boy quietly. 'It was horrible.'

He looked at Michael, and Michael saw the tears in his own eyes – for the station lights were coming on, and the winter was always bitterly cold.

'He's dead now.'

'So what?'

'So it's over. He won't ever do it again, and we must pity him. We'll feel better, perhaps, if we pity him. There's no going back, is there?'

'What do you mean?'

'I mean, we have to go forward. We have to forget, and move forward.'

'How, Michael? I want to go back.'

'You can't.'

'Why not?'

'I don't know, but it's like anything and everything. The pain goes away, and we can be stronger. We're survivors, aren't we? Remember the good times! Remember that afternoon, in the Scouts. You and James, on the ferry – me and James...'

'Where was Luke?'

'Not there.'

Michael smiled, and his young self leaned against him, so Michael hugged the child harder, getting both arms tight around his narrow shoulders. That was the way to make him invisible, and there were just five pieces of orange left. They were blurred as he counted them, and there was another announcement.

'We'll be fine,' he said – and then he said nothing, because he was thinking of Elizabeth.

Had he spoken aloud? His left hand was touching his nose, as if he had a nosebleed – bent forward, staring at the platform floor.

'But will we?' said the tiny boy, curled inside his jacket. 'What if it's never fine? What if this blights my life, and I'm lost for ever in the woods, and the caverns of despair? What if, despite all the years I've had to build things, I end my days alone? Alone in a small flat, where the letters continue to arrive as the invoices did at the council, and opening them becomes unnecessary?'

'I have missed too many payments.'

'*We have to write to you, because the train now approaching is approaching. We have to tell you we have handed the debt to an approaching agency—*'

'And I appreciate that.'

'*You have to stand back, now. If you don't come to an arrangement with us, you will lose your home – stay well behind the yellow line.*'

Michael's head was in his hands again.

'I always do,' he said quietly. My flat is lost, and it doesn't matter, because I don't need one any more. I'm in a tight spot, you see. There are two cards I can't use, because I abused both. They were violated, so I only have one left. That is how I bought my ticket to Crewe, and I will never return to the flat where even the curtains tell the world, or anyone interested, that only the worthless live here – only those who will be found several days after their deaths, perhaps, when Ryan finally notices there are more flies than usual, gathering in the hall.

Michael could give the boy with the bike his watch, except that he was at the far end of the platform – and Michael wasn't wearing it, anyway. It was with his phone. He was surprised to find tears in his eyes. His hands were over his face properly now, the orange peel still on his lap. He was shaking slightly, and the 10.13 had arrived – early, perhaps? The driver had put his foot down, eager to get ahead: it had sailed in from nowhere, like a magic train. It was getting ready to leave, and a whistle blew so cheerfully. People had to stand away now, and let the doors close, for it couldn't wait for ever – it was full of people itching to get to the future, going forwards.

Why had the boy wheeled his bicycle to the end of the platform?

He had boarded, and Michael watched as the train blurred and left the station. Nobody was watching him. If someone was staring at the CCTV images what would they think? He remains behind because he is waiting to meet someone. He is not a man who needs our attention, so we will not lead him gently to the exit, and urge him to sit down quietly on a different bench, with a cup of tea. No, he is a man to be respected, and left alone.

Michael took two deep breaths and smiled.

His objective was to be in Crewe for lunchtime, and there would be another train soon – at 10.23 in fact. He stood up, and the 10.13 gathered speed. He waved to the passengers as they slid away up the line, hoping people would think he'd just seen someone off. He was smiling more brightly than ever now, wondering if he should take his first nip of whisky – which he didn't feel like drinking. He had seventy-five centilitres, decanted into a fruit-juice carton, and he even had a glass because he couldn't abide plastic cups. He needed to be drunk, he was sure of that.

He wiped his eyes, and checked the bag between his feet. The thought of malt whisky in the morning made him feel sick. Another tangerine was the answer, and he'd try to wash it down with a few good gulps. There was a packet of mints somewhere, because the last thing he wanted was to be taken for a sad, empty-headed alcoholic who couldn't even walk straight. Michael was determined to get onto the track and stay upright. Then the rails would guide him, and it was only 10.14. He still had time, as long as there were no cancellations, and as long as he held his nerve.

There was no need to feel sad, for everything would be resolved at Crewe.

He turned, and looked at the vending machine.

Behind him, another train came in, serving the opposite plat-form: its ghost moved across the glass through the treasure trove of sweets which dangled precariously, asking to be bought. Someone must have recently refilled it, just as someone had designed, built and installed it – and what was the result? The result was that he, Michael MacMillan, need never go hungry or thirsty again. The world was looking after him, offering him Twixes and Twirls, and even Maltesers: that most shareable of treats. There they hung, bright and tantalising, and as he put his nose closer his reflection smiled happily back at him. Confectionery could do that: it could always make you happy.

COMING SOUTH

The girl's name was Ayesha.

She was travelling with a guitar, and Michael would not meet her because he was travelling north. It was a conspicuous piece of luggage: a hard, grey case, standing on the seat right next to her. In fact, she was wondering if she ought to wedge it onto the overhead luggage shelf, because the train was getting busier, and the platform was crowded. The last time she'd been on a train, a young man had freed up some space by doing just that, finding a gap for his rucksack above the man sitting in front of him. Ayesha had watched him do it, thinking it was really too big and heavy to be safely stowed – but the owner seemed to know his business. It took him a while, standing with his arms upraised, the sweat patches clear and dark as he turned the thing around and forced it in. Satisfied, he took his seat and it wasn't until a good ten minutes had elapsed that the bag worked itself free and fell onto the head of the passenger under it.

Ayesha had glanced up in time to see it connect.

The victim's skull had been as hairless as an egg, so the blow seemed extra cruel – it had been a neck-breaking crunch that had made him and the woman sitting next to him cry out together. The owner of the bag leapt to his feet, and apologised, but his main concern was for his luggage: he hadn't seen the man's head snap to the side as it took the impact, so he probably didn't realise how much pain he'd caused.

And it had, after all, been an accident.

If anyone was to blame it was the designer of the train, whose priority seemed to have been the aerodynamic appearance of the carriage rather than storage capacity. Or had the designer been responding to a brief created through fear? Ayesha wondered if the train company was frightened that a larger luggage rack would end up being the perfect hiding place for an explosive device? Anyway, the man who'd been hurt spent the rest of the journey rubbing his neck and working his shoulders. He muttered to his wife, and she muttered back: both looked furious, but there was soon nobody to be furious with, because the young man took his rucksack off at the next station, and everyone watched him hurry towards the exit barriers without a care in the world.

'A musician?' said a voice.

Michael might have asked the same question, but he was a long way off, just leaving Bath. It was a man sitting opposite, and Ayesha realised she had made the mistake of staring into space, unoccupied and open to conversation. She would normally curl up with her headphones in her ears, and the journey would be an opportunity to catch up on the music a college friend regularly sent her. Now she was obliged to smile, make eye contact, and reply.

'Not me,' she said.

'Whose is it? It's not lost property, is it? It's not a... God forbid—'

'No, no. It's mine, but it belonged to someone else. I'm just delivering it.'

'Acoustic?'

'Yes.'

'I have one myself. I even had lessons, years ago.'

Ayesha raised her eyebrows.

'I gave up,' she said.

The man was sitting back in his seat: thirty-five to forty years old with soft, neatly cut fair hair and a slightly boyish, sunburned face. He wore a neutral grey suit over a black shirt, and the distinguishing mark was his white clerical collar. He was slim, and his features fell naturally into a friendly, easy smile. She saw that his eyes were soft blue, and he had no anxiety about looking into hers. He didn't seem to blink.

'I probably should have done,' he said. 'Given up, I mean. I embarrass everyone now, especially my wife. Are you going far?'

'Preston,' replied Ayesha.

'Not a town I know. I don't think I've ever been outside the station.'

'You're very wise.'

'Oh, poor old Preston. It's as bad as that?'

'I'm sure it's got nice parts. It's just...'

'You've never found them?'

'I'm still hoping.'

'Don't give up.'

They laughed.

'I'm off to the Lakes myself,' he said. 'Windermere. Do you know that part of the world?'

Ayesha shook her head.

'You should explore,' continued the man. 'I went there a couple of years ago, and it's sensational – it's Wordsworth country, if you like him. We have a retreat there, so... yes. It's a beautiful place.'

There was a silence, and Ayesha wasn't sure how to proceed.

If she produced her headphones, that would be the signal he was probably expecting: he would know the conversation was over. If she spoke again, he'd assume she was happy to spend the whole journey chatting.

'So your family's in Preston?' said the man, before she could decide. 'My name's Paul, by the way.'

'Ayesha.'

'And do shut me up, if you have work to do. Or... I don't know, things to attend to on your phone. I'm just putting off reading some papers. The retreat's a kind of conference, so there's preparation to be done – which I can do tonight. I'm not looking forward to it.'

'Papers for what?'

'For the retreat.'

'And what do you do on a retreat?' said Ayesha.

She knew, really. What she didn't know was why she was asking such a silly question.

'It's an opportunity, I suppose,' he said.

Ayesha went to speak again, but he continued.

'A kind of respite, from the world of work and all the... you know, the day-to-day stuff. It's a chance to think.'

'And how long do you go for?'

'This one is five nights.'

'Five nights of prayer and fasting?'

'Oh, a great deal of prayer. Not too much fasting, I hope. Prayer is the... backbone, or the foundation – I don't know. We're discussing the Church's response to homelessness.'

'Doesn't it have one?'

'Oh, yes. It has a vigorous one. It's not hard to know our Christian duty, because it's hardly a... hardly a complicated theological issue.'

He lowered his voice a little, though they still had the four seats to themselves.

'Nobody's going to stand up and dispute our *theoretical* duty,' he said. 'It's a bit harder, though, when you live in a city absolutely inundated with homeless people, and you... Well, you don't have anywhere to put them, frankly.'

Except your church, thought Ayesha. Or your vicarage, perhaps – which is probably one of those large buildings with lots of spare rooms.

She said nothing, because she knew that a remark like that would provoke a very long reply. If she suggested the Church could do more, he would agree because it was his job to agree. But then he would explain all the practical difficulties, and the need to balance different interest groups or abide by legislation. He would explain why the problem had to be managed carefully because it was complicated. Things were always complicated, unfortunately: there were no simple things any more. She found that she was looking him in the eye again, and he looked back at her with that gentle, friendly, confident smile.

He blinked, at last.

She thought, He is probably a wonderful vicar – if that's what he is. Clergyman. Reverend Paul, helping people and strumming his guitar whilst laughing at himself and trying always to be positive.

He no doubt wanted to be kind, and help people.

'So who's it belong to? The guitar.'

'My brother.'

'And how old is he?'

'He's…'

The silence fell between them again, though there was noise everywhere. Behind her, she heard the internal carriage doors open and the distinct sound of bottles and glasses clinking. The train had picked up speed, and there was a low whistling as it swept along the track, flat fields on either side under an even grey sky. Two women were talking in the seats across from hers, though they were speaking over each other, not listening. Between Paul and herself, though, a silence had opened up that she couldn't quite fill, because he had asked the question out of the blue and she wasn't ready for it. A random question, as she idly pondered what the Church might have to say about homelessness, and what this very nice man might do to help people.

'Why do you ask?' she said.

'Oh… nosiness. Train of thought. My own son is learning, so—'

'How old is he?'

'My son? Fifteen.'

'My brother isn't alive any more,' said Ayesha. 'He died, almost three years ago. I'm… returning the guitar to my parents, who want to give it to one of their friends' daughters. I think it's a daughter – it might be a cousin. Some relative, anyway. It… I think it needs new strings, probably, but it was a good guitar, so it makes sense.'

'Right.'

'He'd left it at my place, you see – and… I've just been looking after it ever since. Or not looking after it – it hasn't been out of its case. It's just been sitting there, so – now, finally… it's off to a new home.'

She paused, and allowed the man to say what she knew he'd say.

'I'm so sorry.'

She smiled, trying to signal that there was no need to be because the world had moved on, and her brother was no longer at the forefront of her mind. She wasn't grieving at this moment. It was some way off, because they had come such a great distance. There was another question, though, and she had experienced it so many times. Would he ask it? How close did this man want to come? As a clergyman he wouldn't back off. Some people were simply silenced when she told them her younger brother was dead: she could feel their fear. Others went out of their way to insist that death was no obstacle in a conversation, and that her brother should be talked about as if he were alive – that was their way of honouring him, and honouring her. She had had such encounters so many times, and she never got it quite right. To not mention her brother, or his death, seemed like a betrayal. To reveal the truth forced people to the next question: 'How did he die?'

'He was killed,' she said, and Paul looked into her eyes.

She thought, He asked about him – and this is his business. He's a vicar, and deals with loss every week. I've put him on duty again, poor man – just as he was looking forward to a chat about guitar lessons and families – a mild flirtation, even – and he finds himself sitting with the blasted bereaved. And he doesn't know what I need, if I need anything. He doesn't know if he can provide it, but he won't back away. It's his job not to back away.

'How?' he said. 'I'm so sorry, and if you don't want to tell me, please… I don't want to intrude.'

He glanced at the women opposite, who were still talking over each other. There was a curious intimacy, and for a moment Ayesha wondered if she wanted to confess her many sins.

'I don't want to ignore what you just said, though,' said Paul. 'How was he killed?'

'He was in a road accident…'

Why was she about to cry? The tears came out of nowhere: from a sudden cloud.

They pricked into her eyes, as if the weather had changed – as if the train had taken her into a different band of pressure, which produced warm rain.

It was Paul's stare that was affecting her, so she looked away and saw that they were going over a level crossing, and one vehicle had stopped at the barrier. Ironically, it was a large lorry, the irony being that Kristin had been killed by a large lorry. 'Killed' was the wrong word, and she should not have used it. The lorry had not set out to do anything bad, and the driver was innocent. The driver had never driven again, so she'd been told – he'd given up his Heavy Goods Vehicle Class One licence, and the firm had found him a job in the warehouse. He wouldn't even drive a car. He had come to the funeral, and he hadn't been able to speak. Nor had she. Nor had her parents. Around the white coffin and the flowers there had been a paralysis that locked the tongue and made your legs heavy.

Thirteen years of life had stopped, and the body was ready now for what nobody could disguise, though they tried. A big, deep hole had been dug, and there was soil standing by. Take him, earth, for cherishing: the white wood must rot away in time, and the cold clay must get to him in the end and soak through the jeans, T-shirt and fleece they'd chosen for this, his final, final outing.

Paul was leaning forward.

She thought he was about to touch her, but he didn't. He said softly, 'I'm a stranger. I didn't mean to intrude, but... sometimes you find that strangers help.'

'Really?'

'Maybe. Sudden encounters, you know—'

'You mean we've been brought together? By God?'

'No.'

She had attacked him, but he was ready for it. He had been in this situation before: God did direct him into these little conflicts, perhaps, so that he might bring healing.

'I wouldn't put it quite like that,' he said. 'But I would say—'

'Maybe God is trying to help me,' said Ayesha. 'By putting us together like this.'

'Look,' said Paul quietly.

He paused.

'I don't have any right to ask you about private, painful experiences... and losing a brother must be one of the most painful.'

'He was thirteen. Eight years younger than me.'

'What was his name?'

'Kristin.'

Paul said nothing for a moment, letting the silence convey his absolute, limitless sympathy. The train hummed, and Ayesha hesitated, wondering if she had the energy to attack him properly. She realised it would be the best way of stemming the tears, which were there in her eyes, ready to flow. The clergyman had seen them.

She smiled, and said something she'd often thought.

'I wish God had helped us on the day he died,' she said.

He looked back at her, waiting.

'I don't know what he was thinking of,' she said. 'God, that is. What happened was that Kristin was cycling with a friend, down a hill. Friday afternoon. And the lights were a bit confusing – we're not quite sure what he thought, and his friend couldn't work it out either. Somehow he thought – Kristin, this is – he thought that he had the right of way, so he went onto the junction, but he didn't. And a lorry... an articulated lorry was coming across and it hit him. He went under the wheels. It wasn't the driver's fault: there was nothing he could have done... he was doing twenty-four miles an hour and Kristin simply didn't see him. He must have checked to the left and not realised there was traffic to the right – I don't know. Maybe he did see it, but it was too late. They went over it, and over it, but the point was...'

She looked at Paul's serious, sympathetic face.

'God didn't really help us very much, on that occasion.'

'No.'

'No.'

She paused.

'If he'd just moved that lorry back,' she said. 'Fifteen metres further back, and that would have been enough. If he'd whispered in Kristin's ear, "Stop." Actually, I say fifteen metres – two metres, because then the bumper would have probably thrown him clear.

As it was, God organised the perfect accident, really. A kind of textbook example of how a lorry can crush a child with no hope of that child surviving. He had multiple fractures, internal injuries and he died at the scene, and...'

'I'm so sorry.'

'I know. We were, too. Everyone was, and still is. I have never met anyone who isn't. There probably are people who'd say, "One less Indian," but nobody's ever said that to me, and so... thank you for being sorry. I shouldn't have told you about him, but I'm afraid you asked, and I loved him.'

'I'm glad you have. It's important that you have.'

'No, it's not.'

'It's important he's acknowledged,' said Paul. 'He lives on, in your—'

'No,' said Ayesha. 'No, he doesn't. Don't say that.'

'What?'

She swallowed.

'What you were about to say – what you said. You've misunderstood, I think. He... he doesn't live on at all, because he's dead, Paul. He... I'll give you an example.'

She swallowed again, amazed at the grief, and furious with the single tear that was halfway down her cheek. She was amazed at her own resolution, too.

'He was in his school's chess team,' she said quietly. 'And the following Tuesday he was due to play in a semi-final against some other school, and he wasn't able to do that. Being dead, he didn't turn up, and... presumably someone else had to sit in the chair and move all the pieces. Another example—'

'Ayesha?'

'Another example of him not living on is that we'd booked a summer holiday together. We were all going out to Mumbai to meet relatives we hadn't seen for ages. Mumbai, then up to Pune, and then to a hill station – an expensive holiday, and... Kristin didn't go. None of us did, but Kristin wasn't able to go because he wasn't "living on" any more. He was in the ground, because God must have been looking the other way, or...'

'Or what?'

'Well. It struck me that God might not actually exist.'

They stared at each other.

'I stopped being an agnostic some time ago,' said Ayesha. 'I no longer think, Oh! Who knows? Maybe there's a creative energy in the world, a spiritual dimension. I realise now what the real problem with God is. You see, there simply isn't one.'

'Ayesha, nobody can explain suffering like that.'

'Of course they can.'

'How?'

His voice was gentle. He had put his face into the fire, and was holding it there. But I am not merciful, thought Ayesha. He asked about Kristin. He wears the dog collar, bragging about his idiot, comfortless religion. He started it, the fucker. Let him have it.

'We live in a godless world,' she said brightly. 'That's the truth of it, because random accidents happen and... this train could be about to derail. This train could collide with another, or there could be a person in this carriage with a bomb, about to cause maximum suffering as encouraged by some crackpot ideology, which will be based on a god, needless to say. It doesn't need much explanation, does it? Until, funnily enough – until you bring God into it. Then it all falls apart because it's so patently absurd. I mean, if God exists... Christ, he must have hated my brother and our family.'

'No.'

'Yes. Because Kristin *died*, aged thirteen. And that guitar... That guitar is no longer needed, so the idea that God brought you and me together and is trying to patch things up in some way, after the event...' She laughed. 'It's so insane, and so obscene, that I can't think of anything else to say.'

'How are your parents coping?' he said.

'What?'

They had stopped at a station, and still he held his face to the blowtorch.

'What?'

People were getting off, and more people were waiting to get on. There was a little girl with a bicycle, and in fact – she looked again – there were two of them. Ayesha stared because they were identical twins. They were eleven or twelve years old, and they took their cycling seriously. Why weren't they at school? Both were on the platform, dressed in tight-fitting Lycra, which drew attention to their remarkable, identical skinniness. They wore cycling helmets and they were very beautiful.

People were climbing aboard, and the poor girls had no choice but to wait behind the crowd. They were frightened there wouldn't be space, and Ayesha could see them pressing their bikes together as if they were one person, reflected, going through exactly the same anxiety in exactly the same way.

Her parents were not coping, of course. She was not coping, and they were not coping – but they were coping better than her gran, who had simply died. Perhaps she would have died anyway, but the relationship between Kristin and his gran had been so intense, and he had loved her in a way Ayesha still found surprising – because he had been a normal, thoughtless, ego-driven boy capable of lying, cheating and even stealing.

He had stolen from the shop close to his school, and been caught. He had been sharp and dangerous, and when she'd held him – when she'd hugged him – she always noticed his bony shoulder, or hard head. He was noisy. He was messy. You knew when he'd been in the kitchen because he left things everywhere, and spilled juice and crumbs because he tried to do too many things at once, like tearing at a packet of something whilst getting the fridge door open with his elbow. Once he'd trodden dog's mess all through the house because he hadn't bothered to take off his school shoes.

But he would make a point of speaking to his grandmother every day. He knew – he was sensitive enough to know – that her day could not finish without her seeing him or hearing his voice, and he submitted to being touched by her. He feigned impatience, but submitted, so when he died her little guttering candle of life stood no chance at all. It simply went out. She had not wailed and screamed: she had simply shrunk, and become very still. Her stillness lasted only three weeks, and then she died in her chair.

'They cope,' she said.

She didn't want to fight – not any more. She should have said nothing. The twins had disappeared, which meant they must have boarded the train – or she hoped they had. People were moving down the aisle, choosing their seats, and she would now definitely have to move the guitar. Sure enough, a young woman had paused, and was looking at her hopefully but nervously, as if she didn't have the right to a seat. She was Asian, and Ayesha guessed Malaysian.

'Sorry,' she said – and she had the most lovely smile.

'No,' replied Ayesha. 'You're welcome. Please.'

A man was getting into the seat next to Paul, and Ayesha was now standing. It was awkward, for the guitar case was solid. The man stood up to help, but it was obvious that there was no room in the luggage rack.

'I tell you what,' said Ayesha. 'Let me sit there, on the outside.'

'I'm sorry,' said the Asian woman, laughing.

'No, please. You take this one, and I'll sit there.'

'I am a nuisance,' she said.

'You're not. You're welcome.'

Ayesha stepped into the aisle, and the woman squeezed past her into the seat. Ayesha sat down again, with her arm round the neck of the guitar case. A minute passed, as the driver waited for something – the right time of departure, perhaps? And Paul the clergyman said nothing. The conversation could not be continued now, but it had happened and Ayesha knew he was reflecting on it, aware that he had made things worse, not better.

Much worse, and he knew it.

He was a good, nice man, and the fact that he believed crazy tales should not be held against him: he probably did more good than she would ever do. In that sense, he probably did bring healing, and no doubt he would run into someone who needed his kind attention.

The Asian woman was checking something on a piece of paper. 'This train is for Burnley?' she said.

'No,' replied Ayesha.

'No?'

'This is a London train. It doesn't go through Burnley.'

'They told me Burnley Manchester Road.'

'No. Definitely not.'

The woman blinked, and Ayesha could read her thoughts: Do I have time? Can I push my way out to the platform? Do I dare? Would I be better staying put?

She made her mind up in an instant, and was on her feet. Ayesha was up again, too, and the poor woman was obliged to apologise once more. There were half a dozen people in the aisle still, but she was small and agile, and she managed to negotiate her way past them, ducking and squeezing through. Ayesha lost sight of her as she got to the doors of the compartment, but the train still wasn't moving: she might just make it. Sure enough, the seconds went by and there she was, and she had a large rucksack with her that she must have stowed at the end of the carriage. She made it onto the platform with seconds to spare, for the heavy doors hissed shut as a whistle blew, and at once the train slid forward.

Paul had produced a folder of papers, and was reading. The man next to him, however, was looking at Ayesha and the realisation came to them both at the same moment, a full half-minute too late. The woman with the rucksack was standing on the platform looking confused, and they were rolling past her.

The man said, 'You know... this *is* the train for Burnley.'

'You change at Preston,' said Ayesha. 'Why did I tell her it wasn't?'

'It doesn't *stop* at Burnley, but yes, you're right—'

'She shouldn't have got off. She needs to change at Preston. Damn.'

Then they noticed the handbag on the table.

'Is that yours?' said the man.

'No,' said Ayesha. 'She's left it.'

*

That night, at supper, Paul told the story of his conversation with Ayesha. He was one of five, and he recounted the details as exactly as he could because he wondered if he could have done more. He wondered if he had been crass. He wanted to think that her outburst might have done her good, but what he really felt was a deep wretchedness, that he hadn't been able to offer any meaningful comfort, and had – instead – exposed her to his own smugness. He had blundered.

'I enjoyed the sound of my own voice,' he said.

He had. There had been flirtation, at the start, and he was deeply ashamed. He had sinned.

He was aching with self-loathing, so he asked if he could say a prayer with those who had listened to the story, and everyone knew it was the right thing to do. They bowed their heads, and Paul asked for forgiveness. Then he prayed for Kristin's immortal soul and implored God to help Ayesha and her family in their wretchedness.

NORTH AGAIN

5

Yes, they would have sacked him for gross incompetence.

He had told so many people that he'd resigned, or taken voluntary redundancy, that he had come to believe both things – it came as a shock when he remembered the complicated truth, and how he'd been cornered by colleagues in an organisation determined to get rid of him. He was on a train, at last, having boarded the 10.23 and taken a seat facing backwards, which he didn't like to do – he much preferred to face the direction of travel. The memory of almost being fired had come from nowhere, as memories often did. An elderly lady sat opposite him, and he nodded at her. She didn't look at all like the council's humanresources manager, but his sacking had resurfaced and the carriage was suddenly full of council employees and the members of the public who were forever downstairs, seeking consultations and explanations. The train might have been chartered specially, for they were all gathered together, pondering his uselessness.

'There's no option, really,' she'd said – the HR woman. 'You can contest it but I don't think you'll find anyone who'd... you know, take the case, Michael. Try, by all means, please. You have twenty-eight days, but...'

But what?

This was years ago, of course – before he met Amy. And people always looked so sad when they did horrible things – or adults did. It wasn't true at school, of course: they had looked gleeful at school, like the boys who'd pushed him into the pond because he had new shoes. Even kind old Mr Trace had a special smile when he so playfully punished you. Michael blinked him away, and remembered when he'd tried to retrieve a parcel from the post office some time ago, without ID. The postal worker had stood behind the unbreakable glass, refusing to hand it over.

'Sorry,' he'd said, without being sorry. 'Sorry, sir – it says on the card. You need ID.'

It had given the man such pleasure.

'I don't have my wallet with me, but—'

'Sorry.'

'I have the ticket, look. I can tell you what the parcel is – it's just a cream.'

The man had shaken his head, weighed down with the responsibility of preventing fraud and theft – a responsibility people like Michael would never understand, especially if they were foolish enough to ignore simple, clearly written instructions.

'Sorry,' he said again.

'Ignorance is no plea, MacMillan. I think we need a little chat, once you've had your lunch.'

'Did Tracey give you lunch? Did it fit?'

Michael was nodding his head again.

He stared at the landscape, trying to remember the name – not of the post-office man, but of the human-resources manager. It might have been Jill, or Jean or Joan. Certainly a 'J'. She was heavy in her chair, like Monica, but whilst she appeared to be sympathetic, there was a toughness under the sympathy before which Michael wilted. His energy left him.

'Please don't sack me,' he wanted to say. 'I can do better. You have to understand that I am not incompetent, or gross – I just need a little time. We all need a little time, don't we? My mother's dead.'

Of course, if he'd said that she would have said, 'In fairness, you've had quite a lot of time. You've had years, Michael, and I'm sorry about your mother.'

'She's just died. I'm an orphan.'

'You're a what?'

'My father's dead, too. A while ago – so that means I'm an orphan, and the world is so... unforgiving.'

'You're a grown man, Michael.'

'That's what I'm not, Joan – and I know I've had time off but I didn't realise what was happening to me. Aren't you just a tiny bit responsible for my welfare, as my employer? You see, I think I'm ill.'

'Go to a doctor, then.'

'About what? About how long I find myself sitting in the office doing nothing, being grossly incompetent? What can a doctor say?'

He had taken time off, of course he had – but those who are ill often put a lot of work into pretending they're not. Looking back, he hadn't simply been poorly, or overworked. He had been... terminally distracted – and this was all before he met Amy, and got other strange, sad jobs. He couldn't blame Joan or Jean or anyone else, least of all his mother. He'd been distracted, as he was distracted now because the woman opposite had a bag of sweets and suddenly he wanted to know what they were. They were in an old-fashioned paper bag, as if they had gone back in time together to the 1970s when things came in bags, having been weighed out on scales. The newspaper shop where he bought his selection was owned by a man called Mr Moorhouse: *Moorhouse* was the name above the door, and it sold sweets, magazines, and a few books and toys.

When he went to the grammar school he no longer passed Moorhouse's, because he took the train, with James and Luke. There was a bus, but the train was faster. Six years of grammar school had prepared him for two years of college and then various clerical jobs, hopping from an estate agent's to an accountancy firm, from which he'd moved to the county council. There he had served the people. There he had proved, over time, to be grossly incompetent in that service – so incompetent that he could not be helped, even after fourteen years of slow, inefficient and finally destructive non-service. He was approaching fifty, and the human-resources manager – Jo, or Jean – had sat with him and his union rep because things had finally come to a head. Things couldn't go on the way they were going, and for his own protection, for his own health... what she wanted to do was protect him from the pressure, as if he was being brought back from a war. It was as if the conflict had proved too much and he was too shell-shocked to perform his duties.

No hospital bed behind the lines, though.

No bandages round his head, and no pretty nurse to tell him he was through the worst of it as she put bluebells into the flower vase. No relationship forming slowly, for they were both shy, and had suffered so much.

'Hold me.'

His mother had said that, and there'd been no nurse at all, sadly, and his GP had always struck him as rather abrupt. Some people were abrupt, out of shyness. If you're shy, you develop strategies to conceal it – you learn to be rude and brisk, and Dr Bonnermorgan had so many patients who were genuinely, visibly sick… his waiting room was full of them. There were five doctors in all, and every one of them saw steady streams of people with diabetes and arthritic complications – there were so many ways of being diagnosably, properly ill. Michael had sat opposite a man with a huge dressing over his eye, whilst a young woman had a wheezing baby that seemed too sick to even cry. The baby had to take priority – there was nothing more heartbreaking than a baby with an illness. Michael would have been abrupt too, if anyone had come between him and a dying child, so he had nothing but sympathy for Dr Bonnermorgan's shy aggression and his natural disgust for malingering charlatans who needed to shake themselves awake and stop fantasising about bluebells.

'What can we do for you this time?'

The doctor had a beard. It was neat on his face, so carefully trimmed – but the question asked was so freighted with uninterest and suspicion that Michael could hardly reply.

'I don't know,' he said. 'It's probably nothing.'

Had he laughed? Yes.

Dr Bonnermorgan had simply gazed at him, and the beard didn't move because his lips didn't open – and Michael struggled to explain a sadness he didn't understand, for he had nothing to be sad about, since bereavement was a station everyone had to pass through – or a tunnel, or simply a long, horrible delay as you waited for the signal to change. It needn't be a derailment.

'I just can't seem to get going,' he said.

'Are you depressed still?'

'No.'

The doctor got straight to the point.

'Are you worrying about something? Is there something else?'

'No, not really. I just seem to be slowing down.'

'What about counselling?'

'Good Lord. I wouldn't know where to start.'

'You start by going online, or reading a few leaflets. I'll send you some – there's good people out there.'

'It's an idea. Thank you.'

He'd found himself back in the reception area, aware that compared to whole swathes of the ailing population he was absolutely fine and lucky to be so. From his toes to the crown of his balding head, and all the way out to his unbitten fingernails: he could stand like Jesus on the cross, and there was nothing wrong anywhere on his unblemished, slowly fattening body. Blood pressure? Absolutely fine. Alcohol intake? That was too personal a question, so he'd lied about that.

'What about diet?'

'Fine, doctor. Everything's fine, actually. Please see the baby. Save the baby, and restore the sight of a truly wounded man. Help the sick for I am a survivor, totally – I have come through, bowed but unbroken.'

It was Steve, though, who confronted him first – and that was Steve from Building Control, in the same annexe as Monica, but on the floor above. He had no problem remembering Steve's name, for Steve looked and sounded like a Steve. He was a man who seemed to know everything, and dealt in black and white. He *had* to know everything, in fact, because people came to him for guidance. 'I want to convert my loft,' they'd say. 'I need to know whether I can do so or not.'

'No, it's not going to work,' Steve would reply. Or, 'Yes, it's possible. I'd better come and see it. I'd better come and measure the ceiling, to check headroom, and then look at the joists to see if they can take the load – because they probably won't be structural timbers capable of supporting heavy furniture. No, you will have to employ a carpenter to reinforce everything, and while he's doing that you'll have to upgrade your plasterboard to twelve or sixteen mill so it's a fire barrier, and no, again, no. You'll have to abandon that chic spiral-staircase idea, because a chic staircase won't allow anyone in the bedroom to escape quickly enough should there be a roasting, blazing fire. You can put in a roof window, yes, but not in the south elevation where you want to put it – you won't get planning permission. Yes, you will need an architect to draw it all up, and you must then submit the application to me and my colleagues on the appropriate forms having paid the appropriate fee. We know the rules, and we don't ever break them – for your safety. For everyone's safety. We are not pedantic people, determined to frustrate your dreams – we are the ones you will turn to in gratitude, for your building will not collapse or burn. You will not drown in toxic smoke, gasping for air – because of us.'

We live by the rules, and keep children safe.

Steve was a down-to-earth man, and worked for the fire service as a volunteer. He was happy in the company of men, and there was a cheerful ease about him that Michael found curiously intimidating, like the smell of a locker-room. He had once had to pull someone off the electric rail by a level crossing, and had done so with a wooden-handled rake.

That's what he said, though he didn't like to talk about it. Michael couldn't remember how it had come up, because he would never have said, 'Steve. Tell me about some awful thing you have seen or done – tell us your worst fire-service story.'

And where had he found this rake?

Perhaps the line ran past an allotment, or a back garden where the owner was standing by his shed, gathering up the leaves?

Steve also played rugby.

He probably had communal showers. Behind Michael's back, he probably used the foulest language, for contact sport required adrenaline, and adrenaline led to men slashing the air with violent words: 'Oh, Christ!' he'd cry, if Michael's name ever came up. 'Michael, in Accounts? That shit-for-brains cunt. Fucking Michael...'

With a pint in his hand, he would speak like that – he might well use that hand grenade of a word. Why not?

Behind Steve's back, Michael would say, 'Ah, Steve. He knows his stuff. He tells it as it is.'

Behind Michael's back, Steve would probably make that foul gesture where the index finger and thumb make a circle. He didn't see Michael as a useful member of the team. Had they been born ten thousand years ago, and encountered each other as members of different hunter-gatherer tribes, Steve would have probably smashed Michael's skull with a stone and stolen his berries. In the open-plan office of the council, he couldn't do that. He was usually polite and they did their jobs in a kind of broad parallel, well away from the rugby pitch. It was a Thursday morning when the confrontation took place.

'I've just had Limston's on the phone.'

Michael was at his desk, and Steve was standing over him.

'Limston's?'

'Builders' merchants. They said they put their invoice in two months ago.'

'Right. I can check that, Steve—'

'I'm not asking you to check it. I'm telling you. They just faxed a copy through to me, and it went in two months ago. June the fifth. Then they followed it up with a reminder, and then an overdue notice, and I've just had the manager nearly at bloody breaking point because we haven't paid them. It's for forty-three thousand pounds. Why haven't they been paid?'

'I don't know. It will be in the system, so—'

'It's not in the system.'

'Then... I'll have to check.'

'What are you doing with the invoices?'

He pulled up a chair, and sat down so he was uncomfortably close. Michael remembered the smell of cigarettes and the power of his arms in a short-sleeved shirt that seemed tight. Nobody else was paying any attention, it seemed – but the tone of voice Steve had used in that last question must have alerted everyone within earshot that a power struggle was under way, and a weaker tribesman was about to be vanquished.

'What are you doing, Michael? What are you doing with the invoices?'

'What I always do.'

'Robbie Limston is a friend of mine. He's asked me to look into this because his bank won't service the debt any more – you know what that means?'

'Yes, of course, but—'

'It means he's got to get money from somewhere, fast, or he risks going under. You know how quickly a little firm like that can go under? I mean, he sails pretty close to the wind. There are months when he hardly turns a profit.'

'Steve—'

'Show me the original invoice.'

There was a very short silence.

'How?'

'Open your folders. Let me see your records for June.'

'I don't think I can. They're in ledgers and the ledgers are filed, and—'

'Go and get them.'

'Steve, what are you so worried about?'

Michael had licked his dry lips, and found that his hands were shaking. The man sitting opposite was not going to be put off and Michael also knew that his own voice was unsteady. He was using Steve's name too often, and the fact of the matter was too awful to confess: he did know where the Limston invoices were, because they were with a number of other invoices – and they weren't in the ledger, because he had almost certainly shredded them. Why had he shredded them? That was what he'd hoped to discuss with Dr Bonnermorgan: an inability to cope, despite his absolutely fine blood pressure.

'You're not doing your job,' said Steve quietly. 'I'm worried that you're not doing your job properly, and… I wouldn't care, normally. It wouldn't be my business. But Robbie Limston is a mate, and he's not going out of business because you're incompetent. When is he going to get paid?'

'I don't know.'

'Look it up.'

'No. I can't. If you... Look. If you have... concerns. If you have concerns—'

'I do have concerns.'

'In that case—'

'Major concerns. Most of us do.'

His shirt was too tight. He should never have bought that size.

'Look,' said Michael. 'If that really is the case, you have to raise your concerns formally, and properly – and I can do a search right away, but... I can't do one because you sit there demanding that I do. I will do a search and get straight back to you.'

Silence. The train rattling on, but somehow silent – and he wished he'd gone through to the next carriage, and found a forward-facing seat. He couldn't ask the woman opposite to move, or he could – theoretically – but it would be so intrusive. She'd got there first, after all, but he was rattling backwards to a place he didn't want to be, and the idea of sitting down next to her seemed positively dangerous.

'It's a simple question, Michael.'

Steve's nose had been broken.

'I'm asking you on behalf of a trusted supplier – when will the Limston invoice be paid?'

'Next week, I should think. They've missed this week's roster.'

'They missed last week. And the week before—'

'For all I know, the original has been... I don't know, queried. It may have been pulled for further inspection, or analysis—'

'Go and get it.'

'No.'

Steve had stood up, and Michael imagined him in his fireman's uniform and how grateful someone would be if he appeared through the flames of his or her burning car. He would yank the door open, and cut the seat belts with a knife. He'd haul you onto his shoulder and out to safety. When you touch the live

rail, you stick to it – so people say. If you touch it with the palm
of your hand, the voltage makes the muscles contract so you find
yourself gripping it. You grip the metal, and all those volts course
straight through your body in their rush to earth, flipping you
like a puppet. The fillings of your teeth pop out. Your eyeballs
turn to liquid and your hair catches fire. The live rail fries you
from inside: you actually melt, even as you scorch. Steve had
managed to drag someone off, though, with a wooden rake. So
Michael sat back, and saw that the woman opposite him had
sherbet lemons – he could see the telltale yellow eggs. She caught
his eye.

'I'm going to see Linda,' said Steve.

I'm going to Crewe, thought Michael. The 14.41 is a through
train, and the rails are not electrified. I won't be electrocuted.

'Linda?' he said.

Linda was Michael's team leader, and she started the inquiry
that turned into a search, that mushroomed into an investigation.
Michael had lost the invoices, he said – but they knew he hadn't.
He had sat at his desk, unable to see the screen for a fuzz of tears
that came from nowhere, and oozed straight back even as he
wiped them. When his eyes were dry they were too dry, and he
couldn't concentrate – and the invoices piled up in their folders,
deep in the desk drawer to the right of his knees. He had no
relationships, but that was hardly Linda's fault, or Steve's. His
mother was dead, so there was nobody to be proud of his non-
achievements, and he had simply run out of fuel. There he was
on the hard shoulder with everyone else screaming by, blasting
their horns.

'Why didn't you ask for help?' she said at some point, in that
kindly voice of victory.

Michael had laughed.

'I didn't think I needed it,' he said – and the woman with the
sweets looked up, for he had spoken aloud.

'Sorry,' he said. 'I'm talking to myself.'

'Pardon?'

He smiled. 'I'm getting into bad habits. I'm talking to myself.'

She nodded, and went back to her book. He was about to say, 'Sherbet lemons, eh?' when he managed to stop himself, and thought instead about Mr Moorhouse, who'd been questioned by the police about something. The 10.23 was not crowded, so he got up carefully, and moved down the carriage. Why had he sat opposite the director of human resources? He could have found a seat on his own, and sat with James.

He went through the connecting doors, and felt even more foolish: there were several tables that were completely unoccupied. He could sit facing the direction of travel, with no neighbours at all: he had all four places to himself, and he wished he had a jigsaw puzzle to spread out, or a deck of cards. Did he want a drink now? No, though he ought to have one. Instead of getting drunk he simply sat and remembered Steve and then Linda, and then Elizabeth, staring at his ghost-self in the reflection as he thought about all the other people who inevitably got involved in his sacking. A disciplinary hearing was just like the fuss at school, for once you start the process everyone gets on board and nobody can stop it. The head of year gets involved, and comes round to see your parents: that makes things better, temporarily, and you are – for a moment – important. Not that he had reported Mr Trace: no, the head of year had come round because he was making so little academic progress, and might have to drop two subjects. Had he been unravelling, even then? By that time, Mr Trace hadn't been teaching him.

'I forgot all about him,' he said.

He remembered Elizabeth again, the first woman he'd so nearly married and then not. Not Amy: he'd nearly married her, too, but Elizabeth had been so different and sometimes he still tried to blame her for leaving him, even though he knew she was to be congratulated. Nothing had been her fault: she'd just seen too clearly, and it wasn't the fault of Polish Pete, the man she was probably being held by now, tenderly, he hoped – though why would lovers be holding one another at this time of the morning, when they had busy jobs? It wasn't Polish Pete's fault, that was the main thing: and for a moment he wondered how people always became trapped in the endless apportioning of blame, and how that disciplinary procedure had been all about narrowing it right down until he was caught in the net, or skewered on that point – that javelin – of indisputable, shameful incompetence. There he was, running as fast as he could as they came after him with the great big skewer. And he tripped. He fell, and rolled onto his back and wham! In it went, just below the ribcage, and he was pinned to the paperwork, blamed for ever as the crowds trundled by on buses and trains. It must come from childhood, he thought, when blame is apportioned extra rigorously, and you have no right of appeal.

'Twelve per cent in your Latin test.'

Whose fault was that? His form tutor apportioned blame, as had his parents.

'It was my fault. I didn't understand it.'

'Why not?'

'I don't know what the teacher's talking about, sir.'

'Who teaches you Latin?'

'Mr Trace. He says words I don't understand – I don't know what a "declension" is. I don't know what "passive voice" means, so I have to pay. That's why I have no defence, sir, when he calls me back at lunchtime, sir. Ignorance is no plea, so he helps me, but… do I really need help?'

Every boy knows: Mr Trace loves nothing more than to help boys pay, and he does so until his glittering eyes get the special glitter. Why tell the story, when everyone knows? What surprise can there be, when we're all abused every day in some way or another? We abuse, because it's what we are: I abuse, you abuse and he was abused. The man reflected in this window, there he is again – and he *will* be abused, pluperfect passive *had been* abused. 'When Caesar came to the water. The water? No, the *river* – sorry, sir. When Caesar came to the river, he called his legions together and said, "Is there a man amongst you who has not been abused? Let him stand forth."'

Michael wasn't smiling.

'"Sexually abused?"' said Lepidus, or Cicero – the names had gone but the text was in his head still: *Caesar's Gallic Wars.* '"Show us a man who has not – *nihil* – never taken the penis into the mouth. Let him make himself known that we may salute him!"'

'Good,' said Mr Trace. 'It's not as hard as you thought, is it?'

The boys laughed when he said that.

No, it wasn't so very, very hard – and Mr Trace was not, thankfully, on this particular train because he was dead, his dust spread wide and ungatherable in a garden of remembrance.

'Did he cum?' said someone.

'What?'

Michael hadn't known what that meant, the first time.

'Come where?'

Screams of laughter, and the wonder and the fear. 'Did he give you something to eat, Michael? Did you get your lunch?'

Everyone knew about Mr Trace, so was everyone to blame? Julius Caesar must have sat in his tent, just like Mr Trace, and in came young Mikilus in his soft leather servant uniform – he'd probably fought for the privilege of fellating the great leader, and perhaps it had even been love? That was how it was back then, before the legislation.

Boys got over it.

Michael slowed down his breathing.

His hands were shaking, so he took the carton from his bag and drank a mouthful of whisky straight from it – then he ate a tangerine. The train was still utterly on time, and would get him into Gloucester soon after noon which was just minutes away, giving him a moment to sweep the peel together and put it in his pocket for disposal in the first litter bin he saw. Nobody was looking at him.

It was this very service that he had picked up all those months ago, travelling in the other direction: he had sat with himself as he was sitting now, looking at himself wanting to be rid of himself. The train had been just like this one, and he'd stepped onto it late one night, to find the vandalised table with its oh-so personal message and the small, polite, helpful Sikh who'd tried to make it go away. He wasn't fond of Gloucester station, but it was coming towards him now: the slow motion of the braking train. It had long, busy platforms which seemed disconnected and spread out, and the trains came in from every direction. North, south, east and west: you could never be quite sure which way you'd end up going, for there were too many options. To get to Southampton, for example, meant going north first of all, and coming back on yourself. If you missed Cheltenham you'd end up lost in the Midlands, but if you got it more wrong than that you might end up in deepest Wales.

Was it the Gloucester station waiting room where they had no chairs? He'd noticed the sign, which was actually a drawing of a vacant seat, and stepped inside to rest. Six people were standing up, and the room was bare.

'Excuse me,' he'd said – at the ticket office. 'What's happened to the chairs?'

'Sorry, sir? I'm not with you.'

'In the waiting room. There's nowhere to sit.'

'Oh! No. They were vandalised, so they've been taken out.'

'But there's nowhere to sit.'

'I know, sir. It's a problem.'

'People are tired. They want to sit down.'

The woman had simply looked at him.

'If the seats are being vandalised,' he wanted to say, 'you repair them. You put staff in to protect them, or CCTV – you can't give in to vandals, because if you do – they've won. It's not important,' he wanted to say. 'In the great scheme of things, it's trivial. But it's as if we're not worth anything any more, and we don't deserve comfort. Civilisation is a myth – we're going backwards.'

The woman handed Michael a customer feedback form, and he said thank you.

When he stepped onto the platform he was almost weeping, for he knew now that he would miss his connection – but he wanted a last cup of coffee, in a mug. He didn't want to drink out of a paper cup, and he knew the café in Gloucester used proper crockery. He deserved china. Why should he drink from paper? He refused to do that when this was his last hot drink, and why should he be sad about it? He had time, and he had to drink more whisky to make himself drunk. Crewe was only two hours away – or two hours and six minutes, to be precise, via Birmingham. Even he could get to Crewe, and if he missed whatever London service he'd been aiming to meet, so what? The trains were hourly, he was sure of it – he'd looked it up and worked it all out, so... 'Please,' he said to himself. 'Stop crying.'

There was a receptacle for litter, and he paused beside it to unload the orange peel, and wipe his weak, foolish eyes. He glanced up to see a camera, and wondered for a moment if anyone was watching him here. Was there anybody at the monitor?

'There's a man with watery eyes,' they'd say.

The bag that held the rubbish was transparent, so you couldn't conceal whatever it was you were throwing away. The bomb-planting terrorist would lift the lid and realise he had been thwarted. Where could he hide his bomb now? He would slink back, shamefaced, to his bomb-making friends. 'It's impossible,' he'd say. 'We have been out-witted.'

Michael looked away, smiling again, and made for the café. He walked past the waiting room and saw that it was full of chairs.

6

Inside, he thought of Spain, where it had been so hot.

Elizabeth saw the advertisement in a shop window, with a photograph of the house – this was after two nights in a hotel, and they had both agreed that what they wanted most was a cottage to call their own. They wanted to cook for themselves, and buy bottles of cheap local wine – not because they needed to save money, but because even the most friendly hotel imposed a formality.

Casa Elouisa was named after its owner. Michael phoned her from the lobby, and thankfully her English was excellent. His Spanish was poor, so 'Habla Ingelzi, senorita, por favour. . .?'

That was about all he said.

'Yes, I do,' she replied. 'How are you?'

The house was available the very next day, and for the whole fortnight, which meant it was bound to be unsuitable and disappointing. They prepared themselves for the difficulty of saying, 'Well, we'll think about it. We have one more place to see.'

'It will be next to a noisy quarry,' said Elizabeth.

'A slaughterhouse.'

'A power station. In the slums. By a brothel.'

'She said she hadn't really got round to advertising it yet. Just a few photos here and there – she hasn't got onto the books of any. . . you know, tourist offices or big brochures.'

'Maybe we'll be lucky.'

They had been lucky all through the holiday, and they were to be yet luckier. The flight to Malaga had been simple, and the hire car was waiting. Michael drove, then Elizabeth took over, and they squealed at every roundabout because it felt so strange to be turning right. He was twenty-six. She was two years younger, and he could still remember the disbelief when one thing led to another and they found themselves going to the cinema, to a pizza house and then to meet her parents. Suddenly, they were on holiday together.

The hotel in Granada was expensive, and it turned out to be a secret jewel behind high walls – an ex-convent with twisting corridors and sudden gardens. They moved on sadly, shaking the hands of the staff who wished them well because love was a blessing, and they had blessed the whole place.

They blessed the car, and blessed the white villages they drove to – villages that were strewn down the sides of high, dry mountains like bleached rubble. Every restaurant they visited blessed them, for they were discovering the wonders of Spanish food: their tongues came to life in their mouths. They were discovering how life changes in the sun, so Casa Elouisa had to be the anticlimax two shy English tourists surely deserved.

It wasn't, though.

Michael ordered an Americano with warm milk, and remembered Casa Elouisa again, with its cool, thick-walled bedroom in which making love had seemed so possible. The barista served him with a smile that was almost a laugh, and her 'thank you' as he handed her twenty pounds sounded to Michael as if he had saved her life. She had the same eyes as Elizabeth, and yet 'thank you' was a phrase said how many times a day?

'Thank you!' she said, taking the note.

It was a new-minted 'thank you,' so fresh and soft, and it was for Michael only – she looked at him as she said it, and sex was not on her mind or his. Of all the station cafés in the world, he had selected this one. He had dignified it – blessed it, again – and the coffee was soon dripping into a cup like oil, the grounds having been tamped and squeezed. The correct measure of hot water thinned the mixture, making the intensity manageable, and it was another girl organising this part of the process. The first took your order and your money, and thanked you – the second made your drink.

She was no doubt nineteen or twenty, the one now holding his cup, but she looked twelve or thirteen, and her short dark hair was pulled behind her ears – she looked like a boy, in fact, James or Luke. Flat-chested, in a too-big shirt with the sleeves rolled, she reminded him of himself. She could have played Oliver Twist and broken hearts, and she was about to pour milk into a jug when she remembered there were options.

'Would you prefer hot milk?' she said.

'Yes,' said Michael. 'Thank you.'

'You're like me,' she replied. 'Strong coffee. Hot milk.'

'I'm trying to cut down, actually.'

'Why?'

'Oh, the usual. Blood pressure. Two coffees a day, maximum.'

'Yes, you mustn't overdo it.'

She smiled too, just like her colleague. She smiled right at him, and she was like the first girl but more beautiful. Her face fell naturally into a smile, just as Elizabeth's had – just as so many people's did... and her eyes glittered like Mr Trace's but differently, for hers were merry and young and she might have been a Romanian Gypsy, born on a bank of wild flowers. She placed the crockery briskly, but precisely, her movements so economical – she didn't know it was Michael's last ever hot drink, but she was preparing it as if she'd somehow guessed. And if she had a boyfriend, did the fellow realise how lucky he was? If she lived with her parents, still – if she wasn't from Europe, but lived in grey old Gloucester – did they realise what a privilege it was, having access still to this person they had created and reared? It wouldn't be long before she spread her wings and left them. As a customer, did he really appreciate the kindness of her attention? Could he write to her manager, and get her promoted? Could he be responsible for her earning a substantial bonus?

Would she take twenty pounds, if he offered it?

She was too beautiful, and for a moment he imagined the horror of her being assaulted. A man could subdue her so dreadfully easily – whilst two men, working together... Michael's imagination plunged, and he looked down at his hands, appalled at the pit that was opening around him. *I'll hold her for you, you hold her for me* – he had read that phrase somewhere, and she wouldn't stand a chance unless she practised martial arts, or unless he came by to rescue her. Perhaps she would be able to fight her own way out of their terrible grip, but she looked too delicate and he could see her thin arms twisted behind her back as the first man dragged her down to the railway tracks, her scream unheard for an express train was passing, screaming louder. There were her parents looking at the clock, just beginning to wonder where she was. And what if the men put her body on the rails? What if those poor parents had to wait at the mortuary to see what was left? He felt a sob rising in his throat.

She smiled, and Michael had to hold the counter more firmly, weak with self-loathing. She turned away. She put the milk jug under the steamer, and for some reason she looked at him again. She should have said, 'Go on. Get out.'

'I beg your pardon. Why?'

'That train for Crewe. The one you said you'd be in front of, old man – it's about to come hurtling through.'

'There'll be others,' he would say. 'I can wait for the later train—'

'You're not going to do it, are you?'

She would be whispering.

'You've not got the balls, so to speak. You'll be back here this evening: "An *Americano, please! – can I have a china cup?"* Kill your fucking dead-self, Michael – do us all a favour.'

She said, 'Where are you off to today, then?'

Shame washed up from his feet again, and he smiled.

'Oh,' he said – and he elongated the vowel to suggest mystery, or uncertainty, or the possibility that he was on some epic voyage.

Don't ask me! That was what his 'oh' implied, and he backed it up with a broader smile and a headshake, trying to mix weariness with the excitement of the challenges he faced. 'I am young, really,' he wanted to say. 'This journey that I'm making today is not to Crewe at all... it's a spontaneous trip that could take me anywhere. I'm free, and the world is wide open – my life is not a disappointment.'

'Up country,' was what he said.

The girl nodded, of course. Her name was Zara – there was a badge saying so. Up country meant north, perhaps – or simply some distance from here.

'I'm going to see my daughter,' he said.

'Where's she?'

'I don't have one!' That should have been his jaunty riposte. 'I caught you out there, Zara! I was joking. Crikey, no! I am a childless man, can you not see that? Smell my clothes. Look at my skin.'

'She's at Leeds University,' he said, because that's where Elizabeth's son was or had been studying, so he'd learned somehow, even as Zara nodded. The rubble of his life was all about him, but he was still holding onto the counter and he felt the tears prick his eyes again as he smiled even harder. Zara was still making his Americano, it seemed – sorting out the milk. She served it at last, and put the jug beside the cup. His time with her was almost up: he had ten seconds left, if he moved slowly. In ten seconds' time he would cease to be a safe, harmless customer, and he wanted more than anything to remain a safe, harmless customer.

He said, 'People who know you are very lucky.'

The blood rushed to his face, in a tide. He couldn't look at her. He heard her laugh, because laughter always diffuses intimacy. She hauled everything back to a safe area, and said, 'Oh, how sweet.'

The word turned him into what he was – a stupid old man – and he moved away before she could think he was dirty, or predatory, or worst of all lonely. No, he was off to see his daughter, in her mind – and a man who was off to see his daughter could not be dangerous. He could have a daughter of university age – he wasn't too old – and she would be looking forward to seeing him. Might she even be joining him at Crewe, on platform number seven?

The Americano was perfect.

It took him back to the county council office where he would sometimes interfere with the percolator to create a stronger brew, and he found himself shunted back to his desk as he remembered the day he emptied its drawers, never to return. The house, however – Casa Elouisa – had been even more perfect. He and Elizabeth had set off on the second day to the nearest big town, and that's where they had found the Museum of Torture.

Why would anyone go to a museum of torture?

Why would anyone remember going to a museum of torture, and remember it now, just as happier thoughts were needed? And who had dreamed such a place up, and obtained funding? In fact, Elizabeth didn't go in. It was a hot afternoon, and they hadn't gone out looking for the place: they simply strolled past it on their way to a terrace so overgrown with bougainvillea that the flowers looked like an eruption. Two espressos, hot and bitter – and across the road a sign in red and yellow, painted in both Spanish and English: *Galería de la Inquisicion!*

'You want to go in, don't you?' said Elizabeth.

'Of course.'

'Go on, then.'

'No. It's shameful. It's sick.'

'You go, and tell me about it. I'm happy here.'

She was, because she had an Agatha Christie novel in her bag, and Hercule Poirot or Miss Marple would be working out who was to blame. The museum, meanwhile, was cool, with several large rooms inviting him to use his imagination as he contemplated other people's pain. There were thumbscrews and hammers. There were slides that would run you onto lacerating blades, and seats with spikes – there was one that let a kind of spear up between your buttocks, slowly. Michael found a grenade with a little handle on the bottom. Pictures revealed that it could be pushed into your mouth: when the inquisitor turned the handle sharp metal leaves opened and cut through your gums and cheeks. It was a punishment from some bizarre, hideous cartoon – except it was real. The thing had existed, and it even had levers to break your teeth, all from the inside. The explanation was in three different languages, and Michael learned that the item could also be inserted into the anus or the vagina.

That was the museum of inquisitional torture, and he had ended up inside it – how? There were several people strolling through, and they all went from case to case, presumably thinking similar thoughts: What ingenuity. What cruelty. What disregard for human rights, and what pleasure in pain – what sadistic delight and what confidence! What relish for the tearing of flesh – so much more creative than simply throwing someone under a train! Of course, the implements came from a very different age, when people were heretics and traitors. That was the age when heresy and treason mattered, and when the mangled body dangling in the city square was a true deterrent. 'See what will happen to you if you break the rules!' In any case, perhaps people didn't feel pain as acutely in the old days? Perhaps they felt so much that they were numb. Michael wondered if agony could reach a peak beyond which there was no feeling. Would you end up in ecstasy? He'd heard that the art of the torturer was to ensure that peak of pain was never reached.

He'd walked through that museum nearly thirty years ago. Elizabeth waited on the terrace, and he left the place feeling shabby. She was deep in her novel – but they'd kissed, and he'd held her tight, blonde hair drawn back and tied with a band, her face very slightly cat-like and her dress so simple. Green and red diamonds, cool in the heat – shapeless, and perfect for her fine, slim body. Days later they were driving out of the town to the little village of somewhere, in search of the *casa* that a woman called Elouisa lived in and rented out – the name of the place had long since faded from his memory. Narrow, turning roads, rising up into the hills – Elizabeth nervous at the wheel, with him navigating. The higher they went the hotter it got, and they knew they were lost moments before they came to the church they'd been told to look out for, for the place was hidden in a forest of volcanic flowering shrubs and the only sounds were the occasional clunk of a goat's bell, and a bee.

'I don't see a slaughterhouse,' said Elizabeth softly. 'It's paradise.'

'Where's she live, though?'

They were still braced for disappointment, because they knew they shouldn't be lucky any more – there was something dangerous in the wonders the gods were offering. They walked past the church, and down the steps, and turned right as they had been instructed. There was a row of cottages, but Casa Elouisa was further down the hill, on its own – it was a pair of huts that the owner had knocked into one. When she had guests, she withdrew into a couple of rooms, and the guests took over the lounge, bathroom, balcony, bedroom and – best of all – the roof terrace, with its view over Eden. When the sun went down the hills turned pink and blue, and the moon came up just like a balloon.

The wine was cheaper than bottled water.

The fridge was old, but powerful: they chilled the white so it hurt their mouths, and they would eat and finish with warm red. Michael had returned, once, on his own. The village was as beautiful, even without Elizabeth. Elouisa was still there, and she remembered him – or claimed to. She had asked if they had married.

'No,' he said, wishing they had.

But they hadn't, and it had been right not to. She had touched him one day, and realised he was all wrong. She must have felt whatever it was that was broken, and thought the logical thing she had to think, for isn't it the engine that drives the species on? I will not have the children I want with this man, because he doesn't want to have sex with me. We can be friends. We will stay friends, but we will not marry.

'We do love each other, don't we?' he probably said, at some point.

'We're not lovers, though.'

'No. Everything is perfect, apart from that. We're not lovers.'

'What's wrong, Michael?'

'Nothing.'

You don't mean to, I know – but you make me feel so very unattractive.

She hadn't said that: she had written it down, in a letter.

He finished his coffee, and watched James and Luke serving someone else. Then he checked the electronic screen – his train was running three minutes late, and would arrive at platform three, on its way to Birmingham. It was going all the way to Nottingham, in fact, having come from Cardiff.

'Thank you!' he called cheerfully – but both baristas were involved in their work. The first was talking to a customer, and Zara had her back to him. In any case, the noise of the coffee machine would have prevented her from hearing his voice. He left the café and used the toilet. Then it was back towards the barriers, and up the steps of the footbridge where he paused to watch a freight train coming through. There would have been an announcement, warning everyone to stand back: '*Stand well away from the edge of platform two. The approaching train is not scheduled to stop at this station.*'

He knew the voice.

They used a man for that particular announcement, and it was still the old-fashioned received-pronunciation type of voice. He sounded just like your teacher controlling the scrum at the tuck-shop window: 'Stand back! Wait!'

Don't get caught in a vortex of air, and be sucked down onto the tracks. Stand behind the yellow line, and hold onto your buggies. Press yourself against the wall – link arms with anyone nearby, just in case you're drawn to the edge and lost. There are no Steves here with a garden rake, so hold on tight!

The engine smashed through beneath him. Every wagon it drew clanked and heaved, for they were all made of iron and steel. Every one carried the same sort of container: the long, hard-edged metal box of sheer weight, bearing down on those severing wheels – he felt the bridge-floor vibrating under his feet – and he could have jumped. It would have been a quick movement, over the vaulting horse at school – he could do it now if he hoisted himself and rolled.

The containers flipped by beneath him, one by one, and his legs were too heavy. He watched them, recalling the sequences in films when the hero – or the villain – would drop from above, to make his getaway. Light as a cat, he would drop neatly into a crouch, steadying himself before running along the whole long length of the train. How many movies used that stunt?

Michael found that he was smiling again.

It was quite ludicrous. If anyone dropped onto the train below, he would be clipped by one of the hard edges and thrown upwards. A man would somersault, and end up either flat on the platform or broken on the tracks – unless he fell between the containers themselves, of course, and slid down under the wheels where he would be rolled, and chopped and dragged by the axles. His clothes would be snagged on bolts and hooks, and ripped clear of the flesh, which would be cut again and again, minced up and mashed. Someone would then have to make dry remarks about needing a bucket.

'He won't need a coffin,' someone would laugh. 'A couple of carrier bags will do for that one.'

'Who was he? Here's a shoe, look at this! There's a card inside...'

'Silly fucker.'

Somehow, in all his fifty-six years of life, Michael had never broken a bone – so he walked on, carefully, and went down the steps. The freight train was gone, and nobody was hurt: there was a rag on the line, but it wasn't a ripped-off, bloody shirt. Everyone had obeyed the teachery voice: *'Stand well back!'* Like children, they had obeyed, and – as a result – they were able to continue with their lives.

No ambulances were needed, and there was to be no cordoning off.

No trains would be delayed just yet: the horror was going to take place later, at Crewe – and it would be screened by trees. The general public wouldn't see.

At 12.36 his train rolled in, and he was relieved to find that it was the type he liked most. It was a stopping service, and the fact that it had eight coaches meant it wasn't too crowded, off-peak. He hurried to the carriage he'd chosen and waited for the door to hiss itself open. He stood back, then, for a lot of people were getting off. Some were in a rush, and some weren't. There were more men than women, and one elderly man delayed everybody because he had a stick and had to climb down carefully.

Fourteen people disembarked – Michael counted them, knowing he would never see them again. They all had one thing in common, he thought: they all had business in Southampton. Whether they were visitors or residents, and whether they were in the middle of a journey or at its end, they were all using Southampton's facilities in some way – except that this was Gloucester or possibly Salisbury, and he was getting confused. It was Gloucester, of course, and they had all been brought together in this tight little clump, easing through the neat little door: they had all arrived, and were almost touching, obeying the rules of courtesy, for if the man with the stick stumbled someone would catch him. If the old lady's bag was too heavy, someone would lift it down for her, and if the pushchair teetered men would leap to support it, laughing and smiling.

'That was close! What a handful! Rather you than me! Are you okay, now? No, not at all. Have a good day.'

'Have a good day, a better day! Hey, you? Have a *fucking* good day.'

Michael smiled at a man who said nothing but smiled at him – then he joined the cluster that could now board. He found himself walking down the aisle behind someone with a snooker cue in a box – another man, who put it up into the luggage rack and took his place at a table. Michael squeezed into the seat further down and smiled again – a smile he hoped was amiable and innocent, for he must have more whisky now: he had delayed too long, and he needed to drink properly. Crewe was just over two hours away, via Birmingham – getting closer.

The passenger opposite looked at him.

'Two minutes late,' said Michael. 'Not bad.'

7

This man was older, and heavier.

He said, 'No. They're not too bad, normally. They let me down a few months ago, but by and large they run to time.'

Michael settled into his seat, and put his bag beside him.

'How did they let you down?' he said.

'Oh, the usual thing. They cancelled the last train. No, they didn't – they shortened the journey. I wanted to get to Bromsgrove, and they were stopping it early. I said to the guard, or... not the guard – the information woman. I said, "How do I get to Bromsgrove? I've paid to get home – I've given you twenty-two pounds. That's a *contract*, isn't it?"'

Michael went to respond, but he wasn't quick enough.

'She said, "Take a cab,"' said the man. '"And charge the rail company."'

He laughed, and Michael's eyes widened.

Again, he went to speak, but the man got in first.

'I couldn't believe it,' he said. 'I mean, there was no way the rail company would reimburse me for a taxi – but that's what she said. I said, "Can I have that advice in writing?" Because I thought if that's the advice you're giving out, someone needs to bloody educate you.'

'Did she write it down?'

'Of course not. She was suddenly too busy, and... you know. You lose the will.'

'What did you do?'

'About what?'

'About getting home to Bromsgrove.'

'I got a taxi. Thirty-seven pounds. I phoned the company next morning, and they asked me to fill in a form.'

'Oh, I've had that.'

'I said, "You cancelled the train, and you know you did. You've got a customer here, telling you he had to fork out extra to get home. *Do* something for me," I said. I said, "If you can't reimburse me, send me vouchers. I'm not *lying* to you, am I? I'm out of pocket by thirty-seven pounds." This was some... I don't know – it was a call centre, presumably. How bright do you have to be to work in a call centre? How many exams do you have to fail to get a job like that? "You need to fill in a form," he said. "I don't want to," I said. "I can send you one if you like." I just hung up.'

'I've had similar experiences—'

'You know what they're going to ask you. Dates, times, proof of purchase. Attach your ticket or receipt. Where did you purchase the ticket, what's your date of birth, what's your shoe size? I can't be bothered with it – not for a few quid. Life's too short.'

Michael took out his carton of juice.

The man's hair was dark and thin. He had combed it back from his temples emphasising the fat round oval of his face. He didn't wear glasses, and he had the kind of fleshy eyes that goggle slightly: there was a ring of shadow round both sockets, caused by the creases of the flesh, and Michael thought they looked almost removable, as if he was trying out a new pair. His mouth was a permanent frown, and whilst he was clean-shaven the stubble on his upper lip stood out like dust or a smudge – you wanted to reach over with a handkerchief and clean it. He was taking his coat off. He should have taken it off before he sat down, because it was awkward now and for a moment he was wrestling himself, tugging an arm free and breathing heavily. At last, it was off and on the seat next to him, and Michael was looking at a patterned, V-neck pullover and a sky-blue shirt. He wore a dark blue tie, but the knot was pulled down allowing the collar to sit wide open – and his frowning, frog-like mouth was open, too, as if his jaw muscles were tired.

At school, he would have been made to tidy himself up. Mr Trace would have taken him aside for a quiet word, for the boys he liked received special attention: he would fasten their top buttons for them, forcing them to stand helplessly prone, with their heads back.

Michael took his spectacles off, wondering how best to clean them. The cloth he liked to use was in the case with his other pair, and that was in the bag. He needed his glass, too, but he didn't want to be delving for that.

He sat still.

'You never win,' said the man. 'They have the power, you see. They have the systems in place. I travel by train as *rarely* as possible.'

'You prefer to drive, do you?' said Michael.

'Not really. Driving's not a pleasure any more, is it? You try getting out of Bromsgrove at five o'clock. Or getting in, for that matter.'

'Is it solid?'

The man was now a talking blur.

'It's appalling,' he said. 'They had a consultation some time ago, the council cretins. "How to Alleviate Congestion," and you didn't have to be a genius. You didn't need fifty thousand pounds a year with an index-linked pension – you needed a bit of common sense so as to stop people parking where the bottlenecks are, and widen the bloody road where the... you know, the junction by the superstore – that's where the congestion comes from. That's why it's gridlocked.'

Michael said, 'I hardly drive at all now.'

'I used to do twenty-two thousand miles a year. This was when the roads were less cluttered, needless to say. I could do Bromsgrove to Hereford in an hour. I could do Bromsgrove to Shrewsbury in one and a quarter. From Shrewsbury, if I took the A5, I could be in Oswestry in twenty, or less. Stop in Wrexham for lunch, and be in Chester soon after two. You could do your job, and get home of an evening.'

'What was your job?'

'Mmm?'

The man paused, as if the question had surprised him.

'I was wondering what job you did, that involved—'

'Tool hire.'

'Oh?'

'Expanded that into plant hire, and ended up with a business that spread all the way into Wales. I didn't want to expand it, but I didn't have a choice in the end. I had so many orders, and... *demands*, that it got impossible. I had a customer in Denbigh – he was a contractor for a quarry – and he told me that there was no reliable plant-hire service in the whole county. He virtually begged me. "Set up something here!" So that's what we did.'

Michael nodded. He took out his handkerchief.

'You must have been busy, then?' he said.

'You know what stopped me?'

'What?'

'Heart attack.'

Michael nodded again, trying to adjust his facial expression to show both surprise and sympathy. He wanted to drink some whisky, but as he went to speak the man struck in first again so Michael was silenced. He talked loudly, with unchallengeable firmness. Most of the carriage could hear him, and a woman in the seats to their side had glanced up irritably.

Michael went to his bag, and found the glass.

'I was taking delivery of one of those mini-excavators,' he said. 'You've probably seen them, but this one was a bit special – it had one of those compactor plates, so it was extra heavy. It was coming off the loader. No, it wasn't, it was *off* the loader – they'd done that before I arrived. We had a local manager, who turned out to be an idiot, but he'd got the thing unloaded, and I was gathering up the paperwork and I felt a pain, right across here.'

He ran a finger over the top part of his ribcage, and sat forward.

'Like a stabbing. Just here.'

Michael nodded.

'Over your heart?' he said.

'What?'

'Over your heart.'

'Right over it,' said the man.

Then he spoke quietly.

'The next thing I knew? The next thing I knew was that I thought I'd been punched or bayonetted. I was on my back, in the mud, and this... manager chap – he hadn't a clue what to do. "Are you all right, Terry? Terry!" And I'm on my back, gasping like a fish.'

He laughed, and Michael imagined the funeral that would have taken place, as mourners gathered round the short, fat coffin. He imagined the strain the bearers would experience as they lifted it.

'I was lucky,' said Terry. 'The chap who'd delivered the digger was ex-army, and would you believe it? Guess which regiment.'

Michael didn't need to. He wasn't given time to, and he wondered if the man's wife regretted the fact that he'd made such a full recovery, and if she fantasised about life without him. Still he was talking, for it turned out the man who'd delivered the digger had been in the medical corps, and if it hadn't been for his quick action Terry would have died in the mud.

'That's shocking,' said Michael.

'I would have died on the ground,' he said. 'End of story.'

'So, luckily for you—'

'He kept me breathing, this chap. And when the ambulance came – and that took ages, needless to say. When the ambulance came, the girl who looked after me – strip of a thing... looked about twelve. She said, "That man saved your life." So it was soon after that I said to the wife, "This has got to stop."'

A silence fell.

Michael now imagined the mute wife, listening attentively – just the way he was listening. He so didn't want to ask another question, but the silence seemed impossible, and the man was staring at him. He couldn't reach for his whisky: he had to stay still.

He said, 'I had a bit of a scare. Two years ago, now—'

'I sold the business,' said Terry. 'I didn't want to, but I said to my wife, "I can't *half* do the job. I can't stand by whilst some fruitcake runs it badly." She said, "Sell it, then." And, well – that was the best advice I ever had, and the best advice I ever took.

We were lucky again. The recession hadn't hit, and I had two separate buyers bidding in the end. I walked away with... I won't tell you what I walked away with. Let's just say that heart attack was probably the best thing that ever happened to me, in every possible way. It enabled me... Listen to this. It actually enabled me to find *other* things to do, so I could live my life. Because that's what I was frightened of, and that's what the wife said. "He'll die of boredom." She said that to my son, who was... he was still at college. Do you know what I said? I said, "I'm going to buy a boat." And that made them laugh.'

'A boat?' said Michael, by accident.

He couldn't stop himself.

'Like a narrowboat, or a sailing boat—?'

'That's where I'm off to this weekend.'

'What kind of boat did you buy?'

The man laughed, and Michael didn't want to know.

'The reason they didn't take me seriously was because they knew I got seasick. We'd been on a cruise, and I'd hated it! *Hated* it. But I said, "I am going to get on the water and learn." We've got an apartment now, in that new Bristol Marina – not a big one, but oh-my-goodness. It looks right over the water, and you just sit on the terrace and... it's a pageant.'

Michael nodded, and saw Terry in his coffin again – floating, this time.

'I never get tired of it,' he said. 'Boats coming in, yachts going out. Ours is moored where we can actually see it, and there's people around to chat to. Interesting people, retired, a lot of them. Decent folk. I've got to get the hull checked over, so we're dry-docking her for a couple of weeks. Then... I don't know.'

'The world's your oyster.'

'Well...'

'You can go anywhere. Where will you go?'

Why had he asked another question? What compulsion was it, when all he wanted to know was how many people might come to Terry's funeral? How many actual friends did he have? And would the decent people from Bristol Marina be there, because they had come to love Terry like a brother? How many pews would he need, because Michael's would be a quick, quiet affair and cars would not be necessary. They would burn him early in the morning: the later slots were more expensive, and harder to book.

Terry was about to speak again when his phone started to ring, and the ringtone was a little trumpet playing 'Colonel Bogey'. He couldn't find it at first, so the volume rose and Michael listened to the opening bars, twice through, the hearse driving steadily out of the marina to the strange, bubbling soundtrack – the tugboats would be hooting, and the harbour master was inconsolable. There were floral tributes fashioned into diggers and ships: *Farewell King of Plant Hire* was written in five hundred white carnations. *Bon Voyage, Dad!*

Eventually, the man found his phone, and Michael heard the voice of Terry's wife. He assumed it was his wife, and whilst he couldn't quite hear what she said, he soon picked up the fact that she was concerned about an estimated gas bill she had received that morning. It sounded as if she and Terry both preferred to avoid estimated bills, and had tried to notify the company so as to register their own meter reading. Something had gone wrong, and Terry's wife needed reassurance, which Terry gave loudly and surprisingly kindly. Michael found himself wondering if they were intimate still, and sexually active. He didn't want to imagine anything of the sort – he wanted a drink – but he could hear her anxiety and it sounded as if Terry cared for her.

Did he care for her?

Of course he cared for her! Why wouldn't he? She sounded just a little fragile, and he could imagine the man steadying her as she stepped onto the terrace to look at all the boats. They probably had separate beds, or even separate rooms, and Michael was in the apartment with them. He didn't want to think about their private lives, but the man had sat back, and he seemed to be sprawling in the seat. The image came like a horrible visitation: he saw the woman bringing Terry to orgasm, and he couldn't stop the sequence playing for the man's mouth was open and his eyes were goggling. She was on the train, under the table on her poor arthritic knees: how would she ever get up? She'd strike her head and her mouth would be unwiped, as unwiped as his own...

He closed his eyes. At last, the picture changed back to the terrace, and they were all simply staring out to sea – the wife, Terry and Michael – leaning on the rail.

Terry would die first, and leave her to her grief. Her children would support her, and she'd move closer to them. She would take out one of those affordable funeral plans, for herself.

Would she meet someone else? Would she meet Michael?

'Terry spoke so highly of you. I know you only had a short time together on that train, but you made quite an impression.'

'How?'

'The way you listened to him. You were so attentive, Michael – are you coming back to the house?'

'I don't think I should.'

'No?'

'I've so much to do—'

'It would be such a comfort, you see. We could stand in companionable silence, looking at the water – we'd be connected.'

He had to get up.

He put the juice carton away, and picked up his bag. He wanted another seat, preferably at the far end of the train – in the last carriage. It was his own fault, again. There was nobody to blame but himself, for he'd started it: 'What do you do?' Or 'Where are you going?' Some idiot question that had opened a valve for the gallons and gallons of drenching, self-regarding, shouting nonsense.

And yet it wasn't nonsense, for the man was interesting.

Terry had lived – and was living – an interesting life. Michael saw him flat on his back in the mud, and it was as vivid as the image of Terry supervising the inspection of his boat's hull – Terry in his sky-blue shirt and loosened tie, nodding his approval, watched by his lovely, decent, nautical friends. The man was rich, and liked if not loved. He had a son. The church would be full, and he would sail to heaven on a river of tears.

Michael felt bruised by the encounter. He had invited Terry to talk, and had ended up weak, silent and even more inadequate – not that he had ever in his life wanted a boat, and not that he cared about the box they'd put him in. The fact that he thought about it did not mean he cared, and it wasn't self-pity – was it? It wasn't, because he had no sympathy for himself: the need to finish, die and exit was a practical, calculated decision as straightforward as a decision not to marry. You saw the rightness, and you acted: it was a question, simply, of getting to Crewe and putting an end to so much needless, repetitive nothingness. The train was eager: it was rattling along as quickly as it could, and the long platforms of Crewe that he'd walked and checked would soon be solid beneath his feet.

He stood for a moment in the lobby, where the carriages joined, and felt the judder of the coupling device. It took the strain and eased again. He looked at the fields, and wondered when people had last been able to open windows, and lean out into the fresh air. Trains had become sealed units, for the rail companies were in a constant state of anxiety.

'Take a moment to look around you,' they cried. 'Take extra care in wet weather. Wear a coat. Are your mittens on? What about your medication? Don't get down until we let you – wait, please! The onboard supervisor wants to dry your eyes and hold you for a moment, because you're important – your safety is important. If you see something suspicious or wrong then please report it. Text us, phone or simply wave your arms...'

Michael smiled, and pressed his nose to the glass.

Some kind of gantry was coming into view, and he could see the engine rolling under it. The track curved, and the next two carriages appeared, then the third. The driver sounded his horn, and Michael saw why: a gang of orange-suited workers were standing off to the side, resting. When he came abreast of them, he noticed one was a woman, and she was staring right at him.

He lifted a hand and waved, and she continued to stare, as if he was invisible to her, or insane. Then she nodded and looked away.

He stood back and felt better. Now was the moment to drink, so he knelt down and poured himself a half-glass of whisky. Amy came to mind again as he sipped it, for marrying her would have changed his life – and he might be standing with her now, or sitting down with magazines and papers. They would be looking at puzzles together, and he would have a role.

'You okay, love?'

'I'm fine. How are you?'

'Fine.'

They would confide in each other, except he could never confide anything worth confiding. They wouldn't be here, though. He would be back at her home, doing something in the garden perhaps. The evening would come at last and they would find themselves on the sofa doing what everyone did: they would be watching television. The television connected to the DVD player, which connected to the World Wide Web as well as the Sky box, so all they had to do was call up a menu of movies, documentaries and sports fixtures that made choosing anything impossible. The screen was hideously big, and the sound system involved speakers in every corner, large and small: they had chosen it together in a store where you walked down aisles of televisions, all showing shoals of fish. Shoals of fish seemed to illustrate the phenomenal quality of the multi-pixilated picture, and the colours had made Michael feel drab.

The world was miraculous. Creation was miraculous, but all he could think about was the money he'd committed himself into spending. He didn't need that intensity of television experience. He didn't need all those clever people taking cameras to the ocean bed, and swimming with them over fragile reefs – all they did was make him feel sad that he would never dive. They reminded him that he knew nothing about zoology, and was doomed to gaze at turtles and stingrays in wonder, thinking, Aren't they amazing?

Were turtles amazing? Perhaps they weren't. If a turtle was amazing, then everything was amazing – and if everything was amazing you had no time to be amazed. You had to guard against being amazed, just to stay sane.

No, he would have preferred a small screen that knew its place and didn't shout about magical worlds of fish. The TV they actually bought didn't bring Amy's daughter down from her room. She – Charlie – preferred to stay in her bedroom when Michael was round. When he wasn't, she and her mum enjoyed good conversation – or so Amy claimed.

'She does like you!' had become a regular reassurance, after she'd blanked him, or stared at him, or said something Michael realised only later was ironic. He seemed to mishear her a lot, because she mumbled.

'Pardon?' he would say. 'I'm sorry, Charlie – say that again.'

'It doesn't matter.'

She was sixteen, attending the sixth-form college, and as far as Michael could see she hardly noticed him, because *he* didn't matter. He was five feet nine inches tall, and he weighed a hundred and forty-two pounds – but Charlie didn't seem to notice him, and always seemed in a hurry to get past. Was he a threat?

Was he in competition with her father, whom she hardly saw? Or was he despised for being the same gender as her father? Perhaps it was simpler than that: her mother was bringing home a dull, stupid, awkward nothing, so what else could she do but despise him? He despised himself, after all, for being interested in her mother, or feigning interest – or trying to generate interest. He had worked at being interested in the hope that he would start to love her, because Amy was a good soul, and she had a sense of humour. She deserved to be loved. Everyone was a good soul, somewhere – and they had come together like two of those not very special turtles, and found themselves pairing off. How many turtles said, 'No, thank you – I'm not interested in you. I'm waiting for another turtle, I'm afraid. I'm so sorry, but I want a partner with fewer barnacles'?

He smiled, and sipped his drink.

It was the choral society's fault, really. Clubs and societies often brought people together: it was what they were for. Neither he nor Amy had a passion for church music – so that was something shared. They shared a readiness to enter the hideous drill hall where practices took place. What else did they share? They shared a dislike of the paper cups in which the tea was served. They shared an ability to tread the long, meandering path of aimless conversation – it was like an escalator that went on and on until you'd lost sight of your destination and point of origin. Yes, he and Amy had found themselves chatting, and that led to their meeting for a proper coffee, and that led to some weak magnet of attraction or need stirring in each of them – some soft bleep as the magnetic fields engaged. Why not see where the connection led?

But he had no affection for Charlie, because she was a stranger.

'Pardon?' he'd say.

'Oh, it doesn't matter.'

He tried to be interested in her – the A levels she'd chosen were dance, hotel management and something he couldn't now remember, and she didn't want to talk about why she had chosen those subjects, so he felt silly for asking about them. He'd get to the end of some idiotic, rambling question, and she'd be gone. The door would be swinging shut, her grunted answer only half-heard again. That was fine, of course: she didn't want to discuss her life with Michael, and it was her home so why should she?

Michael found he was shaking his head, so he sipped his whisky again.

A ticket inspector went by, hurrying into the compartment he'd recently left. Perhaps Terry was having another heart attack? The doors closed automatically, and Charlie was back, pushing past him with a heavy suitcase he had to step aside to avoid. He would have liked a moment of connection with her, and they should have found one. They should have come across a stray kitten together, or a bird with a broken wing. Amy's house had a garden, so there was every chance her cat would have caught a bird and left it mortally injured on the patio. Charlie might have been amazed by his patience, and he would have been touched by the purity of her compassion, which would have turned her back into a child. They would have set the bird on the rockery, and watched it recover and take flight.

It took her a very long time to put on make-up, and one of Michael's agonies was the thought of seeing her half dressed as she emerged from the bathroom – he lived in fear of an accusation or a scream. He had visions of neighbours gathering outside as Amy held Charlie and tried to stop her sobbing.

'He was waiting for me! He won't stop looking at me!'

Sometimes he worried about making remarks that could be misinterpreted, and that made conversation even more impossible. In fact, she thought he was *a frustrated queer*: Amy had revealed this in her final letter to him. The nuclear counter-strike – the retaliatory letter that reduced their idiotic relationship to smoking, radioactive ash.

Not an email: a letter, which he nearly hadn't read.

He had skimmed it, in case there was anything he had to deal with – anything financial, or possibly a threat of vengeance. Her brother had threatened to *break his jaw*, which seemed so specific. If Amy wanted to humiliate him in the street – and if she committed that hope to paper – he should at least make himself aware of it, so he tried to skim the letter, but ended up reading it properly. It was only two sides, and the sheets of paper were small. She had distilled her rage and humiliation – those were two of the words she used – and composed two-dozen cruel sentences designed to cut deep. One of them was about Charlie, and how overjoyed she'd been that Michael and her mother were no more. She had kissed Amy, and hugged her. *She always thought you were a frustrated queer using me to pretend otherwise because it's so clearly what you can't or don't want to deal with.*

The words had lodged themselves in his insides, like shrapnel. They continued to scrape and stab, even when he was still.

'You've got to let someone love you,' she'd said, when the relationship began.

And what was the other cliché, so horrible it had made him sweat? 'You've got to start liking yourself. You've got to learn to like yourself. Stop giving yourself a hard time, stop "beating yourself up"!' That kind of wisdom usually bloomed out of her mouth after a large glass of wine, and he would nod sagely and say something appropriate back.

'You can talk!' That was one of his pearls. 'You can talk, love.'

Love.

'We have to be kinder to ourselves, and each other.'

'We have to learn to forgive ourselves. To start again, because – you know what?'

'Tomorrow—'

'Tomorrow is the first day of the rest of your life. We have to laugh at ourselves a bit more, and take things as they come. Go on – laugh at yourself.'

Michael looked out of the window, and smiled. He smiled and laughed, laughing at himself. He was a clown, gulping neat malt whisky.

'But we did like each other, a little bit,' he said – and realised that once again, he'd spoken aloud.

'That wasn't enough,' he said softly, to the glass. 'Liking each other, I mean. It wasn't enough to justify. It wasn't going to get either of us through – was it?'

'You have to work at it,' Amy said.

He'd seen himself sitting at a lathe for a moment, working at the relationship with some kind of specialist tool. Or watering the little flowerpot and feeding the soil in which it grew, and putting it in the sun until finally there were the buds, and there were the flowers of love – blooming small but vivid, because he'd worked at it.

Their relationship was always about the future.

It seemed always to be based on making preparations: they were always getting ready for the wondrous things that lay ahead. Michael would move out of his flat, and move in with Amy properly and permanently. She would carry on part-time work at John Lewis whilst he would set his mind to getting another job – there were so many things he could do, because he was a 'people person', and it was time he put his experience at the council properly behind him and tried again. Shy, she said – desperately shy – but interested in others. There were retail outlets. There was driving, perhaps? He had a licence.

A taxi? Or deliveries?

He could work in a school, supporting disaffected children one-to-one.

Meanwhile, they had the kitchen to think about – and yes, he stood on the train still thinking about the infernal kitchen. For he had measured the cupboard doors, and got two different quotes for door replacement. It made no sense to 'rip the kitchen out' – which was the violent phrase everyone seemed to use. It made sense to keep the carcasses, because the changes were very straightforward – a tall oven-housing unit where the washing machine currently was, and a couple of extra shelves which could be installed once the fridge had been moved into the little pantry. The kitchen would be transformed.

Gloss white, cream or a colour?

'Gloss white.'

'You're sure?'

'Easier to clean. You see the marks better – not that you'll be cleaning them!'

'And the same handles—?'

'I think we need new handles.'

'Look at this. They'll actually pre-drill holes for the handles – that's worth the extra, I think. But you have to say what handles you're having.'

'Nothing too ornate. Nothing pretentious.'

'Look at these. These are Shaker style.'

'They're nice.'

As for worktops, that's where Amy wanted to spend the money they'd saved elsewhere. They couldn't justify granite, but real wood was surprisingly affordable, and a carpenter could install them in a day. Michael had begun to dread the completion of the kitchen, because the planning used up so many hours, and the discussions were always so wonderfully focused. There would be the most awful vacuum, unless they moved on to the bathroom.

The worktops had kept them going for days.

They had argued over whether they should order one litre of Danish oil to seal them, or two and a half. They had watched a video together on how to cut the hole for a sink, thinking they might do without the carpenter, and thus save two hundred pounds. Michael was worried that his jigsaw wasn't up to it, though.

'I could buy new blades, obviously. Or hire a better one.'

'How much is that? To hire one.'

'Fifty, probably. Once you've paid the VAT.'

'Would they deliver it? I can't pick it up—'

'I'm sure they would, but it'll be extra.'

'Still cheaper than the carpenter.'

Michael had nodded, as he nodded now.

'It's nesting,' said Amy, when he'd pointed out how much time they spent looking at catalogues. 'It's the most basic human instinct. We're building a nest.'

He thought, But we have no young. In any case, we have a nest already – birds don't do what we are doing. We are smothering our fear, Amy. We are still terrified of each other.

He wanted to ask her if they weren't simply swallowing that horrible propaganda, which asked you to believe that a certain type of kitchen brought happiness. That's what advertising did, after all – you didn't need to be clever to see that every advertisement was designed to make you feel inadequate. He had suggested this, and her answer was: 'I want a nice kitchen. We enjoy cooking.'

They did enjoy cooking.

Cooking was an excuse to open a bottle of wine, and the wine woke up the parts of the brain that said, 'We are not frightened of anything. When we are drunk, we can even touch one another.'

He winced, for in the letter she had told him he was a worm. She said that she regretted the day she'd spoken to him, which she had only done because she felt so sorry for him. She hoped he ended up lonely, in a hospice. He had hurt her so badly – a hurt he still couldn't grasp. It wasn't surprising she wanted to hurt him now. It was just like school, when he'd tripped a boy down the stairs for saying something cruel: he had wanted to break bones. Hurting, being hurt: Chinese burns, punches. The needling torment as someone was excluded from whatever group you'd managed to join – that was a particularly vile way of hurting. He remembered the boy Sandham, and how they'd all ganged up on him for absolutely no reason – James as well. They had flung textbooks at his head! The heavy ones they used for O-level physics, and nobody spoke up to stop them. Poor old Sandham had ignored the first, even though it had slammed into the back of his neck. The second had hit his shoulder, and whoever had thrown it had shouted, 'One hundred and eighty!' as if he'd scored a bull's-eye. The third was a direct strike on the poor boy's skull, and the fourth had been skimmed so viciously it had hit him in the jaw. 'One hundred and eighty!' they'd cried, and Sandham had run out of the room, holding his face just like Michael was holding his, pressed against the carriage door. They could have killed the boy, or knocked his teeth out. And afterwards – the most amazing thing – Sandham had simply forgotten all about it.

They hadn't got into trouble, he and his friends.

Psychotic violence had not landed them in trouble, for poor Sandham must have been a good sport, and he hadn't told the teacher – he'd moved on. Perhaps he had bottled up the hurt for ever, and was now a tormented wreck, howling in the night. Perhaps he was unable to be near heavy textbooks? Perhaps not, too – perhaps he'd simply laughed at himself, and put it all behind him?

'I suppose I had it coming, eh!' chortled Sandham. 'Cor, it didn't half hurt – but boys will be boys, won't they, Michael? You take it on the chin, don't you? – you take it in your mouth, sometimes. *Let it go!*'

The train was pulling into a station, and Michael decided to get off.

There would be another train, and he would still make a connection of some kind – he would get to Crewe for the 15.41, just one hour later. He would be on time for that one, and if he arrived later he'd avoid having half an hour to spare. Yes, he had to cross to platform seven, but there was a subway and a bridge. He had once used the lifts, in fact, but he couldn't recall where they were. Not that crossing the station posed any kind of problem: the real problem was the realisation that he was so obstinately, harrowingly sober.

He put the carton and glass away, and when the doors opened he was the first one out, stumbling onto the platform. His knees were shaking, but there was a bench in the perfect spot. He sat, with his bag on his lap, breathing in as slowly as he could. He stared at his shoes, and found that like an idiot he was crying again. The clouds had amassed in his head, it seemed: now, rain was falling.

He smiled, because someone was coming towards him, and the last thing he wanted was to embarrass that person. He really did have just a few hours left – and it would be nice to get through them without causing pain.

'Excuse me, sir. Why are you crying?'

He waited as the woman walked by.

'Excuse me, sir. I'm a Samaritan and I couldn't help but notice the fact that you have tears in your eyes, and... I don't want to be presumptuous, but I can't walk by someone who appears to be in distress. Lay down your burden.'

The passengers were gone, and the tears stopped as suddenly as they started: the sun came out again.

He gathered himself up, and walked to the waiting room.

It was a clean, efficient station, and he'd never explored it before: Bromsgrove, home of Terry and his lovely, loyal, nervous wife. Had Terry got down here, too? Michael hadn't seen him. But he'd been on his way to Bristol, so he said – even though they were heading north, so was that possible? No. Had he not started his journey from home? Had he moved south, or was he staying with friends? Terry had definitely lived in Bromsgrove once, so perhaps he was lying about his journey to the marina? Perhaps it was all fiction, and Terry was off to blow his brains out in the Midlands, or to pick up a Birmingham prostitute – he'd been covering his tracks, the dog, and Michael had swallowed every word.

He should have fixed Terry with a cheery grin.

'You're a sly one,' he should have said. 'Where are you off to, really?'

'That would be telling!'

Terry would have grinned back and winked.

'I don't tell the truth, Michael,' he would have whispered. 'Why should I?'

'Why should anyone?'

He took off his spectacles and rubbed his eyes.

The platforms were blurred now, under a slab of grey-white sky that went from horizon to horizon: typically dull September, life-sapping weather. The waiting area was un-vandalised, and when he walked further, to the ticket office, he noticed exhibition boards. There were photographs of soldiers, and maps with arrows.

Why soldiers, he wondered? He would need his reading glasses now.

He started to read, and as he read a boy called Morris was in need of his help – but they'd got down at different stations, so help could not be offered. The track connected them, of course, but as Michael read the word *Flanders*, and tried to remember where it was, Morris sat hungry and sad waiting for a call that just wouldn't come. He knew in his heart that things were going to end badly.

He had so little money, and he was a long way from home.

IN FROM THE WEST

8

He had no credit on his phone, or he would have called Keenan.

He'd set off in good faith, and had spent his own money on the ticket. He'd got to the café as instructed: nobody had turned up so far, and twelve-thirty was the time he'd been told. Now he sat alone with sixty-seven pence in his pocket, which wouldn't buy him a bottle of water let alone a hot drink. Breakfast – hours ago – had been a sausage roll.

This was Morris.

He was staying with his sister at Newport, and had crept down-stairs so as not to wake up the baby that had woken him twice. No milk, so he drank half a cup of black tea. One sausage roll, from a pack of three: he'd bought them the day before, and there was one left because Ben, his sister's boyfriend, had stolen two. No juice, and no point trying to eat cereal without milk. Other than that, it was baby food and a rancid yoghurt. The sausage roll had filled him, and the deal was always the same: he'd be given money, food and drink. Now he didn't know what to do.

Boots, jeans and a sweatshirt: he sat back with his arms wrapped round himself, keeping his eyes on the window and the door, worried already that he'd missed whoever it was. The woman behind the counter was getting ready to move him on, and he thought about leaving so as to make life easy. Then he looked at all the empty tables and chairs, and decided not to: he could sit where he wanted to sit, surely, since he wasn't being a nuisance.

He wasn't smoking.

He wasn't stinking. He wasn't in anybody's way, but the woman kept glancing at him. A man came in, with a little boy.

The boy was four at the most, and wanted to explore. The man, however, wanted to keep him safe – so they were fighting, and the man was going to win. The little boy did the only thing he could do, which was cry, and the man relented: he ordered his coffee and let the boy run free. Morris watched the child pad about, bumping into a chair. He looked all around the café, and gazed at Morris – and Morris knew what was going to happen next because it seemed to happen all the time. Some people attracted dogs: he attracted little kids. They always wanted an up-close look, and sure enough the little boy was making his way over, as if he were family.

His dad didn't mind, so Morris said, 'All right?' because the boy was standing quite close now, still gazing at him. They simply stared at each other, until the child was distracted and wandered off again. Meanwhile, the door had opened a second time, and a very fat woman appeared, out of breath simply from carrying her own load. The father sat down while she went slowly to the counter, pulling a suitcase. He got the kid to the table, and tore a bun or teacake in half. Meanwhile the woman ordered a latte and a pastry.

His phone rang at last.

'Where the fuck are you?'

'I'm where I'm supposed to be,' said Morris.

'Where's that?'

'I'm in the café.'

'How long have you been there?'

'An hour.'

'Tony was in just after half past. He parked outside, and went looking for you.'

'Where?'

'Cheltenham.'

'That's where I am. I'm at the station.'

There was a silence.

'You said meet at the station,' said Morris.

'Shit. Why the fuck didn't you call me?'

'I've got no credit.'

Keenan swore again.

'Okay, I'll call you back. Stay where you are.'

Morris watched the little boy drop most of his bun.

He would have to go outside soon, because he needed to walk – and he wanted chocolate. There was nothing he could buy here, because the prices were so high: he couldn't even afford tea. Twenty minutes passed, and his phone didn't ring. The woman ignored him, and the man with the boy left.

If he went home, he'd lost money. If Tony didn't come back for him, then he'd still lost money. It had happened before, these stupid mix-ups – and the annoying thing this time was that he hadn't put a coat on, and the sweatshirt he was wearing just wasn't warm enough. He pulled the hood up, and leaned forward so his head was on the table – that was his mistake, of course. The woman behind the counter now had no option, and she was there almost at once, standing over him.

'Come on, angel,' she said. 'This isn't a waiting room.'

'Can I have a sandwich?'

'Course you can. Can you pay for it?'

'No.'

'On your way, then.'

9

For some reason Bromsgrove was remembering its war dead.

There was a photograph of the town's war memorial, so Michael skimmed the first section of text, and learned that the local regiment had fought in Flanders and then the Somme. The Allies were going to throw everything they had at the German defences, and – this was 1916 – the war would be won. The stalemate could not go on any longer, and the tactics were the only tactics anyone could think of. They had always worked in the past.

Michael had to put his face quite close to the display, because the writing was small. He knew that the soldiers would be annihilated – that almost went without saying. Young men from Bromsgrove had packed up their troubles and chugged down from this very spot, on steam trains. They had gone south, and then east to the sea, thence to set sail and be 'entrained' to what looked like villages all around the Somme – which Michael discovered from the map was a river.

He had assumed it was a town in France, or a region. In fact, it was one of several rivers in the area. There were so many words on the information boards, and so many pictures – it would take all afternoon to read everything. In one particular photograph, a man with a moustache was smiling at him. A boy sat close by, and it could have been himself, aged fourteen or fifteen. Michael put himself into the uniform, and imagined the excitement.

He would have asked questions.

'Are we going to see action, sarge?'

'I'm sure we will, son.'

'How long till we get there?'

'No idea.'

'I heard it's pretty much over!' he'd have said. 'We're going to be stuck here and miss the show – aren't we?'

They hadn't missed the show, of course. They had departed, arriving finally at a camp where the waiting started all over again. Then, at last, they moved down to the lines, to replace those who had died, or needed rest. Hideous flares, and the whistling of the shells... he had heard the sound effects in films, and like every schoolboy he'd read the poetry and listened to the slow, sad opening of the 'Last Post'. As a Boy Scout, he'd stood to attention with James and felt the curious ache of loss.

Bromsgrove station must have seen real tears, though: rivers of tears. Tears as the recruits lined up and left, and tears as their remains came back – if they ever did. They didn't, because they were blown to pieces: that's why there were war graves out in France. Again, he realised how little he knew about anything, and so he put his face closer still, and read more text:

The firing died down, and out of the darkness a great moan came. People with their arms and legs off trying to crawl away; others who could not move gasping out their last moments with the cold night wind biting into their broken bodies...

Bodies that could never be reclaimed, though they must have been tagged.

Bodies that would slowly rot, and... Michael remembered a detail from school history about how stretcher-bearers had to kick the dead men hard, in the ribs. That was how you got rid of the rats, which were nesting in their chests.

Had the man with the moustache ended that way? Had young Michael?

The platforms were new, but the lines hadn't changed.

In 1916 old men and women would have sat on benches here, and the names of the lost would have been known to them. The pain would be raw: an ache that made you hold your breath, for surely loss like that made you sit still in case you simply shattered.

There would have been mothers, trying to imagine their sons' and husbands' fear. Had they sat here, trying to comprehend the sheer loneliness of faraway death? He'd been told by someone that a bullet is hot when it hits you – and there were pictures of the rifles they'd used. Clunky old things, slung over greatcoats heavy with rain – boots that must have leaked, and a pack that doubled in weight because canvas soaked up the wet. How could the man with the moustache look so full of hope? Michael stared at him, and the man held his gaze.

He had not imagined being confronted like this, but the town was reaching out to the people of the past. Why was it so hard to imagine anything other than melodrama? The station had been rebuilt with brand-new facilities, and the furniture was the kind you saw everywhere: metal chairs, bolted to concrete in the style of a prison cell. There was a protective glass wall, but it had been designed not to reach the floor – that ensured the space you were in could never be snug, so you'd never be tempted to linger and become a nuisance. Michael tried to imagine the young men waiting beside him, smelling of tobacco and damp wool. He tried to see the ghosts, but they just wouldn't appear. He saw actors only, faking local working-class accents.

'Stand well away from the edge of platform one,' said a voice.

'Why?' said Michael quietly – and for a moment he knew that his time had come, and he didn't need whisky. He could do it, and it had to be done. There really was no need to wait for Crewe.

'Stand well away…'

'No.'

'You have been warned – the approaching train is not scheduled to stop at this station. Stand behind the yellow line!'

He went quickly out onto the platform and contemplated the distance he would have to walk or run, to get onto the tracks. He could jump, of course – simply step into the path of the locomotive – over the top, as it were, if he had the courage. All he had to do was run, now, and dive, and the rails were throbbing. They were pulsing, in fact singing with excitement, for closer and closer came the train and there was no need to brake. The signal is green, and everyone else is standing back. The driver stares forward, for the hardest thing in a train driver's day, apparently, is the mesmerising miles of unfurling track.

Had he noticed Michael, getting ready to jump? Presumably not, and what would he do if he had? The great steel snout was hammering through, drilling into its own tornado. It was a freight train again, and Michael willed himself into its path and could not do it – he hit a wall, and he just couldn't smash his way through – he needed the captain's whistle, and the sergeant's command. He needed to be picked up and thrown.

He stood still, and the gale broke over him. He was rocked back onto his heels as the wagons came past – at least thirty seconds' worth of train, and when the last was gone Michael looked at the rails and wondered what would have happened, and what state his own body would have been in. The severed head had a minute or two of consciousness, so he'd been told: he'd be looking up at the white sky even now, as it faded to black.

What if he'd managed it? The train would be grinding slowly to a halt as the poor driver shouted and cried. The controller in Gloucester or Worcester would have been alerted, and all rail traffic would stop. The Samaritans would scramble a team, for everyone involved in the aftermath needs help – the driver, the passengers, the people on the platform where the incident took place as well as those living close to the line. The dead man's final gift to the world is the traumatising of those forced to look at what's left of him.

He found he was sobbing.

The weather had broken in his head completely, and down came the rain again. He was furious with himself and bewildered. He remembered school, and his failure in high-jump. Physical education, and his inability to vault the horse, for most boys seemed to sail over it but he never did – he'd funk it. 'Funk' was a word from the distant past, but that's the word they'd used.

He was still alive, and didn't want to be. On the other hand, how wonderful not to have been blasted and smeared all over the tracks – not to be smashed to pieces, as if by a shell. He was holding his bag in both hands, and it really was as if the weather had turned – a sudden squall out of a clear sky. He cried and gasped, his lungs snatching at the air, the tears streaming down his face. He cried the way a child cries, and then stopped, and nobody saw him – at least nobody saw him.

And I am crying for myself! he thought, wishing he had something sharp to jab into his own flesh. Not for anyone I have loved, or lost – not for the brave boys of Bromsgrove, or their poor dear families...

He gasped and the fit passed. He stood up straight and put his shoulders back. He mopped his face with a handkerchief, knowing that if anyone saw him now they'd assume he'd been laughing.

He sat down on a bench and waited. A train came by and he didn't catch it. He thought about crossing the bridge and going back south, back to his terrible flat. He thought of Amy and Elizabeth.

Nobody spoke to him, so he ate two tangerines. He had to go on, but it was now a long wait for the 13.55 which was delayed by eight minutes, so that meant he wouldn't get to Birmingham now until quarter past two. How had he misjudged it so badly, and wasted so much time? He'd failed again, funking everything – the 14.41 would hurtle through Crewe, and he'd miss that too. Now it would be a push to meet even the 15.41 – but at least there would be no drama. At least he could get properly drunk and at thirty-five minutes past three he could stagger down platform seven and get himself atomised. Even he could manage that.

Morris was still in Cheltenham.

It was 15.31 and all he wanted now was to go home again. Keenan had messaged him at last, and he was fixing up something totally different, which would mean going on to Birmingham. That might mean spending the night there, but he'd earn something reasonable. He'd get something to smoke and something to eat – it was worth doing, and he had no choice. Maria, meanwhile, was standing on a similar platform up in Carlisle. She was realising she'd done something so stupid she couldn't quite take it in: she had actually frozen.

Ayesha was on the train bound for Preston, with Maria's bag. Maria watched the carriages slide by and she had the insane impulse to chase after them, screaming. She might have tried it, if her legs would only move. She managed to turn at last, but there was nobody to help her: everyone was pushing past. As for the Reverend Paul, he had left the train back at Oxenholme, and was on his way to Windermere, feeling sad.

10

The Herne School is an academy in Crewe looking after more than a thousand boys and girls.

Aaron was twelve years old, and as term had started in the first week of September he was seventeen days into his second year. He was on his way home, having changed into training shoes, which was against the rules. His coat was in his bag, and he had pulled his shirt out of his trousers. That was forbidden too, and three uniform strikes meant you received a detention – but the walk to the railway station was unlikely to take him past anyone on duty. He was with Ollie Jamner, whom he thought of as a friend – and another boy called Khari Aboudi. They were all in the same year, but whilst Ollie was in Aaron's tutor group, Khari was more of an unknown, and most of their encounters had been in the playground or lunch hall. Aaron found Khari exciting and dangerous. He found that he wanted to impress him, and he felt lucky to be in the boy's company because he seemed so fearless. Right now, he was 'on report', which meant he had to carry a folded card with him all day and present it to every teacher who taught him. The teacher would grade his behaviour.

He'd shown Aaron the card. It was meant to be kept neat and clean, but Khari was scrunching it up on purpose, so it was already creased and torn. He'd intimated that he was going to do something unmentionable over it, every night, and the three boys had found themselves howling with laughter.

'Will you tell them?' said Ollie. 'When they open it? "Why's this card so *sticky*, Khari?"'

'I couldn't help myself, miss.'

They crashed in through the doors of the ticket office, calming themselves only when they came to the barriers, where an inspector was on duty. They showed their passes one by one, moving through in sober single file. School started at eight-thirty, so the children were released at three-fifteen. Aaron shouldn't have left, in fact, because he was supposed to be at a play rehearsal until four. He was feeling guilty already, because forgetting was one thing, but deliberately cutting a commitment was forbidden – his parents would be furious. Once you made a commitment, you stuck to it – but he'd got into conversation with Ollie, and suddenly all he wanted was to be out of the building and off the site. He could say that he'd felt ill, or had remembered a dentist's appointment, and there was nothing the teacher could do. If she threw him out of the group it wouldn't be the end of the world. It was worth it, to be with Khari.

Khari had found an empty bench and was climbing onto it. This was bold, since the platform was busy and the benches were quite close to station staff. He'd dropped his bag, and was standing with his hands behind his head. Like Aaron, he wore his shirt untucked, but his shirts were way too big and they were loose and long. The collar was done up, and his neck looked slender. The tie was tied so the knot was extra fat, and whilst some teachers fought against this Khari had got away with it all day, and stood there looking sleek and handsome. Aaron felt a thrill of excite-ment, and he wished he had the same build. The boy's trousers were fashionably tight, and his trainers were unlaced. His legs were wide apart, and he looked at Aaron and said, 'What?'

'What?' replied Aaron.

'What are you looking at?'

'Nothing. Are you going straight home?'

'Why?'

'I don't know. Nothing.'

Aaron was on the bench, next to Khari's right foot. Ollie was checking the train times, though they all knew they had a while to wait. The train they caught came in at 15.55, so he checked it was on time and sat down. Khari put a hand on his shoulder and slid down next to him. Then he snaked his other arm round Aaron and drew him close. He put his mouth close to his ear.

'Hey,' he said quietly. 'Aaron.'

'What?'

'We're mates, aren't we?'

'Yes.'

'Well, there's a toilet over there, mate. Any chance of a blow-job?'

That was the moment a voice said, 'Boys?' – and Aaron was trapped. That was the moment they all looked up, expecting to be reprimanded for the foulness of Khari's imagination – instead, they found themselves staring into the eyes of a nervous, agitated man they definitely didn't know. He wasn't a railway official: he was a member of the public, and they would never forget him.

'Boys,' said Michael quietly. 'Listen carefully, please. Don't speak.'

He had caught the delayed 13.55 from Bromsgrove, leaving the dead behind him. It had made up some time, zipping along the tracks to arrive in Birmingham just twenty minutes later. The Liverpool service was waiting, so Michael took a seat in the very last carriage and drank a little more whisky. He disembarked at the tail end of the long, long platform, and he stood for some time looking at the great tangle of rails.

This was Crewe, at last – and he had fifteen minutes to wait. Platform seven was the next one along, so did he want to use the footbridge or the lift? For a moment he had an urge to simply jump down and cross the rails, as quickly as possible. Then he could start walking, towards the warehouses where a curtain of bramble would conceal him. Nobody would see him hurrying up the line unless there were cameras. If he was spotted, they'd close the whole network and that would be that.

The Samaritans sign told him yet again that there was someone to talk to, and that someone was there to help him. He had tried them, and he couldn't call again – for what could they say? A woman called Ella had helped him most, but to sit there whispering to her would be too intrusive and demanding. Ella had done her very best, and he didn't want to addict himself to her or any of her measured, calm, lovely colleagues – whatever he had done. Whatever life had done to him. He stood still, mesmerised by the beauty of the glinting silver metal and the wonder of the engineering. A hundred and fifty years ago there might have been just one lonely line. There might have been just one train a day, rolling slowly in from Manchester, perhaps? Because that was the old days when railways were a nervous experiment. He smiled at the thought, and took another mouthful from his juice carton.

He was warm and he was ready. He had to set off now and keep moving, for it was so straightforward: one foot followed the other, over the bridge and back along the platform. If he kept moving, people would think he had business on the tracks, checking some complicated bit of signalling. How did his fifty-pound ticket pay for the legions of men and women who kept the industry going? There were experts, no doubt, who understood these things: they spoke the language, and he stood swaying slightly, wondering how he had spent so long on the planet knowing so little. How had he not known that the Somme was a river? For a moment he had a desire to stay alive, and read a book about the war. He could trace the whole of that sad and terrible century – not just in homage to those who had sacrificed themselves, but as a way of understanding how everyone had ended up in this place, right now. On the other hand, why be so ambitious? Why not simply learn how one particular railway line came to be, and why it connected this particular string of towns? He put the juice carton in his bag, and removed his spectacles for a final clean.

'You've missed her,' said a voice.

Michael swung round, the duster limp between his fingers.

'What?' he said.

'She's gone, I'm afraid. She doesn't hang about.'

'Who?'

An old man had appeared behind him – a pensioner – and Michael suddenly wondered if he was referring to some shady liaison with a prostitute. He blinked, hating himself for the absurdity of such a thought. The man blinked back at him, smelling the whisky perhaps.

'The *Proud Isabella*,' he said. 'She came through ten or fifteen minutes ago.'

'Through here?'

'Yes. She didn't stop this time, but she slowed right down. I assumed you'd come to see her. There was quite a crowd, in fact. A couple of hundred.'

The man was carrying a tablet. He flipped the cover and held it out towards Michael. Swiping from the left, he pulled up a folder which opened into a cluster of photo-files, and when he touched one in the centre it turned into the profile of a long green steam engine, with gold trimmings and a black funnel. Michael had just digested that when it was replaced by the same machine crossing a viaduct, and that changed almost at once to a close-up of its nose.

'Beautiful,' said Michael dutifully.

It was half past three, and he had to move.

'You can't account for it,' said the man, stepping close to his side. 'I must have seen her a dozen times, but it's always a new experience – look at this one. I don't know what it is – the noise, or the smell, or the... just the wonder of it. Look.'

He adjusted the angle, and Michael saw that the train was actually moving. It was pulling into a village station, where it was immediately surrounded by children. There was no sound, and he found himself peering into a little world of joyful waving – the children were in fancy dress, wearing Victorian-style bonnets and waistcoats.

'Where is that?' he said.

'That's the Dales, that is – just outside Settle. Look at the pistons, though.'

The camera was closing in on the wheels.

'Four thousand horsepower, near enough – and there's two of them.'

'Are you an engineer?' said Michael.

'More of a mechanic, really, but it's become quite a hobby—'

'Where was it going? Today I mean.'

'What?'

'The steam train. Where was it going?'

'Milton Keynes.'

'Did it have passengers? Was it—'

'Oh, God yes. The tickets went months ago. Months ago.'

'You should have bought one.'

The old man laughed.

'Not this time,' he said. 'You can't go every time, can you? I have in the past, and I will again. Today I just came out for a few photos – it's an occasion, isn't it?'

He tapped something, and Michael found himself inside one of the compartments, looking out at a level crossing. Again, people were waving, and the excitement made him feel slightly bewildered. Michael tore his eyes away, and inspected his new acquaintance more carefully. He was even older than he'd thought, and frailer too. He could have been eighty, or even eighty-five, and his teeth were so perfectly white they had to be dentures. Sure enough, the upper plate slipped, and he saw that the man's face was unnaturally pale and beginning to crumple. He wore a dark grey cap, and what hair Michael could see was ragged and random, as if white clumps of dirty white cotton-wool had stuck to the sides of his head. His eyes were watery and he had a skinny throat.

'I was going to take my great-grandson,' he said slowly. 'Then we realised it was during school, and he told me he wasn't inter-ested anyway.'

'Wasn't interested?'

'In seeing her. He said it was a bit boring, trains.'

'That's a shame.'

'Well… there's so many other things now, aren't there? Phones, for example – computer games.'

'Yes.'

The dental plate shifted again, and now Michael noticed his hands and how bony they were. He was hunched forward, holding his gadget in both, and he was a little breathless. Michael stood, unable to move, for the train on the screen was still chugging silently along past houses, and he didn't want to be like the man's uninterested great-grandson. On the other hand, he could feel a speech coming, which he knew almost by heart because he had heard it before – or some variation. The man was about to list more of the things young people found more interesting than trains, and they would all be electronic things. The man would laugh in wonder as if the laugh could make the terrifying new world harmless. Yes, he could use a tablet, but he had still become unnecessary. Technology wasn't interested in him, for he just wasn't the market: his market was stair-lifts and mobility scooters, and trousers with elastic waistbands. Funeral plans, too.

'I have to go,' said Michael.

The man didn't hear him. Instead, he touched Michael's arm very gently.

'Listen,' he said. 'I said to the oldest, the other day, "What's so important that you've got to bring your phone to the tea-table? Who are you talking to?" He said, "I'm texting." I said, "Why?"'

Michael gazed at him.

'"Why?" I said. "Stop bloody fiddling! Talk to your gran. Talk to a real person for a change." If it was up to me, I'd make them turn the damn things off, and leave them at the door. They can't have a proper conversation any more – not like my generation. In my day, we talked to each other. We communicated.'

'Yes,' said Michael.

Had the man finished? There was a sudden silence.

'They are different,' said Michael. 'Things change, I suppose.'

'Yes. And you try having a conversation with a young person.'

'I know—'

'They look scared. They haven't got the ability to listen, you see. And I don't think that's progress. Is it?'

'What isn't?'

'What?'

'Sorry, what isn't progress?'

He looked over towards platform seven, and there it stood – long and empty, and impossible to get to. He needed to drink the rest of the whisky, for that's what he'd planned to do as he walked down onto it. He'd planned to let the liquor hit him hard and fast, and that would be the fuel he needed. The old man talking was holding his sleeve, though, as if he needed to feel the material.

'All this technology,' he said. 'Are we better off for it? That's what I ask myself, you see – are we better off now, than in my day?'

'Yes,' said Michael.

'It's not progress, is it?'

'Yes. I think it is.'

'How?'

The man wanted to know, it seemed, and now he was looking out at the tangle of rails in much the same attitude as Michael. Perhaps he felt desperate too? If that was the case, they could walk together, holding hands. They could even share the whisky, and steady each other.

'I think we're better off,' said Michael.

'In what way? You tell me, because I don't think it's progress, you see.'

'Well, I'll give you an example—'

'I'm not sure we're any happier,' interrupted the man. 'All these gadgets... because that's what they are, in the end. Toys, really, and are we happier for them?'

'We can stay in touch,' said Michael quickly. 'With the people who care about us – we can talk to them. If your... grandson, let's say, misses the last bus, he won't be stranded in the dark. You'll know he's safe.'

'He'll be on the phone for a lift, that's why. In my day, you would have had to walk.'

'Yes, but you'll be able to keep him safe.'

'Were we in so much danger? In the old days?'

'I'm sure we were. Yes – definitely. *I* was.'

The man said nothing, and Michael swallowed.

'We are so much better off,' he said. 'Your great-grandson has access to so much knowledge now. With one touch on his screen he can do just what you're doing. He can call up recordings and information. He can listen to ideas, from people who think more deeply than he does. He can get advice, and find out about other people and what they might be going through. I think that's progress – I do.'

'Playing computer games. Is that good for you?'

'Don't you play games?'

'No. Not for hours on end in a room all by myself, no. Not games where you... There was one he was playing the other day, it made me feel quite nauseous. He had a flamethrower. He was a soldier, with a flamethrower, squirting fire all over people. That was the game, and he was on it all afternoon – twelve years old. With some friend halfway across the country, so they don't even have to see each other.'

Michael nodded.

The man would talk about sexual predators soon – and he would have to stand there listening. He glanced at the old man again, and wondered how many months of life he had left, because he wasn't well. He would be getting home as the light faded: his wife would see how weary he was. She would set his supper before him, and what would it be? What did a man this old eat on a Thursday evening? Meatballs. Fish fingers. A lamb chop? Had they discovered the ready-meal, and the supermarkets' money-saving deals? Chicken tikka masala with oven-ready naan bread and a free dessert.

He gazed out at the tracks and thought of Amy, who had used Waitrose, especially when they had special offers. The freezer was full: she would be working her way through it without him. Perhaps Charlie had organised another celebration meal, and they'd clinked glasses at his absence from the table. Monica had used a supermarket out of town, and Elizabeth? It didn't matter, but now he couldn't move his feet.

They had sat at her table – Monica's table, not Amy's. Did it matter who was who? Were they interchangeable now? Monica liked fish, and they'd spent an evening poring over a brochure from a supermarket that specialised in frozen food. It had come through the door and there were photographs of salmon, bream and haddock fillets. Prawns, king prawns, cod and trout – you could buy them as they were, or in sauces, and you could almost smell the sea. They had gone out to the store the next day, and bought six haddock steaks for three pounds.

'My word,' they'd said. 'Very tasty.'

'This is good,' they had agreed. 'Oh, this is a meaty fish. Crikey. How much was this? A bit of butter and it's... this is... This is amazing.'

Ross-on-Wye was the place they went together once, and somehow Monica had chosen the worst bed-and-breakfast in the country, imprisoning them both in a small, mean room with two single beds. They found out too late that the guttering over the window was broken, which meant the rain came down hard and splattered on the sill. They wouldn't have cared on a fine day – but that night a rainstorm hit, and above the nagging, sawing wind was the gushing of water. He had lain awake, not deserving Monica's patience, and she had begun to suspect that. They both yearned to be home, away from each other – and yet their friendship survived, because they both needed somebody to phone.

Why do two adults of the opposite sex who like each other not sleep together, when they are both single? Why are they not drowning the sounds of the storm with joyous, experimental sex? Why isn't one of the beds straining and heaving, the legs scraping the floor until the neighbours can't stand it and hammer on the wall?

A short train had appeared, and was choosing its platform. Michael looked at the driver as it approached and saw how focused he was – the last thing he wanted to do was run somebody down, even if they wanted to die.

'Pornography,' said the old man suddenly. 'That's what they're looking at, half the time.'

'What?' said Michael.

'Aren't they? Parental controls? Do me a favour.'

'How old's your great-grandson? You said he was twelve.'

'Twelve, yes. No... eleven.'

'And he's looking at pornography?'

'No.'

'Sorry, you said he was.'

'No, I didn't. I'm just saying it probably won't be long. That's what they do, isn't it? You read about it – they send pictures of each other, and before you know it your best friend turns out to be your worst enemy. Too late – she's sent the whole lot to everyone else. Every day, you hear about it. Then they're changing their gender.'

Michael nodded.

'Boys become girls,' said the old man. 'They put on a skirt, and then they swap back again. They end up not knowing what they are, and I blame the pornography – I do.'

'When did you first see pornography?' said Michael.

'What?'

The man thought he had misheard, and was putting his ear closer to Michael, so his head was on one side. There was a station announcement, but the words were inaudible.

'When did I what?' said the man.

Michael tried to speak clearly. He knew he smelled of whisky, but he wasn't going to search for a mint now.

'I was asking you,' he said. 'When did you first see a... you know, a pornographic magazine or film?'

The man looked baffled. 'Why are you asking me that?' he said.

Michael so nearly said, 'It doesn't matter.' He so nearly diffused it again, but for some reason he decided that the topic had to be examined, properly.

'You're saying your great-grandson sees images,' he said patiently. 'Or *will* see images, at the age of eleven – that's what you're saying. And you're telling me that, as if it's unusual or... I don't know – a new thing. Part of the danger of technology, and the age we're living in. But it seems to me that boys have always found ways of looking at pornography.'

'Not at the touch of a button.'

'Perhaps not, but—'

'There's so much of it.'

'Does that make such a difference? Didn't you borrow or buy magazines? That's what I'm asking.'

'I didn't know where to get them. No, I didn't.'

'You never looked at pornography?'

'What?'

Michael's astonishment must have been clear in his voice, for the man was looking at him with just a trace of fear.

'No,' he said, as if the idea was offensive to him.

'You must have, though,' said Michael.

'Why?'

'Because everyone does. *Mayfair. Penthouse.* There was a boy at my school who got them from somewhere, and hired them out. Fifty pence, I think, for a weekend. What about the *Sun,* for goodness' sake? When does a boy first see a copy of page three?'

'That's a very different thing.'

'But it's not.'

'Not what?'

'It's not different. It's the same—'

'It's totally different.'

'How?'

'Well, for one thing—'

'You think the pictures are more tasteful? More... artistic, or what? Less naked?'

'Ah, but they don't display themselves, do they? Page three is a joke – just a... woman's bare chest for a bit of fun.'

'A pair of knockers.'

'What?'

There was a pause, and then the man chuckled, and looked away.

'I don't know,' he said. 'All I know—'

'That's what we called them,' interrupted Michael. 'That's what people called them: a right good pair of knockers. "Look at the size of them, eh?" That was how we spoke. That was the kind of thing you'd hear on television, but it was all part of something else. We'd made her body horrible, so it was something to leer at. To lust over. Do you know what I mean? And there was something disgusting about it, always. You know? You'd take the magazine home, and you had to hide it. So sex becomes a shameful thing, and I'm just wondering – how do you grow up normal if you glimpse a woman and she's... turning herself inside out, in a magazine? It used to terrify me. I used to hate it. And I used to worry that I was abnormal for hating it, while wondering if everyone hated it, but couldn't say so. Do you know what I mean?'

The man said nothing for a moment, and then he sighed. Michael waited, wondering if his companion was about to say something wise. It was the most serious speech he'd made in weeks, or even months – and he'd made it to a stranger who now seemed to be pondering his response.

'You're talking about the objectification of women,' he might say. 'You are. You're talking about attitudes that – yes – *can* go unchallenged, or... fail to change. It's sometimes hard to learn new behaviours, isn't it? That's what you're saying, mister.'

Michael would nod.

'Yes,' he would reply. 'I don't know how I became what I am. I can't blame magazines, or Mr Trace. Can I? I just long to understand it.'

'Who was Mr Trace?'

'My Latin teacher.'

'What happened? What's he got to do with it?'

Michael would tell him, and perhaps they would stand together with bowed heads, and finally clasp hands. The old man's voice would drop to a whisper.

'Me too,' he would say.

'What? You too?'

'Yes.'

'Are you lost, too?'

'I've been lost all my life. What happened to us? How did we end up here – in Crewe?'

'Crewe.'

'Why Crewe?'

The old man was still, but he said nothing at all and the silence only got longer.

He held up his tablet, slowly, and took a photograph of the rails. He stepped to one side, and Michael realised he was actually filming, panning slowly from right to left to take in the whole side of the station – and there could be no reason for it, for who would ever ask to see that sequence of film? Who was waiting at home, yearning to watch an empty section of this particular station on a September afternoon? If Michael walked onto the line now, would he carry on filming? Would he show it to a journalist, and get his great-grandson to upload everything onto some website where the world could enjoy Michael's last moments, and comment on them?

'Phew, look at this one – whoa! #Splat! (57 likes)'

The old man flipped the cover, and put the tablet under his arm.

'That's it for today,' he said softly. 'I've run out of time.'

'Is it late?'

'It is for me. I'm ready for a cup of tea.'

Michael smiled.

'Where do you go for that?' he said.

'Oh, here and there. Different places.'

He didn't want Michael to know. He didn't want the conversation to resume – he just had to get away.

'Goodbye,' said Michael.

'What?'

'I said goodbye. Have a nice afternoon – it was nice to chat.'

The man nodded.

He turned and walked carefully off. His legs were not reliable, and he should have had a stick. Michael didn't watch him for long, but turned back to stare at the warehouses. He thought of those poor women again, forced to expose themselves in magazines. The ones he'd seen had held their legs wide open so their genitalia were like a wound, and he remembered hard, glassy eyes – a sense that he was looking at corpses, mutilated by a madman.

Deep in thought, he didn't hear the announcement, or the approach of the train he'd been waiting for. It was suddenly on him, hurtling in from behind on his very own platform – not platform seven after all. He'd missed the warning and there it went, its slipstream rocking him so hard that he found himself cowering. It really was the train he'd planned to be in front of: the absolutely punctual non-stop express, just a blur of red blazing through at fifty miles per hour with a confidence and purpose that Michael found shocking. Even if he ran at it, he'd simply be bounced off the side. He'd spin and tumble like a clown, and there he'd be on his back looking up from the ground – would he laugh at himself, he wondered, as the staff gathered round him? He'd have to listen to his very own announcement:

'If there's a doctor in the station, could you please make your way to platform...'

'Let me go,' he'd say. 'Don't save me.'
'There's someone coming, pal – stay still. Don't try to move.'
'But I must.'
'Has he got water? Give him a snack – call the refreshment trolley!'
Would they wrap him in a blanket, and hold his hand? Was that the best shortcut to love, in fact? You smashed yourself up so badly someone had to be tender. Was that the way to a relationship? Michael smiled, knowing he should be dead by now, and knowing that it wasn't a question of why any more, but why not? He could not stand another pub, or another café, nor another trip to the supermarket with a small wire basket waiting for the yellow-sticker girl to price down the end-of-the-day stock. No, please no: not another evening in an armchair, or an excursion to somewhere he didn't want to be. The choral society, again – he could never again face that. The ceramics group – he couldn't face that nonsense either. Evensong, or the cake-and-coffee group. The Japanese season at the club cinema, which was a bus ride away, all for a quick chat with the person who tore his ticket: a

quick, jaunty chat. No, this wasn't self-pity. This was... a decision just to stop.

It wasn't even a decision to stop, it was a *need* to stop – even if the 15.41 was almost out of sight. After he and Elizabeth had split up – which was after how many years? Did it matter? After they went their separate ways, he had found himself in an airport chapel. They had split up for good in Newcastle, because it had become clear that there was no point meeting again, and he had to stop chasing her. He was no longer simply visiting her: he had accidentally started chasing, like one of those persistent dogs who wants to carry on running for a ball you've got tired of throwing. She was on a course, and he had insisted on visiting her at her hotel – she'd invited him, for sure – but he was unaware that he'd become an obstacle. Had he turned thirty? Whatever he was, she was two years younger and she needed to get round him and move on. She was too polite, though, and so scared of causing him pain. It had come to a head, somehow, and he had left the same evening and found himself in the city centre, walking, as the solitude soaked in and changed the very temperature. He walked across some massive, mighty bridge looking down at oily water, and he'd found a cheap room somewhere. She didn't text him, and he didn't text her, for she had found a way of saying, 'Michael? Stop.'

He hadn't taken the train home, because an airline was experimenting with cheap flights – you could fly for a pound. He'd taken the bus to the airport, and before long he had exchanged his seat on that for seats in various waiting areas – then it was a seat that rose up into the air, and there was England way below with all the roads and railways laid out like a map. For a while you could see the intersections, and the loops and curves – and then it was covered over in cloud. He smiled about it now, but it was the only time he'd ever been on a plane hoping it would crash. How selfish! But he remembered that hope so vividly, because even as he felt concern for the other passengers, he was wanting a nosedive to oblivion.

They landed softly and safely.

He came into the arrivals hall feeling sheepish, and aching with the knowledge of what he'd lost. She was right to bail out, and he would never ever doubt that: Elizabeth had saved herself, as he'd saved Amy. In the lift he saw that there was a chapel in the basement, so despite his annihilating disbelief in all gods, Christian or otherwise, he decided to find it – and it wasn't easy to find. It was beside the lost-property office, neat and tiny, and knowing he was the only one there he let himself go for a moment. He sat on yet another chair with the tears plopping onto his trousers, sobbing as hard as he'd sobbed on the platform at Bromsgrove, perhaps – or maybe harder. He was back in school, sobbing his twelve-year-old heart out, and did it matter?

No. A hand had been placed on his shoulder, and it was the minister – whom he hadn't even seen. He'd thought he was alone, but the minister had appeared out of nowhere for the once-a-day service and put a gentle hand on his shoulder, just like Mr Trace. He stood behind him, and the hand was warm.

'Lay down your burden,' said the minister quietly. 'Come unto me, and lay down your burden.'

That was all he said, and Michael remembered the infinitely soft, unassuming tone of love. He had held the hand for three or four seconds, and then let it go.

Now, he needed to get more drunk – it was the only solution.

Back he went, towards the barriers, and when he saw schoolchildren he realised it was later than he'd thought and that the day was disappearing. There were about twenty of them, girls and boys – and they were all in green blazers, though some had coats over the top. Three in particular caught his attention, because one was standing on a bench in a striking pose. He had high, sharp cheekbones and startling eyes – he was a warrior. The second was sitting down, without a jacket – and Michael realised it was James. The third was himself.

They didn't notice him, and he turned away quickly.

His twelve-year-old self was on the bench again, and there was a vending machine close by. Michael stopped and looked back: the boys hadn't moved, and he knew he had to be quick. He would do something that he had never done before, or even thought about doing – it suddenly seemed like a simple, lovely gift, but he had to be brave. His feet seemed welded to the platform suddenly, and he had thrown himself forwards, overbalancing almost.

'Sorry!' he cried, for he'd almost collided with someone. He had to take a step back and start again, focusing on the big metal machine.

He got there, checked that it took both coins and notes. Change was given, but he didn't want change – with trembling hands he fed one of his three precious twenties into the slot, and then made his selections. He was smiling now, for there they hung: all the chocolate bars you could ever want. He lost count of the items he chose, and they all fell silently into the tray at the bottom. He pressed more buttons and down they came, one after another. They piled up like treasure: twenty pounds' worth of sweets.

Nobody was watching, but he still lost confidence. He was gripped by a fear that what he was doing would be caught on camera, and that an official somewhere was standing up from his seat in disbelief. There was a man, behaving suspiciously! What was he about to do? He was going to offer sweets to innocent, vulnerable children – the most obvious prelude to something vile.

'If you come in my car, son, I'll give you some sweets.'

'You give me sweets, mate – I'll cum in your mouth.'

That was a joke from his grammar school.

'If you come in my car, son...'

It was too late, though – for the machine's tray was full, and the thought of everything being wasted was as unbearable as the misunderstanding, and the hard eyes of the transport police.

The boys would never forget it. He remembered what it was like, after school. You never had enough money. You never could buy the sweets you needed, and gorge on them – and sometimes you had to gorge. You deserved to after the routine horrors of the day.

He plucked up all his courage, and walked towards the bench. They were all sitting down, and the one who'd looked like himself still had the same hair and the same frightened eyes. The one in the middle had provoked him, and Michael saw the f-word on his lips even as the other two howled with laughter. Then he was in front of them, and it was too late to turn back.

'Boys,' he said – and they jerked to attention.

They were staring at him.

'Listen carefully, please. Don't speak. You see that machine over there? The vending machine?'

They looked, and so did Michael. Nobody was using it, so he still had time. The boys were silent, and you could almost smell the apprehension, for some inviolable code was being broken and they were just on the edge of panic.

'Be quick,' said Michael. 'It's out of order, and there's so much stuff, just... lying there. Hurry.'

He turned at once and walked away. He kept walking, making it obvious that he didn't want any further contact and therefore couldn't possibly be dangerous. He was a harmless, drunk stranger who had spoken and gone. He only dared look back when he'd returned to the far end of the platform, and the boys were just visible. They were at the machine.

They appeared to be on their knees, reaching through the flap: they had found the treasure, and they would never forget him.

Michael sat down on the nearest bench, and found he was shaking. He was hot and cold, and out of breath, but the boys would never forget the moment. They would never forget *him* – just a man with earnest eyes, stopping to pass on a bit of wondrous good luck. Young Michael would never, ever forget that day – so he took the whisky from his bag and poured another drink. Could he go forwards now?

He allowed himself to smile, and then he started to laugh. The 15.41 had come looking for him, in a way. It had even changed platforms, hunting him down! And he'd still managed to miss it.

He was obstinately, utterly alive.

STUCK

11

Her wallet was gone, as was her passport.

So was her tablet, her phone and her tickets... the horror was taking hold even as she watched the last coach get slowly smaller and disappear. Her bag was sailing away all on its own, and her plans had been wrecked in an instant. Her bank cards were gone, as was the cash she'd withdrawn – and even the directions she'd been given. That meant her trip was at an end, but more importantly it meant she would probably have to pay hundreds of pounds to get replacement documents – if she could get replacements, and what if she couldn't?

It got worse, because she wasn't insured. Someone could use the cards, and she might be liable. The phone she'd lost was a cheap one, but it held all her contacts and it wasn't backed up. How much cash had she been carrying? A hundred pounds at least, because she'd used the ATM just outside the station. As for the tablet, it was the tool she used most to keep in touch with family. It was laden with photographs and videos, and there was the dongle that went with it. As for the passport, she didn't want to think about it because that was simply priceless.

She struggled to breathe. The tablet could be replaced, but the passport was the thing you didn't lose – almost as precious as life. It was the product of countless hours in labyrinthine queues designed to crush your very soul: you inched through them, working out what bribes you could avoid and what bribes you'd have to pay. Inside was her work visa. She could get a duplicate, probably, but at what cost and with what complications? How long would it take? Her husband would be too angry to speak, as would her sister! 'We're supposed to be saving money,' they'd say. There would be no sympathy because in the end this was something you just didn't do: you had to be truly, truly stupid to do it. You did not leave your life on a train.

She closed her eyes, unable to move. People moved round her, but she didn't notice them. Lost property was never returned, and her bag would be with someone else already. Why would it be handed in when it could more easily be slipped over the passenger's shoulder, and taken home? If the woman with the guitar had picked it up, nobody would challenge her. Of course, she might be honest and alert the train crew, but there was every chance they'd have a scheme of their own for dividing up the spoils, and even if they were honest, and took it to the right desk how long would it take to get back to her? Where would she have to go to claim whatever was left? The train was going way down south to London.

A man in uniform was standing some way off, and she managed to take a few steps towards him. More people overtook her, crossing from right to left and left to right – for a moment she wondered if she'd ever reach him, and he was helping somebody else anyway. He was laughing, as if the world was a funny, entertaining place. The customer was laughing too.

'Yes, love?' he said, turning towards her.

She said, 'I've left something on the train.'

Her voice had changed.

'Which one?' said the man. 'The one to Euston?'

'Yes. The one that just left.'

'Something valuable?'

He was old, and he looked experienced. He looked kind, too – and she knew she was about to burst into tears.

'Very valuable,' she said. 'Very, very valuable.'

Her mouth was dry. She was feeling dizzy. Somehow, she described the bag and listed its contents, and – as she did so – the tears started and she had to stop talking.

'Let's get you sat down,' said the man gently. 'Let's go somewhere a little bit quieter, okay? Give me your rucksack.'

He eased it off her shoulder, and took her arm.

'You'll be fine,' he said. 'What's your name?'

'Maria.'

'Maria. I'm going to take you to the help-desk, Maria, and we'll see what we can do for you.'

'I'm so sorry,' said Maria.

'We all lose things – there's nothing to be sorry about. You were in a hurry, were you?'

'I was on the wrong train. Yes.'

He was holding a door open for her.

'You go first. You left it on the table, or the seat?'

They entered a waiting area, where twenty chairs stood bolted together in two strict, back-to-back rows. The desk was at the far end – a raised counter, with a computer and a rack of leaflets.

'Were there other passengers, sitting with you?'

She nodded. 'It was crowded. Yes.'

'In that case, it might have been found already. Your phone's in the bag, yes?'

'Yes.'

'Could we try calling it? Or is it locked?'

'I don't understand, sorry.'

'Do you need a code for the phone, to unlock it? Or could somebody just pick up, if we called the number?'

'I think someone could pick up. I'm sure they could, yes.'

'Shall we try that first?'

'How?'

The man smiled.

'You sit down,' he said. 'You can use mine.'

Maria nodded and sat down. The next moment, his phone was in her hands and she saw the panel of digits. For a moment she had no idea of her own number: she had to close her eyes to think. It came back to her and she tapped it in. She mis-dialled, and had to start again. Her hands were actually trembling, and in the end he did it for her, taking her instructions. They heard a soft bleeping as a satellite somewhere received the transmission, bouncing the signal back towards a train that was miles away, hurtling south. The connection was made, and there was silence. Silence, so she put it close to her ear and there was a faint, hesitant ringing. She bent forwards slightly.

'Please, God,' she said quietly. 'Please help me now. I will do anything.'

12

Michael poured another drink, then tipped it back into the carton.

He had decided not to use the waiting room, so he couldn't see any screens. All he knew was that he had failed in his objective, first at Bromsgrove, and now at Crewe. Gloucester didn't count, because he'd never seriously contemplated leaping from a bridge. Crewe, however, was an abject failure and he wasn't sure what to do next.

The boys had been a distraction, as had the steam-train enthusiast. Every day was unpredictable, it seemed – but in such worryingly small ways. You never knew whom you would meet, and internally you never quite knew how the brain would deal with the wash of stimuli that came at it the moment you woke up. One smile could change everything, just as a sharp or impatient word could send you spinning off your own fragile axis. If the steam-train man hadn't been there, would he be dead? The steam-train man had been there because of the steam train, so his being alive still was the responsibility of those who had organised its journey to Milton Keynes – and as for the three boys, why had they chosen that particular bench?

Things came together for no reason.

He lost his thread, and looked for a tangerine. There were three left in the little net but one had escaped – it was lurking in the corner of his shoulder bag, as if it didn't want to be eaten. Another train was leaving as another arrived. There were twelve platforms in all, and how many trains per hour? They seemed to have been coming and going almost constantly, most of them stopping, of course – but some in too much of a hurry. Some shrieked through as if their drivers had lost control. Somebody, somewhere was in charge, and yet it seemed such a jostling free-for-all – a race! A three-coach train revved its engines and departed: Michael raised a hand to it, and knew he was properly drunk at last. Young Michael must be on his way by now, heading for home with chocolate round his mouth as he tried to account for his incredible luck.

He smiled, and sipped from the carton.

Drinkaware told him that he should have a maximum of fourteen units a week. Fourteen units was a bottle and a half of wine, or thereabouts, and he had learned to love wine with Elizabeth. That was over twenty-five years ago, and the love had blossomed time and time again – most recently in a privately run off-licence he'd found, called Vines. It was quite a walk from his home, but worth the journey because the two lesbians who owned it were so friendly. They were knowledgeable, too, and shared their knowledge joyfully. They indulged Michael, talking about vineyards and soils but cutting it short, because they were sensitive to his ignorance and knew when to stop.

This was reassuring, because he'd been trapped some years ago by a salesman who seemed to think he'd found a soulmate. He'd been working at the council then, so he had spare income and slow old Monica liked wine too. The man had got it wrong, though: he'd phoned Michael and tried to sell him wines that hadn't been bottled yet, assuring him that the discounts available if he bought three cases would mean that he was paying next to nothing for some special grape from a south-facing valley – and Michael had listened, unable to interrupt except with questions, which invited more and more information.

'I don't know,' he would say. 'Let me think about that. That sounds good—'

'It's a really good deal,' said the salesman. 'I did something similar last year.'

'Did you?'

'It's a no-brainer, really. You can't go wrong, because the wine will be bottled and you get it so much cheaper.'

'Let me think about it.'

'Shall I call you tomorrow?'

'Not tomorrow—'

'What about the weekend?'

The kitchen designer had pursued him, too, as had the supplier of solid-wood worktops, and even the carpenter who was going to fit them and didn't seem to have many people needing his services. Everyone worked hard, trying to do business as the profit margins shrank and Michael asked for indefinite thinking time because now he had no money. His phone number had been sold on to so many people: so many new friends, all chasing business. Everyone hoped he'd need this service or that – he tried always to be polite. He could not bring himself to be abrupt, because rudeness was an assault and always left him shaken. His phone network wanted to talk to him about changing his contract, or taking advantage of deals the company was doing because it had seen an opportunity to save him money – why did the company present itself this way? It infantilised everyone, Michael most of all as he sat with the phone clamped to his ear.

'With the friends-and-family coverage, everybody wins. It's insurance for you and for your loved ones. I've just bought a policy, and I have to say I can't believe I waited so long. It really does do what it says, you know? And if you take out a direct debit...'

But he couldn't, for there was no money left.

If they had known he had so little, would they continue to call? A stupid question, but even when he told them they'd insist that credit was available and the price might go down if he were to 'avail' himself – if he were to 'take advantage of' – and sign up to whatever it was... you got the impression sometimes that if you weren't spending, and taking on debt, you weren't really alive. Michael had given in, taking out small loans and then larger ones – and he'd paid some off, while others had simply grown secretly, tumour-like, until they couldn't be confronted. It meant more paper in the drawer.

Vines was a nice place to buy wine, and if the women noticed that he drank too much it wasn't their place to say so. His mother had known, and told him – then she'd died.

Amy had tried to train him into drinking more water. A glass of water for a glass of wine, and with her he'd been able to spend some evenings completely sober. Then she'd get depressed, and order a couple of wine-boxes, which meant you lost all track of how much you were consuming. Two days ago, he had left Vines for the very last time, and he felt he was saying goodbye to family. He wondered if the woman who'd served him had thought about him as he pulled the door shut. She might have watched him go, before saying to her partner in the office, 'That was Michael'.

'Michael again – really?'

Perhaps she would ask an affectionate question: 'How was he?'

'He didn't look too well,' the first woman would say. 'He looked... sad. He said goodbye very seriously, and shook my hand.'

'Why?'

'I don't know. He's a sensitive man, and I think he *is* sad. He's the kind of man we...'

What?

'... the kind of man we ought to be friends with. He's intelligent and honest. We should invite him for dinner. We should ask him if he's thought of joining our cycling group, or better still – more reasonable and practical – the tasting circle.'

Michael smiled.

He often bought their wine of the month, but on that last visit he'd surprised them by investing in a bottle of Tomatin malt whisky, from the Highlands. It was behind their heads, high on the rack, priced at fifty-three pounds seventy-four... and he used his untouched, special credit card, to check it was working. He'd withdrawn the sixty pounds cash afterwards, so the whisky was the first transaction. The woman didn't show any surprise at his purchase – why would she? She was too professional. In any case, surprise was not the word: mild curiosity would be more likely, along with appreciation.

Perhaps they had been secretly stunned.

'I just couldn't believe it,' the one who'd served him would say.

They were in bed together – the lamps turned off.

'What?'

'Michael MacMillan.'

'What about him?'

'Why would he buy Tomatin malt whisky? He's never done that before.'

'Some celebration?'

'I wish I'd asked. I wish I'd said, "What's the occasion?" I'm not going to sleep now, am I?'

'You can ask him next time. Or I will.'

'Tomatin malt – he knows his whisky.'

'He's a good man.'

'Sensitive.'

'Deep.'

'Let's hope he's enjoying it with the one he loves, eh? Where's he drinking it, the old soak? Mystery man!'

They would giggle, and then they would hug. They would get on with whatever they did in bed, which was beyond Michael's imagination, and he hated himself for both failing to imagine it and trying to – what did it say about him? What would a judge say, if he was ever on trial for being so stupidly sordid? What would a jury think? Twelve men and women shaking their heads, astonished that people such as Michael still existed.

'You have displayed in this courtroom only self-pity.'

The judge was pitiless, and his voice would have to be loud and fierce.

'For those you have hurt, wounded and insulted you show nothing but *contempt* – and for that you will pay. You poke your nose into other people's private lives, wallowing in your sad, primitive adolescence – how have you failed to develop, man? Take him down…'

Michael smiled, for there would be no trial, and he would never know what his friends at Vines had thought, said or done. What he did know was that the whisky he'd chosen was fabulous. He took the glass out of his bag again, and set it on the arm of the bench. He allowed himself another measure, so as to stay happily, wistfully drunk – it was a kind of topping-up.

Anyone watching would assume he was sipping healthy juice, so he sat back and the bench seemed ever more comfortable. The station roof was remarkable, and Crewe itself seemed the right place to be. The drunkenness was gorgeous and warm – it was like the central heating coming on.

He poured again, but kept the measure small.

It was like stepping out of the wind into shelter. It was like turning to find the one you love has waited for you after all. It was like being allowed into your mother's bed, when something had frightened you as a child, or you'd simply felt the ache of being alone and awake in a house where everyone else was asleep. It was like getting home when you'd missed the last train, and had to walk through the rain – the whisky was his home.

He looked at his ticket.

It was invalid now, of course, for he had accomplished that journey whilst avoiding its climax. Obviously, he could go anywhere – if he didn't want to stay where he was.

Obviously, he could do exactly what he wanted, and the live rail was available if he didn't want to walk up the tracks. He had a limit of six hundred and fifty pounds on the card, and had spent one hundred and ten. He could spend the rest however he chose, and they would have to write the debt off – because he had no guarantor.

Would they try his brother, or even Amy? They'd have no luck.

He had a vision of himself in a comfortable, first-class carriage, and now that he was drinking the fine old malt it seemed right. He would wait until he was truly, uncomplicatedly happy, and it would be easy then: he would step out onto whatever station it might be, and do the business there. He would put good old Crewe behind him, and keep going north. It would be easier not to know which train was going to kill him. It would be easier choosing a platform and line at random, and setting out between the rails.

He would wait for the dark. The darkness would be intense on the track, and he would plod on until whatever train it was kissed him goodnight and sliced him into however many pieces ninety-six wheels would cut you into – if it was a twelve-coach train, of course. Crewe had helped him make a better decision, so he opened his mints and put one in his mouth. Then he cleared away the little pile of orange peel, and set the carton and glass back in his bag. He walked through the barrier to where they sold tickets.

The schoolchildren were long gone, but they would talk about him tomorrow.

'We should write that man a note,' said his younger self. 'We ought to thank him.'

'Where would we send it, though?'

'We could tape it to the vending machine. Or to one of the pillars – we could make a card...'

'We should tell the police, Michael. They'd protect us.'

'Do we need protection? From what?'

'From Mr Trace!'

'But he's dead. We've been through this. He's ash and dust – he's gone...'

Michael found himself at the sales counter, frowning.

A man of his own age stood staring back, ready and willing to serve. The glass between them was thick, but there were microphones. He wouldn't have to shout, and he was still completely alive: his legs were working and his spine was keeping him upright. His hands, too, were behaving exactly as hands should – resting rather neatly on the shelf whilst cradling a wallet, which they opened so efficiently without even a tremor. His fingertips would have no problem easing the card from its little pocket, and presenting it.

'I'm going further north,' he said carefully.

'Very good. Which station?'

The man's voice was made thinner by the tannoy, but he was friendly and he even looked interested.

'Glasgow.'

'Okay, there's various options for Glasgow. Have you decided on a route?'

'I haven't, no.'

'You're going today?'

'Yes, please.'

The man studied his computer.

'I was wondering about first class,' said Michael. 'And ideally, I think I want "any route". A bit of flexibility in case I change my mind.'

'I can sell you an anytime ticket,' replied the man slowly. 'But it's usually cheaper if you book a particular train. There's not that much in it, actually. You're travelling now?'

'Yes, please. Today and tonight.'

The man peered harder at what must have been very small print.

'All the cheap fares are advance fares, I'm afraid. You want the next service?'

'If possible. Yes. That would be great.'

Why didn't he just say 'yes'? Why did unnecessary words extend everything he said?

'The best I can do, first class, is two hundred and seventeen – and that's via Preston.'

'What's standard?'

'Standard is one zero nine.'

'I think I'll go standard.'

'I would. But I can't book you a seat, I'm afraid. You should be all right, though – it's not the school holidays.'

'Thank goodness. It will be soon.'

'Don't say that – they've only just gone back.'

They talked for another two minutes. They talked about the East Coast line, and the speed restrictions that were still in place because of the old, crumbling infrastructure. Ultimately, though, the transaction ended. The card worked, and the tickets were there before him.

'Thank you,' said Michael. 'You made that very easy.'

'Not at all.'

Should he now write to the train company, and express his appreciation? He wrote so many letters in his mind, so the phrases were always ready: *The service I received today was, by your standards perhaps, merely professional. For me it was outstanding.*

He liked to avoid hyperbole, but he wanted to share his humble gratitude.

Your salesman couldn't have known, or, Your saleswoman no doubt meets people like myself every day. However, may I say the interaction I experienced. . . the friendly and courteous service, as if I was the only customer that mattered, as if finding me that particular item was his or her most important duty – I find it astonishing that your staff routinely treat people with such. . . What?

He could not write or even say the word 'love' because it wasn't, and his own idiocy silenced him again.

'Bye now.'

The man nodded.

It was love, though, in a way. It was a generalised love, which focused specifically on him just for a moment. Impersonal, except it was received so personally.

The people in retail were genuine servants, and he loved them because they probably didn't realise how many lives they saved every day. The smile, and the encouragement to have a good afternoon – or the quiet, tender 'take care' offered by boys, girls, men, women. . . it brought tears to his eyes.

He had once been in a pharmacy, and an elderly woman had tripped and fallen. She'd come crashing down because of a shallow step, and he had been the one to help her, and comfort her, and call for a chair. He had shown her love, because she had been so vulnerable, and terrified that she had broken a bone. She feared she'd ruined Christmas, which was only a few days away. She feared her family would be furious because she'd had such a stupid, avoidable accident. Michael had crouched in front of her and turned himself into a doctor, and a counsellor. He'd become a husband, or a son – he'd been Jesus.

'You ought to go round to your GP,' he'd said.

'It's nothing,' she insisted. 'I'm fine.'

'You say that now, but it could be a fracture.'

'It can't be. It mustn't be.'

'Listen to me. Let me call you a taxi…'

He had been both husband *and* son, as loving as he had tried to be to his own mother – and it was funny how the taboo of touch simply disappeared. For some reason he had the right to put his hand on the old lady's arm, and crouch so he was almost pressing against her. Years ago, some colleague in the council office had joked about how to deal with members of the public who were upset. You offered comfort, and that was the time 'to slip it in, while they're distracted'.

People had laughed.

Michael thought about it now with horror, ambushed again. When you were comforting someone, this colleague said – if a member of the public was upset and needed your support – that was the time to get your arm round them, and 'slip it in'. He meant have intercourse with them, while they were vulnerable – that's what he'd meant. Roars of laughter at the inappropriateness, the sheer daring of the wag that could joke about sexual assault – 'to slip it in and do the business'.

Sex, again – like the smell of your own sweat. You could never get away from it, and the letters in your head never got written. They would be conceived after half a bottle of wine, and for thirty minutes they would exist, charming the violent world into something tearfully peaceful, for the recipient would no doubt read his prose and be transfixed in wonder. It is worthwhile, they would think. We are appreciated. Soon, the letter became a misjudgement and an overreaction, the outburst of a drunk who won't let you go: 'I love you. I fucking love you, mate.'

Where he lived, people got drunk in the street.

Drink turned them into needy children, or aggressive children. The young man in the flat below his – Ryan was his name – seemed quiet and stable for days on end, and then he'd turn into pure paranoid menace. The booze hardened some, and softened others, and left everyone so ashamed they had to drink again.

Amy was a drunk, really, which meant they would have been married drunks.

But the man who had sold him his ticket did absolutely not need his love. He was only doing his job, and was probably as capable of being vain and difficult as anyone else – why turn him into a saint? What if he went home to humiliate his wife, and make her miserable? What if it was worse, and he was tormenting a child? Michael groaned, for he couldn't stop the vision. The man was suddenly in his stepson's room, and he was demanding something too horrible to contemplate. He'd paid for a new school uniform, and the boy owed him – or was it a girl? Let it be a girl, and it was her trip to France, or state-of-the-art phone – and at the end of a long day in the ticket office it was payback time, behind closed doors. Michael tried to stop thinking, but on it went like a film and his eyes saw the images even when they were closed. The girl turned back into a boy, and it was himself, and the man was holding his head gently, stroking his hair.

'Try it. Just try it.'

Lunchtime, and the other boys screaming in the playground. The blinds were down, and the little bolt drawn for privacy. *Caesar's Gallic Wars* was there on the desk, and the hand was applying just a little more pressure. Michael's hand was shaking, and he couldn't get his brand-new ticket into the slot, for he was hot in his blazer. He could not write to the station man, because any letter from Michael would give him an affirmation and a confidence that might prolong the suffering, even if he looked so kind. You never could tell, for kind-looking men did bad things. They showed love, only to slip it in and do the business.

'Let's talk at lunchtime – bring the translation.'

The barrier gates snapped open, and he was through.

What had his mother told him, years ago? As a little girl she'd been 'touched up' by the lodger – and she'd told her own mother, Michael's gran.

'He touched me up, in his room.'

'Don't go into his room, then.'

That's what she'd said, and there was an unchallengeable logic to the advice. 'Don't go into his room. Walk away.'

Michael found a bench.

He was on the wrong platform, so he walked down the subway and back to number five. There, he found another bench which looked across the divide to the one he'd just left. He wasn't on it any more, of course: he'd moved, so he couldn't see himself. As for young Michael, he'd be home by now, unless he'd stopped off at James's house. Some afternoons they did their homework together, working through the Latin, and the science and all that French vocab he'd forgotten.

He smiled.

The apple-juice carton looked so innocuous. The glass he had brought was opaque. The whisky was warm. And it came from a tiny Scottish town, and he knew that because he had visited the distillery with Amy, to whom he would now be married if he hadn't written that dreadful letter. What he wanted to remember, though, was his Highlands holiday, and how he'd hoped she'd let him do that particular tour on his own, because he knew she wasn't interested in whisky. Why had she insisted on coming with him? Hadn't she realised she was spoiling it?

'It was nice,' she said afterwards. 'Such a con, though. All they want to do is sell you stuff.'

He'd laughed, because he'd bought two bottles and a box of Tomatin liqueur chocolates.

'Of course they do,' he said.

Secretly, he'd wondered what she expected. It was the distillery's business, after all, and it would have been strange if they'd suddenly started giving their whisky away. 'You've taken the trouble to visit us, sir. Have it for free.'

'Such a con, though, Michael. All they want to do is sell you stuff.'

'I know.'

'And it's not cheap, is it?'

But it was, for all that time and skill.

He had wanted to understand the distilling process, because he had such gaps in his knowledge. He didn't know what malt was. He didn't know why spring water mattered, and he hadn't even known what a bonded warehouse was for, because he'd never thought about it. Thousands of barrels of whisky were simply left to sit for ten years, or fifteen years... it shouldn't have struck him as odd, but it did. Time made the whisky better, so you paid for its age.

He sipped the liquor and tried to taste the oak. The oak soaked into the spirit, and nobody had come up with a way of faking that process. A woman called Vicky had shown them round, and there was someone else on the tour – a bilingual Scandinavian – who seemed to know his stuff. He had asked technical questions, but Vicky dealt with them all, succinct and utterly in charge – the Scandinavian man had ended up looking rather foolish.

Amy had said, 'Boring twat,' under her breath.

Boring twat.

They had made love that night, unsuccessfully. 'He's not much good in the bedroom department!' A letter he could write, and questions he could ask. He could handle a complicated conversation with a ticket salesman, and he could disguise whisky so it looked like juice – and he could provide sweets for schoolboys he'd never ever see again, and make them happy. Relaxing into sexual intercourse, though – that was something he had never ever been able to do, and he sat on the bench pondering the fact, returning to it, turning it over and over as the trains came and went.

It all came back to sex. So what?

He would not jump onto the tracks now, for that would waste the ticket. Better that he simply went to Preston, on the 16.48 – for the train appeared to be absolutely on time and why should his chopped body delay it? The next one had been cancelled, he noticed, and the train company was genuinely sorry. The apologies were available at the touch of a button, and they'd found an actor who sounded so sincere: *'We're sorry for the delay...*

*We're sorry to announce, and we're sorry – so sorry, in fact, that
we are holding back the tears, feeling only shame. Don't tell on us,
please! We're sorry. . .'*

Michael laughed.

His own train would take him north, and he could decide
about the onward route when he got to Preston. He would go
right back up to the Highlands, because he was remembering the
perfect, isolated station two hours or more beyond Glasgow, and
express trains definitely came through it. The track was unfenced
for miles, and there was a night train from Aberdeen or Inverness
– the poor driver would see him in the headlamp, of course, but
that couldn't be helped. Michael would be illuminated, as if by
a searchlight. He could turn away, though – in fact, he could
walk backwards once he'd heard it coming, or he could put his
head down and run, and the man at the controls would blast the
horn and never see his face.

Michael sat back and sucked a mint.

Poor Morris had made it up the line towards Worcester, but Michael had never met him, and therefore didn't know that there was a new plan. It seemed that Tony really had gone to the wrong café, somehow, and refused point-blank to drive all the way back to Cheltenham. The idea now was obvious: to sort someone in Birmingham.

'I don't have any money,' said Morris.

'I know that,' said Keenan. 'Go to Birmingham. Can you get through the barrier?'

'I don't know. Maybe, maybe not.'

'If you get through, I can fix you up with Aziz. That's the best I can do, because—'

'Fix me up with who?'

'What?'

'Who have you got in Birmingham?'

'It's a guy called Aziz – I thought you'd met him.'

'Never. What's he like?'

'He'll look after you. He's okay, he's a good man. Young.'

'What time?'

'I don't know yet. I'll call him, and he'll call you. There's a park, near the station – he'll only want an hour.'

'It's a long way to go if he doesn't know I'm coming.'

'That's why I'm going to call him, Morrie. Worst-case scenario is we wait till tomorrow, so just stay put.'

'How much is it worth?'

'What?'

'I said, "How much is it worth?" One hour.'

'I don't know. The usual, I imagine. Have you got anything on you? Any stuff?'

'No. I was going to get it from Tony.'

'Then it's the usual. Are you up for it or not? I don't want him messed about.'

Morris cursed silently.

'Yes.'

'What?'

'I said yes.'

'I'll call you back, then. Or he will.'

He waited another forty minutes, and the call finally came. Birmingham was on, for as soon as possible. He got there at 17.02 having avoided the train guard. As for the station barriers, you waited for someone with a suitcase and the gates opened wide enough for you to follow through. As long as nobody was watching, away you'd go. He didn't have Aziz's number, because Aziz didn't want him to have it – and that was normal.

They would meet in the park. They would find a hotel, which Keenan always insisted on – and the sex would be quick. He'd be paid in cash, and home before midnight.

NORTH AGAIN

14

Ayesha had set Maria's handbag in front of her, on the table.

She hadn't wanted to touch it at first and she certainly didn't want to look inside. To do so would be intrusive. The man in the seat opposite suggested she should, though, to identify the owner.

'If there's a phone number,' he said, 'we can call it.'

'I should have kept my mouth shut,' said Ayesha. 'I should have said I don't know.'

'She did say, "Is this train going to Burnley?" That's what she asked you.'

'I know, but I should have realised.'

She sighed.

'I make this trip twice a month – I should have known. She was a complete stranger, wasn't she? A backpacker.'

She unzipped the bag and peered inside. There was a tablet, and beside that a cheap, pay-as-you-go phone. There was a long, slim wallet too, which was clean, smart and new and when Ayesha opened it she saw banknotes and cards. When she saw the passport tucked into a side pocket, she felt even worse. The poor woman had lost everything at a stroke: *Pilipinas* stood out in gold, so she was clearly miles from home. Ayesha flipped the cover open, and Maria looked up at her, smiling shyly.

'Is there a number?' said the man.

'This is her phone. We can't call her.'

'But is there any other? Like a contact for emergencies?'

'I don't know.'

'Look in the back. See if there's a next of kin.'

Ayesha turned to the last page.

'Next of kin,' she said. 'There's a number for a sister by the look of it, but the address is Manila.'

'What time is it in Manila? Do you want me to check?'

He tapped some digits, and turned his own phone sideways to see the results of his search. He brought the screen closer and tapped again.

'They're ahead of us,' he said at last. 'It's ten past nine in Manila – you could try her.'

'What could she do, though? "Maria Ruiz", that's her name.'

'Whose name?'

'The woman who owns this bag.'

'Her sister might know someone. There might be a mutual friend you can send it to.'

'She's stuck,' said Ayesha. 'She's got no phone, and we've got all her money – we've got everything. Could we call the rail station? Get them to make an announcement?'

'You could try.'

'What station was it? Carlisle?'

'It might be better if we just hand it to the guard. Let him do it.'

Ayesha nodded.

'I'll take it to him,' she said. 'I'll go down to the buffet car, and see if I can find him. Can you look after my stuff?'

She stood up, and put the guitar on her seat. She walked carefully through the carriages, for the train had picked up speed. The woman's phone rang as she emerged from the third, plaintive and urgent. Ayesha stopped and fumbled for it. She held it close, and for a moment she couldn't remember which button you had to press for a connection – the ringtone wailed on, desperate as a crying child. She found the right one and put the thing to her ear.

'Hello?' she said.

There was a pause, and she heard an anxious, distant voice: 'Hello? I think… Hello?'

'Hello.'

'I think this is my phone, yes?'

'I think it is,' said Ayesha, steadying herself. 'You left it next to me, on the table.'

'Hello?' said the voice.

'Hello. Hi, can you hear me?'

'Yes, but not very well—'

'You left your bag on the table. Is that Maria? I've got it here, Maria – it's safe. Where are you now?'

'I'm sorry, I didn't hear everything.'

Ayesha found a seat, and pressed the phone closer. She could hear a station announcement, and the speaker above her head chose the same moment to come to crackly life, the volume high.

'Good afternoon,' said a voice. 'This is your train manager speaking, and I'd like to welcome those passengers who joined at Carlisle...'

Ayesha ducked low and closed her eyes.

'Hello?' she said.

'This train is for London Euston,' said the manager happily. 'We will be calling at Oxenholme, Lancaster and Preston.'

He hesitated, but Ayesha knew that he was far from finished, and that everyone on board would now have to endure the full long list of station-stops, for they had already endured it twice. They would then hear all about all the snacks and beverages – alcoholic and non-alcoholic – and that would probably lead into an earnest, paternal encouragement to keep all one's personal possessions with one at all times. The man was unstoppable, and poor Maria strained to make herself heard. To Ayesha she was a tinny whisper, calling from a distant planet.

'I'm sorry,' she said. 'I just can't hear you.'

'What?'

'Wait. Wait...'

She got up and headed back the way she'd come. The train manager spoke slowly, as if what he relished most was his time at the intercom. Somebody's toddler was in the aisle, but she managed to move past and get into the little vestibule as the open doors decided to close, and knock the phone from her hand.

'A variety of toasted sandwiches,' said the manager, but his voice had dropped away a fraction. She snatched the phone up again.

'I'm here,' she said. 'Can you hear me?'

'Pardon?'

'I'm here, Maria. Your bag's safe, okay? I'm holding it—'

'Hello?'

Ayesha swore quietly.

'I've got your bag!' she said. 'Nobody's taken anything, and it's perfectly safe.'

There was a short silence.

'Thank you,' said Maria.

'Where are you? Where are you at the moment? Are you still—?'

'I'm on the station, still.'

'Carlisle?'

'Hello? I'm on the station, yes. I'm at Carlisle, I think – Carlisle.'

'Okay,' said Ayesha. 'It's easy then. You don't need to worry, okay? I've got everything with me, and we can meet up.'

The doors opened, and the toddler's mother appeared. The toddler was now in her arms, and had started to cry. He was taking a deep breath, for someone had hurt or upset him and he needed to express his grief and rage.

'Hang on,' said Ayesha, moving to the side.

'Crisps,' said the train manager. 'Peanuts.'

'Do you have my passport?' asked Maria.

'Your what?'

'My passport, in the bag—'

'Yes, I promise. Everything's here. And you're going to Burnley, aren't you?'

She had a finger in one ear.

'Sorry, when—?'

'Where are you heading? You said Burnley.'

'Burnley Manchester Road. Yes—'

'So you need to change at Preston, I think. Is that right?'

She moved back into the carriage, for the child's howl was deafening.

'Yes,' said Maria. 'I think so.'

They were rattling over points, and for a moment Ayesha contemplated finding the alarm and slamming her hand on it.

She could bring the whole train to a halt, and have a simple, quiet conversation.

'Yes,' said Maria again. 'I have to change at Preston. You're right.'

'Then I think it's going to be very straightforward,' replied Ayesha. 'I'm going to get down there myself, okay?'

She had never spoken so carefully or clearly.

'Take the first train you can,' she said. 'You get to Preston. We'll meet in the café, in front of the footbridge. There's a big bar-café, right in the middle. I'll be waiting for you.'

'At Preston?'

'Yes. I won't leave until we've found each other, and I'll have your bag with me.'

'In Preston? Now?'

'Yes.'

'Thank you. Thank you so much—'

'You mustn't worry,' said Ayesha, and for some reason her eyes were full of tears, as if the loss were her own. 'It's perfectly safe, okay? My name is Ayesha.'

'Ayesha?'

'Yes.'

'Okay. Thank you, Ayesha. I'm Maria.'

'I know. I'll see you soon, Maria. A couple of hours, at the most.'

The station man was smiling.

Maria handed him his phone, and he handed her a tissue. Her rucksack was against her chair, but she pulled it closer so it was tight against her knees. For a moment, she couldn't speak.

'I have to go to Preston,' she said at last. 'I need to get the next train and find this person – Ayesha. I don't have a ticket, though – all my tickets are in my wallet.'

'You don't have a ticket?' said the man.

'No.'

'Then you'll have to stay here.'

'What?' cried Maria. 'No, you don't understand. I can't, I—'

'I'm joking,' said the man gently. 'I'm joking, Maria – I can issue you a special pass right now, free of charge. Special circumstances, special pass – that's the least of your worries, okay? We'll get you to Preston, so...'

He looked at the screen above their heads.

'You've got about twenty minutes to wait. Problem solved, eh? By the sound of it.'

Maria nodded, but found that the words she needed wouldn't come.

'You see?' said the man. 'We can always sort things out. It's never as bad as it looks, is it?'

'No.'

'You thought it was the end of the world, didn't you?'

Maria looked at him.

'It nearly was,' she said. 'I'm so lucky. Thank you.'

Michael's train was busy, so he wasn't sure where to sit.

An elderly couple sat either side of a table, halfway down the carriage, so he apologised for the intrusion and joined them. There was a new mint in his mouth, and his shoulder bag was neatly zipped.

'Filling up,' he said.

'It always does, this one,' said the man.

He had been forced to pick up his coat to make room, so Michael asked him if he wanted it placed on the overhead rack.

'Thank you,' said the man. 'That would make life a bit easier.'

'Give us a bit more space,' said his companion.

'Just don't let me forget it.'

Michael laughed.

'So easy to do,' he said. 'We've all done it.'

The woman had a tablet, and next to that was a deck of cards. They both had paper cups, and there was the usual detritus of milk cartons, stirrers and sugar sachets, suggesting that the trolley had recently passed. Michael sat down, wondering if it would return, and whether it would be selling sandwiches or not – he should have bought one at the station. Every service was different, after all, and the catering had to be planned to meet different passenger needs. The people who organised these things were not reckless, and the last thing they wanted was a surplus of unsaleable food. Were there people monitoring how many items got bought and how many ended up wasted? Of course there were. There had to be – there would be computers receiving the data, and managers sifting the figures. A sandwich would cost three to four pounds, and the mark-up on that had to be three hundred per cent at least, which Michael didn't begrudge if only because pushing the awkward, laden trolley down narrow aisles looked so hard. Those doing it were heroic in his opinion, begging people to move their luggage, feet, children and pets, even as passengers were constantly trying to squeeze past... Was it a job he could do? He wouldn't last a day.

On the other hand, was there any job he could do? How had he become so jobless and unemployable? How had he become such a liability at the council? The whole staff, divided as they were by envy and intolerance, had come together to dismiss him. Looking back, it may have been the only thing everyone had ever agreed: that he, Michael, needed to be fired because his desk drawer was full of unpaid, unprocessed invoices which he occasionally shredded. His school desk had been just as cluttered, as was the one at home.

He said to the woman opposite, 'How are you?'

'Oh, very well,' she said.

'Where are you off to?'

'Settle.'

'Settle?'

Michael raised his eyebrows.

'Somewhere I've never been,' he said.

'You should definitely go,' said the man to his right – her husband, presumably.

He sat in Michael's peripheral vision, so they were shoulder to shoulder. They were both well dressed, and could be brother and sister, or old friends. They could be lovers, too, escaping from the grind of long, tedious marriages having met at the choral society, or a book club – but they looked very much like man and wife, if only because they played cards together, and looked so comfortable. Their clothes were from the same catalogue, and Michael should go to Settle, apparently – the man felt confident enough to suggest it, as if he knew instinctively that Michael would appreciate the place. Michael couldn't help but wonder if there was any specific reason, and he nearly laughed. He knew he was drunk.

'Nice place?' he said lightly – and he just managed to prevent the mint flying from his mouth.

'Oh, it's beautiful,' said the woman – and her voice dipped for the first syllable of 'beautiful' to turn it into two. She gave the second that special emphasis, for Settle was clearly *very* special. A lot of towns and villages were beautiful, but this one, it seemed, was enchanted.

'They haven't been allowed to spoil it,' said the man. 'It's got its problems, of course it has. Traffic, needless to say, in the summer—'

'But the main street,' said his wife, cutting in neatly. 'It's an absolute picture. They have a flower festival.'

'Really?'

'It's magical.'

'Do you live there?' said Michael.

'Well,' said the man. 'Yes and no.'

Yes and no? Yes, they did, but no, they didn't – and did Michael dare get his juice out, just to top himself up? The bag was on his lap, so it wouldn't be a difficult manoeuvre – but would these two people notice the smell? They wouldn't suspect the colour, but the scent might alert them to the fact that they were sitting next to someone drinking neat whisky.

'Ah,' the man might say, as he expanded his nostrils. 'Do I smell a Tomatin malt?'

'You do!'

'Good man!'

His hand would be extended, and they would shake firmly.

'I have a flask of my own,' the man would say. 'Just here! Untouched!'

They might suddenly become the firmest of friends, bonded by their relish of good whisky and the whole Highland culture. What was more likely, however, was that the stink of Michael's surreptitious boozing would mark him out as dangerous or unpredictable. In any case, weren't they just too wrapped up in Settle and the wonders of the main street where they did and didn't live? They might not even notice, let alone care.

'We're buying a flat,' said the woman. 'It's off-plan, and we haven't quite completed. We're off for a third viewing.'

'Congratulations,' said Michael.

'Thank you.'

'Life's going to change, then. Do you have family there?'

Of course he didn't really want to know. He didn't want to hear the details – he shouldn't have asked, and even as he opened his mouth he was full of dread. He was looking harder at the woman, and he saw the brooch she wore, and the necklace, and the ring on her finger. There was nothing ostentatious anywhere, but it all sent the subtle signal of good taste and Southern wealth. How much would an off-plan flat in Settle cost? A lot, obviously – but they could afford it because they both had pensions, and his had been the climax to some well-paid business-orientated job, and he'd probably retired with stocks and shares and a whole investment portfolio that generated thousands of pounds. Why weren't they travelling first class? Small economies, or maybe the train had no first-class facilities – or maybe it was in the hope of meeting ordinary, down-to-earth people like him. Perhaps a friendship was about to be born after all, that would last until death. Michael would speak at both their funerals, or they would speak at his.

He reached for his juice carton.

'Pardon?' he said.

He had missed something, and he nearly belched.

'We have a grandson,' said the woman again. 'He's at Giggleswick.'

'Oh?'

'Just started.'

'Giggleswick?'

There was a school at Giggleswick – he'd heard of it for some reason. But was it in Settle?

'Giggleswick,' he said again. 'I know the name.'

'He finished his first year this year,' said the woman. 'He's just starting GCSEs.'

'Wonderful,' said Michael. 'Is the school close by?'

'It's in Giggleswick, yes.'

'Is that a place?'

'Yes.'

'A town?'

'Yes. A village, really. Two miles or so from Settle.'

'Oh! So you'll be on hand to... what? Look after him.'

'Oh, his housemaster does that,' said the man. 'We'll be lucky to *see* him.'

Michael produced his glass, and poured himself a measure of whisky. The liquid didn't bear any resemblance to apple juice, especially in such a small quantity. It came out of the carton differently to juice, and the fumes suddenly seemed so strong they might be flammable. If someone lit a match the glass would fill with fire, and when he put it to his lips it did feel savagely hot. He knew he was sweating, and when he breathed out he knew his breath was toxic. The mint was now in the way of his tongue, so he removed it and put it on the table, where it sat like a small, white pebble.

'Giggleswick,' he said quietly.

'He's a boarder,' said the woman. 'Absolutely loves it.'

'Is it a boarding school?'

There was a fractional pause.

'Yes,' came the reply.

'So he lives there, really? That's his home.'

Michael was aware of the burning round his gums.

'You'll see him for weekends, I hope. He'll need somewhere for weekends, so this... place of yours. It could be just the thing.'

The woman was looking at the mint, and Michael could see that she knew what he was drinking. He could sense her distaste, and he felt his hand shaking slightly. Perhaps she had known from the moment he sat down – from the thin, cheap waterproof he was wearing, and the jumper underneath it. From his watery eyes, and his nose and cheeks – they carried the early signs of bursting blood vessels. He could pass for the dignified professional only until he was sitting still, and now he was the object of the woman's merciless scrutiny. Her eyes were blue, just like Monica's.

'Weekends are for sport,' said her husband.

'Are they?' said Michael.

'Oh, he's rugby mad,' said the wife.

'Same as his father.'

'Same as you.'

Michael smiled. 'Wonderful,' he said.

The little dance had come to an end. They had both communicated everything, and were now heavy with self-satisfaction.

'So what do *you* do, my friend? And where are *you* going?'

That was a pair of questions neither he nor she would ever ask.

'Tell us about *your* grandson, if you have one.'

They wouldn't ask that, either – so Michael told them.

He said, 'I don't have a grandson.'

'No?'

'No. But I suppose... Giggleswick. That's a private school, isn't it? Like Eton. I suppose—'

'Oh, it's not like Eton,' said the man.

'No?'

Michael turned his head, and looked at the profile beside him. The man had white hair, which was neatly cut – the fringe healthily full and pushed back in a wave. He had skin that suggested an outdoor life – a boat, probably, like the man who'd been on his way to Bristol Marina. This chap was almost certainly the type who sailed, and would be on the committee of some sailing club which would be just up from his house overlooking some estuary – and there was something in the way he'd said, 'It's not like Eton,' that suggested he had intimate knowledge of the place, perhaps because he'd been there as a boy. Had he been a youngster, kneeling on the cold floor of some traditional old classroom as his housemaster sat open-legged in front of him? Had he possibly even been the housemaster, his poor wife still in blissful ignorance? Or was that all simply myth, prejudice and prurience? The old, unfunny joke about public school: 'Backs to the wall, lads! Sir's coming!' The man was carefully not looking at him, so Michael tried again, desperate to haul his mind away from the sexual images that flashed and flashed again, leaving him blind and empty-headed. This man had never performed oral sex on anyone, and if he had it didn't matter. Or perhaps it did.

'No,' said Michael loudly. 'I don't have any children at all.'

The woman said nothing, and nor did he. What was there to say, now they knew he was drunk? They couldn't really ask him why not, and commiseration would have been presumptuous. A light-hearted 'Lucky you!' would have been misplaced, because for all they knew Michael was alluding to the fact that he'd had children once, and they had all been burned alive or murdered, which accounted for his descent into alcoholism.

'How much does your flat cost?' he said.

'Oh, Lord,' said the man quietly. 'Too much.'

'It must be an expensive area, Settle. Is it more than a million?'

'No, no.'

'How much?'

'I'm not sure. The, er...'

'I thought you were buying it. Have you not agreed a price?'

The man finally looked at him and smiled. 'Yes. But it's just not something I want to discuss,' he said politely. 'It's a bit... you know. Personal.'

'Confidential?'

'There's nothing confidential about it, but—'

'What are the school fees at Eton? Giggleswick, I mean.'

'They... vary.'

'Expensive, though.'

'Not cheap.'

'Then there's all the other expenses,' said Michael carefully, working to disguise the tremor in his voice. He was working hard, anxious to avoid rudeness. All he wanted was polite normality.

'Uniform, I expect. Cricket bats. Rugby kit. Food and drink, and trips to France. Outings to... where do they go? Museums, I suppose. The zoo.'

He poured more whisky.

'I expect there's a lot of expense,' he said. 'That's why I didn't have children. My wife wanted them, passionately.'

He turned back to the woman.

'I said I just don't think it's practical – from a financial point of view. We could have had them. It wasn't as if... there were obstacles. She had ovaries, after all.'

He laughed.

'I had what I needed. But... in the end, you have to make a decision. One girl, one boy. One of each. Or none of each, and I decided – we decided, with the expenses – no children for us. So she... left me, and we decided not to get married after all. We hadn't been together that long, but we knew it wouldn't work, so she went her separate way. I'm going up to the Highlands, now. Changing at Preston, possibly – or I might go a bit further. Change somewhere else, and change everything.'

'A long trip then,' said the woman.

'Oh, yes,' said Michael. 'Where are you going?'

There was another short, charged silence.

'You're off to Settle,' he said. 'You told me that. What's your... what's your grandson's name?'

A tiny pause, then, 'Percy.'

'Oh, Lord. I suppose...'

He floundered.

'Does he get teased about it?'

The man said, 'About what?' And Michael noticed irritation in his voice.

'About being called Percy,' said Michael.

'Why would anyone tease him about his name?'

'It's unusual.'

'Is it?'

'Isn't it? How many Percys do you know?'

He laughed, because it was funny.

'I can't think of a single one,' he said. 'It's a nice name, I'm not saying it isn't – and I wouldn't tease him. But boys, you know – they can be very cruel. They can be very intolerant, and... I can just imagine them... You know – teasing him. No mercy for Percy. But – hopefully, he'd tell someone, wouldn't he? They have all these helplines, now – counsellors. People believe you, I think, and... My closest friend was – well, it doesn't matter, really.'

The man said nothing, and the woman had picked up her tablet.

'Have you got any photographs?' said Michael. 'Of the new flat, I mean. Not of Percy, though... how old is he? Young, I imagine.'

She didn't speak.

Michael sat and finished his drink. The silence seemed terribly, tragically heavy to him – for to not answer a direct question was quite a significant rejection, and it meant he couldn't ask another. He had to be sensitive to the fact that the couple no longer wanted to talk, and that was because he was drunk and had been... Not invasive, but certainly lacking in the good manners he normally upheld in every situation. He had been tactless, and intrusive. He had been stupid, too.

He said, 'I'm having a little bit of a problem.'

He said it quite quietly.

'It's not really a problem one can talk about. So I don't. It's not like... If it was cancer you might just say it. I suppose you wouldn't. But... I don't understand why you want me to visit you in Settle.'

'We don't,' said the man.

'You did.'

There was a silence.

'A moment ago you did, but... I just don't think it's my kind of place, and I genuinely don't think I could afford it. Unless things change, dramatically, and there's not much chance of that. I'm... comfortable. Compared to so many. There was a picture in the paper—'

'Look,' said the man. 'Please don't take this the wrong way, but would you mind if we didn't chat any more?'

'Chat about what?'

'Would you mind if we didn't?'

'Didn't what?'

'Talk.'

'No. Not at all. I don't think we were talking, really. I don't think we were having a conversation. You seemed to want to tell me about your personal life—'

'That's not quite true, but—'

'I don't think I asked you if you had any grandchildren, and I don't think I asked where this boy, Percy, went to school – or what his name was. Or if I did, it was because—'

'Let's drop it, please.'

'Of course. But... when I was at school, they called us by our surnames. Maybe there were lots of Percys and I just never knew. My friend was James, but... Crikey. We called him "Seyton". James Seyton, and we were very fond of each other. We were good friends, but... we lost touch.'

Michael closed his eyes, and suddenly felt so weary he thought he might lapse into coma.

'As you do,' he said.

If he fell asleep now, the man would have to climb over him when he got off at Settle. Wherever Michael was going would flash by and he would end up on some awful, unknown terminus and have to come all the way back down the same old line, looking at himself in the darkness.

The man and woman said nothing, but he could feel their anxiety and it made him sad. He had caused them anxiety and embarrassment, and there was no way to put things right: to speak again would make it worse. On the other hand, sitting in a silence that seemed heavy with tension was unbearable. He felt bad, and he knew they did too: they were feeling the same emotions as he was feeling, but they could not find a way of sharing them, or releasing them and that was the saddest thing – how they couldn't shake hands now. They couldn't hold each other and weep. He could not turn to this man with white hair and hug him – unless a miracle occurred. No: they would get to Settle, or wherever they had to change, and perhaps they would laugh with relief as they stepped down onto the platform.

'Poor man,' they would say. 'Lonely.'

They would nod, and she would say, 'Drunk.'

'Really?'

'Didn't you notice?'

'Notice what?'

'Didn't you smell it? He was drinking neat whisky.'

'He wasn't!'

'He *was*, darling. It was in his juice carton.'

'Crikey.'

That would be their explanation of the awkwardness: that the man beside them was an alcoholic, and alcoholics were by their nature embarrassing. They would not think of him again, because Percy was coming to supper – they had a table for three booked in some very nice restaurant, probably an Italian. Boys liked pizza, or Michael had. It had always been such a treat. Percy would arrive, flushed from his exertions on the rugby pitch, a picture of wild-eyed health – like James, in fact. His hair would be mussed from a quick shower, and he hadn't had time to dry it. He would be young enough to embrace his gran and kiss her, and he would probably hold his grandfather too – what did it matter, who hugged who? James would bring a friend, perhaps – like young Michael – and they would sit at the table together, laughing. They would be teasing each other – Percy-James and Michael, together – as they chose their different toppings; in jeans and casual sweatshirts, or perhaps not? Perhaps they had dressed up for the occasion, and looked grown up in neatly pressed long-sleeved shirts and ties, their collars fastened properly by Mr Trace, who couldn't stand an untidy boy and would always touch the soft part of your throat, fastening the top button.

'That's better,' he'd say, stroking your neck. 'Come and find me at lunchtime. Have your lunch, and we'll talk.'

Jackets on, despite the heat. The boys had dressed up, because it wasn't an Italian restaurant at all, it was Settle's finest celebrity-chef bistro, popular with the rich and famous. He could hear their laughter, and the landscape was woodland, with farmers' fields in between and a sudden rush of white flowers, close to the train. He, Michael, was having a little bit of a problem but they hadn't felt able to ask him what that was, for fear that he would tell them – and it wasn't their concern.

Into a tunnel they went, and it was surprisingly long. Would they ever, ever come out or were they going slowly deeper into solid earth? Might they just possibly run deep into the thick, gooey clay and slow down and down and down as the tunnel roof got lower and the wheels clogged... might they be entombed for ever?

One thing was clear: they would never be friends.

What did he want them to do, these poor fellow travellers? And out they rushed, into a new world where everyone could breathe again for there were houses, with long gardens and sheds. What did he want? Did he want a dinner invitation?

'Don't leave us, Michael! You must meet Percy! Why not? A table for four!'

What then?

'No, stay the night! We're just getting to know you!'

What did he want or expect, or need? Were they going to install him in the spare room of an off-plan flat that didn't exist yet, and never let him go? The woman would say, 'Listen. You're not going anywhere until we get to the bottom of this little problem of yours. We have room! We have that little ensuite guest room, Michael.'

She would be so unbearably kind, and he – the husband – would be distant but wise. His respect for and love of all human life had been forged in the army, where he'd probably commanded troops as a brigadier or colonel. He'd seen his share of bloodletting, of course. He'd seen his own men blown to pieces by the IRA. Not as bad as the First World War, but you still had bodies cut to ribbons, spread around the tracks with shoes in the grass...

and the invoices. Oh, the invoices: they had piled up only because he hadn't been able to deal with them, or his mother. He hadn't been able to enter the details onto the spreadsheets. He had hit an obstacle, and could not concentrate properly, and he had been getting headaches because Elizabeth was so long gone as to be one of those old legends you told yourself round the campfire like a sad, drunk Red Indian reliving the good old days when the buffalo roamed.

The house in which they had never lived together was so, so dark. Every time he typed numbers into the appropriate box, it seemed it was the wrong box. The numbers were sometimes right and sometimes wrong, and it seemed to take such a long time to enter one single invoice, particularly as he became ridiculously, obsessively correct. He would have to have breaks – and that meant trips to the kitchen area, where they had the coffee machine and the fridge. It meant time away from his desk, but nobody ever challenged him because nobody was actually waiting for him to complete a task: the invoices were loaded onto spreadsheets and the finance department dealt with them as and when they came in.

His desk was his sanctuary.

He really had pretended it wasn't happening, and slow, sweet Monica hadn't asked or probed. After his resignation-dismissal he had continued to leave for work, except he had gone to the park instead. He had taken the bus to the playing fields. Then, he had done two circuits of the perimeter by which time she would have left the house – but she wasn't living with him. He and Monica had never lived together, so he was misremembering. Who had he been pretending for? Not Monica, not Amy – so had it really been himself? He tricked himself into thinking he was still going to work, and hadn't been let go, just as he was tricking himself now – for it suddenly seemed he wasn't ever going to kill himself either, having tried and failed in both Bromsgrove and Crewe. He should have grabbed the steam-train enthusiast and frogmarched him down the tracks. He could have tripped him over and knelt on his chest, and that would have stopped him talking about nothing. He would have coughed out his dentures, the poor man.

'No, mister! No!'

They would have been cremated together, for half Michael's head would have lain against the old man's severed shoulder: a jigsaw for the morticians, making them truly inseparable. If only he'd met the 15.41 – and he was about to be sick.

It would be over now, and Percy's grandfather would never have had to move his coat, or say, 'Do you mind if we don't chat any more?'

Do you mind if we don't chat any more?

Michael swallowed, and smiled at the thought, realising that he still didn't have the courage to do anything other than chat. He would find it, though – the courage. It might be at the very bottom of the juice carton, and it might mean crazy, bendy legs that could hardly carry him – but he would find it, and dance down the railway line.

The train had slowed, and there was another one next to it travelling just a little bit faster. They were racing, and everyone was carefully not looking at each other.

So many people, treasuring their lives! And he would wake up wondering what his was for and how he had come to have no purpose. How he had come to be so unconnected, for all the strings and strands had stretched until they'd broken and the most meaningful and important thing he had done in the last week was to help Vivienne in the flat opposite with a broken blind – a misaligned toggle, in fact. He smiled at this thought, too – and then laughed. The other train was winning, and he nearly said, 'Come on! Faster!'

She – Vivienne – had rung his bell, which was a rare occurrence. She had apologised for disturbing him, but the blind had come off the wall and she couldn't see to fix it. Did he mind? No, he didn't. She hated to be a nuisance, but she wasn't being one if only because she was giving him the chance to show how high his spirits were. She was allowing him to play the role of 'busy man'.

'You don't have to come now,' she'd said.

'No, I've just got a couple of errands in town, and then I'll be over.'

'Are you sure?'

'Absolutely.'

The blind did not need replacing or even repairing – she had knocked it somehow, and the rail had come away from its plastic toggle. It was thirty seconds' work to fix it, and Vivienne had been so grateful. With both his parents gone, he couldn't phone anyone to say what he'd been up to, and how he had single-handedly reattached an elderly lady's blind. He was orphaned, but so were most people: your parents died in the end, because that's what parents do. They were up in heaven, no doubt, except heaven was the place nobody with a brain could possibly believe in, unless they hadn't escaped their childhood. Why not believe in it, though? Why not take comfort? They would all meet in heaven and he could tell them his important news:

'It was only the toggle, Dad. She'd knocked it.'

'What kind of toggle, son?'

'You know – one of those plastic curtain tracks. They have toggles at the back. You just have to locate it in the groove, and turn it.'

The nagging, desolate sameness: it was shaming.

It was the grief. It was the pushing against doors that were jammed, or swung open so you found yourself in rooms you didn't want to be in – and they were passing houses again, for the other train had veered off somewhere, or derailed down an embankment and was blazing behind them as they shot forwards victoriously into some suburb, where people really lived. The rooftops spread, and all that stone and slate had been quarried and hauled, the mortar mixed for a town to rise even as the young man on the other side of the carriage watched something noisy on his phone. Michael could hear the inane, barking laughter of a cartoon, and the young man seemed riveted. Everyone was forced to share the squeaking nonsense – and he wasn't six years old! He didn't have the excuse a child might have. No, this man was in his early twenties – he was a robust, intelligent-looking Asian man, and a hundred years ago people like him would have been stuck in the mud of the Somme, with bullets sizzling in their chests. He'd have been caught in the open as the machine guns opened fire, and he would have fallen backwards, or sunk to his knees, astonished and breathless. Six hours of cold, slow suffering lay ahead, as he cried for his mother. Now, he couldn't even muster the courtesy to wear a set of headphones – despite the sticker on the window: *Please consider your fellow passengers!* Once again, the train company wanted to look after everyone. It was aching for a little peace and goodwill, and once again it wasn't working.

It was the nothing that wore you down.

The nullity of encounters like these wore Michael down, for he would not be on some touchline cheering Percy and James as they raced towards the goal. If he watched the boys and girls playing football or hockey, someone would notice him and think, Predator.

Percy needed protection, and would get it.

Percy lived a busy, driven life. Percy rushed from his lessons to the changing room, and then off to school-supper before he dropped exhausted into his boarding-school dormitory bed, too tired for the pillow fights he'd outgrown. The expensive flat would be left to him in his loving grandparents' will, and he would marry, and have a baby of his own. The grandparents would die happy, and Percy would wear his grandfather's watch, which Michael could see on the man's wrist. It was a wind-up model, of course, and every time Percy wound it he would think of the sweet, strong old man who had given it to him, and how wonderful their times on the boat had been as young Percy learned to navigate by the stars and steer the craft deftly into harbour. Percy wouldn't be the kind of man to walk out into the thin, scruffy copse of trees at the back of his flat with a rope. Never would Percy find himself blinded by tears, hissing, 'Do it!'

'What?'

'Hang yourself, you crippled bastard! You've mended the fucking blind, so get it over with – do it!'

No, no – and no again. Michael screwed the cap onto his fruit-juice carton, and put it in his bag with the glass and the half-sucked mint. He decided not to say goodbye, because the couple were so ostentatiously concentrating – one with the tablet and the other with a Kindle. He stood, put his bag over his shoulder, and set off to the doors at the end of the carriage, away from the chirping, giggling phone. He walked through two more, and found a pair of empty seats in the third – but he walked on into the little vestibule again. If he could open a door, he could throw himself out: but the doors were locked, and you couldn't even get the windows down. The toilet was out of order, so he couldn't drown himself – though of course it probably wasn't out of order at all. It was simply too expensive to maintain, or they didn't want it vandalised.

'We would unlock the toilets, sir, but people keep using them.'

Michael smiled again, because that's what someone had said to him once, on a station called Fratton. 'We have to keep the facilities locked, sir. They get smashed up if we don't.' We would provide seats, but we're worried people might sit on them. We would put the heating on, but you might get comfortable and never leave: better to be cold, with the wind racing through the freezing, doorless shelter. That's the world: live in it.

They were approaching Preston.

'We will shortly be arriving in Preston,' he was told – and he watched the town rolling in, the train easing into its very heart. So much work had gone into the place, and the work would never stop. People came and went, working and serving – designing, building and expanding. Michael stood at the door, but it remained obstinately closed until the guard decided it was safe to disembark. He or she pressed a switch, and the door opened slowly, even as a little step appeared before Michael's feet. Those waiting to board hung back, allowing him to disembark first: they formed a committee to studiously ignore him as he passed through, and walked towards the iron bridge that would lift him over the rails to all the other platforms.

What if he hadn't been there? That little crowd would not have had to wait. They would have pressed forwards, three seconds earlier.

He passed a boy standing in a glass tunnel. It was the waiting area, with anti-vandal prison-cell seats – seats you could hose down quickly. The boy was probably younger than Percy, and he appeared to be on his way home from school, late as it was. He was keying something into his phone. A sports bag lay heavy between his feet, and he had a backpack too. Eleven years old, probably, in a too-big blazer: Michael noticed him because once again it was himself, and he'd finished all those sweets. He'd put on a different uniform, too, and the thoughts were spilt – they seemed to hit the ground and smash, and he found he was standing absolutely still with his eyes tight shut, balancing.

The boy wasn't him, but it might have been James.

He had loved James with the fantastic storybook desire to save him from fires, and be necessary to him. James Seyton, with his effortless grace – did it matter? There were people pushing past, just avoiding him as he stood marooned, for he had liked James so much, and still thought of him as a friend. He had felt the flutter of his heart whenever they met. They had taken the train together, and it didn't really matter, for the emotions were old now and his love for James had simply been a first tentative outing, like the first small clambering steps that would take him ever higher up the rock face he'd been lost on now for so many years, climbing and clinging, unable to get down. It just didn't matter, for the tracks were everywhere and a train would come.

But he had joined the Scouts with James.

Oh, he could see the two of them still, in beret and scarf – and James was a better athlete than eleven-year-old Michael. He could see James the day they'd worked a little ferry together – that was some Scouting nonsense, no doubt – hauling on a rope to drag the craft across the pond, so they'd both been soaked but only James had taken his shirt off and carried on bare-backed, and extra specially splendid, for you couldn't be aware of your beauty then; the word had no currency and he had no idea why he found himself ejaculating that night as something visited his dream and left him damp, sticky, shamed and more scared than he'd ever been – with nobody to talk to but Mr Trace, who wanted to see him again about his low mark in a recent test.

'I'm afraid you'll have to pay.'

If he was homosexual, he needed to embrace it. It wasn't a criminal offence any more: one was allowed to be gay. It was encouraged, for gender meant nothing, the pronouns only revealing how narrow-minded and repressed some people were. There were so many partners out there, and rights to be claimed – there were attitudes to be challenged, too. If he could find James again, they could recall that time on the ferry together, and he could explain that no, he wasn't homosexual – or, if he was, he had so successfully deceived himself that he might as well not be. What was he, then? How had he evolved or faded or fallen into this?

'Does it matter?' James might say, holding both his hands.

No. Not at all.

It just didn't, because take any soul from any of Preston's long, dark platforms, and they would all have similar irrelevant predictable stories, and silly anxieties about their silly childhoods. They would all end up the same: neatly boxed in the back of a hearse, queuing for the crematorium – and once you'd noticed one of them, they seemed to be everywhere. You couldn't go two miles without a sign reminding you that this town had a crematorium too, and it was closer than you thought, and what you were breathing probably contained a speck or two of somebody – not that it mattered. If he could only stop, then no one would have to listen any more – he wouldn't have to listen to himself. The self-, self-, self-pity, like morning mist, would evaporate as soon as the sun came up.

'You were never clever enough,' he said, aloud. 'Too stupid.'

He opened his eyes, and the young boy was still there, turned away, wearing yet another set of headphones. He was loved and might even be in love. He might have met his own James,

Percy or Michael, and if he hadn't he would do soon: and then he would be enmeshed. Michael walked on, and found the platform had tilted. He had to work hard, because it was suddenly so steep that he needed all his puff just to get to the bridge.

He felt like crying, of course – so he laughed.

He climbed up the footbridge, holding the rail.

Up the stairs, along and down again – and did he want tea in the central café-bar, with its many sets of doors? No, so that meant climbing another set of stairs whether he wanted to go back the way he'd come or onto a platform on the far distant side of this ridiculously wide station, where trains were behaving just like trains, grinding and roaring. The footbridge was heavy old Victorian iron, and had been built long before anyone worried about those who'd lost their legs in the war: it would outlast everyone who dared climb it. The roof was high, and if there were lifts he couldn't see them, so up he went again, and he thought of the famous picture: the infinite stairs, leading you round and up for ever. This bridge wasn't like that, for it did its job simply enough: he could see a taxi rank one way, beyond the ticket office. Platform two was suddenly to the right, and he glimpsed people on it, stirring in expectation as a little purple train came in, just like a noisy toy.

'Never, ever clever enough,' he said to himself, smiling – and even as he realised he was muttering aloud, the train company told him it was sorry. It was still so sorry, because the purple train was just like all the others: it was running twenty-two whole minutes late. Those in charge knew they might be causing the most terrible inconvenience, and he thought for a moment that he ought to find the station manager and assure her or him that it simply wasn't so: there was no inconvenience at all, because he no longer had any destination in his mind, and all he wanted was another tangerine. Why hadn't he eaten one already? He still had two or three left.

'Don't apologise,' he would say to the manager. 'Lay your burden down.'

'We *are* sorry,' said the announcer.

'Don't be,' replied Michael. 'I have nowhere to go.'

'You do, sir – surely. You have a ticket to Scotland in your wallet.'

'But I have no schedule, and I want you to know that I understand. Trains will be late sometimes – I have the imagination to understand that.'

The manager's eyes would fill with tears.

'We do our best,' he'd say.

'That's just what I mean, sir!' Michael hissed.

He leaned on the rail for a moment.

Sir, he thought quietly. Sir or madam. Person in charge. I *know* you do your best, because we all do. You're trying to help me go north, but look at the network spreading out of this town – look at the rails – and look at all the things beyond your control. You have electrical problems. You have wear and tear. You have to deal with vandalism, while thoughtless people like me fling themselves under your wheels. How can you hope to get it right, ever? If a train gets in on time, we should line the platform, cheering the miracle.'

Michael breathed in, and smiled again: Glasgow had ceased to exist.

The Highlands were suddenly a fiction of someone else's past – he would never reach them. No, not now: for he had a new plan. He would take the little purple train because it was there, close by – he could see it, and it was real. It was short, neat and noisy and he wanted suddenly to know where it went. If it went in a circle, he'd stay on it for as long as he could, and if he couldn't die on the tracks perhaps he could die more comfortably, in one of its seats? He'd met someone, years ago, who told a story about travelling on the Tube in London – the Circle line, in fact – and discovering that the man he'd sat next to was dead.

He was sitting next to an actual corpse.

'So what did you do?' Michael said.

'I didn't do anything,' said the somebody. 'I didn't want to get involved, so I got off at the next stop.'

'Did you report it?'

'No.'

How long had that solitary former person been going round and round on the Circle line? How many passengers had decided not to get involved, and when had it slumped so far forward that it couldn't be ignored? Perhaps it had rolled onto the floor, and people had still stepped over it? Another dead person, dammit – where's the guard?

He reached the purple train, and climbed on board.

No, no, no: he would never get back to the Highlands, because they were in the past and this was a train to the future – where it was actually going he still had no idea. Someone would tell him, or the destinations would soon start to scroll endlessly across the display panel, for you couldn't avoid knowing where you were bound for very long. At that moment he was happy to sit, uncertain whether he'd be taken forwards or backwards. His ticket might be valid, but it was equally possible he'd have to buy a new one.

So what?

He chose a seat, and closed his eyes. Meanwhile, elsewhere, Morris closed his – and he was hungry, too, for he had reached Birmingham and still hadn't eaten. He'd got through the station barrier, but he wasn't bound for Preston because he had no business there. He was wishing he was home in Newport and, like Michael, he'd lost all sense of purpose and direction. Yet again, his phone wasn't ringing as he waited for a call he knew in his heart just wasn't going to come. He was supposed to meet this man, Aziz, for just one hour – but unfortunately, Aziz had changed his mind.

Aziz had forgotten the arrangement he'd made just minutes before, so he didn't call Morris to tell him he was no longer wanted. He didn't call to say he wouldn't be calling – for Aziz was a busy man with hardly enough time to call even his heavily pregnant wife who had been trying to reach him for an hour, in floods of tears.

His phone was turned to silent. Why? There was a good reason, and it was because the substance he was using was so pure it had just lifted him into a different zone, and inner-city Birmingham had become a paradise of dancing, weaving cars – his gums were tingling, and he was feeling finer than he'd felt all year. His own vehicle seemed to throb and hover, powered not by petrol but by smooth, loud music, and it felt like a boat. Lights were coming on, each one opening bright as a flower, so the thin young boy in the park was far from his mind. Aziz didn't want a boy ever again, he was past all that: instead, he would go straight to the restaurant which overlooked the canal, and he knew that tonight would be the best night since they'd opened.

He didn't need anyone.

Morris needed him, but they would never connect. Morris had found the park, and sat on the bench getting colder, even as Michael peeled that second-to-last tangerine. He sat, and his phone just wouldn't ring. His hood was up around his ears, and he was at that stage when he had to calculate very carefully whether or not to stand and walk for warmth, or stay in his seat to save energy: not a deadly stage, of course, but an uncomfort-able one, and what he longed for most was a burger, or a cigarette. A joint, a burger and a ticket back to his sister's: all of that was obtainable for less than fifty pounds, which is what he didn't have unless Aziz paid him the agreed seventy, plus expenses. He checked his phone for missed calls, and the cracked screen only reminded him of his sister's boyfriend's temper. Two sausage rolls! And he'd known they weren't his.

He had known they belonged to Morris.

There were things Morris knew, and things he didn't. One thing he didn't know was who Dorothy and Ken Trott might be, and why their names were written on a plate by his left shoulder. Morris hadn't noticed the plate, and he'd never seen the Trotts who used to sit in this very park at this very spot. He'd never shared their pleasure in the roses, or been even loosely connected to the moment when they made a big decision: that on their deaths a certain amount of money would be left to Birmingham City Council so that this very bench could be dedicated not to the prostitutes who cruised around it every evening, but to their years of tender love. *In memory of Dorothy and Ken Trott, who loved this view*: that's what was written just below Morris's neck, as he sat getting colder, waiting for Aziz who didn't want him. And he didn't know that he'd been spotted until it was too late.

When the young man sat down next to him, he got the very strong sense that it would do him no good to run. He would do much better talking his way out of the park, and right out of Birmingham – for it was definitely time to go.

That was when his new friend spoke to him.

'All right?' he said.

Morris said, 'All right.'

'What's your name?'

'Morris.'

'Where you from?'

He paused, then decided to be truthful.

'Just outside Newport,' he said – and his mouth was dry, because there was someone else now, leaning on the back of the bench, and he could hear him breathing. There were three of them, in fact – and there was a boy his own age just down the path. They had surrounded him.

'Newport?' said the man quietly. 'What's a Newport queer doing in Birmingham?'

'Nothing.'

'No?'

'Waiting. For a friend.'

The man laughed, and leaned in close. He spat, then, full in Morris's face – and someone grabbed him by his hood. They wouldn't let him fall to the ground: it was easier to keep him on the bench, for they could use their fists and their feet, and take it in turns. When they were ready, they rolled him onto the path, and stamped on him.

CONNECTION

17

Maria caught the 15.58 and it was on time to the second.

She reached Preston at 17.10 and she got down carefully, for the rucksack was heavy on her shoulder. She still couldn't understand how she had left the bag on the table, for without it she felt incomplete. Why hadn't she noticed, when normally she checked so carefully? She stood in the café doorway and saw a young woman waving. The next moment the handbag was in her hand, and she simply started to cry.

'You're so good,' she said. 'You sit here all this time – that's so, so kind.'

'Do you want to check what's inside?' said Ayesha.

'Yes. No! Thank you.'

She was laughing, too.

'Well then, what do you want to drink?'

'Nothing, thank you.'

'Have something with me. Just… relax for a moment. Do you want tea or coffee?'

'Just… tea, please. Thank you.'

'Herbal? Mint?'

'Honestly, no. Just… everyday tea. Breakfast tea.'

Ayesha had found a corner table, and her brother's guitar was propped against the wall. Maria sat down, the rucksack beside her – and she wiped her eyes. She couldn't stop smiling, for the bag looked and weighed the same. She held it to her chest and unzipped it. She removed the passport first, and then she took out the wallet: there were all her cards and train tickets, and there were the banknotes. Everything was safe again: order had been restored, and the temporary separation had already started to seem less important. Her bag had had an adventure of its own, but now it was back where it belonged. Incredibly, their journey together could continue, and her family need never know. When Ayesha returned, she was carrying a white china cup, and the string of the teabag trailed over its edge.

'You know you asked me something,' she said, setting it down. 'You asked me if the train we were on went to Burnley.'

'Which train?' said Maria.

'The one we were on together, at Carlisle. You sat down, and asked me if the train went to Burnley. Well... I didn't realise it, but you were on the right train. You didn't need to get off.'

'It was the right train?'

'Yes. You had to come here, didn't you? So as to change at Preston.'

'Yes. So...'

Maria thought hard.

'Why did I get off?'

'Because I told you to. By mistake.'

Maria digested this, and smiled even more broadly.

'I needed to come here,' she said. 'And here I am.'

'That's right. But that train – the one you were on – would have got you here faster. I just didn't think quickly enough, and suddenly I opened my big mouth, and—'

'I was getting down, running.'

'You were getting down, and it was my fault. All of this is my fault, so the least I can do is buy you a cup of tea. Is there anything else you want?'

'No. Thank you.'

Maria started to laugh.

'I am very lucky,' she said. 'Everything is okay, because of you. Look.'

She opened the bag again and removed her passport.

'My life,' she said. 'My visa and my work permit. I am so, so lucky – thank you.'

'You must stop thanking me. If I hadn't—'

'You're a very kind person. And I make you late! Where are you going?'

'I'm nearly home. I'm not late at all.'

'You live here?'

'Close by. My parents do, anyway. I get a bus from here.'

'You waited for me.'

Maria was laughing again. She brushed the tears away and shook her head.

'I just felt so guilty,' said Ayesha. 'Where are you going, by the way? Are you camping somewhere?'

'Camping?'

She looked down at the rucksack.

'No,' she said. 'I have a hotel. But everything is here, for walking. I don't have a suitcase.'

'It's more practical. Easier to carry.'

'Where are *you* going? You told me – your parents.'

'I'm going to see them,' said Ayesha. 'I'm returning this thing... this guitar, amongst... you know, other things. I was going to see them anyway—'

'You play guitar?'

'I don't.'

'My husband plays. I sing, he plays guitar.'

'This belonged to my brother, but we've decided to give it to a friend. Is your husband meeting you, or...?'

'Meeting me where?'

'For the walking holiday. In the hotel.'

'No.'

She paused.

'He is working. United Arab Emirates.'

'And you're from the Philippines? I've never been there.'

'You must come. Are you Indian? Or... Where were you born?'

'My parents are Indian. I was born in Bury.'

'Bury?'

'Near here. Not far.'

'I worked one year in India.'

'Whereabouts was that?'

'Mumbai.'

'Right.'

'So noisy. Like Manila.'

They sat in silence, and Maria blew across the surface of her tea and added sugar. Ayesha didn't need to look at her phone to know the time, for there was a clock on the wall opposite, and a series of information boards. They were sitting, it seemed, on the site of a First World War canteen, where thousands of hungry, thirsty soldiers had taken refreshment on their way to the front. There were signs announcing this, and the writing was so big you had to read it: *In 1917, every single day, three thousand two hundred and fifty men were served by volunteers.*

She looked at Maria, and they smiled at each other.

Conversation had come to a natural end, it seemed, but the meeting was going to be prolonged by the same hot drinks the soldiers must have sipped, here in this very spot. Not that the delay mattered, for the buses to her parents' house were regular and she'd called to tell them she had to meet someone first. In any case, she didn't want to go home. She wanted to see them, of course – but seeing them was always so hard.

Why had she assumed Maria was single? It was because she looked so young, and the rucksack had marked her out as a student traveller. Her English was good but full of short hesitations, and her face switched between anxiety and open joy in half a second – the muscles were always at work. She had very dark hair, drawn back from a small, oval face, and it was held somehow under a denim cap. She wore a light pink waterproof, and a crucifix was just visible against her throat. She had small, fine hands that tapered to carefully painted nails, and she looked up from her tea suddenly so their eyes were locked together for a moment. Maria's were almost black, and luminous. She smiled and her teeth were perfect.

'Where's your hotel?' said Ayesha.

'I don't know.'

She laughed.

'Some... very small place. I have a map, but first I get to Burnley.'

She drew a ticket from the wallet.

'Burnley Manchester Road. Do you know Burnley Manchester Road?'

'Don't ask me.'

'Why not?'

'Because... Because I gave you the wrong information, earlier. You shouldn't trust me.'

Maria laughed again.

'I see, you're joking! – of course I trust you. But honestly... Listen. I take the C4 bus from the railway station. The C4 bus goes to the hotel, so they say. I hope it does. I hope it will come.'

'You seem well prepared,' said Ayesha.

'I stay two days in the hotel. One long walk.'

'And that's holiday?'

Maria nodded.

'Very special holiday.'

Ayesha smiled, wishing that conversations like this didn't have to be interrogations. Why only two days? What's so special? Will you be alone, and if so won't you be lonely? Or is it an organised walking-adventure you booked weeks ago with friends? And why Lancashire? What is your job here, or was I right in my first assumption, that you're studying? If so – if not – does your extraordinary beauty make your life difficult, and what is your experience of this strange, strange country?

'My brother died,' she said suddenly.

Maria's eyes opened wider than ever.

'He died, and I'm taking his guitar back home – I can't even remember why I'd been looking after it. He came to visit me, but I don't know why he left it. He did, though – and it's time it went somewhere else.'

'He died?' said Maria softly.

'He was in an accident, just over three years ago. A road accident, and... it affected us all pretty deeply. Well, it would.'

Ayesha smiled, and Maria stared at her. The passport was on the table still, and she had her left hand on it, as if she was worried it might be snatched. She was leaning forward, and Ayesha thought again how thin, small and frail she looked – the rucksack was huge beside her. Kristin's guitar stood in the corner, and the case was dusty. Inside was the instrument itself, bought for his eleventh birthday, because he had borrowed a friend's and learned a number of chords, so he clearly needed his own. He deserved his own. She had heard him once, at an early stage of the process, practising a song in his bedroom – his unbroken voice surprisingly sweet and in tune. She had made him record himself, and the recording... she had it, and could play it easily if she ever wanted to. So far she never had. The most unbearable thing, or one of the many most unbearable things, had been the disposal of his possessions – the shoes that had kept his feet safe and warm, and the coat with some particular shopping story attached... the coat he'd wanted and argued with his mother about, because it wasn't strictly right for school, but he wanted it if only because it wasn't strictly right for school. And he'd got his way – the indulged, spoiled, over-loved Indian son. Over-loved, and thus forever tempting fate. Don't show your love, for the gods will be jealous of it. They will destroy it, out of spite. But how could you not over-love Kristin, who lived so entirely in the loving present? He brought electricity into the room, and left everything charged. She had under-loved her brother, whilst their gran had simply not been able to face the world without him. Without his love, there was no world, and it had slowly stopped spinning.

Her own was darker now. It really was as if a light had been turned off, the switch removed from the wall.

She felt a hand on her wrist.

'I'm so sorry,' said Maria. 'How old was he?'

'Thirteen.'

'Thirteen? Oh...'

For a moment, Maria looked stricken, as if she couldn't comprehend the horror of such a loss. Ayesha nodded, and the hand remained, its grip a little firmer.

'Do you have brothers, Maria?' she said.

'I have four.'

'Four?'

'I am the oldest. There are seven of us.'

They sat in silence again. Maria kept hold of her wrist, but it didn't feel intrusive. It felt as if she was imparting something, even though Ayesha had no idea what that might be, and could feel herself fighting. She was fighting the desire to confide more, and fighting the sense of comfort she was deriving from physical contact, whilst fighting her own despicable weakness and need for attention – if that's what it was. Most of all she was fighting the fact that she would never see her little brother again, which was a truth she had known for just over three years and yet seemed to stab her all the time, as if shards of something had lodged in her heart and cut it when she turned, or took a step – that re-realisation of the truth. For it hadn't been a dream, or a hoax, or a horrible film... Kristin had cycled into the path of a lorry, and there had been no miracle to prevent him being lost beneath its unforgiving wheels. People sympathised, but after all the sympathy and tears, he still wouldn't and couldn't do the one thing she wanted: he couldn't walk into the kitchen.

'Where's your tie?' she might have said, if it was a school day.

'Oh. Shit.'

'Kristin!'

'I forgot...'

She looked at Maria again, and the ache was almost too much.

'I get so tired,' she said quietly. 'I never knew how tiring it is, just to be sad.'

'Yes, it is.'

'Does it pass?'

'What?'

'This. That's what I want to know. Am I ever going to be just... normal again? Because that's what I want.'

'No,' said Maria.

'No?'

'Of course not. How can you be?'

'Why not, though? You don't think so, but... Are you a counsellor?'

'No, I'm a dogsbody,' said Maria. 'I work in a hospice. I am very good at cleaning, and my... my husband is a driver, and some construction. But to lose a brother, or anyone that you love... I mean *love*. How can you be the same? You would not want to be the same.'

'I want to be the same.'

'If you were the same, then what you had... What you had with him – it would not have been worth anything.'

She spoke slowly, struggling with the tenses.

'I don't know.'

'I do. What we have with people... with those we love – there is nothing more important. What is more important? Tell me.'

'I want him back, Maria.'

'What was his name?'

'Kristin. And he won't come back. He's gone, and I can't bear it.'

'Yes, you can.'

'I can't. I'm not bearing it. None of us can.'

'You are, though. You are bearing it, and... we must. You want to stop?'

'To stop what?'

'You want to die?'

'No. Yes. Sometimes I do, but...'

'You can't. Not yet.'

Ayesha groaned, and the hand on hers tightened.

She went to speak again, if only to ask the simple question, 'How can I go on?' But she found the words wouldn't come. She breathed in, ready, but her throat had closed and her mouth felt slack. She shook her head, and found she was staring at Maria's tea, which had hardly been touched. Seconds passed, and the silence stretched – and there were no more words worth saying. The Filipino woman had said things she had needed to hear, and that was enough. The café was busy, and there was a buzz of chatter. There was a platform announcement, halting and semi-audible, and someone was rolling a suitcase across the tiled floor – just everyday, constant noise.

It was so loud. She would never make herself heard over the top of it.

'I must go,' she said.

She pulled herself together and stood up. The hand slipped from her wrist, and Maria nodded and smiled.

'I really hope you have a good holiday.'

'Thank you,' replied Maria. 'And thank you for looking after my things.'

'I'm sorry I told you to get off the train. You know which one you're getting now?'

'I think so. Burnley.'

'That's platform two. Don't get confused by the different Burnleys – you want Burnley Manchester Road, yes?'

'Yes. Platform two?'

'Over the bridge.'

She was standing, and their hands came together for the last time. The next moment, Ayesha had the guitar under her arm and her bag over her shoulder. She went through the automatic doors. She went up the ramp to the exit, and paused a moment to retrieve her ticket. A guard glanced at it, and let her through, and suddenly she was amongst the taxis, heading up the slope to a bus stop at the top. The bus she needed was due, and she saw it at once: it was stuck in the heavy rush-hour traffic, indicating left.

She showed the driver her pass. She took a seat at the front, knowing that in thirty-eight minutes – if she stayed on the bus – she would be home. She had to stay on the bus, and get off at the right stop. She had to walk up the street, and press the doorbell. Those were the things she had to do, and if by chance she saw a young boy in a black blazer, she would not look away. She would look at him.

It wouldn't be Kristin, but she would try to smile.

EAST

18

Maria went over the bridge to platform two.

The train arrived twenty-three minutes late, and she stowed her rucksack in the luggage area. She walked down the aisle to a seat a few places in front of a man who had just stood up, with the remains of a tangerine in his hand. She didn't look at him – she just noticed the bright colour of the peel – and he didn't notice her. He was deep in thought, for it had occurred to him that he still hadn't bought a sandwich. Wherever the train was going, there wasn't going to be a buffet car, or even a trolley. He decided to get off again, and would have done so had it not been for a woman with three small dogs on three tangled leads. She had luggage, too, and created such an obstacle he turned and walked the other way, to find he was now blocked by someone with a buggy. It seemed easier, in the end, to sit down, and before he knew it the doors had closed and they were rolling backwards.

His last tangerine would have to do, and that would be no bad thing – nothing would be wasted. The juice carton was a different story: it was still more than half full, so twenty-five pounds' worth of Tomatin malt would soak into the earth and stones, unless he forced it down his throat even as he lay between the rails, or rolled himself across them. It would only need one, in fact, for the wheels would sever whatever he asked them to sever, even if one felt for the poor, poor driver. He'd heard that some poor souls saw the ghost of whoever they'd run down: they saw him or her, standing by the tracks. The worst thing, apparently, was the sheer helplessness – the inability to swerve and the knowledge that the brake couldn't help… You had to blast your horn hoping he or she would change his or her mind and step back out of the way. Some drivers never recovered, and some thought they had, only to be plunged into mental breakdown years later.

He could write a note of apology, and pin it to his jersey – or fold it into his shoe, perhaps, with the debit card.

They soon came to the first station, and stopped.

It was Lostock Hall, and some people got off as other people got on – it looked like the same number, in fact – a fair exchange. The authorities had placed planters along the platform, with flowers and shrubs. The paintwork was new, and he was reminded of an elderly man he'd read about who intended to photograph every single station in Britain. His retirement was going to be full of meticulously planned journeys up and down the British Isles – Michael had read about it in some newspaper, and he wondered if the man would see his mission through to the bitter end, or realise halfway that he had embarked upon something so absurd and unnecessary that it brought tears to the eyes. Retired people claimed to be busy, and he suspected that most had become skilful in misleading themselves.

'That phone never stops!' they cried. 'Oh, my God, and now it's the doorbell!'

Anyone could fill the day photographing stations. You could glue matchsticks into long bridges and towering cathedrals, but all that meant was your life was shrinking. His had shrunk into something so small he could hardly see it himself, and whoever penned his eulogy would be hard pressed to write more than two or three sentences. Not that he wanted a eulogy, and not that he wanted to think about it now.

Would the job fall to poor Monica? Perhaps the brother he never saw would feel obliged to come all the way up from Cornwall, if that's where he still was? Perhaps he would take Monica for tea, and they would sort the funeral out together.

'No eulogy. Who's going to be there?'

'We should say something.'

'What?'

'People liked him. In the council, I'm sure they did.'

'I thought they kicked him out years ago. What about the DIY store? That was his last pay packet – did he have any friends there?'

'No.'

The train was rolling backwards again.

He had sold his first house to Monica's son, who was in his early thirties, and a good businessman – Trevor was his name, and he hadn't thought about him for such a long time. Trevor had tried to help him, agreeing to buy Michael's home quickly after he'd got behind on the mortgage payments.

He stared at his knees and remembered how he'd moved back to his mother's, and looked after her until it became impossible. She'd gone into care and the only flat he could afford was on a troubled estate where the council housed those in desperate need. The fences were broken. There was a barking dog, and litter – the litter seemed to have accumulated over years, and it blew listlessly round and round in circles.

Nobody would ever pick it up, so Michael did for a little while. His street was dominated by rows of bins, and the people he saw wore clothes that were fading before his eyes. It was as if his eyesight was getting dim, or failing to register colour. Vivienne, who lived opposite and had the troublesome blind – she was so pale she looked bloodless.

Was it the food, or the lack of exercise, or simply the lack of sun? Was it deeper than that? Was it lack of hope? He was surrounded by the unemployed, unemployable working class that didn't work, and he fitted in so neatly. The broken class, and he'd used the last of his money to buy his very own one-bedroomed box right in its weedy heart.

He should have bought bunting, and cheered it up. He should have bought a second-hand guitar, and filled the world with music. Pots of paint, balloons – flowers and seeds... He could have made it work. Instead, he cowered in his sitting room, moving in with Amy when he knew it was wrong. He chewed the last segment of his last tangerine, remembering how wrong it had been. Amy had encouraged him: she had been truly wonderful, and had he ever really thanked her? No – he had hurt her. The Do It Yourself store had been her idea, because she'd read an article in the local paper saying it was recruiting. She'd given him the confidence to apply, insisting he needed a new start. She'd poured her energy into him, and through her he'd managed to get onto the store's training programme: he would be a sales assistant. No buses went out to the retail park, unfortunately, but that didn't matter because years ago her brother had left a bike in her shed.

'He's forgotten about it, Michael. You can fix it up, and cycle.'

She solved the problem, and he repaired the punctures.

He bought new brake blocks, and found the tools he'd used as a boy: the little round spanner, and three-in-one oil. The ride out was hard, and there was no way of avoiding a major dual carriageway. In the wind and rain it was horrendous, but he got there and completed the course. They gave him tough black shoes with safety soles, and green overalls. They gave him five green T-shirts, and after the council job where he'd always worn a collar and tie he felt like someone in a theme park – 'the elves', they were called.

He really had started again.

The train went over some points, clattering – and nothing mattered, really. Everything was funny, in the end. Someone came by on their way to the toilet, helping a toddler for whom the journey was a wondrous adventure. The child paused in front of Michael and stared at him, seeing what? Some wide-eyed monster, perhaps, like the dead man going endlessly round the Circle line. The child didn't scream, though – she smiled. Her mother urged her onwards, and Michael smiled back and waved his fingers: the child did everything so, so slowly, and savoured everything she saw. She wanted to linger, and perhaps her mother was savouring everything too – the world was new again for her? The Asian woman's rucksack caught the child's attention, and she needed to touch its straps and play with the zip.

'Come on,' said the mother gently. 'That's not yours.'

Michael swallowed his fruit, and fast-forwarded to the realisation that he had become the butt of the younger workers' jokes. Fast-forward to the interview, then, with a team leader accusing him of sexist behaviour because he had made a silly joke of his own and an angry, hassled co-worker had reported him. Rewind to school, where a weak silly joke could earn the derision of the friends you craved, and forward back to the present to discover the same state of affairs existed in a multi-billion-pound DIY empire: Michael, in his green elf-trousers, had misjudged it again.

'Did you call her a silly girl?'

This was said by his team leader – a man in his early twenties called Tim.

'I probably did. Yes.'

He poured himself a small glass of whisky, and smiled again.

'Her contention,' said Tim, 'is that you disrespected her because of her gender. You demeaned her, Mike – and I have to agree.'

'She was being silly, Tim. The joke wasn't offensive.'

'"How many feminists does it take to change a lightbulb? One to change the bulb—"'

'All right, it's a bad joke—'

'"And the other one to say, 'It's not funny.'" That's going to offend some people, Mike.'

Michael smiled, wishing Tim would use his proper name.

'We were telling those kind of jokes,' he said.

'Perhaps you shouldn't have been. And if you have a problem with Sunita, you should come to me.'

'I don't have a problem with anyone.'

'We have procedures to deal with tensions and... disagreements.'

One particular Tuesday he had got embroiled in an argument about Rawlplugs. It was his third month, and things had been going reasonably well, though he was spending less time at Amy's place. His benefit had ended, replaced by his earnings from the store. A minor glitch had delayed the first payment but it didn't matter. He wasn't starving: he knew the bank transfer was imminent. Of course, the weather had got worse, and it was colder than ever cycling to work, but he told himself it was all part of a fitness regime and he was cutting down on the wine, or trying to. The girl he'd called silly was away, learning how to mix paint,

and her friends were studiously ignoring him: all he wanted was
to do his job.

Was that a fiction in itself? Michael looked at the houses,
and then at a swathe of allotments so carefully tended they
made him want his own. The train was slowing down, and
the station seemed for a moment to slide towards them like
stage scenery, and there were the actors in their places. A
couple sat on a bench, as if they weren't on a platform at all
– they could have been relaxing on a pier, gazing out to sea.
Someone was hurrying down the steps of a footbridge and a
neatly dressed woman stood ready to board, tapping something
into her phone.

Did anyone simply want to do their job? That was absurd:
everyone seeks validation, and wants to be useful. He wanted to
be liked, so how had he got into an argument about Rawlplugs?
In fact, he hadn't argued, but it hadn't mattered – it had felt like
a fight.

Perhaps everyone is on a high wire, he thought as he sipped
his drink. Everyone is inching along step by step, trying not to
look down.

'Mate,' said the man. 'Where's *Instafix*?'

'I don't know,' said Michael. 'I don't recognise the name. What
is it exactly?'

'Oh, fuck,' said the man quietly.

He looked at Michael as if he were an idiot.

'*Instafix*,' he said again. 'Like plasiplugs, but better.'

'Are they…?'

Michael faltered.

'What are they for, exactly?'

'Cavity walls,' said the man, as if everyone should know.
'Plasterboard?'

He had a wire basket in his hand, and his wife – or lover – or
sister – or transgender brother – was carrying something from
the garden centre. It was an orchid, and she, they or he held it
in both hands so the wand of the stem swayed in front of their
face, which looked as if it had been crying.

'I think we've got our own brand,' said Michael. 'For cavity walls, I mean.'

'You don't do *Instafix?*'

'I don't recognise the name, but—'

'I thought everyone did it.'

'Let's have a look. If we do, it'll be with the fixings.'

The man was younger than Michael, and his shoulders were huge. The sleeves of his sweatshirt were rolled back to reveal massive, meaty forearms wrapped in bright tattoos. He walked awkwardly because his gigantic thighs forced his legs apart. Michael led him past nails and screws, and they came to a rack holding a variety of brightly coloured packets.

'This is where I was,' said the man. 'I've looked here already.'

'I know we've got something for plasterboard,' said Michael. 'What about these?'

'No good.'

'No?'

Michael had taken a little box from the rack, and looked at the diagram that showed how the contents worked. He put on his reading glasses, which were in the breast pocket of his overalls.

'"Ideal for plasterboard,"' said Michael. 'I used these—'

'You're not listening to me,' said the man. 'There's no point trying to flog me something that won't do the job. I've tried them.'

'You need something bigger?' said Michael. 'What is the job, exactly?'

He was trying to be helpful. He was trying to engage, but the man seemed to find the question intrusive.

'It doesn't matter what the fucking job is,' he said. 'They don't work. They're crap.'

'They do say they're for plasterboard.'

'They don't work.'

'It says here,' said Michael. '"The perfect fix for—"'

'They don't fucking work, mate! This is what you do, isn't it? You sell people over-priced fucking crap, and you don't know what you're talking about. "What's the job?" I told you what I wanted, and you try and sell me some... shit you want to sell me.'

Michael floundered.

'They're for plasterboard,' he said lamely.

'Oh, fuck off,' said the man, turning away – and Michael couldn't think of a reply.

He stood alone in the aisle, flayed, as the couple left him, and he replaced the packet with a hand that had started to shake. He tidied the area a little, though it didn't need tidying – and what he didn't find out until later was that the man had gone straight to the service desk and complained about him. Once again, he found himself sitting with Jo, Tom or Tim – whoever it was this time – having to justify himself, for the accusation now was that he was recommending the wrong item and had been patronising.

'I thought it was the right item,' he said.

'Well, you have to be very careful,' said Jo or Tim – who clearly didn't want him on the team any more. 'If you're in any doubt, call one of the guys and get a second opinion. Graeme's good. He knows a lot about fixings.'

Yes, he did – Graeme knew everything about fixings, and called Michael 'Mikey'. Michael had spoken to Graeme several times, and the impression he'd always got was that Graeme knew a lot about every item in the store, because he was one of those men who did every job in his own house, by himself, with infinite patience and total success. He had a soft Scottish accent, and a habit of looking at your toes before his eyes travelled slowly up to your chin, as if he was assessing your weight for a hanging. If they had to do something together, like yard work or unloading, Graeme would always encourage him.

'Try to get under it, Mikey,' he'd say. 'Oh, no, *no* – hold the edge. To you, a little. Turn it! *Oh...*'

He always seemed disappointed. Sometimes he operated the big power-saw in the special cutting booth, and he did it so carefully. He'd been trained to slice sheets of chipboard, and Michael nurtured a guilty hope that one day there would be an accident, and he'd have the pleasure of picking up Graeme's severed hand.

'Is this yours, Graeme?' he'd say. 'Where do you want it?'

Why would he ever call upon a man like Graeme? And as for the big man who'd wanted *Instafix*, Michael wondered what he'd done to upset him, really? All he'd wanted was to help. Of course, it occurred to him that the man might have received bad news moments before their encounter, or been in the middle of the worst confrontation with his wet-eyed partner, or lost a vast sum of money, or a chance of promotion – or a baby, even... there were a hundred thousand things that could collapse and make you yearn to stabilise yourself by lashing out at a random stranger.

Still, it hurt – and he was still mouthing the man's words, here on the train.

It hurt as he cycled home, and it hurt more because he felt so foolish for being hurt. What should he have said? What *shouldn't* he have said? Or was the root of the problem simply his idiot, irritating face that invited abuse? Should he go to work in a mask, and speak through a tube?

They changed his shifts the next week.

They didn't consult him: suddenly he was on six-thirty starts. Suddenly he only had thirty hours instead of the thirty-eight he needed. The next week it was twenty-six: just over two hundred pounds for the week, with so many debts to service. The spores of poverty, there on your fading clothes.

Work in a pub: bar staff required.

Work in a café.

Work from home, on the telephone, perhaps? It just didn't matter now, but he had tried. Deliver newspapers. Deliver leaflets. Stop people in the street and get their views on particular products. Work with children, work with the sick – you seemed to need years of experience to do either of those things, but cleaning pubs and houses? That kind of job was easy enough to find. He was offered work by a firm called Mina's Cleaners, and the manageress contracted him to spend two hours cleaning a pub six miles from where he lived, starting at half past five so he could get to another – three miles beyond – at quarter to eight. Four hours' work would bring in just under forty pounds, and if he did it every day that would double his income *if* he could persuade the DIY store to give him shifts that started at eleven.

Jo was away, so the acting team leader – that was Tim or Tom again – changed things in Michael's favour. So began a week of cleaning and... it didn't matter.

It just didn't matter, but why did people use toilets so that their excrement smeared the entire bowl and seat? How did vomit get on walls, behind the pipes? Why did the pub have so much brass to polish, and why was the hoover so lacking in suction even after he'd emptied it and checked every single joint?

One of the pub managers phoned Mina.

'I don't think he's been in,' he said. 'It's a bloody mess.'

Mina relayed this faithfully, and Michael explained that he had been in, and he'd spent two hours doing his job as the land-lord slept upstairs. Yes, he'd missed the brass plaques on some of the doors, but only because the women's toilets had been particu-larly foul, and someone had moved the mop. He'd given up hunting for that, and cleaned the floors on his hands and knees, but the landlord thought he hadn't been in – or that's what he claimed, because he resented paying Mina her commission and wanted a confrontation. Michael was thus sucked into another world of anger and accusation, but this one had real shit and sick – and when Jo returned she put him straight back on early mornings.

'I can't do them,' said Michael.

'You've got to be flexible,' said Jo.

'I have another job,' said Michael.

'Everyone wants to avoid the early shifts,' said Jo. 'You have to do your bit—'

'But I'm getting too many.'

'You're getting no more than anyone else.'

'That's not how it feels.'

'That's how it is, Mike. That's the truth. If you can't do early mornings, you can't be on the team.'

The team. Last one to be picked, and first to be let go. He couldn't vault the horse, and he couldn't even dive off a platform in front of something as huge as a train, or sort himself out at Crewe – so Mina paid him, deducting money for an insurance scheme he hadn't known about. And it just didn't matter – for the world is a beautiful place, and the woods and fields spread to the horizon getting ready for sunset, so you must not let yourself be dragged down by small-minded people. The whisky was so full of old oak, and you had to rise above calamity as you crept back into your flat and listened to someone else's TV through the floor and the sound of their hacking cough. You could try, couldn't you? You could reach out, perhaps, and offer cough medicine, forcing a friendship out of that. One day he hadn't turned up at the DIY store, and the next day he was late.

Then he went in and sat for too long in the rest area.

Then he took too long to stack the fence-posts.

Then he ignored someone.

It was the only way he could fight back, and meanwhile he had gone for a Health MOT and dismantled a wedding, and could they have married, really? It had seemed like just another fantasy, which is why he drifted into it and had finally woken up.

The station they'd arrived at was busy, and the carriage started to fill up even as he wondered if he'd got the sequence of events wrong, and perhaps the fence-post incident had been before his long stint in the rest area, for he was too close to tears. A young girl sat next to him, and when he went to speak she thought better of it – perhaps she had spotted a more comfortable seat, or she smelled liquor… Michael doubted that, because his juice carton was back in his bag, and he'd just started another mint. Now he was somewhere else, and there was a great big mosque that looked grand, gold and new.

Another child peered at him through the gap in the seats in front, and someone nearby spoke at length to a person in the office querying a detail about a drawing which Michael had no choice but to try to follow, because it seemed to involve the distance from the eaves of the roof to the top step and whether or not the distance could be legally decreased. Perhaps phone reception was bad, because the man spoke with exceptional clarity:

'No, no,' he said. 'Take a look at BS1319. 1.3.1... What? No, what does it say? No, look at what's in parentheses...'

He wouldn't ever reach Glasgow, let alone the Highlands – that was most definitely off now, because this train wasn't going to either. Where would he get off? If he got down at the next stop, he could probably make it home – but home wasn't home, which didn't matter because... He was luckier than many. Once again, the train was slowing down – had he gone to sleep? The fields had been ploughed up and turned into scrapyards – they were going backwards past a lorry park, where drivers had abandoned dozens of long containers. Haphazard wire fencing had been strung all around them, and the brambles were thriving. Over a bridge they went – over an inky canal, too narrow now for barge traffic. Soon they were amongst carpet warehouses and factory outlet stores, and there were no people to be seen. There were jaunty flags, though, and banners advertising sales: this was his country. This was the country he'd learned to navigate, and was lucky to live in.

His parents had set him on his feet, to toddle into this future.

When they came to the next station, he saw it was busier than the last, and he at once saw Amy with a pushchair, and Ryan from the flat below. There was a girl who resembled his next-door neighbour from childhood, and the old woman could have been his poor, dead mother so he closed his eyes and tried to breathe through his mouth. The guard told everyone to remove luggage from seats, pointing out that a cancelled train had made this one extra busy. He apologised for that. He was sorry, because he knew everyone's journey was being inconvenienced – but he was powerless. What could he do? He sounded like a nice young man, who genuinely cared – if he'd had the power to pull a few extra carriages from the sidings and bolt them on, he would have done so. His Northern voice was polite and genuine: Michael knew that if he communicated all his problems to such a man, the man would listen. He'd clasp his shoulder, and say with absolute sincerity, 'Let me get you a form, Mike. Do you have access to a computer, Micky? Because you might find it easier to go through our website. You can get up to half your money back, Michael, sir – Sir Michael – if you just lay your burden down.'

Michael smiled.

A man in a brown kurta sat down next to him, studiously avoiding eye contact, his beard and dress announcing the fact that he was Muslim. He had fat, hairy fingers which he used to hold his thighs.

'Busy,' said Michael.

'So busy,' replied the man softly.

Silence. On they went, backwards. He wanted to hold this man's hand – it was so much bigger than his own.

'They cancelled a train,' he said – his voice working almost normally, except that it had a rasp he didn't recognise.

'Every week they cancel trains,' said the man. 'I take this train on this day, at this time, every single week. Most times, I don't get a seat.'

He laughed to himself, and Michael looked at him wondering for the hundredth time about the significance of beards, and why God wanted people to grow them. If it was a badge of virility, that seemed primitive. If it was homage to the prophet, or simply a gesture that said, 'I believe in this particular nonsense...' surely both were good, sound impulses that connected you to an almost infinite number of people with similar needs?

It was the beard of a patriarch: a triumphant beard, grey as a squirrel.

'They take my money,' said the man. 'I say, "Please give me a seat. Can I not expect a seat?" "Sorry," they say. "We have had to cancel a train, or... some other service is running late, or slow – there is overcrowding today. So sorry."'

He shook his head.

'"We do not guarantee you a seat,"' he said. 'That's what they said to me once. "We cannot guarantee seats." "Can you guarantee air?" I said. "Can you guarantee we will not suffocate?"'

He laughed.

'You know, this train should not be stopping.'

'Stopping where?' said Michael.

'Anywhere. This was the non-stop service, but they turn it into the stopping service. You cannot make timely progress, because of me.'

'I'm sorry, I'm not sure—'

'This is the stopping service now. We will stop everywhere.'

'Right.'

A silence fell.

'Are you going far then?' said Michael.

'No,' said the man. 'Only to the next station. Where are you going?'

'All the way. North.'

'North where?'

'Newcastle.'

The man laughed.

'That's a long way.'

'A couple of hours, I think.'

'And what will you do in Newcastle? You have family there?'

'No. I'm just... doing a bit of business. Then home again. South.'

'Very long way,' repeated the man, laughing again. 'I go to my father's house, just fifteen minutes. Back again, to and fro – I'm a taxi driver.'

'Really?'

'Twelve years. Before that, a foundry. That is what my father did also.'

'Where are you from, originally?'

'Pakistan.'

Michael nodded.

'That's somewhere I would love to go.'

'Then go you must. What is to stop you?'

'Oh...'

'Go tomorrow.'

Michael laughed and the man laughed.

'There's nothing, in some ways,' said Michael. 'But – I don't know. Fear of getting lost, perhaps, and... not knowing the language.'

'You don't speak the language?'

'No—'

'Why is that a problem? You will find, everywhere you go, everyone speaks English. And *wants* to speak English. You will be very popular! People will queue up to practise their English with a real English gentleman.'

'Do you go back?' said Michael.

'Of course. Every two years.'

'Good.'

'The most beautiful country in the world. Apart from this one.'

He turned suddenly, and smiled.

'Go, my friend – please. Before you die.'

19

Michael wanted to be silent, but the man was staring at him as if waiting for the next question.

The smile slowly faded, and he looked away. As for the train, it had found another bridge, and this one took them past factories and factory yards. Most seemed to have closed, but it was hard to say for some had the occasional vehicle outside. The sun really would be setting soon, and they passed a great stack of tyres.

'We lived in a very rural part of the country,' said the man, not needing the question after all. 'My father's house. Very large house, with a lot of land. He was a wealthy man.'

'Why did he come to England?'

'I don't know.'

The man laughed.

'We ask him that question, my brother and me. He came when I was ten years old, my brother was eight. "Why did you bring us here, Daddy?" That is always the question. He was rich, but there was no money, and the farm was very poor. He took a job in the foundry and two weeks ago... he died.'

'He died?'

'Ninety-three years old. He died in the hospital.'

'I'm sorry.'

'Now we have to go back, of course – to have the memorial. We bury him here, but the memorial will be a very big programme, near Lahore.'

'You have a big family?'

'Me? I do, yes. My father had just two boys. I have five. Two girls, five boys.'

'That's a lot of mouths to feed,' said Michael. 'How old are they?'

'My oldest is twenty-eight. My youngest is at school, still. Sixteen.'

Michael found himself nodding.

He knew very little about Islam, but all his expectations were being confirmed, and he wondered how he could ever penetrate such an extraordinary culture. He would be asking questions for ever. Why this? Why that? The man spoke good English, but Michael presumed he spoke his own language at home, and was no doubt more eloquent and comfortable speaking it.

'You grew up in Pakistan,' he said.

'On the farm, yes,' replied the man.

He laughed.

'My brother and I, and our friends. We would set off early in the morning with a little food. My mother would not see us again until sundown. That was in the holiday, that was... if we had no chores. Playing all day. Swimming. Walking. Climbing.'

'Fighting?'

'Fighting? No. Yes. Sometimes – I don't know.'

They sat in silence again, and Michael pondered the things he was curious about. He had heard that Muslim boys and girls were required to commit large sections of the Koran to memory, and he wondered why. Was the book like a manual, offering advice when you faced a moral question? Or was it simply a demonstration of love for the text? Were the children working from the original, in Arabic? If so, there was even less hope for him, because he'd have to learn a whole new alphabet. He'd have to read from right to left, too, which would turn him into a child again, unable even to decipher letters – sounding out syllables that had no meaning. He could kneel and stand, and put out his arms, but he would never be part of it, so Islam would not save him. The man would soon become impatient with his stumbling misunderstandings, and Michael would be alone. Physically, the man was very big, and his laugh was surprisingly merry. It had a teasing quality, and Michael could imagine him telling filthy jokes, which didn't quite square with a religion that always seemed so serious, with strict disciplines and unsmiling faces. This man was a version of Steve from the council – the volunteer fireman – but without the malice. Both were men of total, terrifying certainty.

Prayers, and the rituals that went with prayer. The washing of hands, the removal of shoes, and the sheer organisation of a mosque – of so many people in rows, with the women on one side and the men on the other. Days punctuated by prayer at specific times, the closeness to God marked every few hours – by dress, by gesture, by food, by language and most of all by day-to-day conduct.

Michael found himself yearning for such a life. Paradise might be waiting, if he could only join this man's team.

'Why are you going to your father's house?' he said.

What an absurd question.

'Today?' said the man.

'Yes.'

'Oh, everyone is there. Everyone has come, and I think there are more than seventy people.'

'A meeting, then? Seventy people in your house.'

'More. Many people came from Pakistan, you see. To see him – or his body, I should say.'

He laughed.

'At the hospital, you know – the nurses did not need even to touch him.'

'In what sense?'

'Mmm? To feed him.'

'What, you had family to do that?'

'To wash him, yes. To clothe him. To help him. To nurse him. The nurses... they did not need to do anything, even at the end. It was his family who helped him to pass, and prepared him and... we did everything. He was never alone, and that made him very, very happy.'

The man said goodbye as they came into Accrington, and Michael watched him step off the train and walk down the platform. Suddenly he was out of sight and Michael knew then that he should have followed him – he had missed his chance to talk to a prophet. As the train moved off, he was in silly, stupid tears again, and he got to his feet. The peel from his tangerine fell onto the floor, and he dried his eyes as they left the station, just as the sun turned red and flashed in his face. He gazed backwards, hoping for a last glimpse – but the bend of the carriages made it impossible, and they were balanced on the most colossal viaduct, teetering high over a glorious town. Should he press the alarm?

'I need to get down!' he would cry. 'I need God!'

The train wouldn't stop, and if it did they wouldn't let him jump down onto the tracks and run back to the platform. In any case, it would be too far now. He'd be detained by officials or even arrested – and how would he get back to anywhere and leap in front of anything, ever? He stood helplessly, and the windows were all too small. He couldn't get his head out now, and smash it into a concrete post, and in any case a pre-recorded voice was soon shrill in his ears: Burnley or Manchester was the next station, Manchester Road? It was the next station-stop, and there were people on the train who wanted to get down at that place, too. There were more people, determined to carry on with their lives here on another random stretch of greyness, with Accrington long gone. The Asian woman, for example: she was on her feet, putting away a tablet. There was no hesitation, for she was one of the great army of people who knew her destination. He stood aside to let her pass, and watched her pick up the rucksack. She stepped off the train with it, even as a jogger came through the park in Birmingham, and passed an empty bench. Semi-conscious Morris had been flung into the undergrowth nearby, and she spotted him.

She called the police.

Ayesha, meanwhile, was with her parents, hoping they wouldn't object to her opening a bottle of wine – and poor Morris was too weak to speak, and couldn't see because of the blood in his eyes. Michael could see, and he saw that the platform they'd arrived at had no barriers: you exited through the ticket office, and its glass doors were wide open, the rucksack passing through.

He watched it, for it spoke of open countryside and fine, healthy hill-walking. This was Lancashire, and he had a notion that just beyond these towns there were wide moors. He stepped forward, wondering if now was the moment to break free: the rucksack was disappearing just like the Muslim man, and he had nothing in his head at all. The station was more forlorn and anonymous than any station he had ever visited. Its chilly, concrete blankness seemed extra-specially brutal in this particular light, but there were still a few seconds left to him before the train doors closed. Why Burnley? Why this place, when there were so many others? Even as he stepped back, he heard the warning bleep, and why he changed his mind again he did not know. He dived forward, and the doors caught him in their jaws. For a moment, he was stuck and crushed – but they opened almost at once, releasing him. Out he fell, stumbling with his bag, and there was nothing in his head worth having – how he longed to empty it, once and for all. He steadied himself, and just stayed upright. He looked around for the rucksack but it had floated away, leaving him alone again.

He turned, to reboard the train.

The doors closed in his face this time, and the train was a sealed unit, moving out.

The passengers who'd seen him stumble were staring at him, positive now that he was drunk. He glimpsed himself in a variety of windows, gazing back as he raised his hand to wave as usual, to nobody and nothing. His own image waved happily back. The train departed, and he was left looking at a length of track that was streaked in red. The sun was red, and the signal was red, too. His hand was in the air, and his fingers were splayed out wide – so he lowered his arm and put the hand into his pocket.

OS GRID REF:
SD837321 TO SD299810

20

Maria didn't notice him.

She showed her ticket, but the inspector hardly glanced at it, and when Michael came through the man turned his back completely – not out of rudeness, but because something was flashing on his screen. The station concourse was very small, and two pensioners waited in silence while a handful of other people fanned out across the car park. Maria stood still with her rucksack, checking a piece of paper.

She crossed to the other side of the road, where there were two shelters. At the second, a bus was waiting – Michael saw her and followed. He watched her speak to the driver, and once she'd bought her ticket he backed away. Then he changed his mind and approached.

'I've forgotten where this bus goes,' he said.

'Oh,' said the driver. 'Where are you going, sir?'

'I'm going all the way, but—'

'To Bacup?'

'That's your final stop?'

'Bacup is, yes.'

He pondered a moment, struggling to breathe.

'Good,' he said, climbing on board. 'Could I have a single to Bacup, please?'

If the driver was surprised by Michael's nervous uncertainty, she didn't show it. She pressed a few digits on the ticket machine and told him the fare. He produced his second twenty-pound note – still so clean and pure – and she didn't grumble as she hunted for the change. She counted the coins carefully, and when she handed him the notes she actually smiled at him. For a moment he wondered who would be getting her children's tea, for it was after seven o'clock and she looked like a mother. If her husband was out of work, perhaps he was doing the cooking? He hauled his mind back to the moment, and said, 'How long's the journey?'

'We get into Bacup at about ten past eight.'

She spoke slowly.

'When do you start? Have I time to do something?'

'To do what, my love?'

'To find a shop.'

'No.'

'Oh.'

Michael smiled.

'So you were waiting for the train?'

'We connect with the train, yes.'

'I'd better get out of the way then. I'll make us all late.'

She laughed, and he was grateful. She had heard what he said and even acknowledged its casual merriment – she liked him. The engine was on, but Michael noticed that she didn't pull away until he was actually seated: she waited as he chose a place at the back of the bus, and he could feel her giving him time to settle safely. There were only five other passengers, three of them travelling alone. The other two were teenagers, who were sharing a pair of headphones. There was an elderly man, a middle-aged woman and the backpacker, who'd now found a space for her rucksack and seemed to be checking her paperwork again. She was holding it close to her face.

The doors had closed, and he didn't know where he was going.

They eased gently away from the kerb, and the next moment the driver was heaving the vehicle carefully over the railway tracks, determined not to jolt her precious load. The tracks stretched left and right to vanishing point – and Michael had time to look in both directions, and see the width of his new world. He was on his way to Bacup, but he'd never heard of it. A road sign mentioned Burnley Town Centre, but they were going in the opposite direction, uphill, and they were soon on some kind of ring road, or bypass. There was a lot of traffic, but they seemed to switch lanes effortlessly and suddenly they had taken a turning at random and were spinning off to the right, past an old mill. This was where the dark, satanic mills had stood, of course – for this was England's pleasant land. The houses were dropping away now, and they were moving out of the town.

He was totally lost, and the red sun was caught in a web of bare, black trees. It was unable to stop sinking, and he could see dry-stone walls overgrown with thorn hedges, and the fields seemed surprisingly small. Some contained sheep – the grass sloped upwards, and he glimpsed the occasional farmhouse. They passed a telephone box, and a pub that wasn't open yet – if it was going to open at all, for it had an abandoned look.

They picked up another passenger, who knew the driver well enough to exchange quick, interested enquiries – and once again the bus didn't move until the newcomer was seated. The driver checked her mirror and wasn't in a hurry: it was more important to ensure nobody got hurt. At once, the road turned back on itself, and they were climbing even higher. He caught views of wide skies, and the sun's rays had reached that point when they painted layers of cloud: there were ridges of deep pink, so part of the sky was deeply furrowed and even bloody. The driver found a lower gear and took them to a hilltop, and suddenly the culti-vated land fell away and they were out on the wildest of moors – just as he'd predicted. Michael realised he had crossed a border into sheer wilderness. They were driving into wilderness, and the light was fading quickly – even as he watched, the clouds above were losing that bright, dramatic red as if the batteries were dying. The day was draining away into darkness.

He would be abandoned in some tiny town.

He would find a pub, and take a room, perhaps. If that wasn't possible – and why would it be, out in the wilderness? – he'd have to sit in a bus shelter and wait for that same sun to do its business elsewhere and rise again. It would rise, and it would rise on him if he let it. Of course, the bus he was on might simply turn round, and it could take him all the way back to the station they'd just left – in which case he'd be at Burnley Manchester Road again, retracing his steps to the opposite platform so as to

catch another train south or west. He'd buy a ticket with a card
that couldn't last much longer – or perhaps he'd try to dodge the
fare. In fact, he'd enjoy being caught doing that, because he'd
relish the attention.

'I'll need a name and address, sir.'

'Of course you will,' he'd say. 'I'm sorry. I'm just… caught
short, so to speak.'

'What I'll have to do, sir, is put down that I issued a penalty
fare and you couldn't pay it as of now. So what will happen is
the company will write to you, and make arrangements for
payment.'

Could he give a false address?

They'd be wise to that kind of ruse. If he had nothing with
which to identify himself, perhaps the transport police would
appear? Too busy to investigate lewd graffiti, they would be
there for his misdemeanour, ready at the next station – ready
to take him into an office and treat him with the infinite
patience of those who knew what to do when a man had no
money.

But at what point did things become menacing?

He would have to raise his voice and insult them. Perhaps if
he'd finished the whisky he might manage to be unreasonable?
He might throw a punch and shout, 'God is great!' – then everything would change. How long before you found yourself sitting
bruised and cuffed on a metal bed, your shoelaces gone? You'd
sit, knowing there was nobody coming to claim you. No mother
to sigh with disappointment, and no wife or brother or son – no
partner, even.

No Monica, no Amy. Absolutely no Elizabeth.

He would be like a piece of left luggage that nobody was
looking for.

Michael smiled, for self-pity was never far away. It had rolled
in again, straight off the moors – the mist came down and left
you staring through the bus window at the reflection that followed
you round the world: your own, foolish face mouthing the words,
'So what?' And as he met his own eyes again, he didn't want the

journey to end. The world was getting so much more dangerous, and the black rocks were getting spiky and dramatic, rearing up in the dusk – there was a soft booming sound, too, and he realised it was the wind. You hardly heard it on the train, but out here the driver had to sail her bus hard into a gale that tugged and heaved.

He heard the ticking of the indicator, and she pulled into a layby.

Nobody was waiting to board, but the two teenagers were getting off – and they also knew the driver, and said goodnight to her. The light was all but gone, and Michael craned his head round as the bus set off again – and they weren't in a village. He hadn't noticed so much as a house, and yet that was the destination for the two teenagers. They were farmer's children, perhaps, used to a bracing walk in the dark – they'd been doing it for years, and could have done it blindfold, over the cattle-grid into the farmyard, the sheepdogs barking in joyful welcome and the warm yellow lamp in the kitchen blazing like a beacon.

Bread in the oven, and a broth warming on the hob. A newborn lamb in the farmer's arms – an extraordinarily late birth, admittedly. He'd be trying to feed it milk from a bottle, and the youngest boy – a child of seven, perhaps, in his pyjamas – would be sitting close, knowing he now had a special pet which would follow him everywhere.

'You two!' said the farmer's wife, in a broad Northern accent. 'You must be right frozen. Sit down, there's tea in't pot.'

'Saw a stranger on't bus, Ma,' said the girl.

The accents were getting broader.

'A stranger, eh? A stranger on't bus?'

'He weren't a walker, because he had nowt wi' him. Just a little bag, really.'

'Was he wearing boots?'

'No, Ma. Shoes. He was all on his own as well, starin' out at nothin'.'

On they went, and he was breathing quickly again.

If he got down at the next stop, he could simply walk onto the moors until he was too tired to go on. He could drink the rest of the whisky, and stagger another half-mile – but would he die of exposure? This was hardly the South Pole where a man could tramp heroically out into oblivion. In a snowstorm, the deadly cold tricked you into feeling warm and sleepy – that's what he'd read. The danger zone was when you wanted to sit down and rest for a moment, for you'd never get up again. He had heard about a woman in the wilds of America who'd parked her car because she needed to relieve herself, and headed into the woods to find privacy. Rangers found her body months later, and deduced that she'd stood up, lost her bearings and gone the wrong way. She never found her car, for the disorientation had got worse and she'd wandered further and further from it. She hadn't plunged down a ravine or been attacked by bears; she'd simply got weaker, and more dehydrated... And she'd had time to write a note of farewell and surrender. The rangers found her curled up under a tree, and she hadn't wanted to die as he did – if he really did. Because he did, but he couldn't – so maybe he wouldn't. He could not take the plunge, and yet he knew he had to try, because the options had so clearly run out and it was the one item left on his particular menu. It was the chef's special, and the waiter had recommended it. There would be a waiter talking to Percy's grandparents right now, in the bistro of that beautiful Yorkshire town. They would be choosing their wine, while he moved further and further into nowhere.

Michael closed his eyes to erase the scene, and when he opened them again he saw that the rucksack was moving. The bus driver had stopped again.

'You're sure?' said the Asian woman.

She sounded anxious.

The engine was still running, and the indicator was ticking. The light had gone, so the bus seemed to have come to rest in a black box.

'It's down some steps,' said the driver. 'You'll see it.'

The hiker laughed.

'I can't see anything!' she said, and the driver laughed too.

Michael stood up as the doors opened, and hurried to the front. The rucksack was disappearing, and Michael watched it go.

'Is this you too?' said the driver.

He nearly said, 'No. Sorry.' The words were on his lips, for to get off the bus was suddenly a momentous, irreversible decision: there would not be another. On the other hand, he could make out walls, and he could see a parked car.

'I think it is,' he said brightly. 'Thanks ever so much.'

'This isn't Bacup, love.'

'No, that's fine – this is good for me. Have a nice evening.'

'You too.'

'Drive carefully!'

'Oh, I'll try to.'

He couldn't prolong that little burst. The driver had to close the doors and continue: she had her other passengers to think about, and a schedule.

'Oh! What time is the next bus?' That would have been a forgivable extension, and might have given him the moment he needed to change his mind.

He didn't think of it in time, though, and the doors were closing. The handbrake grated, and the wheels crunched over loose stones. The bus became a yellow lantern, and he watched it slalom carefully through what must be a small village. He watched it disappear and reappear. It climbed up the same road, but its headlights were dimming and then suddenly – as if the world wasn't round at all – it reached an edge and tipped itself into oblivion.

He – Michael – walked forward.

There were a dozen houses at the most, though there may have been more down hidden lanes. Some of the front windows were illuminated, but there wasn't a single street light. The wind now buffeted him, as it had done the vehicle, and his waterproof was no protection: he was instantly, violently cold.

He retraced his steps, and explored the other way. Overhead was a great spray of stars, but no moon. There were steps to his right, which the driver had referred to – they took him to an abrupt corner and another, steeper flight down. Seconds later, he was at the bottom, in a car park. There was a sign, lit up by two weak bulbs: *The Golden Fleece*, it said. *Welcome*.

21

Maria checked in quickly.

Her reservation was entirely in order, and the manager had kept a table for her in the bar. They stopped serving food at nine-thirty, so she had time to freshen up – it wasn't quite eight o'clock. No, she didn't need help, and she could manage her own bag. Within a few minutes the door was locked and she was sitting on the bed.

Single rooms were always a little sad, but she had a ritual to ward off that sadness: she opened the handbag she'd lost, and removed her wallet. Inside was a small concertina-shaped photo book, and the next moment the room was full: her husband, children and parents were in front of her. They looked up, and she said their names quietly. There was no disapproval or recrimination: there was only the simple reminder that whilst she felt so far away, they were even further. Nothing stood between them but time and temporary distance. She said a prayer, and thought about the woman she'd met in Preston whose name she had already forgotten – she said a prayer for her, too.

She put her tablet and phone on charge, and then she unpacked.

The shower was weak but welcome. She turned the television on, just to hear voices, and got ready to go downstairs again. She didn't hear Michael as he walked along the landing, past her door.

He had entered the pub, wondering what to do.

The bar wasn't crowded, and nor was the restaurant area. He was in a new state of uncertainty, though, because nobody could expect a room in a place like this if they hadn't booked one in advance. People didn't walk into hotels any more: they planned their journeys. He would be met with suspicion and rejection, and he couldn't face inventing some story about a broken-down car. He knew what he looked like: he looked desperate.

The pub would not welcome him.

He was about to turn around and leave when the receptionist arrived.

'Hello,' he said. 'How are you tonight?'

Michael saw a frank, friendly face. The man looked busy, without being rushed or hassled, and he was looking into Michael's eyes as if he saw only a normal, harmless customer.

Michael licked his lips, realising he was actually frightened.

'Good evening,' he said. 'I'm fine, thank you. But... I'm in a bit of an awkward situation.'

'How can I help?'

If anything, the man was concerned.

'I need a room, please. For tonight.'

'That's easy. Just tonight?'

'Yes, please.'

'Because tomorrow we're chock-a-block, one of those walking parties, but tonight... I'll double-check.'

He had turned away. He was looking at a computer screen.

'Tonight, you're in luck. Single or double, sir?'

'Single, please.'

'Room twelve. It's one of the nicest rooms we have, I think. It's a double, but I don't think that matters – we can upgrade you.'

He clicked the mouse.

'Bed and breakfast is eighty-five, and I can cancel the supplement. Dinner as well? That's one hundred and four.'

'I think I'll go for bed and breakfast.'

'Not a problem. Have you stayed with us before?'

'No.'

'Then if I could trouble you to fill in the card – your name, phone number. Are you parked in the car park?'

'I came by bus, actually.'

'Oh.'

The man was surprised, but there was still no suspicion or fear. Why should there be? Perhaps people's plans did change just like that, and this was more common than Michael had thought.

'What time would you like your breakfast?' said the man.

'Seven-thirty, please.'

'Seven-thirty.'

Michael took his wallet out. He had one twenty-pound note left, plus all the change from his fare – clearly, the credit card would have to work its magic. He watched its progress as it was slotted into the payment machine, feeling deep in his bones that this would be the moment of terrible truth, when everything would grind to a halt. The smiles were about to fade, and the trust would evaporate.

'I need a *valid* card, sir.'

'Of course. Could you try that one again, please?'

'I can try it, certainly.'

The man's voice would drop in register, and the 'sir' would seem just a little ironic. Two beads of sweat rolled down from Michael's armpits, but he tapped in his personal number, and after the hesitation and consideration, the card was approved. The debt must be four figures by now, but the payment went flying through as if the cash was on the counter, and the man tore the receipts out with a flourish. Suddenly – magically – there was an old-fashioned key on the desk, attached to a wooden fob.

'I'll just fill in the form,' said Michael.

'Or you can do it in the bar, if you want a drink.'

'I think I'll... do it here, and come down for a drink later.'

'Very good. Can I leave you to it for a moment? The room's up the stairs, turn right. Everything's signed, and... will you need a hand with luggage, or...?'

He had realised the guest had nothing, apart from his shoulder bag – and what was in that?

'I'm fine,' said Michael. 'Like I say, I'm travelling light.'

The man replied, 'If you need anything, like a toothbrush – or a razor... There'll be someone on call right through the night.'

'Thank you.'

'See you later.'

Michael reached his room, and sat on the bed.

It was larger than the bedroom in his flat. The bed was big, and the pillows stood fresh and white beneath a bright cushion that matched the curtains. There was a little dressing table or writing desk, but half of that was given over to a television set. The other end was dominated by a kettle, with tea, coffee and biscuits in a jar. There was a chest of drawers, and over it a painting of a woodpecker. Everything was clean, and he thought how unfair it would be to die here – it would be even more unfair than under the gaze of a poor train driver. But the man at reception had offered a razor, and it was conceivable – if he asked for one – that he might dismantle it for the skinny blade. Was that not expected of him? A seasoned spy would take it apart in an instant, and slash away with the little shard of super-sharp metal: the veins could be open in seconds, if you'd had the training. But to do that here, where the bedcover was so pale, and the carpet so carefully hoovered – it would be monstrously rude.

When he'd worked as a cleaner he'd come upon ingrained dirt: the dirt of filthy shoes and filthy habits. Spillages, and the daily dropping of food that got ground into the fabric – no time to clean up properly, and no will to do so either. Let people drink in their own mess. This place, in contrast, was loved. Perhaps the cleaner was the owner, and his or her personal pride went into every careful stroke of the duster. How would he or she feel when the moment came? The guest in room twelve still hadn't appeared, and the gentle knocks on the door still hadn't roused him.

'Was he by himself?'

'Yes. Came by bus, or so he said. Said his plans had changed.'

'Knock again.'

It would be way past checkout time, so they might suppose he'd disappeared as mysteriously as he'd arrived – they would have to look.

Michael sat with his eyes closed.

The manager would bring a duplicate key. What if Michael had left his own in the lock, so he couldn't get it in? That would cause terrible inconvenience. The hotel staff would have to find a ladder, and put it up to the window, and if the curtains were undrawn they might see evidence of his presence, and realise he definitely hadn't left. They would knock again, more loudly, and at last the decision would be made: they would have to drag the poor locksmith out, all the way from the nearest town. Ten minutes would pass as he jiggled Michael's key onto the floor – no need to break down doors, this wasn't an arrest. This was simply gaining access with a rising sense of dread, for everyone now knew the guest wasn't sleeping, or wearing headphones. No: there was a dead man awaiting them, and the only uncertainty was what state he might be in.

In the bath, up to his nose in cold, red water?

Or does the water drain over ten hours, through a leaky plug? Who would pull him out, and how? What equipment could they bring to prevent the crazy comedy of his corpse slithering out of the tub and slapping the lino?

He put his head in his hands, but the thoughts uncoiled.

'Stop the film,' he wanted to say – but now he was remembering an old friend or acquaintance… someone he'd got chatting to, perhaps? She'd worked in the Salvation Army, and he recalled the lovely, serious slogan, *Where there is need, there is the Salvation Army*. Utterly devout, utterly committed – she had been summoned to places once the police and fire brigade had left the scene. She had been trained to break bones – to break arms and legs – so as to get corpses into body bags. That's what she told him, because he had asked about her nights on call, and pumped her for the details.

'What do you do? What have you seen?'

She told him. The body in the bed grew stiff and couldn't be moved. If there was nothing suspicious about the death, that was part of her job: to break it down. She had broken limbs across her knee.

He found that his eyes were closed tighter than ever, so he opened them. He slowed his breathing down, and filled the kettle. As he waited for it to boil, he cleaned his glasses and ate two biscuits. Then he washed his face and had a cup of coffee. He felt glad then, that he was alive and in such a pretty room. He felt ashamed, too, for bringing such horror into it. He felt like opening a window, but instead he got undressed and had a shower.

'Stop it,' he said. 'Stop thinking.'

He started to sing, very quietly:

'And did those feet...'

He stopped, wondering where the old hymn had come from, and how it came to be buried so deep.

'And did those feet. In ancient times. Walk upon England's pastures green?'

He paused, and tried the next part.

'And did the holy. Lamb of God. On all our pleasant pastures... seem?'

They weren't the right words, but the tune would never leave him. In the absence of a school song, 'Jerusalem' had been used in every end-of-term assembly, roared out by eight hundred boys, the music teacher hammering at a piano. Never had he pondered the meaning of the song's questions and demands, but they were there in his brain and on his lips – the singer wanted a bow of burning gold for some reason, and arrows of desire. He was calling for a sword, and then not just a chariot, but a chariot of fire, knowing that the clouds had to burst open at some point so Jerusalem could rise. It would rise here, of course, right next to this hotel.

He stood, lost in thought.

He made the water colder, and that increased the power of the shower jet. He sang more loudly, repeating phrases as he sluiced himself down, and when he stepped back into the room wet, dripping and white, he was surprised at how quiet it was. Everything around him was beautifully still, and he smiled because nobody had been hurt, and no one had died. At five to nine, he went downstairs and ordered a glass of wine, for which he paid in cash. The backpacker was there, at a table on her own. She was studying a map but she looked up at him suddenly, and he knew at once that she recognised him.

He saw the surprise, and then a flash of unmistakable fear.

'Hello,' she said.

'Hi.'

It was quiet in the bar, and she knew he'd followed her. There was music, but it was soft and he found there was nothing he could say – so they simply looked at each other.

22

'How are you?' he said at last.

'Good, I think,' said Maria. 'I don't know. How are you?'

'Good. Lovely place, isn't it?'

'So nice. Very nice.'

There was a silence again.

'You live here?' she said.

'Where?'

'This place. This... area.'

'No,' said Michael. 'I'm passing through.'

'Like me.'

'Yes.'

He tried to relax, for it occurred to him now that he might have been wrong. She hadn't recognised him, and what he'd taken for fear might have been nothing of the sort. They hadn't actually made eye contact on either the train or the bus – and they certainly hadn't spoken. She had been so busy with her tablet and maps, so why on earth *should* she have noticed him? She had spoken because it would have been rude not to.

'What are you planning?' he said. 'You look as if you're off somewhere.'

'Where?'

'Pardon?'

They stared at each other, and he wondered if she had misheard.

'No,' said Michael. 'Sorry... I was asking where you're heading. You look like you're planning a walk.'

'Tomorrow, yes. I'm going to Higher Lee Ridge.'

'Very good. Lovely.'

'I hope so.'

She looked at the map again, and stretched her thumb and finger over it.

'Seven miles, I think,' she said. 'Seven miles back too, so... early start.'

There was a vacant chair tight against the wall, and Michael was close to it. She noticed it too.

'Can I see?' he said, nodding at the map. 'Can I join you for a second?'

'Of course.'

'I don't want to intrude,' he said. 'You're probably with friends.'

'No, sit down,' said Maria. 'Please. I'll make a space for you.'

'Don't worry, no – I can squeeze in there. Are you sure? You're probably enjoying a bit of peace and quiet.'

'No, please – you're welcome.'

She laughed, and Michael eased himself into the seat opposite hers. She drew the table back slightly, and he tried to sit in a position that suggested he was about to get up and leave. He would leave, too – as soon as he'd glanced at the map, he'd find an excuse. She would have headphones somewhere, and be yearning to use them.

'Higher Lee Ridge,' he said. 'What time are you heading off?'

'Oh, eight o'clock. Maybe half-past seven – I don't know.'

She was unfolding a leaflet.

'Have you looked at the weather forecast?' he said.

'No. You think I should?'

'I don't know. Always wise.'

'Maybe it will rain.'

'It's bound to, isn't it? This is England.'

She laughed again, and shuddered. 'No,' she said. 'I don't want to look at the weather forecast. If it snows, it snows. I have waterproofs.'

'You're very determined, then. That's good – you're serious.'

'What?'

'About your walking. You're serious.'

'I'm very stupid,' she said. 'I will get lost, and... what if they never find me?'

She carried on smiling, and he knew he must tear his eyes away because the smile seemed too full of joy. He put his wine glass down, and as she unfolded the leaflet he saw that she had made careful notes on it. There was a drawing he'd noticed at the check-in desk, which seemed to feature one walk in particular. He picked it up and studied it.

'"Higher Lee Ridge,"' he read. 'This is where you're going?'

'That's where I *want* to go, yes.'

The hotel was marked by a red circle, and a black dotted line ran round the car park they had both crossed earlier. It took you up the steps they had descended, and you then had to walk along the road. The road must be the one the bus had taken – and after fifty metres or so, you veered off to the right across open country. The leaflet showed woods and a stream. It showed a viewpoint and what appeared to be open moorland. He turned it over, and saw that the dotted line continued past a 'shepherd's store', and zigzagged. Then it was moorland all the way, and Higher Lee Ridge appeared to be a narrow, exposed pathway leading to a dramatic peak. The final sketch was of that peak: a kind of stack or column, with views in every direction.

Six hours, said the text. *In fine weather. Not suitable for young children or the infirm. No climbing, but steep final ascent.*

'You've come up here to do this?' he said.

Maria nodded.

'I have two days only,' she said. 'A friend told me, "You have to see this place. Higher Lee Ridge – you have to see it."'

'Why?'

'I don't know. It's incredible.'

She laughed.

'Can I get you a drink?' he said, as lightly as possible. 'Wine, or a juice?'

He hated to ask, because the words felt like such an obvious proposition. He was older than her, and he was a single man who had appeared suddenly and asked to sit with her. She had been the first to speak, but only out of courtesy – or even nervousness. There were empty tables, and he could have gone to one. In her position, he would be getting worried.

'No,' she said. 'Thank you but... I am sleeping.'

'Early night. Good.'

'I was up very early today. I was travelling all day, and I lost my bag.'

'You lost your bag?'

'And I found it again. Someone helped me, but...'

She sighed.

'I am so tired. You know this place? You know Higher Lee Ridge?'

Michael looked at the leaflet again, and decided to tell a lie. It wasn't the first of the day, for he'd told people that he was going to the Highlands even after he'd abandoned the idea. He'd told the boys on Crewe station that the vending machine had malfunctioned, and he had an idea that he'd alluded to a son or daughter at the café he'd used in Gloucester. He hadn't lied to the steam-train enthusiast, and to Percy's grandparents he'd tried hard to tell only the truth – they just hadn't wanted to hear it. Now, looking at the leaflet, and letting his gaze shift back to the blackest eyes he had ever seen, he said:

'Yes. But I haven't been there for a long while.'

'You know this walk?'

'Oh, I wouldn't say that—'

'But you've done it?'

'Once,' he said. 'As a boy, I think – a while ago. When I was a boy.'

'Is it easy to follow?'

He smiled, and she smiled back at him. He could see her anxiety so clearly now: she really thought she was heading into the wilds. He lied again.

'Yes,' he said. 'I was thinking of going tomorrow, in fact – but a little later than you.'

'You're walking that way? To the Ridge?'

He was nodding.

'I hadn't decided. But I'd like to see it again.'

'Are you going alone?' she said.

'Yes.'

'Then we could go together. You could take me? You could guide me?'

'I don't know about that. I could try, but it's quite easy, I think – you don't need a guide.'

'I do. I will get lost!'

'I...'

He paused.

'Look,' he said. 'I can't just push in on your walk. Are you sure you don't want to do it alone, at your own pace?'

'No. I would like to walk with you. It would help me.'

She was staring at him, and still he wasn't sure if she had recognised him. Would she say so, if she had? Perhaps she had been distracted? And yet there had been so few people on the bus.

'What's your name?' she said suddenly.

'Michael MacMillan.'

'I'm Maria.'

She was lifting her hand and extending it. They shook hands.

'How is your day, Michael MacMillan?'

'It's been good,' said Michael.

'And we'll walk together? You promise?'

'If you're sure. Yes.'

'Then I'll see you for breakfast. Thank you.'

'Seven o'clock?'

'Seven o'clock, yes. Perfect.'

'At this table?'

'This table, that table. I don't mind which table, but I'll be here. Seven o'clock, Michael – you don't change your mind!'

She looked at him and there was nothing in her eyes except relief.

He sat at the bar after she left, with another glass of wine.

Was it really so implausible? She had not recognised him from the train – that was to be expected, but he still couldn't believe she hadn't noticed him on the bus, because he'd climbed on board after her and passed her in the aisle. They were the only two passengers to alight at a remote moorland spot in the pitch dark – but she simply hadn't been aware of him. Her priority must have been working out where the hotel was, of course, and he had followed at a distance – not because he had sinister designs, but because he'd been so uncertain as to where he was going.

That was the truth.

Now, however, he had set himself up as a protector – or as someone with knowledge and experience. He should be dead, but he wasn't. Crewe station would have got back to normal by now, and he should be where? In a mortuary, of course. The shoe that was on his foot should be in a plastic bag, the details from the debit card logged into a computer. He should be a police officer's routine nuisance, but instead he was holding a glass and the deep red of the wine made him think of all the blood that was still circulating in his veins, unspilled.

He could put the glass down on the table.

He could pick it up again and taste the wine.

By saying so little to Maria, and nodding his head, he had been promoted to someone not just safe but useful... essential, even. For whatever the weather threw at them, he would have to guide her over the moors to some place he'd never heard of called Higher Lee Ridge: he would have to follow the dots and the dashes. He had been there before, apparently – but a long time ago. He could hear his own voice as the wind buffeted them both, and they stared at the sodden map.

'I'm sure we're close,' he could say. 'I recognise that stile, that... sheep.'

He hadn't suggested he knew the way intimately, so they could navigate together and he would simply give her the reassurance that if they did miss their way, they would do so together. The problem, of course, was that this was a wilderness, and it was bound to rain.

It was bound to rain, and he had absolutely no equipment.

23

Perhaps there was a God after all.

Morris's right eye was swollen shut, but he hadn't been blinded. One finger was broken, so the hospital would provide the splint – it would take time to heal, of course, but despite the savage kicking he wasn't crippled. The bottle of wine on Ayesha's table was empty, and her mother had cooked a leg of lamb, which they'd all enjoyed: they had enjoyed each other's company again, and had been so carefully kind to one another. Most miraculous of all, though – most fortunate and unexpected – was the existence of a little cupboard in The Golden Fleece that Michael found when he visited the loos. It said *Drying Room*, and when he opened the door he found shelves and racks of boots and waterproofs.

Morris would spend that night in a waiting room.

Ayesha would sleep in the room next to Kristin's, and try not to wonder what he'd look like if only he'd reached seventeen. She had seen his ghost, just once – or hoped she had. It might have been her own reflection, but she wanted it to be him, flickering back from wherever he was. She lay in bed remembering the times they'd slept side by side, when he was little, and how he'd made her squeal by putting his ice-cold hands on her skin. If his thin ghost slipped in beside her now, she wouldn't make a sound.

She closed her eyes, willing him to appear – as Michael looked at the abandoned clothes, and wondered if he dared borrow them. He knew he shouldn't stand there for too long, in case he was disturbed, but it did seem extraordinary that his problems had been so easily solved. There were two cagoules, and they were both far more robust than the skimpy thing he'd been wearing. There was a big red coat and a pair of waterproof trousers next to it. There were various socks and three pairs of proper walking boots, the soles thick with hard, dry mud. Above them he could see a woolly hat, a single, solitary glove, and even a football scarf – but could they be lost property? He should ask the manager, obviously, but the thought of being thwarted at this stage was unbearable – and it mattered, because he couldn't do a fourteen-mile walk over the moors in his own shoes. He scrunched up the toes of his left foot, and felt the debit card.

He would rise early and take what he needed.

He would risk using it, because it wouldn't be theft – by late afternoon he would be putting everything back in exactly the same place, and Maria needed a guide.

In fact, she didn't – he was sober enough to know she didn't. If he failed to appear at breakfast, she would set off at eight o'clock, fiercely alone with the leaflet in her hand and the map in her pocket. If the sun was eclipsed by the moon, and the ridge plunged into unnatural darkness, Maria would still be following those dots, and she'd get to whatever summit or stack he'd seen in the sketch – he knew she would. He had promised to lead her, but he would be the follower.

He lay in his bed, and the wind got stronger.

He could be in a ship, way out at sea. He could be in any random room, and he felt such a long way from the place he called home, where he had caused such pain. He had been right to withdraw from the wedding, though, and at this moment, he belonged here. If his credit card could go on for ever, this is where he would stay – and who knows? He might become essential to the hotel in some way, and find his pub-cleaning skills were suddenly appreciated.

Nobody polished brass like he did, they would say.

Nobody took the time to get under the toilet seat, and bleach the urinals so thoroughly, giving the disinfectant time to act before the water cleared it – was there an award the hotel could win for sheer cleanliness? Would someone write a letter, aston-ished that public spaces could be so immaculate?

He remembered James again, for no reason.

They did litter duty together on Tuesday after school, and he remembered James climbing a tree to get at a crisp packet that had stuck in its twigs. He'd taken his blazer off, and hauled himself higher and higher as everyone cheered. He remembered Amy, and making love with his eyes closed and knowing the lies between them now formed a very high wall indeed – he couldn't scale it or tunnel under it, and walking round it would take for ever. The lies prevented progress, and he was so tired of his own head, tired of his own imagination... the lies told and thought until they stiffened into truth.

To whom could he talk? If there was only a way of shunting backwards, and owning up to poor, dear Amy with all her special range of vulnerabilities and hopes. He would have liked to call her now, or text her a straightforward *So sorry* – except he'd chosen not to bring his phone. He'd left it on the bed beside the envelope. In any case, it would make things worse. You never knew what rage people carried inside, any more than you knew the real extent of their grief, or their joy, or their sheer hollowed-out emptiness.

'But I'm still alive,' he said quietly.

A red light glowed on the TV. The kettle switch was blue. An alarm of some kind in the ceiling winked very faintly: the room was alive, too. Maria was nearby – he wasn't sure where. They'd had a few more minutes before she left the bar, and he'd asked her where she was from. The Philippines, she'd said – which were way off in the South China Sea, somewhere near Japan. What an accomplishment it would be, simply to get to whatever ridge it was called – wherever it was. It would be a day spent better than many, and with that thought in his mind, he realised he was about to go to sleep, and the bed felt softer.

He thought of his mother, and the gentle face he no doubt misremembered, before she got so ill. Elizabeth, Monica, Amy – the girl in the Gloucester station café. The boys on the platform at Crewe, and his silly brother. There were so many other memories too, pounding just like the wind, begging to be let in. The wonder was that soon he would be sleeping, with every likelihood of waking up again, for breakfast.

Maria was thinking, too.

Her husband had texted, just a thoughtful midnight text of love and good wishes: the same as usual, for he was on late shift. It was extra sweet after his disapproval, if that's what it had been. Perhaps his misunderstanding had been borne of her failure to communicate, but he hadn't wanted her to make this trip. Now, in bed, she was imagining sleeping with him. Jao's hard back was turned away from her, covered only by a sheet. Miguel, their youngest boy, was climbing in between them, silent and hopeful. Just minutes before they'd been making love, so what did that say for the child's timing? He was worming his way in, all six years of him, unnerved by the rattling of the roof, or perhaps the knowledge that his father was off again soon, as his mother made top-secret plans – was she leaving too?

'Just for a little while – I'll be back soon!'

But what was a little while in the life of someone six years old? It was so hard to know what any of them really compre-hended, and harder sometimes to know what they cared about – but Miguel was super-sensitive, unsettled and needy, and he slid between their bodies, moulding himself into her arms. When she held him tight he seemed to melt into her as if he was only in her imagination – he could almost be there in the hotel bed, as she rolled onto her side and caught the fragrance of his hair.

Inconceivable how sweet a child could smell, and how he could pad across the room wide awake but be so instantly asleep, and reassured – how his skull was already a magical miniature of Jao's.

She held his ghost. She held it tight.

Morris was numb with fatigue, the pain dulled by sheer exhaus-tion. Ayesha ached for Kristin as she listened to her parents talking next door – his ghost was so shy. Perhaps ghosts feared rejection?

The fan turned and swung, breathing over Maria and her family every ten seconds.

Jao turned and reached for her. He found he was touching not her but their youngest son, and she was behind him with just the same eyes, light coming not from the stars or moon but from the street lamp.

'We are making a better life.'

'Of course.'

'We're lucky, aren't we?'

It was just one of the memories Maria used, to ease herself into sleep – that precious, holy time of three in one, whispering while the other children slept. The wind rattled the window, but it was the harmless edge of a typhoon heading out to Manila Bay. Someone was walking across the landing outside, trying to be quiet, and she heard a door close softly.

She thought of the man with the kind eyes, whose name she had forgotten. He was quietly reassuring, and she now had a guide – she texted Jao to let him know, yearning to speak to her sister. Manila time ran seven hours ahead, so the house would be full of just the same soft breathing and snores as The Golden Fleece. Another hour before her district came to life, but the first jeepneys would be stopping already for those on the earliest shifts.

Her mind was full of numbers, and she tried to erase them.

The hundreds earned, and the hundreds sent. The thousands borrowed, and the thousands invested or promised – always set against the hundreds deducted and never seen, and the unforeseen expenses such as her housemate's birthday – the contributions to which you could never say no, and to which you *should* never say no. She saw little Nikko's eyes for a moment, and it was him beside her, replacing Miguel. She'd had to watch his birthday through the screen of her tablet – and she couldn't resist the urge to call up the photographs right now, whatever the pain: she sat up and drank a little water. Two more years for her, and five for Jao... and there was Nikko, and here was she.

She opened another folder, and wondered if she could bear the whole birthday movie, and listen to her children's voices. No, she couldn't. Instead, she would listen to the rain that had already started, and thank God she had a guide. She was glad to be here, of course, but when had she last endured such solitude? The man's name was Michael! She remembered it, and knew he'd been sent to look after her.

She thought of the woman – Ayesha – and the bag, and went through the consequences of losing it again. Still she couldn't believe her own stupidity, and Ayesha's kindness came back to her, as did that sudden revelation of her terrible wound – a wound that now seemed frightening, for it reminded her how easily a child is lost.

'Will I ever be the same?'

That's what Ayesha had asked, as if she wanted to go backwards. She'd told her no, and she shouldn't have done: she should have said yes. The woman wanted reassurance, as everyone did – as she, Maria, did right now so far from home... why hadn't she offered it? And what was the dead child's name?

She remembered the guitar, but not the boy's name, so again he'd been forgotten – and Ayesha would be wide awake, no doubt, aching with a pain only God could take away, if she believed in him. Maria knew that God came to her through dreams, and that when she was most desolate, sleep would bring the kind that didn't simply nourish and revive: no, they resurrected.

And God had brought her Michael MacMillan.

She prayed for her own family and then for Ayesha. She prayed for the soul of her little brother, and suddenly remembered: his name was Kristin. And Kristin's ghost stepped into the room and stood looking down at Ayesha, and Ayesha was fast asleep dreaming about him. Morris slept fitfully, aching all over, and Michael found that he was still so, so glad – just to be alive.

He was alive in a bed, not dead in a drawer.

24

'Through the car park,' he said. 'I remember that much.'

'It says that here,' said Maria, checking the leaflet. 'The first bit is easy, and we don't get lost. Soon we get very lost – but not yet.'

She was laughing already.

'We can't,' said Michael. 'It's going to be signposted all the way.'

The red coat was too big, and he felt like a lifeboat man ready for the storm. It had capacious pockets, so he'd folded the waterproof trousers into one of them, and put his packed lunch into his backpack. The hotel had provided that. The boots he'd chosen were a little tight, so he was wearing only his normal socks. He had taken the woollen hat too, and it was already on his head. As for Maria, her waterproof was purple, and it was belted in tight to her waist. The hood was up, and he watched as she secured it with flaps under her nose. The rain was on its way, and the wind was rising. It had pounded all night, rehearsing for a day of wild storms.

'Okay,' said Michael, smiling. 'Follow me!'

He led the way to the stone steps, and ascended them to the road. The bus stop was further down, its tiny shelter empty: they passed it, and Maria paused, producing a small, compact camera. She took a photograph carefully, and they moved on between two rows of squat, heavy houses. An arrow pointed them along the turning to the right – which Maria also photographed. Then they came to a farmhouse, where another arrow was embedded in one of the granite gateposts: it directed them through the farmyard and up round a barn. Up again, and now the path took them into the trees, so they were cutting through a wood, rising all the time. It was steep, but good to be out of the wind.

'I think you're fitter than I am,' gasped Michael, when they stopped to rest.

He was panting. She wasn't.

She lifted the camera and took a shot of the way they had come.

'Will you take one of me, please?' she said.

'For the folks back home?'

'Of course.'

She posed with her hands on her hips, and he couldn't see the smile because half her face was covered. She realised, and pulled the hood back: he took a second picture.

'You have a camera?' she said.

'I don't.'

'You don't have a phone? You must do.'

'I don't even have a phone. I left home without.'

'Why?'

'No reason. Nobody calls.'

'You are very brave, I think. When we get back I can send you my pictures. Are you on Facebook?'

'I'm afraid not. I don't really do all that. I just... never get round to it.'

'We use it all the time. You ready now?'

'For what?'

'For going on!'

'Yes – of course.'

The trees grew thicker, and they crossed a stream. Then, just as the leaflet predicted, the footpath divided and the track on the left took them up again. Ancient trees stood either side, and it grew darker before the canopy lifted and lightened, and the wood turned yellow. They went through ferns and brambles, still climbing, and came to its edge. There they paused, a little nervously, for the land beyond was so different. It was stark, bare and brown, offering no shelter at all. The footpath was reassuringly clear, but it led into a kind of infinity – a plateau that was ominously empty of people.

'What made you come here?' said Michael.

'Somebody at my work,' replied Maria. 'They were telling me about it – on and on.'

'What did they say?'

'That I should come and see the view. I told them, "Every time I get holiday, I try to do something." I try to get away, so—'

'Like a walking holiday, or—?'

'Like an adventure. Like seeing some new place. A gallery, maybe.'

She was taking another photograph.

'I don't have much money, though, so it's not easy.'

'It's an expensive hotel. Isn't it?'

'Of course.'

'The train fare, as well – it all mounts up. Do you have a railcard?'

She laughed.

'I don't have a railcard. Do you have a railcard?'

'No. I meant to get one, but…'

'What?'

'Sometimes you just don't get round to things, do you?'

She put the camera away and looked at him.

'Why are you here, Michael? You are not on holiday.'

'How do you know that?'

'You told me last night. You said you were doing some business, but… I did not like to ask about business. People tell me I am very… what's the word?'

'Nosy?'

'Not nosy. Like a policeman – like asking questions, always.'

'Inquisitive. Suspicious.'

'Suspicious, yes! People say I am like a detective, always asking why and what and who. So I try and remember not to. What is your business?'

She laughed as she said it, putting a hand over her mouth.

'You see?' she cried. 'A bad habit!'

'I'm in the cleaning business,' he said. 'What about you?'

'Oh, I work in a school, and I work also in a hospital. And I work in a restaurant.'

'But there's only one of you.'

'Yes, but I am a superhero. Joking...'

She laughed.

'You have three jobs?' he said.

'The school is in the day. The hospital is in the evening – it's a hospice, not a hospital. The restaurant is just three times each week, early morning. That's cleaning, also.'

'And this is London?'

'No. This is Scotland, near Dumfries.'

'Dumfries? Why?'

'You know Dumfries?'

'No.'

'I work through an agency, and they say, "We have a place for you in Scotland: Dumfries." I say, "Thank you very much," and I buy a ticket.'

'Do you live alone?'

She looked at him.

'I think you are the policeman now,' she said.

'I'm curious.'

'I don't live alone. I live with some Filipinos and some from Malaysia. We have a flat, out near the football stadium. You like football?'

'No.'

'So what do you like?'

'Oh, walking. Talking.'

'Good,' she said. 'Come on, then. We should be doing more of the first one – the walking, I think.'

'Not the talking?'

'No.'

She set off, and Michael fell into step behind her. The path went through weedy grass at first, but that soon thinned and they were obliged to walk in single file. The wind had risen, of course, and though it wasn't strong enough to blow them over they needed to concentrate, just to keep their balance. There was no point trying to speak, so Michael pieced things together, shocked as usual by his own ignorance. His image of Maria as a student was idealised nonsense, for her working day must be twelve or fourteen hours, and she seemed so frail. He watched her back, and her careful, elegant movement forward, and noted the fact that it was just as he'd predicted: she was leading him.

He was lucky, too. If he wasn't there, she would be moving over this landscape alone, and she would be making slightly better progress because she wouldn't have stopped to talk. She might be half a kilometre further on, and if she paused to turn and look backwards she would not see an awkward man, sweating already in a bright red coat. The landscape would be empty of him, and it would be only her.

Where would he be, if things had turned out differently?

He would be in some place he didn't want to think about, because it was impossible to visualise. Something stopped him seeing himself broken and discoloured, and the idea of him being cut to pieces was simply beyond imagination... was the brain wired so it couldn't process such a thing? A mortuary in Crewe, or Bromsgrove – Preston, even. Accrington – where the nurses were forced to put on gloves to move him? They hadn't had to touch the Muslim man's father. He had been surrounded by family.

He tried to imagine the darkness of a closed box, or a zipped-up bag – and he couldn't. Instead, he walked on and let the wind surge around him. His boots were getting slightly heavier, and they were rising steadily into the gale, towards a twisted thorn tree – there was nothing else. The tree trembled in the wind, and when they got closer they saw there were actually three sheep huddled under it, which broke cover and ran bleating away. Soon, it was behind them, and they reached the undramatic crest of the hill, where a shallow dip took them through boggy ground towards a peak that was higher. Up they went. The same path continued in the same single furrow.

The brown slopes folded into each other, and if your legs kept working you could walk them for ever – Michael could walk right across England. In the far distance they spotted a little stone hut, and Maria stopped.

'The shepherd's store,' she said in his ear.

'I think so,' he replied. 'You see? You don't need me.'

She laughed.

'I do,' she said. 'Don't leave me! But when we get there we should have something to eat.'

'That sounds sensible.'

'What?'

'I said that's a good idea.'

'Are you tired?'

'No. Are you?'

'Yes.'

'I thought you were fit.'

'I thought so too. You're fitter than me. How old are you, Michael?'

'Fifty-six.'

'Thirty-three. Are you married?'

'No. I'm like you, I think – obstinately single.'

She screwed up her eyes.

'Obstinate means...?'

'Stubborn. Someone who knows what they want. Do you think you'll marry, when you go home? One day, perhaps?'

'I don't understand you,' she said.

'Will you marry? One day?'

'I'm married already.'

The wind took her words away, and he had to move closer.

'Say that again,' he cried.

She pulled the flaps of her hood open.

'I said, "I *am* married! I married twelve years ago. I have six children."'

He simply stared at her. 'That's not possible,' he said.

'Why not?'

'Because... where are they? Where's your husband?'

'In the Philippines, of course. My children are in the Philippines, and my husband is working overseas.'

'In Scotland?'

'No.'

'Where?'

She laughed.

'Listen,' she said. 'Let's get to the house, okay? We sit down, out of the wind. We have some food, and... oh my God, you will wish you had not asked me about my family.'

'About what?'

'What?'

Another gust had snatched his words away.

'What shouldn't I have asked about?' he cried.

'About my children, Michael!' she yelled. 'I will show you photographs, and then I will start crying. It happens every day – three times a day.'

Another gust of wind hit, and Michael steadied her. There was rain now, very fine but also very constant. She got her camera out, and this time took a photograph of him. Then she turned and plodded on. It occurred to Michael that if Maria had made this trip alone, she would be getting nervous now – or he supposed she would, because he knew *he* would be. If he was out here on this exposed, blank hillside all alone he would be thinking only of the disasters that might befall, and how he should give up and turn back.

He would be worrying about getting lost.

Maria's presence meant he wasn't scared at all, and he wasn't thinking of the future: he was experiencing the moment, in all its misty wetness, measuring his footsteps to a destination that must be getting closer. Before long, he could see that the house was smaller than he'd thought – and it wasn't even a house. They reached it, and it was a carefully, beautifully built cube of rough stone, with a tin roof. It had one large wooden door which was padlocked shut – but it afforded them all the protection they needed, for they could sit against the most sheltered wall.

They didn't speak for a while, because they had serious business to attend to: the packed lunches needed to be unwrapped, and there was tea to be poured. Maria had a thermos flask in her bag, and there was a flat space to rest it. She handed Michael her lunch-bag, and he unwrapped her sandwiches: she had chosen cheese. He unwrapped his own, and he had chosen ham. Like her, he had a bag of crisps, so he opened both packets. She poured tea into the flask's plastic lid.

'You like sweet tea?' she said.

'No,' he replied. 'I never have sugar.'

'Oh, dear.'

'What?'

'I'm afraid I put sugar in already. In the hotel.'

'That's fine.'

'I didn't think about you.'

'But it'll do me good. I think we both need the energy.'

'That's true. Are we halfway yet?'

'More than halfway, I think. Where's the map?'

Maria pulled the leaflet out of her pocket, and it was sodden. He laughed, because it looked so sad, and she laughed too.

'Disaster!' he said. 'We'll never get home.'

'No, we have the other map,' she said, giggling. 'We won't get lost! Anyway, you've been here before. You remember this place?'

'Not really. It's very vague.'

'You must try. I think this is a very old building – you must have come here, and sat against it.'

'It was a while ago,' he said. 'But listen – I think we should have just one sandwich each, and save the other two.'

'In case we have to spend the night here?'

She was laughing at him, and he was shaking his head.

'No,' he said. 'But I think the last part will be hard. We'll need an extra boost.'

'A what?'

'An extra boost. An... injection.'

'Yes. You are very wise, Michael. I think, without you, I might have given up.'

'There's still time to do that.'

'You want to give up?'

'Do you want to?'

'Of course not. I don't have a choice.'

She took a sip of tea, and passed the cup to him. He took his first bite of ham sandwich, adding a few crisps. He waited, then, and the taste exploded: he hadn't had that particular combination for years. For a moment, the ham stuck to the roof of his mouth as it always had, and always would, and she watched him as he worked at it with his tongue. Yet again, she was grinning at him, as if he was a clown.

'Why don't you have a choice?' he said at last.

'I do. I do, really... but...'

She bit into her sandwich, and he saw the same ecstasy cross her face as had crossed his. He waited as she chewed and swallowed.

'I told someone I would definitely come here,' she said. 'Someone who... this is a secret, okay? Someone who is paying for my hotel. Paying for the train, also.'

'Who?'

'I must not say.'

'Why not?'

'You could get me fired.'

'Why? And why would I want to get you fired?'

She laughed.

'It's because of all the rules,' she said. 'You're not allowed to take money from people. Patients, I mean. In the hospice. If they find out, it could be a big problem for me. So you keep it to yourself, please.'

'Keep what to myself? I still don't understand—'

'The fact that I just told you... That this person who is paying me... And you should drink the tea, before it gets cold.'

He took a mouthful as instructed.

'So who is he?' he said.

'It's a she. She's a patient and we talk, and I meet her grand-daughter. She is very old – very sick – and she is saying all the time, "You must go to this place, and that place. England is so beautiful," she says, "and you must, must, *must* go to Higher Lee."'

'Why?'

'She came with her husband, years ago. It's very beautiful, I guess.'

'And you came all the way up here because she... What? She organised it?'

'Yes.'

'She paid for the hotel?'

'She did that, with her granddaughter. I said I could not take any cash, but if they made it possible then I would love to go. They made the booking.'

'Is she dying, do you think?'

Maria looked at him.

'It's a hospice, Michael,' she said. 'They are *all* dying, yes – and this is not my camera. The granddaughter lent it to me, and so I am looking at all this scenery for her. My eyes will be her eyes, if you understand me? That's what she said.'

'I do understand.'

'Good.'

She frowned.

'I could not go back and say, "Yes, a very nice hotel, thank you – but I got lost!" She would never forgive me.'

'How old is she?'

'I think eighty-five. I must hurry back, or she will be gone! I'm joking.'

Michael sipped the sweet tea again and returned the cup. He took another bite of his sandwich, and she did the same. He had an image of the old woman now, in her hospital bed, and he felt only admiration.

'Look,' said Maria. 'Look at that...'

The wind had died suddenly and the mist rolled back. They could see into a long valley, and at its far end – even as they watched – the sun managed to break through. What was strange, though – and impossible – was that when they looked the other way, the weather was so different. The clouds were dark grey turning to black, and the rain was visible like a soft curving curtain. Maria held her camera up, and Michael noticed that this time she was filming: she panned from left to right, taking in the extremes. The next moment, the valley disappeared.

They finished the sandwiches and wrapped the remaining two up in film. Maria had the rest of Michael's crisps, and they drained the cup of tea. There were two biscuits: Michael had taken them from the jar in his room, feeling slightly guilty.

'Shall we save them for later?' he said – for Maria was looking at them, too.

'I think we should. How much further is it?'

'About an hour?'

'One hour to the ridge. Then up to the top. Then all the way back, and home – if we're alive.'

'Are you ready?'

'Of course.'

'Come on.'

She patted his pocket.

'You should put on your waterproof trousers,' she said.

'You're right.'

She watched him as he removed them, and let them flap in the wind. He crouched, and unzipped the ankles to make them wide, but it was still difficult to work the legs over his boots, and standing up it was impossible. He managed to get the left one over his left foot, but he was tottering – and he had to sit down. Only then did he realise she was now filming him, and was finding the whole thing funny. When he pulled the trousers up to his waist, she was bent double with laughter: the folds had made his abdomen and hips stick out. He adjusted the waistband, and it was his bottom that looked ludicrous – Maria was helpless.

He started to laugh himself, and she just managed to hold the camera still. At last, the trousers were on and he could move more easily. He took out a handkerchief and wiped his face. She took it from him and wiped hers. He rearranged his coat, and she adjusted his hood.

'Ready?' she said.

'Totally.'

She did her own hood up tighter, for the rain was now merciless – and they stepped out into it.

25

He had been on walking holidays with his father.

He had hiked as a young man, too – but he hadn't pushed himself this hard for a number of years. He wasn't unfit, and the cycling he'd done to the retail park had given him some leg muscle and even some stamina. Nonetheless, the ground grew steadily steeper and he was finding it hard. He was finding it harder and harder to believe he was there, too, and the thought kept occurring that he could have stumbled into the afterlife, with all memories of the train's actual impact miraculously erased. Walking in this tunnel of wind and rain, he tried to imagine at what point his particular afterlife had begun, because it might have been on the bus with the angelic driver, or when he stepped into the hotel with the helpful manager. Had he even died at Preston? For clearly, Maria was his guide.

There she was, just ahead – and she seemed so real.

She was tireless, too, and kept up a pace that was a little faster than the one he would have set, had he been in front. They were in single file again, and the muddy grass had given way to rock. The path was a vivid gulley, and there were no choices to be made, for it never divided – it had been scored through, and they were two brightly coloured bugs worming along with their heads down. The leaflet said they wouldn't need to climb, meaning they wouldn't need ropes and crampons. What they did need was courage, for they were approaching a long ridge, and the drop either side was worryingly steep.

The path was like a tightrope.

It slumped at first, as if the rope was slack. Then it was a constant, gradual ascent, and at the far end there was a tall, bare, chimney-shaped stack. It seemed strange, suddenly, that a thin tourist leaflet could encourage you to risk your life – for that's what they were about to do.

Maria crouched down, and Michael knelt next to her. Turning back was unthinkable but they needed to take it step by step. The wind was as strong as ever.

'What are you thinking?' he said.

'What?'

He had to put his mouth close to her ear.

'What are you thinking?'

'That it is very dangerous. Difficult.'

'Yes.'

'What are you thinking?'

'The same thing.'

'What?'

'I am thinking the same thing. Very dangerous!'

'Too much wind. Maybe this old lady is trying to kill me.'

'You want to go back?'

'I can't hear you—'

'I said, "Do you want to go back?"'

She laughed at him, and her laughter was flung away. Then she took out her camera and photographed the way ahead. She managed to turn it on Michael, and he made a frightened face.

'Smile,' she said.

'How? I'm feeling sick.'

'But it's the last photo, Michael, before you blow away!' she cried. 'Joking! Come on!'

She tightened the straps of her backpack, and checked her bootlaces. He pulled his hat a little lower. There was no point in delaying, for there was nothing to plan or discuss. Maria pushed on, and the next moment she was walking upright again.

Michael followed, still negotiating the gentle descent. He found that his boots fitted neatly into the well-worn path, and best of all he discovered it wasn't as narrow as it had seemed. There were handholds of a kind, too, for the track was snug against a shelf of knee-high rock, which acted almost as a hand-rail. If you took care, and went slowly, it was safe enough.

Of course, Maria was quicker than him. She was nimble, and was getting close to the end. She was using both hands, and he could see that she had found a certain rhythm as she walked. The wind pressed him back, and he inched forward more carefully. When he saw that she had turned and was filming him, he managed to wave, but when he took another pace something strange happened. He found his legs were locked, and he couldn't go any further.

She must have sensed it, or perhaps she saw his face close up in the camera and knew something was wrong. He opened his eyes to find that she was next to him again – she had retraced her steps.

'What?' she said.

He laughed.

'What's the matter, Michael? Are you resting?'

'No. I'm not feeling very well.'

'What do you mean?'

Her face was very close. It had to be, so she could hear him.

'I'll be okay in a minute,' he said. 'I'm just feeling... a bit sick. I think it's vertigo.'

'You're not going to faint, are you?'

'What?'

'I said, "You're not going to faint?" Do you want me to help you?'

'I don't think you can.'

'Do you want my hand?'

He shook his head. It was noticeable that she'd come close, but she hadn't touched him. She could see that he was shaking, and knew that touch would make things worse.

'You've done it before, yes?' she said.

He nodded, and closed his eyes again.

'Five minutes,' she said.

'I know. But then we have to come back.'

'Going back is easy.'

'Is it?'

'You can do it. You just have to take your time.'

He looked down, and imagined falling. He wouldn't die, because he'd bounce and roll – and he might hit his head, of course – but that would be unlucky. He would roll down the steep shale, and slither to a gradual halt way, way below. Then he would have to find a way up.

'You go on,' he said. 'I'll follow you.'

'You sure?'

'Yes. It's raining – I need to move.'

The rain was lighter, and cool on his face. Then, as he smiled, it was as if someone somewhere had adjusted the tap, for without any warning at all he was underwater. He stood hunched in a solid, merciless downpour – and it was hard not to take the assault personally, because it was so fierce and drenching. He pulled his hood up over his hat, and she leaned forward and did his zip up for him, taking it right to his nose. Hard rain was battering them both again, and it streamed off their waterproofs. The only other sound he could hear was Maria's tinkling laughter: once again, she was finding him funny. She turned her back and set off. He followed, and a few steps on she turned to check he was with her. She went slowly, and he went slowly too, through sheets of water. One step at a time, keeping the purple waterproof as close as he could.

Incredibly, he was dry inside.

The waterproofs formed such an impregnable skin that he felt warm and safe – and he realised that he and Maria were now crawling through solid cloud, for visibility was next to nothing. When the thunder came, he mistook it for an air-force jet at first, for it had that same savage, ripping quality – tearing at the sky. Then the final roll burst in a detonation so loud it hurt his ears, and there was no possible response except more laughter. Maria turned back to him, horrified.

'We can do this!' she yelled.

Would they be struck by lightning? That would be the ultimate experience, he thought. Rained on, thundered at, and finally electrocuted. He would be burned onto the rock, and where was Steve with his rake? He laughed again and lumbered on – Maria went just ahead of him. They were ascending the last section, for the path was widening. The thunder hit once more, but the next moment they had reached the stack, and it gave them the security they needed. Not only was its base broader, but there were wide crevices to lean against and hold on to. It soared high above their heads, just like a tower, and though the rain poured on they spotted cover. Maria climbed on all fours, and he followed her into a shallow cave.

'You're okay?' she said.

'No.'

'You're not?'

'I'm still shaking. How are you?'

'I thought maybe you had a heart attack.'

He wiped his eyes.

'I nearly did,' he said. 'What would you have done, if I had? You're trained, aren't you?'

'This is my holiday, remember? I'm not on duty.'

'Then let's have some tea.'

'You think we deserve it?'

'I need that sugar.'

'I have a treat for you, then. And for me, too.'

Maria drew her bag round onto her knees, and pulled out the remains of their lunch. He unwrapped the sandwiches and passed one to her, feeling her fingers as she received them. They munched happily, and he watched her swallow. He saw a piece of cheese on her chin, which she wiped away, and when she drank, the liquid was so hot she spilled some down her front. They ate the two biscuits, and she then produced a great slab of chocolate. They sat close as she unwrapped it, the foil revealing thick, brown, nutty squares. When the first dissolved on his tongue, the sun came out, and he saw the horizon.

He swallowed.

'I was lying to you, Maria,' he said. 'I've never been here before.'

26

'Lying?' she said. 'Why?'

'I don't know.'

'Lying about what? You said you knew this place.'

'I don't. I was lying.'

She laughed.

'Wait,' she said. 'I showed you the map, and—'

'And I lied to you. You asked me if I'd ever done this walk, and I should have said no, but... I thought if I said yes, you'd think it was a good idea if we went together.'

He paused, and she stared at him.

'It sounds stupid,' he said. 'I know that. You would have probably thought it was a good idea, even if I'd told you the truth. Two heads are better than one, and all that – but... I suppose I wanted to pretend to be knowledgeable. And useful. So it seemed safer to say I knew the area, but... I don't. I've never been here before in my life.'

'Oh,' she said.

He decided not to look at her.

'These boots aren't mine,' he said. 'Nor is this coat. Didn't you see me on the bus?'

'What bus?'

'The bus you got from the station. To the hotel. Didn't you see me on the train? I was sitting about three rows behind you.'

He could feel her gaze, so he was forced to lift his eyes. He could see only confusion on her face.

'I didn't see you anywhere,' she said. 'You got off the train at the same stop as me? Burnley?'

'Yes.'

'You got the same bus, to the hotel?'

'Yes.'

'Oh.'

'I wasn't following you, Maria. I saw you get off the train, and I had nowhere to go, so... I don't know why. I'm not a dangerous lunatic, I promise. But I had no destination in mind, and suddenly I was off the train and on the bus. It was a whim.'

'What's a whim?'

'A whim?'

'I don't know that word.'

'It's when you don't have a plan. Spontaneous, sudden. On impulse.'

'But you had a reservation at the hotel.'

'I didn't.'

'You must have done.'

'I didn't. I just turned up, hoping. By that time it was late and dark... I nearly stayed on the bus, in fact. But... I didn't have anywhere to go, you see, so it made sense to stop at the hotel – not because you were there. But the next minute, you were in the bar with the map, and you said hello.'

He paused.

'I should have said something earlier, I know I should. At breakfast, maybe – but I was very scared you might not want to go on the walk with me. You might think I was a... madman.'

'Are you?' she said.

'What?'

'A madman?'

'No.'

She looked at his feet.

'But they're not your boots,' she said. 'Where did you find them?'

'In the hotel. They have a drying room, and I think they must belong to someone who forgot them.'

'Or someone who's looking for them, maybe.'

'Yes.'

She laughed and then stopped.

'I don't really understand this. Where were you going, really? You were on the train, the same as me. You got off the train—'

'I didn't have a particular place in mind.'

'You must have, Michael. You don't just... catch a train and say, "Let's see what happens. Let's see where I go." Or maybe... Are you very rich?'

'No.'

'Michael?'

She was looking at him harder.

He had pulled his hood down when the sun came out, and now he took off his hat. He met her gaze, then turned his head away. He looked at his knees, but he knew she was simply staring at him and wasn't going to stop. It was warm, and his coat was steaming. The rock was a soft grey, and tiny flowers had taken root in the fissures. The clouds were rolling back in around them, of course, but at that moment you could see for miles, and the hills and peaks interlocked so naturally. He could see downwards, too, and on his right the land fell away in a series of dramatic steps, like cliffs. You could see the caverns of despair, and he smiled as he re-remembered his poem, aged eleven, and the A grade he'd been so proud of. *Come with me*, went the first line:

> *Come with me, to the caverns of despair.*
> *They boil in tears and freezing air.*
> *You will cross them, if you dare:*
> *The icy caverns of despair.*

He had remembered the whole verse, and he closed his eyes with embarrassment.

Maria said, 'Why do you say you had nowhere to go?'

'Because it's true.'

'You have a home, though.'

'I do.'

'You have family.'

'Not... really. Not as such. I have a brother, but I don't see much of him. And—'

'You have a job? Or are you retired?'

'I am... I'm kind of without work at the moment.'

'But you have money.'

'No.'

'Nothing?'

'I do have some. But not very much, and... Actually, I don't have much at all.'

'So why are you here? Sorry. But I'm more confused than ever.'

Michael laughed, unable to meet her gaze.

'I'm trying to explain it,' he said. 'I'm not sure I'm going to find it very easy, but what I told you was the truth. I just... didn't know what to do.'

'What is the matter with you?'

She said it very clearly.

'Are you sick?'

'No.'

'So tell me. What is the matter?'

She was sitting close, not touching him but looking at his face. She didn't seem frightened, or even worried – or not for herself. She had pulled her own hood down and loosened her coat. He glanced up and saw a black jersey, and again got the impression that she was small but very strong. His eyes drifted to his knees again, but she was waiting for an answer. He tried to find the words but they weren't there – and he felt his throat tighten. He blinked and laughed, and still she didn't speak. All he could hear was the wind again, finding its way round the rocks.

He said, 'When I was a boy...'

And he stopped.

'What?' she said.

'Something bad happened to me. I think several bad things happened, and for some reason... I have never had the strength or the... whatever it is you need, to get back from it, and... just lately. I don't know. I find I can't get away from it. You don't want to know, and I don't want to say any more. But I've come to realise I can't get away from it. I'm stuck with it, and it won't let me go, and...'

She was looking at him.

'That's what's the matter with me,' he said. 'It's nothing.'

27

'What happened?' she said.

'Oh... nothing, honestly. Not a lot.'

'Michael, I can't hear you properly.'

'Nothing. Nothing at all that matters.'

He stopped.

'It doesn't matter.'

'I think it does. Were you hurt?'

He shook his head.

'What happened to you, Michael? Tell me.'

He took a deep breath.

'I was asked to do things,' he said. 'It was a while ago, obviously... and they were of a sexual nature. A man at my school.'

'You mean a teacher?'

He nodded.

'Yes.'

'When was this?'

'Oh, like I said – a long time ago. I was... just a boy. I was eleven.'

'What did he do to you?'

'Well...'

His throat was tight again, but she had asked – and he managed to laugh. She had paid him the compliment – the honour – of asking, and was waiting for his reply. How strange that he couldn't speak, and that despite all the words he knew, the ones he needed simply weren't there.

He tried again.

'He didn't do anything *to* me, actually,' he said at last. 'It just started to happen. I think the first thing he did, or the first time it happened... I think he just took my hand. He liked to touch, you see – he was very physical. He liked to punish boys, not...

he wasn't a sadist. He didn't really beat you, but he played games, and one time... This was after he'd got into the habit of one-to-one meetings, or sessions. "Little interviews", you could call them. And... I suppose I ought to say I was not the only one. There were other boys, boys he liked more. Boys he found much more attractive than me, I suppose. But he – one day – took my hand and exposed himself. And...'

'What? "Exposed", meaning...?'

'I don't think you want to hear this.'

'Tell me.'

'I can't.'

'What happened, Michael? Say it.'

'This has nothing to do with the walk, or why I got off the train.'

He laughed and wiped his eyes.

'You asked why,' he said. 'You asked why I was, you know – or... what the situation was. So I don't know. It does seem to stem from... or in my mind, like I said... I've never quite put it into perspective, because he was a sad, wretched little man, looking back. And being objective, a very lonely one – and he must have been so scared, so... in torment, really. But he made me, or got me, to touch him. Touch him, between the legs. His... penis.'

There was a silence.

'Many times?' she said.

'No. Five times, in all. And once... the last time, was the last time because I got very scared. I cried, because...'

'What?'

'You don't want to know.'

He laughed again.

'I do.'

'You don't.'

'Michael. Look at me.'

'No.'

'Please look at me.'

'If I do... if I look at you, Maria, I don't think I'll be able to talk. Or do anything – I'm so sorry, but... the last time...'

He closed his eyes, and – inevitably – the tears squeezed from under his eyelids and rolled down his cheeks. He felt his lip trembling, and he was back there even as the rocks seemed to tilt for a moment and slip him all the way through the years. The sun was warm, and the wind nagging as usual, but he was in the classroom, and however many times he got out of it, somehow – like a comedy or a farce – there he was again, for the green door was closed. Its little bolt was drawn so they wouldn't be disturbed. The blind was down, and the fact that it was lunchtime meant no children were allowed inside the building without special permission – which was what he had. He was allowed to be in room five, on the top corridor of main school, because he had a meeting with Mr Trace. He was there again, behind the teacher's desk.

The man had his gown on, and Michael was in a chair too, just opposite. *Caesar's Gallic Wars* was open, and his pencil case was right beside it.

'Try kneeling down,' the man had said – so softly. And the next thing he knew, he was on his knees, and Mr Trace had his hand on his shoulder, and then on the back of his neck. So gentle, so easy and surely so easy to resist – but somehow not. For he was bowing his head, and the head of the penis – just the head – was inside his mouth. And the next moment, and the next moment – a succession of moments, for the hand kneaded his hair, and pushed him lower and lower. Up again, and lower – for how long? For one full minute perhaps, or even two?

He said to Maria, 'He made me… suck him. And… that's what I did. He didn't make me. I just couldn't find the words to say no, so that's what happened.'

She was listening.

'It was a kind of joke,' he said.

'A joke?'

'Yes. A joke that… this might happen to you, a bit like the way people say, "Backs to the wall, lads." If someone has a reputation, or they used to call it "wandering hands" – you'd know that you kept your distance. And, likewise… other boys would say it. "He'll give you a mouthful." "Was it hard?" "Did he give you something to drink?" I remember that one. "Did he give you a drink?"'

'Meaning…?'

'Yes. Meaning… did you fellate him? Did you bring him to climax? – but I didn't really know what any of that meant, then – and they probably didn't either. You always pretend – you pretend to know more, and I'm still doing it. It's like a… compulsion not to ever admit you don't know, or you're out of your depth. Do you understand?'

'Yes.'

He was silent for a moment.

'How old was he?' said Maria. 'An old man?'

'I don't know. Forties, so… not really. Younger than me. And people laughed, because everyone found it funny that he did what he did, and if it *wasn't* funny, then we had no way of talking about it. You just had to get through it, and – in the end – it was just so seedy.'

'Seedy?'

'Nasty. Depraved. Sad, and… I don't know why I let it get to me. I don't know why it matters. The man's dead. I don't hate him, and when I think of him now, I… Now I imagine what a wretched, empty life he led, and what he must have thought of himself – and I can't lay it all on him, anyway. Because it was a school where everyone, or most of us – maybe not all of us… were so very cruel, you know?'

'Michael—'

'Vicious, really – more so than I think boys need to be. The place was charged with sex and porn and hormones, and nobody ever saying anything normal or tender. No love you could admit to – love was a weakness.'

He sighed, then smiled.

'So you learn to protect yourself, don't you?'

'Of course,' she said.

'Of course. You're not going to expose your feelings, to be trampled on. And this man… Mr Trace. I actually liked him. He paid me attention, and even at that age – especially at that age – in that kind of school… attention is what you want. Need. So I did it, five times, and on the fifth occasion I… yes, I did what he asked, and… sucked him off, as they say. And it didn't take long, thank God – and that was the end of it. He didn't ever

ask me back, because he could see I was scared, I think. He...
came in my mouth, and I couldn't believe it. I was just there,
on my knees with this hand on my head... both hands, I think
he had. And yes, he did. He came in my mouth, all over me –
and I... choked. And started crying, and...'

He was quiet for a moment, remembering.

'Oh, dear,' he said quietly. 'How do you make a joke about
that? I must have wiped my face. And... I stood up, I suppose,
and went about my business.'

'You didn't tell anyone?'

'I forgot about it.'

He laughed and shook his head.

'I went out, and I went back to the form room... and the other
boys came in when the bell went. "Did he give you lunch? Did
it fit?" But... everyone got teased, and it was soon forgotten. We
were in different sets the next year, and I didn't have him as a
teacher – we never spoke again, I don't think. And all his life
– the rest of his life – he might have been terrified I'd say something, or another boy would. He liked other boys much more
than me, so I think I was just a little snack. There were some
he couldn't keep his hands off, and he always had his hands on
them – doing your tie up, and fussing at you. And you bury these
feelings so deep, you see. You get them under control, and you
hide them away. You get on with your life, or most people do
– but for some reason, Maria... I don't know why but they just
keep coming back, and won't let me go. And you did ask – thank
you so much for asking. Because somehow I got rewired, or took
a wrong path... I don't know what the right way of putting it is.
And lately it's been like the most terrible, terrible weight, that
I just have not been able to keep on carrying. I'm not normal,
and I'm so sorry to talk about it, because it's so... disgusting. But
that's who I am – that's me. That's why I had nowhere to go,
and why... I was going nowhere.'

He paused and sighed. A silence fell, and at last he said:

'Shall we change the subject?'

28

'I don't think it's easy to change this subject,' she replied.

'No. But I think we should.'

'Why?'

He shook his head, but he couldn't think of an answer.

'I think you are very upset by it,' she said. 'I don't mean to be so stupid – it is obvious that you are very, *very* upset by it, Michael.'

'Yes, but everyone has their cross to bear.'

'Yes, they do.'

'I was eleven years old. You'd think I'd have got over it by now. I told one other person, once. I told this boy who'd been in my class at the same time, though we'd never been friends. This was fifteen or twenty years ago. We met up and the subject came up – good old Mr Trace. What did he do to you? Horrible man, he loved touching your arse under your blazer – any excuse to slap your arse. You dropped a pen, you got a word wrong, or the ending wrong… "Come out here! That has to be paid for…" And everyone laughing. So I… I told him. Not about the sucking, but the holding his… you know what. We'd had a few drinks, and he couldn't believe it. He thought I was making it up at first – I said, "Loads of us did. Didn't *you*?"'

'"No," he said. "Never." I said, "You must have. People joked about it." "Never," he said. So… maybe it wasn't as many as I thought – who knows? Then he said I should tell the police. That's what he said to me.'

He paused.

'Did you?' said Maria.

'No.'

'Why not?'

'I couldn't. I couldn't imagine what good it would do. Mr Trace would have been an old man, if he was even alive. I thought, Do I want revenge? No. Do I want my day in court, so I can talk about it? No, I do not. Am I so scandalised by him, and what he got away with? Am I looking for compensation? Like I said, Maria... I just feel pure, sad pity for the old sod, the old... twisted-up, sad sod who probably spent his own childhood being played around with and... fucked. Sorry.'

Michael paused.

'You just pass it on, don't you? But what I really feel is... why can't I forget about it? That's what I'd do, if I could – I wouldn't go to the police. I'd have it burned out of me, like you can have your eyes corrected these days by a laser. I'd get them to just burn that memory out, and... maybe things would adjust. Then, you see – I'm talking too much, aren't I?'

'No.'

'I am. You didn't come out on this walk to listen to this.'

He laughed.

'But... the other thing you do... or I do... is wonder if you haven't just found a really good excuse for having had such a strange and rather wasted life. You think, I've found someone to blame! I can blame the filthy old pervert in my school – let's crucify him. But who can't find someone to blame? Everyone has a similar tale to tell, don't they? We get bored listening, because it's everywhere.'

'Is it?'

'I think so. Another priest. Another football coach – whatever it is. And the thing is, whatever he did or didn't do, my life would have been roughly the same – the same mixture of good and bad, and luck and bad luck. I don't pity myself, or... if I do, I don't want to. People get played about with! They do. Kids. Boys, girls – girls in particular. Fucked about with, and picked up and handed round. Abused, raped – I wasn't raped. It's a modern thing – a Western thing, I'm sure of it – we hunt for excuses and... reasons for why life isn't as good as it should be.

Tough shit, life's hard. You had a man's cock in your mouth –
just... get over it.'

He was nodding, and trying to laugh again.

'Get over it.'

He breathed in and swallowed. He put his hands over his face.

'Why could I never get over it?'

29

'I don't know,' she said. 'I don't know why you can't get over it, I mean. Everyone I meet, in the hospice, for example – everyone has different stories.'

'You work in a hospice. And this is meant to be your holiday.'

'Yes—'

'And you're listening to just another old bore. You must have heard this kind of nonsense all day, every day—'

'Michael, no. That's not true.'

'Let's change the subject.'

'Why?'

'Because it's... not going anywhere. I shouldn't be using you like this – it's me that's the problem.'

They sat in silence.

'I don't know the answer,' said Maria at last. 'I don't know why we carry this pain, or why some people do. And you're wrong about the people, in the hospice, I mean. There are happy people and sad people—'

'And the war. The First World War.'

'What?'

'The war.'

'What about it?'

'That was trauma. That was *real* trauma, on an industrial scale.'

She smiled at him.

'You've lost me this time, Michael. What has the First World War got to do with what happened to you?'

He shook his head and frowned.

'It was clear a minute ago. Now it isn't.'

'I think you are a very clever man.'

'Not true.'

'You are a very sensitive man.'

'No. I'm just selfish, and selfish people talk about themselves…
and fail to look up. We just look down all the time. Can I tell
you where I was going, before I followed you?'

'Where?'

'Up to the Highlands. Scotland. I was looking for a railway
track… a station, actually. It was going to be Crewe, but I changed
my plan.'

He licked his lips.

'Go on,' said Maria.

'I went to the Highlands, years ago. Have you ever had a malt
whisky?'

'I don't know.'

'Do you drink?'

'Of course. What do you mean?'

'Look at this. Wait.'

He had slipped the juice carton into his bag at the last moment.
He hadn't imagined drinking liquor in the course of the walk,
but the hotel manager had said they were in for changeable
weather. He'd thought it might be wise to have something
warming, and as he retrieved it Percy's grandparents came to his
mind. For a moment he expected to see them, but the idea of
those two elderly people hauling themselves along the ridge in
their expensive clothes was so ludicrous it made him smile. He
was safe from them here, and from all the others. As for the cup
he and Maria had used for tea, it was now empty, so he poured
a small measure and let her smell it.

'Brandy,' she said.

'Malt whisky.'

'You drink this?'

'Sometimes. And it might keep the cold out. It might give us
a boost.'

'My husband likes whisky. He drinks too much.'

'Do you love him?'

'No.'

'What?'

She laughed.

'Michael, of course I do! What kind of question is that? He is... better than me, so that makes me angry sometimes.'

'How is he better?'

'In every way.'

'I can't believe that.'

'You must meet him, then. He's so patient.'

'Is he an angel?'

She looked at him.

'I ask the same question,' she said. 'Sometimes. And I think the answer is yes. He drinks, like I say – but all that means is maybe angels need to drink from time to time. You believe in God?'

'No.'

'Oh, please... you must do. How can you not?'

'I can't, and... Maria. I can't imagine anything nicer than this. Drinking this with you, in this place – so let's not talk about God. We'll only fight.'

'He's looking after you now.'

'He's not.'

'He's watching you.'

'I wish he was. I wish he existed, and I... I'm glad you think he does. I would never dream of trying to take him away from you.'

'Okay. We'll drink to my God and get drunk.'

'You get drunk. I'll carry you back.'

'I don't get drunk. Except – that's not true...'

She thought about it.

'I got drunk six days ago. And I have told... nobody.'

'Tell me.'

'No.'

'You'll feel better.'

She smiled at him.

'I'll feel ashamed, Michael – will that make me feel better? I *am* ashamed, because I made myself sick on the carpet – so I am not going to tell you anything. I will have one sip, to keep out the wind.'

He passed her the cup and watched her lips. He took it back and she watched his. The whisky rolled over his gums, as it had the previous day, and he tasted the oak and the spring water. The caverns of despair were still visible, as were cloud formations he could not name, and Vicky the Tomatin tour guide appeared briefly, with all the interesting facts he'd now forgotten. He saw Amy's face again, and felt only shame. She turned into Monica, and Elizabeth – and suddenly it was his mother. He looked at his hands and saw they were still doing their job, holding the little cup steady – they were still able to pick things up and put them down. There was more chocolate and more whisky. There was a bag of unopened crisps and two small bottles of mineral water.

'What were you going to do in the Highlands?' she said.

'What do you mean?'

'Tell me.'

'I don't know what you're asking.'

Maria smiled.

'Yes, you do,' she said. 'You told me you were looking for a railway track. First Crewe, and then the Highlands, so that's what I'm asking. What were you going to do, when you found this track?'

'I was...'

'You were going to kill yourself, Michael. Weren't you?'

He nodded.

'Yes,' he said. 'I thought it was... probably for the best. It did seem like the best option, all things considered.'

They sat in silence for a long time, watching the weather.

'You want to meet my family?' she said.

'That would be nice. One day.'

'You want to meet them now?'

He looked at her.

'How?'

'Be truthful, please. Do you want to meet my family?'

'Yes,' said Michael. 'Very much.'

30

Maria delved in her bag and pulled out something flat, in a plastic case. She opened it to reveal her tablet.

'I think you're lying to me now,' she said softly.

'About what?'

'You're being polite. You're saying what you have to say, but—'

'I want to meet them very much,' said Michael. 'Or see them, at least. You've got photographs?'

'Oh, yes – and I get revenge now.'

The tablet was coming to life.

'You do know the Philippines?' she said. 'You remember where they are?'

'Near Japan.'

'The South China Sea – very good. Okay, first we have Jao. This is my husband.'

She was flipping folders open, and the first picture she enlarged showed a robust man with close-cropped jet-black hair and Chinese eyes.

'Jao,' she said. 'We were married twelve years ago. Sweethearts from the same barangay, nice wedding – this is him now, you see? Very strong.'

Michael saw the same man in jeans and a T-shirt.

'What does he do?'

'He is a construction worker, driver. Cleaner.'

'Where?'

'Right now? This minute, he is in UAE, United Arab Emirates. He's like me, he is part of an agency. But no work in the UK, so he earns money over there.'

'Good money?'

'Not bad. For us, it's good money.'

Another photograph flipped up.

'That's his mum, you see? And that's his dad. That's him again. And the money's okay – you can live very cheaply. Like me – I live very cheaply, and all the money goes home. We have a house now. You want to see our house?'

'Yes.'

'Say no.'

'Why?'

'Because if you say no, I won't show you my house—'

'I want to see your house, Maria,' said Michael. 'More than anything else in the world. Let me see it, please.'

'Okay.'

She opened another folder and pulled up more pictures. He saw a team of Filipino men, setting blocks out on a patch of mud. In the next, the walls rose up on foundations, and window frames appeared. Children watched, then disappeared: now the roof was on, and the children were inside. It was a bungalow beside a tree. He saw the other side: there was a door and they shifted to the back to a pig-pen. They moved up the hill, and he realised he was looking down, at a village, and the bungalows were surrounded by emerald green.

'That's where you live? Is that Manila?'

'That's where my mother lives. We build the house for my mother – this is outside the city, maybe a four-hour drive. One day, we go and live there too.'

'It's so beautiful.'

'You think so? We have the title now, so it's registered.'

'And the children? How many do you have? You said six.'

'Six, yes. No condoms, you see.'

'What do you mean?'

'It's a Catholic country, Michael. The Pope says no condoms, so my husband agrees with him. I said to him, "Two is enough," and he agreed. Then suddenly, it's three. Four. Look at this one... wait one minute. Give me one more whisky, just... very small.'

Her fingers closed the photos that he'd seen, and another folder opened. This time a girl seemed to spring out at them both. She had white flowers in her hair, and you could almost hear her laughter. Maria clicked again, and she was calm, smiling a smile that brought tears to Michael's eyes. She clicked again, and the child was fast asleep in her father's lap. They were on a bus, and her long, dark hair fell over her face, but she was still smiling – pretending to sleep, perhaps.

'Her name is Max,' said Maria.

'Max?'

'Max.'

She took the cup and sipped.

'Eleven years, now. Next came Lucas... you want to see Lucas? He is very bad – a very bad, naughty boy. Every time I call, "What is Lucas doing?" Every week, something he shouldn't be.'

'At school?'

'School. Home. In the street—'

'What does he do?'

'Always the wrong thing! Talking when the teacher says don't talk. Running, jumping, falling down. He is very beautiful, but...'

The photograph came up and Michael looked at a boy who was staring back over his shoulder. He wore a white shirt, and the camera had caught him by surprise – his eyes were wide. The next one showed him bare-chested, posing, with a smile as sweet as his sister, and the next showed a whole family group: there were a dozen people, their arms wrapped around one another. Lucas was yelling at the camera, and the joy in his eyes seemed to tilt the world – Michael found that his mouth was open.

'Beautiful, yes?' said Maria.

She leant a little closer, and pointed them out one by one.

'Max,' she said. 'Lucas again, shouting. My husband, his mother and father. My mother. That is Nikko, number three – we call him the monkey-boy. Miguel is four, Roxanne is number five... and the baby is Roselle. So we have three of each, and no more. Until the next power cut.'

She opened a close-up, and Michael realised her breathing had changed, as if she'd swallowed something and it had lodged in her throat.

'Eight years old last week,' she said quietly. 'My special.'

'I've forgotten the name.'

'Nikko, Michael – keep up.'

'And he's your special? Your special child? In what way?'

'Every way. He is a boy at school, and a monkey at home – so crazy, so wild. Climbing up and up. He has no fear.'

'They're gorgeous.'

'They are. They're all special, of course—'

'But of them all? Nikko's the most.'

'Yes.'

She shrugged.

'Always gentle. Always kind.'

The boy's hair was so long he had to lift it up out of his eyes, and he wore a vest that would have fitted his father: it came to his knees, like a dress. What could he possibly be looking at that gave him so much pleasure? He met Michael's eyes, and Michael had to look away, for the child's hope and hunger for life were too intense.

'That is his new shirt,' said Maria. 'For basketball.'

'Look at his teeth.'

'What about them?'

'They're perfect.'

'Of course. But too many sweet drinks and bad food. My sister is not as strict as me, but... it's his birthday there. After I spoke to him – look.'

She opened another, and his face was a mess of cake – but he was still smiling through the cream, holding Michael with shining eyes.

'After I said goodnight to them all,' said Maria. 'That's when I got drunk.'

'Why?'

'Because I wasn't with my son, Michael. Why do you think?'

'Oh! Because—'

'It was his birthday, and I was here. He was there.'

She laughed, but he could see the tears in her eyes.

'Who looks after them?' he said.

'My mother and my sister.'

'And...'

He was about to say, 'And you really miss them, don't you?' But he just managed not to. Better not to say ignorant things, he realised. Better to let the agony peak in silence and pass – better to let her go through the pain, and remember why she was putting herself through it. Six children, all those miles away without her – their mother in a strange place, on a rock with a total stranger. For a moment Michael just managed to remember how important an eighth birthday was for a child – how the day came slowly closer, and became the biggest event the world had ever known until it finally passed, and you had to wait for the next. Maria had not been there for it – did that mean she was missing six birthdays every year? Sitting in some room in wherever it was she lived: Dumfries. Between the hospice and the school, and whatever that third job was – thinking of her three boys and her three girls, changing daily without her. And if anything bad happened, neither she nor Jao could protect them. If something went wrong, what could she do? If they were sick, or somebody did something monstrous – if they came home too upset to speak, changed forever – where was their mother when they needed her most?

'How often do you speak?' he said quietly.

'Every day.'

She called up a more formal photograph. The six children sat with her and her husband.

'Have you spoken today?'

'Before breakfast, yes. They go to school,' she said, and he saw her wipe her eyes.

'That is their school dress, you see. Max, Lucas, Nikko, Miguel. It's a nice school – not a government school.'

'Expensive?'

'Of course. But they study.'

'Even Lucas?'

She laughed.

'Of course. He knows how angry we will be! And he is... He is also very clever. So smart... and oh, Michael, look at Max...'

'How long do you stay in the UK?' said Michael gently.

'I've been here two years. If I am lucky, two years more.'

'Then home for good?'

'I hope so. Please God.'

'Please God.'

'You don't believe in him. Why do you say that?'

'I'm pretending to. What about Jao?'

'How long for him? Ah, he will stay working, for as long as he can. You don't understand, I think. To have work here, or there – where he is... We are very, very lucky.'

Now she had started to cry.

'I'm sorry,' she said. 'Take no notice – this happens every day. I say to my husband, "Three times a day!" But... look. This is Nikko and Roselle, together – see how he holds her? He loves everyone so much, and he says to me, "Mummy..."'

For a moment, she couldn't continue.

Michael put his arm around her, and she leaned against him.

'Wait,' she said.

'What?'

'There's a signal. Wait – you want to speak to them?'

She wiped her eyes, laughing.

'My sister will be angry, but I don't care. Okay? They are eating now. What's the time?'

'I don't know.'

'It's twelve o'clock, just gone, so seven in the Philippines. You want to meet them? Speak to them?'

'I don't understand—'

'We have a *signal*, Michael. You don't use computers?'

She had opened the tablet's little bag again, and was searching for something.

'Yes,' said Michael. 'All the time.'

'For calling your friends?'

'No. You're calling them now? Maria...'

'Hush. Wait.'

'We're on a mountain.'

'So what? You have a signal on a mountain, always. The bes

She had a plastic clip, and he watched her fingers as they inserted its tiny cable into some hidden socket or port. Then she was closing windows on the screen and opening new ones. She called up a grid of numbers somehow, and tapped them until they spun and expanded – they were like petals, which came together and resolved into an image of a little house. She was signing into something.

'They will think you are a scary man,' she said. 'Joking.'

Cartoon people appeared, waddling across the screen: truncated bodies with cartoon eyes that blinked together. Then the tablet was alive in every sense: it was buzzing and chirping, and he saw that she was completely serious, and making a connection across those thousands of miles. You really could stand in the middle of a wilderness, and reach out to another continent. She was doing it, and presumably somewhere in Manila a phone or another tablet was ringing and shuddering, and someone was walking towards it.

'Is this expensive?' said Michael.

'No,' said Maria. 'I mean, yes. Very.'

Her sister's phone rang soon after seven in the evening, Manila time. The satellites took the signal, bouncing it around the curve of the world until a face appeared on the screen, just a little concerned.

'Maria?' said a voice. It was so far away: so thin, and so distant.

'Maria... *Ok-ka lang*? Are you okay?'

31

It was her sister, and the next moment Max was beside her.

They were in the street, it seemed – Michael peered, trying to work out what he was looking at, but everything moved too fast. They were holding a phone, presumably, or a tablet, and it spun as they walked and turned, allowing him a glimpse of what might have been a barber's shop. Someone was reclining in a red chair, but that flashed past and there were people moving around some kind of tricycle, with an old man on the saddle. There was a din of traffic and the blasting of horns – over that, more language that he couldn't understand.

Maria was saying, 'Wait. Wait!'

'Are you okay?' said the voice.

Maria was talking fast, and the words sounded to Michael like a kind of birdsong, interspersed with her usual laughter – the street was suddenly full of tables, and he saw bottles of beer. A taxi was parked behind or in front, but they were moving into a shack of some kind, and it was immediately darker. All at once, the picture settled, and they were in a bedroom or a lounge – he could see a mattress, but then a table and a stove with saucepans. A lamp illuminated an old woman's face, and within seconds three children had gathered, shoulder to shoulder.

The language bubbled, and the phone was passed or grabbed. At last it was still again, and now there were no children at all, but only the sister.

'I'm fine, I'm fine!' cried Maria.

The children returned.

There were four of them this time, and still the strange syllables looped and danced, peppered with cries and laughter. He recog-nised Max, but then her head was pushed aside by the little boy with long hair – it was eight-year-old Nikko, alive and jumpin at the screen. What did he have to say that was so urgent? And what could be so funny?

'Okay, no,' said Maria. 'Okay – stop. You speak in English, please. Max!'

Somehow, she organised them – she couldn't silence them, but there was some semblance of order, and Michael gazed at faces that gazed back at him. He hid behind Maria, and the giggling continued mixed with shouts from somewhere and more car horns. Maria was adjusting the volume, and spoke in her own language still. Max and Lucas and Nikko. The other was a boy, but Michael couldn't remember his name – and he looked sleepy, his big eyes blinking.

'Say hello,' said Maria – but she was saying it to her children. 'Say hello, please. This is my friend, so we speak English.'

'Hello, uncle!' shouted one of them – it was Lucas, whose head was almost shaved.

For some reason, they could not stop laughing, and then they started to wave. Up on the rock, Michael looked at the hands waving as Maria laughed with them – for she was excited, too. This was the second call of the day, he remembered – did that make it illicit? Was that why they were so, so excited? – because calls had to be rationed, and this was late and extra-special?

She hushed them.

'Go on, Michael,' she said. 'They want to hear your voice. I tell them you are my bodyguard, and I say you're looking after me.'

'What shall I say?'

The children shouted with joy, and he realised they had seen him properly for the first time. Maria was angling the tablet so they had a clear view of his idiot face. She was offering the device to him.

'Uncle!' cried Lucas. 'How are you? How are you?'

Again, his throat was constricted.

Yet again, words seemed so hard to come by, but he took the tablet from Maria and brought it closer. The children were laughing, and when he put his nose near to the glass they screamed. They were waving still, and he could feel an ache, and a fear that he hadn't felt for years. On top of that came the realisation that he didn't deserve what was happening, because he shouldn't be here. He was wearing another man's coat and another man's boots. He should have been dead by now. Whatever he said next would have to be intelligent, or even profound – he wanted to say something appropriate to the occasion but he couldn't find a single worthwhile syllable.

He put his hand up and waved, and this time it was the daughter who spoke.

'What is your name?' said Max.

He licked his lips.

'Michael,' he said firmly.

'Hello, uncle.'

Inspiration came at last. 'What are *your* names?' he said slowly.

They told him. They introduced themselves and each other. They pushed to be closer to the screen and Michael could only stare in wonder. They told him their ages, in slow, hesitant English.

'Where do you live?' said Lucas, and Michael told him.

'What is your age?' said Nikko, but his sister shushed him, and there was more talk in their own language. Maria took the tablet from Michael, and held it steady for him.

'We have had a long walk,' he said.

'Oh,' said Max. 'Good.'

'Your mother and I. We have been walking – together. We have come many miles.'

He could hear his own robotic voice, and wondered why he was speaking so awkwardly, as if he had only just learned how to talk. It was as if his mouth had been sewn up for years.

'The weather,' he said. 'It's been quite… changeable.'

Lucas said something in his own language, and Max pinched him. He writhed and squealed, and Maria had to shush them again. Whoever was holding the phone dropped it and picked it up, and Michael felt drunk. He felt as if he were reeling.

'When are you going to bed?' he said.

'What?'

'When is your bedtime? Sleeping.'

'No sleeping,' said Nikko.

'You have school tomorrow?' he asked.

'No school!'

'No?'

'Yes.'

'When?'

'What? Yes!'

They nodded, and Max found a school book from somewhere and showed him a piece of writing. Again, the phone seemed to spin and he caught glimpses of a barred window with a crimson curtain. There was the table and the chair. The children's English fractured back into the local tongue, and all the time there was the same excited, teasing laughter. At last it was still, and the children's faces filled the screen.

'This our house,' said Max.

'It looks lovely.'

'You see Roselle? Here...'

The picture slipped away, and Michael found he was looking at a baby in someone's arms. She was fast asleep – in fact, she appeared to be concentrating hard on not waking up or opening her eyes. He heard the blast of an extra-loud car horn, and still she slept. Then Maria was talking in her own language, and the phone closed in on the baby, and turned around to reveal who was holding it: bald Lucas reappeared, grinning happily, and he was joined by Nikko who stuck his head up between his brother's outstretched arms, and filled the screen with his own wild, shining face.

'You come here, uncle,' said Nikko.

'Where?' said Michael.

'You. Come here, Philippines.'

'Come to the Philippines? To visit, you mean?'

He laughed.

'Yes.'

'No.'

The little boy put his nose closer, and Michael found he was looking into a pair of huge, dark eyes again, behind a sheet of hair. Fingers lifted the hair away, and the eyes were too much – they were Maria's eyes and her husband's eyes. Eyes you could look into all day, for in a dazzling moment he realised how a child's eyes could nourish you. These were the eyes of one you would protect with your life – with your sword and shield, as the clouds unfolded and Jerusalem rose up out of the rock. Never would you be separated, unless some terrible cruelty tore you apart and put you on the other side of the world. For a moment all Michael wanted was to help protect this boy – his brothers and sisters too – and keep them safe. He didn't know them, and they had nothing to do with him: but that was all he wanted.

He needed a sword and shield, and Maria was holding him.

'You come Philippines,' said Max gravely. 'We wait you here.'

'No,' said Michael. 'Not easy for me.'

'Yes! Very easy.'

'You come,' said Lucas.

'You come here,' said Nikko. 'Promise, uncle? Promise!'

And for some reason, Michael lost his composure completely, and started crying again – and that made Maria cry. They sat together in the sun as the children laughed at them, and the car horns blasted outside. Michael and Maria looked through the little tablet, holding it in their hands – gazing at a world so far away, but so close they could feel the heat and smell the fumes. At last, Maria put her hand on the screen, and the children touched her fingertips. She made Michael do the same, and he realised that was the signal for God bless, goodnight, goodbye – we are apart, but close. Goodbye – we are touching... I love you.

Maria ended the call, and they were alone again.

They dried their eyes, and they stood up. Then, slowly and carefully, they walked all the way back to the hotel.

NORTH AND SOUTH

32

Michael's things were behind the reception desk.

He had forgotten that the room was only available for one night, and the staff had been obliged to prepare for the next guest. They were very kind. They found him a sleeping bag and even a mattress, so he had supper with Maria and slept on her floor, squeezed between the bed and the wall. The next day, they caught the bus to the station, where the 10.12 to Blackpool was only one minute late. They boarded together, and got down at Preston.

Maria was heading north, so Michael took her to the platform. Her connection was eight minutes late, and there was an apology because the person speaking knew that there would be inconvenience. Another train came through but this one didn't stop. Everyone was advised to stand behind the yellow line, and it crashed through in a hurricane of silver and red. Those last eight minutes seemed extra-specially precious – a little gift from the railway company.

He kissed her on the cheek when they parted.

She held him very close for a long time. For a moment he worried she might miss the train, but she let him go at last and he stood back. The doors closed, and he then had the wondrous experience of watching her choose her seat quickly so that she could sit down and wave. They waved to each other until the distance made waving absurd, but he carried on anyway in case her eyes were better than his. He turned, aware that people had noticed him and might even be envying whatever relationship he had with the woman they'd seen board the train. He was aware, too, that he really had been waving to someone. He had not been pretending.

He crossed back to his own platform, and passed through Crewe just after twelve-twenty. He got back to his flat shortly before six. His room was still his room, and when he saw his own two hands setting his bag down on the bed, letting go of the strap, he stopped for a moment and stood motionless – catching his breath – for the note he'd left was unopened. His clothing was there, and his phone was on the bedside table exactly where he'd left it, next to his watch.

There was one message, from Maria.

All good??? it said.

He could hear a television coming up from the flat below. Now and then came the cough he recognised as Ryan's. He texted back, *All good. You?*

Yes. Work tomorrow.

He put the phone down and opened the drawer of his desk. He took out all the letters and started to open them, one by one, throwing away the envelopes. Soon, the contents lay in orderly piles and he carefully punched holes so as to transfer them to a ring-binder. Everyone wanted his money, it seemed: the council, the water company, the various banks who'd sold on his debts – they were queuing up to prosecute him. There were letters from solicitors and bailiffs, and they threatened, so politely, to take everything he owned. In fact, there was only one thing they couldn't take – and that was his life.

In the morning, he would have to talk to them.

There had been one encounter on the train south.

At Birmingham New Street he changed trains, and as the service was busy he found himself sharing a table with a young man who'd got on board just ahead of him. He was a boy, really, and he was hunched and slow, and as soon as he took his seat he put his head on the table. Michael found himself looking at a grey hood that was stained by grass, and fingers that were wrapped in a splint. There was an unpleasant smell as if he'd wet himself, and the part of his face that was visible was heavily bruised.

They travelled in silence for several miles, and then the door behind slid open. A clink of bottles followed, and a woman appeared pulling the refreshments trolley.

'Tea, coffee,' she said. 'Anything to eat or drink?'

Michael said, 'Yes. Thank you. Could I have a coffee?'

'Of course.'

He couldn't place her accent, but it sounded Eastern European. Her uniform was just a little tight, her hair drawn back from her face emphasising a nose that was long and sharp. The efficiency of her movements dazzled him, and he wondered if she was being timed. There was so little space on the trolley, for it was laden and she needed not only a tray and wallet for cash, but also the little machine for cards. She was a magician.

'Anything to eat?' she said.

'Yes,' said Michael. 'Could I have a sandwich? What do you have?'

She had to stoop to see into the sandwich shelf, and she went through the list briskly.

'Egg mayonnaise. Chicken tikka. Tuna and sweetcorn and… that's it.'

'Could I have the egg, please?'

'Egg mayonnaise. Brown or white bread?'

There was even a choice of bread. The egg mayonnaise sandwiches had clearly proved unpopular.

'Brown,' he said quickly.

She put the box on a paper plate, with a serviette tucked under it. She placed a lid on the coffee cup, and used another, smaller one for milk tubs and sachets of sugar. She inserted a wooden stirrer, and set it all down carefully, close to Michael's hands.

'Biscuit?' she said. 'With the coffee?'

'No, I mustn't,' he said.

He was about to say, 'I'm trying to be careful,' when he decided not to. The woman didn't need any further information, and she had many more carriages to serve before turning around and dragging the whole apparatus back again. How many responses like that could she tolerate?

'I'm being careful. Don't tempt me! I'm sweet enough, thank you.'

She was working out his bill when he noticed that the boy in the sweatshirt had turned his head. It was still resting on the table, but he'd opened his eyes. Both were swollen, and the left one was so damaged it would hardly open at all.

He had a drowned look.

Nonetheless, he was staring at the sandwich. She had placed it quite close to where he'd been resting, and Michael saw that the skin round his ear and down his neck was a mixture of livid crimson, yellow, black and violet. The right side of his mouth was slightly open, because his lip was torn.

Michael handed over his third and last twenty-pound note, and took his receipt and change. The woman thanked him, and he thanked her so she thanked him again and moved on. Michael rearranged what she'd given him, putting the coffee by the window.

He said to the boy, 'You don't look well.'

He spoke softly. There was no idiot jauntiness, because the face was so badly marked it was upsetting him – and he found a quieter, gentler tone.

The boy, however, just grimaced – Michael saw his nostrils twitch and the lips effect a kind of sneer. Was it a smirk? Or a wince? Maybe it was just that quick, animal reaction to warn off a predator? He looked no more than fourteen – he had so much growing to do, but he looked lean and starved and the skin that wasn't discoloured was unhealthily pale. His clothes would have fitted someone so much bigger: it was as if he'd put them on and shrunk.

'What's wrong?' said Michael.

'What?' said the boy.

'You don't look very well. I think you need a hot drink.'

The boy raised himself up, painfully. He sat back in his seat, and looked out of the window. That meant he was as far away from Michael as he could be, and his shoulders were up round his ears. The hood of his sweatshirt put his whole face in shadow, but the injuries were still visible. Conscious of them, he put his left hand up to his nose as if to wipe it, but kept it there. His eyes drifted towards the landscape again.

'What would you like?' said Michael.

The boy didn't look at him.

'She had coffee. Tea. Hot chocolate.'

'No money,' said the boy.

'What?'

'No money.'

'I'm going to buy you one. You need a drink, all right? What do you want?'

The boy said nothing. He shook his head, and his arm moved higher so his whole face was covered. He settled lower in his seat, as if all he wanted was to sleep, undisturbed.

'I think you should have a hot chocolate,' said Michael quietly. 'Wait there.'

He got up and walked down to the trolley – it was almost at the doors, because nobody had made a purchase. He placed his order and bought a KitKat. Then he bought a chicken tikka sandwich, and made his way back to his own table. The boy seemed to be dozing, and Michael set the items down in front of him.

There was no movement.

Michael climbed back into his own place, and busied himself with his coffee. He got the cardboard carton open and removed the first of the egg sandwiches. Then he reached over and opened the chicken, as if the boy might struggle with the seal. Minutes passed, and the train sped through fields. At last, the boy huddled forward and took the hot chocolate. He sipped it, and Michael saw again that his right hand was bandaged.

'Thank you,' he said.

The train was slowing down, and it was like watching a bird come a little closer, to take a crust. He was like a mongrel dog, or a rat, even.

'Have you had an accident?' said Michael.

The boy shook his head, but again it was a flinching movement.

'Where are you going?'

Silence.

'Home,' he said at last.

'Where's home?'

The boy shrugged and gazed out of the window again. The train stopped but they weren't at a station. Michael ate his own sandwich, quietly, and said no more. He finished the coffee, and couldn't help but notice that the chicken sandwich remained untouched. He wondered if the boy was a vegetarian, or if his choice had been foolish: how could the poor soul eat spicy food with torn lips? It was possible that he simply couldn't bring himself to accept a gift, of course, because gifts come freighted with obligations. He didn't want to be in debt. All through childhood, thought Michael, we are told never to accept the approaches of strangers, for strangers will want something from us – the price will be too high. From Hansel and Gretel onwards, we're told the same thing: never take the sweets.

'If you come in my car, I'll give you five pounds.'

'Give me ten, mate – I'll cum in your mouth.'

Michael closed his eyes, but for some reason the joke now seemed simply crude and ignorant. Why had it ever alarmed him?

He looked at the boy again, and the clothes made him feel sad. They suggested the cheapest of the cheap high-street stores – were they bought by his mother, still? Were they borrowed or interchanged amongst brothers and friends? Except he wouldn't have friends. He would have 'mates', and Michael could almost hear them, because a pack always met up quite close to where he lived. You'd hear the mumbling and the sniggering – there might be a skateboard or two, or even a bicycle riding in tight circles. They always wore what this boy was wearing now: they conformed to uniform regulations as they must have done at school, but instead of shirts and ties it was now this: the costume of the unskilled, jobless poor.

The boy picked up the sandwich and took a bite. Sauce immediately ran down his chin, and he winced. It stained the bandage on his hand, so he licked his fingers quickly, and Michael thought of rats again.

He wanted to say something, but he couldn't think of a single question or statement that would take them forward, and the train was obstinately still. They were simply stuck.

The boy smelled worse now – the stink of urine was strong. Had people urinated on him, perhaps? He couldn't be incontinent, but he might have been so drunk last night that he'd lost control. Was he coming back from a wild party? Was he actually the son of some wealthy couple? Was he at university, even?

'How old are you?' said Michael.

The boy swallowed.

'Sixteen.'

'What's your name?'

'What?'

'Your name. If you don't mind me asking.'

'Morris.'

There was a silence.

Morris swallowed the last of the first sandwich, and went straight on to the second. He pushed it into his mouth and ate hungrily. Then he drank and wiped his lips, and started on the chocolate bar. He ate with total concentration and without pleasure – the eating was mechanical and fast. Michael didn't want to stare at him, so he gazed at the wasteland outside, trying to ignore the reflection in the glass.

He said, 'A hundred years ago...'

The boy made no sign of hearing or listening – but it didn't matter. Michael wanted to tell him something.

'A hundred years ago,' he said. 'You would have been off to France. I'd have been too old, I think – but a sixteen-year-old... I think conscription had started, but the other thing I read was that – this might surprise you – young men lied about their ages, because they were so keen to join up and fight. Twelve-year-old boys would walk miles, apparently, trying to find a... recruitment office that would take them.'

The boy sipped the chocolate.

'And I met someone yesterday,' said Michael, 'who had three jobs. She made me think I need to find work, because... I don't do much any more.'

The boy wasn't looking at him.

'What happened to your eye? Tell me.'

The boy creased his brow for a moment, then looked away. He was about to speak, when the doors closest to them opened and a friendly voice said:

'All tickets, please. All tickets.'

The boy said, 'Fuck.'

'What?'

He went to stand up, but winced as he did so. Then he seemed to lose interest in the movement, and slumped back down. In any case, the guard was at the table across from theirs, waiting as a man and a woman delved into their pockets and bags: there was no escape. Michael produced his ticket, and waited for what was now inevitable.

'Thank you, sir – tickets, please?'

The boy looked up, and the guard stared at him.

'Stolen,' he said.

'What's that?'

'I had my wallet stolen.'

The guard looked at him more carefully.

'Where have you come from?'

'Birmingham.'

'Birmingham? What kind of ticket was it?'

'I don't know. Just a... return.'

'Any proof of purchase? A receipt, or...?'

The boy shook his head.

'Where are you going to?'

'Newport.'

'Long way. Do you have cash, or a card?'

The boy's head twitched again.

'ID?'

'No.'

'Okay,' said the guard.

He was a big man, with a very heavy stomach and a very thick neck. The train company had given him a uniform, but he couldn't wear it smartly: the collar of his shirt was wide open and the tie was loose. His jumper was too tight, and standing in the aisle he looked hot and uncomfortable – but he was determined to be friendly. He was getting no pleasure from the boy's discomfort, and it occurred to Michael how hard men like this must have to work to avoid confrontations. They were being scrutinised, too, and their conduct had to be faultless and professional: there was a camera just ten paces away.

The man was not a bully.

'The problem we've got,' he said, 'is that without ID we can't do it on board. What I'm going to have to do, therefore, is ask you to get down at the next station, and they can take a few details there. Is that okay?'

'I'm not lying,' said the boy.

'I'm not saying anyone's telling lies, sir – I'm just saying—'

'I've got nothing on me.'

'Nothing at all? Did you tell the police?'

'Yes.'

'How did you board the train without a ticket?'

The boy shrugged.

'Did you not mention this to anyone at Birmingham? The fact that you'd had your ticket stolen?'

The boy shook his head.

'I just want to get home,' he said quietly. 'I just... I just got the train.'

'Were the barriers open?'

The boy nodded.

'You see, I understand that, and I can see you've had some trouble. But the problem is, son... boarding a train without a valid ticket is an offence. So I have to charge you a penalty fare, and—'

'How much is it?' said Michael.

The guard looked at him.

'We're not travelling together,' said Michael. 'But I can help. What would the fare be, please?'

'From Birmingham to Newport...'

The guard looked down at his ticket machine, and the boy looked out of the window.

'With the penalty fare, it will be... I can tell you in a moment.'

He pressed buttons and checked a piece of paper. Everyone in the carriage was working so hard to ignore what was happening – it was a collective effort, and Michael felt the torture of embarrassment as he waited to hear the figure.

'Forty-three eighty.'

'That's with the penalty?' said Michael.

'No. We'll do it as a single, but I can't emphasise this enough – if you lose a ticket, you're best off talking to staff at the station where you board, and they will try to help. You can't travel on a train without a ticket.'

'That's very kind of you.'

Michael presented his card, and there was another fifteen seconds of suspense as the connections were made. At last, the transaction was allowed and the guard gave him his receipt.

'Thank you,' said Michael. 'Do you know why we've stopped, by the way?'

'Red signal. Service from Worcester coming through.'

'Right.'

Then, as if they hadn't spoken, the guard moved on.

'Tickets, please, all tickets,' he said – and Michael pushed the one he'd bought over to the boy, who said nothing at all.

Michael remained silent, too. He was wondering who the boy lived with, and what might be waiting for him when he finally got home. He wanted to know who had assaulted him, and why – but he couldn't ask.

'We have to work,' he said quietly.

The boy ignored him.

'We can't not work,' he said. 'We cannot throw ourselves away.'

He wanted to say more. He wanted to say, 'We might meet again. We might bump into each other some time in the future – it's not impossible. Will you have recovered when we do, and moved on? We can, surely... but what if we can't?'

He wanted to take the boy's hand, but Morris was staring out of the window.

Michael wondered if he dared write his number down and hand it over.

'I don't know you,' he could say. 'But it seems to me you need someone. If you need more help, I will help you – because you're young, and something bad has happened to you. I don't know what you've done, but nobody deserves to be beaten the way you've been beaten. That doesn't mean I can help, because maybe I can't – but you *can* trust me.'

He went to speak, and then thought better of it.

Inside his bag was a pen – but he couldn't make the move. To pass on his number would be too much like a proposition, or the act of a mad evangelical who was saving souls. On the other hand, who was looking out for this one? Who was waiting for this poor, injured boy, worrying about him – longing for his safe return? What if there was nobody?

Michael set his bag on his knees, and opened it. The pen was there, in a pocket – but still he didn't dare.

'I'm alive, Morris,' he said. 'I want to live.'

Morris turned and looked at him.

The left eye was all but closed, while the right one seemed to gleam. The train was moving slowly forward again, and Michael pulled out the pen and the first piece of paper he could find. It was the leaflet that had guided Maria to Higher Lee Ridge. As he removed it, he saw a flash of bright orange. There was a tangerine left after all, and it had lodged itself beneath his spectacles case.

He put it on the table.

As for the leaflet, he had laid it out on Maria's dressing table to dry, and she'd been about to throw it away. He had saved it. It was torn, but he wrote his phone number carefully beside one of the pictures, and below that he wrote his name.

His name was Michael MacMillan, and he underlined it. Then he thought of Terry, who was in Bristol at the marina. He thought of Percy, which was short for Percival: he would be in a classroom, or on a playing field. His grandparents had not revealed their names – unlike Scottish Graeme, Sunita, Jo, Tim or Tom, and all those old colleagues at the council. There was Steve, and the HR woman – Jean. There were lots more whose faces had faded, but they could all be in the next carriage – they were following him, in a way. What about the wise Pakistani in Accrington, in a house with seventy people who had gathered around his father? What about the woman on the bench, way back where his journey started? Had she made it to wherever she was going, and met up with her daughter? An anonymous steam-train enthusiast had saved his life, and he'd met himself at the vending machine – that nervous boy, who might be telling his friends about the madman on the station even now. He would be checking vending machines for the next year, recalling his find for the rest of his life. As for Bromsgrove's war dead, Michael couldn't remember a single one of them. Not one of those brave, frightened young soldiers had lodged in his memory, unlike Maria's six children. He could name each one: Roselle, the baby. Next to her was Roxanne, and then Miguel. Max was the oldest, and Lucas was one year younger. Nikko was the monkey. As for their father, his name was Jao.

He read his own name again: Michael MacMillan. He pushed the leaflet across the table, and weighted it down with the last tangerine.

'Contact me, Morris,' he said. 'If you want to.'

The train rolled into a tunnel, and came out again. He thought about Elizabeth, and then Monica. He thought about Amy, whom he'd hurt so badly, and closed his eyes.

FAR EAST

33

When you land at Manila's Ninoy Aquino Airport, your first impression may be negative. The walk through the terminal is a tiring one, and there are usually eight or nine long queues in the immigration hall. You inch forward, and the Filipino officer in the booth will only give you the most cursory glance, because he or she sees so many different versions of you every day. He or she isn't likely to see you as an individual: sadly, you have come to seem the same as the last and the next. Your visa will be stamped into your passport, though, and through you will go. You have permission to enter the Philippines.

Michael entered and stood beside the carousel.

The bags were appearing, one after another, and in a short while he saw his own.

He picked it up and checked his instructions. They were printed in a large, clear font, because he didn't want to go wrong at this crucial stage:

> Go through customs, out of the building – walk across the road past the yellow taxis, go past the hotel meeting point, the way goes left and right: GO TO THE RIGHT!!

He did as he was told, handing a form to the man at the customs desk. He turned left past a line of banks, where a young woman urged him to take an airport limousine.

'No, thank you,' he said – and the woman smiled at him.

'Where are you going?' she said.

'I don't really know,' replied Michael. 'I'm meeting someone, I think.'

'*Mabuhay*. Welcome to the Philippines.'

He stood still and looked at her. She seemed completely sincere.

'Thank you,' he said and moved on.

A pair of glass doors opened onto a dark roadway, and he felt damp heat. It was nearly midnight, local time, and the air was unnaturally warm. He was frightened now, for he was leaving the protected zone and the world was suddenly full of crawling taxis. They were yellow, and their engines were reverberating: the road was actually a concrete tunnel, and he could hear the constant squeal of tyres. Ahead, he saw the hotel meeting point, so he crossed with the crowd. His new manager had asked him where he was going.

'Somewhere nice?' she said. 'Winter sun?'

He'd told her that he wasn't sure, and that he had no definite plans. It was a lie, but he hadn't wanted anyone to know the truth: the trip felt like a private adventure, and he couldn't believe it would actually happen. He couldn't even imagine getting to Heathrow airport, and the idea that you could simply sit in a succession of seats, and end up on the other side of the world – that seemed absurd.

So much had changed.

He had lost his flat, because his polite appeals for more time had fallen on deaf ears. He'd given in to a compromise: repossession was avoided, but he'd had to sell quickly and take the first serious offer. Now he had a new doctor, and was on a waiting list to see a counsellor. He worked in a supermarket, and his job was not so different from the DIY centre: he unloaded stock and shelved it. He took turns on the tills, and had completed a short course that allowed him to supervise the self-service area.

He emailed Maria and Jao every week.

The airline he'd chosen was the one that they always used. It catered for those determined to economise whatever the inconvenience, so – as a consequence – he had been awake for the last thirty-six hours and his eyes felt raw. He'd flown via Kuwait, and the plane had been full of cheerful overseas workers who were returning home – he was the one white face amongst them, and they cheered the captain as they came in to land.

A man had turned to him:

'Hey, Joe!' he'd said. 'Welcome.'

Joe was the friendly name for a Westerner, it seemed.

Now, Michael stopped.

He'd come through a short pedestrian subway, and he was in the open air. There was a solid stone wall in front of him, so his fellow passengers streamed left and right, manoeuvring trolleys as quickly as they dared. Some were running, and he realised how the exit system worked. If your name began with any letter between A and L, you went to the left: that's what the sign said. Everyone else – M to Z – went right, and it was a simple way of spreading the arriving crowds out safely, to avoid a crush. Both channels took you down broad concrete ramps, which curved around a floodlit meeting area. Those waiting for their loved ones positioned themselves at the appropriate exit, and looked up in expectation. It meant there was less chance of a stampede.

Michael checked his paper again, and went to the right. As soon as he saw the masses below, he was filled with dismay. There were hundreds and hundreds of people, even at this time – midnight – and the noise was now deafening. Everyone stood in brightly coloured clusters, and most were gazing at the ramps, aching to get their first glimpse of mother, father, son, daughter, brother or sister. Some had banners, and others held placards, and the atmosphere was that of a sports stadium when the home team is winning. He could hear people howling as they waved and clapped, but what made the scene seem extra chaotic was that a line of buses was inching through the centre towards a subway. They were nose to tail, honking their horns. Some people were boarding and others were getting down – it was a constant flow of joyful, anxious chaos.

He stopped.

He had never seen such confusion, and his legs felt weak. He stared down, aware that a lot of people round him really were running, for they had spotted their families. The crowd surged as reunions took place, and he watched men disappear into scrums of women and children who hugged and kissed them, and wouldn't let them go – he could see an old woman in floods of tears, her hands raised in triumph. He stood alone, wondering how he would ever find Maria, if she had actually managed to come for him. She'd said she would, but he knew the journey to the airport took four hours and she was bound to be delayed. In any case, they would never find each other. He should have insisted on taking a hotel, for he had never felt so overwhelmed. Every face was Filipino, and he was watching such personal, private rituals of joy.

Why his eye alighted on a particular group, he didn't know.

Perhaps it was because everyone in that particular cluster was staring at him, and even at that distance he felt their gaze? Perhaps it was the fact that one of the children was on a man's shoulders, waving her arms slowly in full circles? What he knew was that it had to be an optical illusion, for the woman standing in the middle looked so like his friend – and she was flapping her hands at him, calling something he couldn't possibly hear.

He knew it wasn't her, because it couldn't be – he deserved nothing.

He felt his knees simply give way, and he clutched the wall for support. He was back on the ledge, in another storm, and the tears blurred his vision. He had to wipe them away fast in case the illusion disappeared – he had to clean his glasses. It was Maria, Jao and all of the children, and they were screaming his name. He did manage to wave, and they were frantic in their response – for a moment, he heard a howl of 'Michael!'

They could not come for him, for families weren't allowed up on the ramp. They had to wait whilst he got himself together and walked on. They had to wait as he stumbled all the way down, on rubber legs. When he got to the bottom, he still couldn't get to them – he had to go through a final cordon of airport officials, and he had to take more steps. He was like a deep-sea diver with a suitcase.

At last he was through and somehow they were face to face. Maria's husband was shaking his hand, whilst the eldest boy – this was Lucas – Lucas took the bag. He knew that Maria would embrace him, but what he didn't expect was that the children wanted to as well. For some reason, all he could think was how late it was, and how kind they were to come all this way when they could have been in comfortable beds. Hands were reaching out, and he thought, You don't know me. You don't know me at all, so how can this be allowed?

Roselle was placed in his arms, and he wasn't quite sure how to hold her. Roxanne was presented next, and he did his best, still not sure what to do or what to say. He went down into a crouch, then, so as to greet the others – and he almost fell. They were saying things, but he could hardly hear.

'Uncle,' they said. 'Welcome, uncle!'

He heard their names, and he hugged first Max and then Miguel. Lucas still held the suitcase, but hugged him as best he could, and when he saw Nikko he went to pieces completely, for the boy leaned in and kissed him. He kissed Michael gently on the cheek and then reached for his hand – and Michael let himself be led. He was guided like a blind man, towards a waiting bus. The children helped him with infinite care, and the next moment they'd found seats and they were moving.

'So,' said Maria. 'How was the journey?'

Michael shook his head and laughed. There were absolutely no words, so he didn't try to answer. Roselle was in his arms, and the family were squeezed around him as if they always sat together, in just this way. He kept nodding, realising that if he hoped to speak – if he was ever to find his voice again and say anything worth hearing – he would have to study hard and find a whole new language.

ACKNOWLEDGEMENTS

Train Man started on a train, and was meant to be a radio drama – but that didn't work out, so I turned it into a novel. Michael is based on an old friend who killed himself years ago on a railway line. I don't know if the Philippines would have saved him.

My apologies to those who notice the occasional liberties I've taken with timetables and geography: sometimes you just need to get where you're going.

My agent, Jane Turnbull, was the first to read the book critically and suggest improvements. I'm deeply indebted to her. Clara Farmer helped enormously, as did my copy-editors Harriet and Mary. I'm grateful to Mike Smith, Maria Yambao, Steve Lewis and Sam North.